rolled onto her side and t  ody
upwards but that also prov her
front and tried to push her ole.
She managed to shuffle her on
her stomach. She had made o a
halt, exhausted. With an a to
look at her watch. It had taken the entire morning to move a few feet.
To reach the phone in the drawing room would take days, possibly a
week, especially as there were the steep kitchen stairs to negotiate.

'Bugger, bugger, bugger.'

Tom had been right. She needed one of those confounded cord-
less telephones he was always going on about. Or even one of those
alarms around her neck that she had been so annoyed about when he
suggested it.

'Bugger, bugger, bugger, bollocks.'

The Japanese kimono she wore as a dressing gown had rucked up
round her waist; her long silk nightdress now barely covered her
knees. She hated to think how she would look to whoever found her.

On her wrist the little diamond-studded watch was disappearing
into swelling flesh. Her hand was swollen too, multiple rings digging into her fingers. Her left wrist throbbed as much as the right.
Evelyn didn't need to recall much about her time as a nurse to realise
that her wrists were very badly sprained, or possibly worse.

'Bugger!' she muttered one more time, and then, taking a deep
breath, she shouted as loudly as she could, 'I hate being ninety!'

Kate Glanville was born in West Africa to Irish parents. She now lives with her three children in rural West Wales. For many years she has practised as a successful ceramic artist supplying tiles and tableware to many leading shops and galleries around the world. From childhood she has been passionate about writing stories. Kate is the author of five captivating and poignant novels.

By Kate Glanville

A Perfect Home
Heartstones
Stargazing
The Cherry Tree Summer
The Peacock House

Kate Glanville

THE PEACOCK HOUSE

ACCENT

First published in 2021 by HEADLINE ACCENT
An imprint of HEADLINE PUBLISHING GROUP

1

Cataloguing in Publication Data is available from the British Library

ISBN 978 1 4722 7991 0

Typeset in 10.5/13pt Bembo Std by Jouve (UK), Milton Keynes

Printed and bound in Great Britain by Clays Ltd, Elcograf S.p.A.

Headline's policy is to use papers that are natural, renewable and recyclable
products and made from wood grown in well-managed forests and other
controlled sources. The logging and manufacturing processes are expected
to conform to the environmental regulations of the country of origin.

HEADLINE PUBLISHING GROUP
An Hachette UK Company
Carmelite House
50 Victoria Embankment
London EC4Y 0DZ

www.headline.co.uk
www.hachette.co.uk

For Harry, Daisy and Tomos – a constant source of love and laughter. You are all wonderful. X

And for the late great Perry the Peacock who shared our life for a little while and provided inspiration for this book.

EVELYN

Dismal. It was the only word that Evelyn could think of.

Dismal, dismal, dismal – it ricocheted around her head as she stared out of the bay window. The rain ran in unrelenting tears down the diamonds of glass and the wind moaned through the gaps around the ancient frame.

Outside there was a world of nothing. The garden had completely disappeared into the thick, grey mist. It was hard to imagine the view; the sea in the distance, the mountains that swept down to the shore, the rooftops of the houses that clustered around the crescent bay.

Evelyn turned and looked around the enormous bedroom; it was much too big for the mean little fire that crackled in the grate.

Flopping down onto the eiderdown she stared at the ornately plastered ceiling. Its Jacobean swirls reminded her of a wedding cake. There had been no cake at her wedding to Howard, rationing had made sure of that. The war had also made sure there had been no white satin dress, or trailing bouquet, though she wasn't sure the war could be blamed for the lack of other things a bride expected.

It had been two years since her wedding day, nearly two years since she had been banished to the land of rain and rocks and shrouding cloud. *Two years*, Evelyn whispered and saw a chilly puff of air escape between her lips.

1

This would be her second Christmas in Wales, in the huge house, with only her mother-in-law for company at the dinner table. So different from the boisterous Christmas dinners at Wilton Terrace where there had been jokes and riddles, and indoor fireworks, and endless bottles of champagne from the cellar. There had always been a huge fir tree in the hall, soaring up through the stairwell; Evelyn and her brother and sister had to stand on ladders to decorate it. At Vaughan Court they didn't have a tree.

'They are unpatriotic!' Lady Vaughan had declared when Evelyn had dared to suggest they put one up in the drawing room. 'We will take no part in Germanic traditions at Vaughan Court.'

She wondered if Howard would come to visit this year. She doubted it. His work in Whitehall was much more important than a wife, especially when he had everything he wanted in London. She tried not to think of the letter; the swirling writing, the sickening scent of violets, the words that had suggested an intimacy Evelyn had no experience of. Instead she glanced over at the jumper she'd been knitting; her mother-in-law had suggested it as a gift for Howard.

'It will give you something to do,' Lady Vaughan had said.

The colour of the wool was hideous, it was all that they had in the town.

Evelyn closed her eyes and wished for something to happen, anything, anything at all, as long as it was something more exciting than the life she had.

She opened her eyes at the sound of the rain beating harder against the windows. The moaning of the wind grew louder, more like a howl, and then a roar. She sat up. The windowpanes started to rattle in their leaden frames and for a moment everything seemed to darken, as though the shadow of some colossal beast had passed by outside. Then there was a bang, an explosion. The whole room seemed to shake; Evelyn thought the windowpanes might shatter. Jumping up from the bed she tried to crane her neck to see from the window, but everything was fog. She heard shouting below her. The boys.

A crash, there's been a crash on the mountain.

Without even stopping to think she wrenched open the bedroom door and ran. Racing down the long corridor, she had no time to scowl at the beastly portraits, the Persian rugs slipping beneath her feet. She almost tripped as she took the steps of the marble staircase two at a time. With an ungraceful skid she crossed the black-and-white-tiled hall and pulled at the heavy oak door until it opened and she was outside.

The rain had turned to sleet, slivers of ice pricking at her cheeks; her hands were already turning numb. Ignoring the cold, Evelyn ran around the side of the house. The boys were smudges ahead of her, already scrambling up the steep path.

Peter, Billy.

She called their names and set off as fast as she could, following them upwards, clambering over rocks and boulders. The smell of smoke was thick on the wind and high above her on the mountain-side something was giving off a ghostly glow.

EVELYN

March 2016
Vaughan Court

She could see a lot of dust. She wondered when she had last swept under the dresser. *Why* would she have swept under the dresser? Who would ever have been able to see the dust unless they happened to be lying on the cold flagstones of the kitchen floor, their face turned at such an angle that they could see the accumulated dust beneath the dresser.

In the gloom she could make out several fragments of broken china and a wizened apple. There were some little bits that she hoped were ancient raisins and not rat droppings, and a marble that had probably belonged to Robert. He had loved marbles; he'd kept his collection in a big glass jar. He would have been upset to lose such a beautiful one; Evelyn thought she could even remember the search. Why hadn't she thought to look beneath the dresser? Too busy probably. Fifty years ago she had been very busy, constantly juggling: the house, the garden, her writing, the charity, the school. And Robert and Howard had both, in their different ways, required a lot of her time.

Now Evelyn had a lot more time, though she would rather not be spending it lying on the kitchen floor. She was cold. An icy draught blew in from the open door. She knew she must try very hard not to go to sleep. She must somehow keep herself awake and make a plan. It was proving much more difficult than she had originally thought.

Her gaze travelled back and forth. She was getting used to the gloomy light beneath the dresser. There was a hairpin, and a fork, and something round and shiny – a coin maybe, or a toffee wrapped in foil? If only she could reach it, she was getting hungry.

At the very back, against the skirting board, there was a pen. It was an old-fashioned fountain pen that could well have been there for decades, maybe before Evelyn's time. Her mother-in-law had been forever making lists: sweeping into the kitchen with a hundred things for Nelli to do, shouting at the poor girl when she couldn't read her handwriting, encouraging Mrs Moggs to punish Nelli in cruel, vindictive ways. Evelyn shut her eyes. Even after all these years she didn't want to remember Lady Vaughan, or Mrs Moggs.

Evelyn dreamed that she was shut in the cellar with Nelli, cradling her in her arms, telling her everything would be all right.

Evelyn woke up. Something was sitting on her leg. Claws digging into the papery bare skin.

'Get off me, bloody bird.'

There was an irritated flap of wings, and a swish as a long train of feathers passed across Evelyn's line of vision. A beaky face bent down and peered at her. She wondered how long the peacock had been using her as a perch.

'Go away.'

Tap, tap, tap.

Another peacock was pecking insistently at the coronation biscuit tin as though in protest. The seeds that it had contained would have long ago been consumed. Evelyn could still hear the ringing clatter of metal on slate as she had tripped over the doorstep, the hail of birdseed scattering onto the floor, her agonised cry as she hit the ground.

She had put out her hands to stop the fall. There had been a searing pain somewhere indefinable, but after a few moments she had felt fine; a little breathless, a little shaken, but fine. She'd breathed a deep sigh of relief and tried to sit up. That was when the pain had come again. In both wrists. Infuriatingly it seemed impossible to raise herself without the support of her wrists, and now they were useless. She

BETHAN

Aberseren, North Wales

Bethan had imagined a long line of taxis waiting outside the station. She'd imagined sliding onto the warm seat while the driver put her suitcase in the boot. He'd have jumped back into the car with a smile.

'Where do you want to go, love?'

'Vaughan Court, please.'

'I'll have you there in no time.'

A flick of the windscreen wipers and they would have set off, wheels splashing through the puddles. Maybe there would be a male-voice choir coming from the radio, or Tom Jones singing 'Green Green Grass of Home'.

But there was no line of taxis; there were no drivers, or male-voice choirs or the sound of Tom Jones. There was only the unrelenting drizzle and an empty station car park illuminated by a streetlight, even though it was three o'clock in the afternoon.

Bethan peered towards the car park entrance and rubbed her hands together wishing she had brought a thicker coat. In London it had been a warm spring day; her vintage Burberry trench coat had seemed perfectly sufficient. She had never dreamed that the sun would not be shining at the end of her journey. In her memories the sun had always been shining in Aberseren.

After ten minutes she knew she'd have to start walking, if only to keep hypothermia at bay. She vaguely remembered the direction.

9

There were only three to choose from; the coast road north, the coast road south or the steep hill straight ahead.

'Between the mountains and the sea,' that was the way her granny Nelli always described the location of Vaughan Court. To Bethan it was hopelessly romantic; like her memories of Evelyn and the house, and her memories of Wales.

Granny Nelli had told her so many stories about her homeland; beautiful ladies emerging from lakes, mythical palaces under the sea. To Bethan it had always been a magical land where giants roamed and women could turn into birds. So different from Battersea where she'd grown up. As a child she'd longed for their annual visit to North Wales, and as an adult she'd spent hours on top of buses or on the Tube thinking of those fairy-tale memories that intertwined with dreams, so that she was never sure what was real and what she had imagined.

But nothing seemed mythical or romantic now. Bethan pulled the heavy suitcase over the slippery pavement while cars splashed water up her jeans as they passed. She was glad she'd chosen to wear her Dr Martens boots. Her mother had persuaded her to wear sensible shoes, warning that Welsh weather could be temperamental.

'You can say that again,' Bethan muttered as the wind began to pick up.

Her long red hair whipped her cheeks; the wild curls that she had tamed with straighteners that morning were already springing back to frizzy life. Bethan stopped and pushed her hair back from her face, her fingers brushing against the little swallow earrings her grandmother had left her in her will. They'd been a gift to Nelli from Evelyn. Bethan thought that Evelyn might like to see that they were still worn and cherished by her friend's granddaughter.

Bethan set off again. The road seemed much longer than she had remembered. The row of multi-coloured cottages leading from the seafront turned into imposing Victorian villas. Most of them were B&Bs or guest houses; one rusty sign declared it belonged to a *Luxury Boutique Hotel*. Its garden bordered the graveyard of the chapel with its long-arched windows and imposing grey façade.

Beyond the chapel there were more houses; a scattering of mock-Tudor semis that soon gave way to an endless line of bungalows, with neat front gardens and sentimental names. She noticed the entrance for a golf club that she didn't remember: *Red Rock Golf Club, Restaurant and Spa* was etched into a monolithic piece of slate at the bottom of a daffodil-lined drive. In the distance she could see a low cedar-clad building with smoky windows and a line of smart cars parked outside. Bethan imagined a Jacuzzi and lavender-scented relaxation rooms. She imagined being wrapped in a fluffy white robe while skilful fingers massaged her aching feet and a waitress brought her a large glass of Chardonnay and a bowl of chips.

She pushed away the fantasies and forced herself to keep on going; surely it wouldn't be much further.

The bungalows petered out into a patchwork of fields scattered across the craggy foothills of the mountains. Sheep huddled against wind-raked hedges and looked as damp and miserable as Bethan was beginning to feel.

At last the familiar golden weathervane appeared, sitting on top of the carved bell tower. The Vaughan family church was much prettier than the austere chapel in the village. It perched on a low hill, opposite the gateposts of Vaughan Court. The only time Bethan had been inside it was for her grandmother's funeral many years before.

Evelyn had insisted that Nelli should be buried in the churchyard after all her years of service to the family and her further years of managing Oak Hill School.

The coffin had been wicker, tied with hundreds of multi-coloured ribbons, each one representing a child that had spent time under Nelli's care at Oak Hill. It was carried in and out of the church by old men Bethan didn't know; her mother had explained that they were local men who'd known Nelli as a child in Aberseren, and one of them had worked at Vaughan Court with her before he'd left to fight in the Second World War.

'I was the boot boy and she was the scullery maid,' he'd said afterwards, through a mouthful of egg sandwich. 'We started on the same day; fourteen, we were, only left school the week before. The

11

housekeeper had already given us both a thrashing by teatime. It worked wonders, mind, we knew what was expected, not like youngsters today.' He'd looked sternly at Bethan. 'Bring back discipline, that's what I say.' Bethan's parents had glanced at each other and suggested that Bethan might like to go and play outside.

Bethan had spent the funeral service staring at the stained-glass windows, each one telling a story that Bethan's atheist upbringing had failed to impart; she could only guess about the lambs and lilies and burning trees. Afterwards they had stood around the grave, the sadness of the occasion at odds with the brilliant blue of the sky. Bethan had buried her face in her mother's skirt as they lowered the coffin into the ground.

Later, Bethan and Robert had looked for peacock feathers in the garden and Evelyn had given them both the biggest tube of Smarties Bethan had ever seen. Robert had jumped up and down in excitement even though he was a middle-aged man. Bethan tried to remember how old she'd been – not more than eight because when she was nine, she and her parents had started going on holiday to France, when previously they had always visited Aberseren with Granny Nelli for a week. Nelli would stay with Evelyn and 'catch up', as they used to say. Bethan and her parents would stay in the Red Rock Caravan Park just beside the beach; Bethan had loved it, day after day on the sand. Sometimes Robert joined her and they'd dig huge holes and wait for the tide to come in and fill them.

After Nelli died, Bethan and her mother would make the long drive to Aberseren once a year to see Evelyn, but only to stay one night. 'The Call of Duty', Bethan's father used to call their visits. 'She's my godmother,' Bethan's mother, Annie, would say. 'I worry about her living in the middle of nowhere, all alone in that great big house. She must be lonely since poor Robert died.'

As a teenager, Bethan had refused to go to Wales at all; Aberseren was so boring compared to London, and Evelyn seemed judgemental, peering with curiosity at Bethan, who'd been a spotty girl trying to mix Goth with Boho, struggling to hide her red hair under various shades of blue or purple. Bethan had decided that Evelyn was snobbish and opinionated, and the Regency romances she wrote were dull and dated compared to the authors Bethan liked to read, and the kind of books Bethan wanted to write.

Now, Bethan wondered how she could have been so disparaging of Evelyn. Evelyn Vaughan, *the* Evelyn Vaughan. Her books were loved by millions of readers all over the world; her stories had been adapted for television, and some had been made into films. Bethan thought about everything she'd read on the internet in preparation for the interview. Evelyn had set up Oak Hill School for children with learning disabilities; she had been an advisor for several Government select committees on disability rights. She'd given speeches in the House of Lords and had numerous awards for her campaigning work. She had an MBE and various other honours; Wikipedia made it seem that she was practically a saint. Bethan was amazed that such a woman could have been her granny Nelli's best friend. She had never understood how a scullery maid and her mistress had become so close.

Bethan walked past the church and through the big stone gateposts of Vaughan Court. A long drive wound steeply upwards with no sign of anything but bare trees and battered clumps of daffodils. Her eyes stung from the rain that trickled from her hair. She suspected that her mascara must be halfway down her cheeks. The hem of her Burberry coat was splattered with mud and her handbag slipped again and again from her shoulder until she gave up and slung it across her chest.

She knew she was not going to make the impression she'd hoped to make on Evelyn; successful freelance journalist – as stylish as Evelyn herself – ready to get to work on the interview with professional efficiency. Now she was going to drip all over Evelyn's beautiful carpets. She'd have to ask for a towel and take off her boots to get them dry. The new notebook she'd bought at the station that morning was probably damp in her handbag; Evelyn would think she was an amateur. Bethan already knew she'd have to explain about *Frank*; she hoped that Evelyn would understand the concept of an online women's magazine.

Bethan silently cursed Mal, probably somewhere on the M25,

warm and dry in the new Nissan they were supposed to share. She wondered if he was alone and pushed the thought away. She'd been determined not to think about the late-night messages that pinged on his phone, the long sessions at the gym, the weekends when he had to go into the office.

'It's the new project, Babe. You know how important work is for me.'

Now this was her project, her important work. She hoped the interview with Evelyn would lead to more commissions. She hoped she'd be able to give up the day job at the café and finally feel like she could call herself a journalist, maybe one day even write the novel she'd dreamed of writing since childhood. She looked up at the scene in front of her. It looked like the setting she'd always imagined for the story she'd never quite been able to conjure up.

The mountains were like a stage set; a dramatic backdrop of craggy rock and glowering cloud. Bethan tried to imagine protagonists roaming over the wild landscape, but they were ghostly and unformed. They quickly faded and she found herself thinking again of Mal and wondering where he was, and who he was with.

Something rustled in the bushes. Bethan turned; through bare branches she thought she saw a flash of blue.

'Hello,' she called out, her hand tightening on her handbag. 'Is there someone there?'

There was no answer. She noticed that the bushes flanked an overgrown path that led off the drive towards a wooden shed, like a child's Wendy house; it was shrouded in ivy, with a single circular window visible above the foliage, and an arched door. Bethan peered towards it; a memory came back to her, something upsetting, something that made her heart beat harder. Bethan hurried on, picking up her pace, wondering if she'd made a mistake. Maybe this wasn't the drive. Maybe this was just some mountain road that wasn't going to take her anywhere but the top of Snowdon. She checked her phone; there was no signal let alone 4G. At least the rain had stopped.

Then suddenly she turned the corner and there it was.

A shaft of sunlight broke through the clouds, shining upon the rosy façade of the house, lighting up the gabled roofline, tall twisted chimneys and high pink sandstone walls that interspersed the mullioned windows. Wide slate steps led up to the ancient oak front door. Above the door she saw the ornately carved portico, with the large stone lion she had loved so much as a child. He sat on top of the portico, his paw resting on a shield, his ferocious gaze forever staring out to sea.

Bethan's heart lifted at the thought of the fire that would no doubt be blazing in the hearth, the comfortable chintz sofas, Evelyn in some elegant outfit, pouring tea into bone-china teacups. Maybe there would be sandwiches or a cake. Bethan was starving; she'd had nothing but a bruised banana and an M&S sandwich since breakfast.

As Bethan approached she stopped and stared. The house was no longer as perfect as it had been in her memory. Slate tiles littered the gravel on the ground, and some of the windowpanes were broken. The portico was riven by a deep crack and the lion teetered at a perilous angle. Smashed stone lay on the steps and when Bethan looked more closely, she could see that half of the lion's shield had fallen away.

Everything was very quiet. Bethan shivered as the sun disappeared behind the clouds. She took a step towards the large oak door. As her hand reached for the ancient iron bell-pull something let out a long and very high-pitched scream.

The scream was followed by a scuffling noise, much nearer. Bethan turned and saw a flurry of blue and green as a peacock flew down and landed on top of the stone balustrade a few feet away. Its long tail hung down as elegantly as a bridal train.

Bethan smiled. How could she have forgotten about the peacocks? As a child she'd never called Evelyn's home Vaughan Court, she'd always called it The Peacock House. It had been part of her summer holidays to come and see the beautiful birds. She'd had a collection of their feathers in her bedroom in the little flat above her parents' pottery studio.

Another peacock strutted around the corner. It stopped and looked at her, its head on one side.

15

'Hello, handsome,' Bethan said. 'Did you make that horrible noise?'

The peacock ruffled his feathers and proceeded to open his tail into a magnificent fan.

Bethan turned back to the door. She pulled the handle of the bell-pull and heard it chiming deep inside the house, but no one came to let her in.

Leaving her suitcase by the door she walked back down the steps onto the gravel that surrounded the house. Her footsteps crunched as she made her way around the corner. From this point she could see the knot garden. As a child she had loved the intricate pattern made of box-hedge flower beds; a geometric jigsaw of roses and lavender and geraniums. In the middle there was a fountain topped with a cherub that had spouted water from his open mouth. Bethan had once tried to imitate him with her orange squash during afternoon tea on the terrace. Bethan's mother had been mortified but Robert had clapped his hands in delight and Evelyn had said it was quite all right and given Bethan a linen napkin to wipe her face.

Bethan stood on the terrace and looked down, searching for any sign of Evelyn in the garden. Another peacock hopped up onto the balustrade a few feet from her. Bethan took her phone out of her pocket; she couldn't resist taking a photo. She thought she'd send it to her mother to let her know she'd arrived; Annie had been so enthusiastic about the interview.

'I can't wait to read it,' she'd said the night before when Bethan had popped in to see her parents after work. 'Granny would have been thrilled that you are writing about Evelyn. I'd have come with you if we weren't so busy getting ready for the exhibition.' Bethan had looked around at the piles of dusty white bowls and vases on the studio floor; her father had been working day and night to throw them on his wheel, and now they were waiting for Annie to add the brightly coloured patterns that would bring them all to life.

Bethan took a step towards the peacock and photographed some close-ups of his tail, thinking that the feathers might provide some inspiration for her mother. She wondered if Mal would like to see the peacock too. She put her phone away and walked round to the back of the house.

Within seconds she had her phone out again, snapping pictures of a tall cedar tree festooned with peacocks. It seemed that every branch had a peacock sitting on it, like Christmas ornaments. There were peacocks everywhere, not just on the tree but several on the high wall of the kitchen garden, more on the ridge tiles of the stable block and one standing, tail displayed in all its splendour, on top of the bonnet of a little pale blue MG convertible. Bethan could remember Evelyn taking her out in the car almost twenty years before. Evelyn had worn dark glasses and a leopard-print coat; to eight-year-old Bethan she had looked impossibly glamorous even though Evelyn must have been in her early seventies then.

'Evelyn,' Bethan called out. 'Evelyn, are you here?'

The peacock on the car let out a high-pitched cry, another answered, and then another, until a whole cacophony of screeches filled the air.

EVELYN

She was running, scrambling over rocks and boulders, her feet splashing through streams with no care for the soft indoor shoes she had on. Behind her, Billy and Peter were calling to her, telling her to wait, but she couldn't wait, she had to get to the plane. The smell was awful, noxious fumes of fuel and burning rubber. She could see the tangled, twisted mess of metal, she could see the body slumped inside the cockpit. Flames were licking at the glass.

'Stay back,' the boys were shouting. 'Bloody hell, she's gonna blow.' But Evelyn ran on, slipping on a tide of shale.

Only a few more steps. She could see the pilot's dark curls, his features slick with sweat. His eyes were open. He was trying to speak. She couldn't hear him. She reached out to try to find a way inside the cockpit. It was so hot. Then the plane began to fade in front of her, disappearing into swirling mist, the heat replaced with a bone-chilling cold.

Jack!

Evelyn woke up. She was still on the floor.

The birds were making a lot of noise outside. She wished that they would do something more useful; like go down to the village and tell Tom she needed help. She tried to look at her watch again but now it was much too painful to move her arm. She thought it must be teatime and then she remembered the girl. The girl was coming at teatime. Was that today? Evelyn tried to think, her brain a mass of muddled dates and times and people – Jack's handsome face amongst it all, his dark eyes looking down into her own, his breath on her lips.

Evelyn tried to focus on the present.

The girl had written a letter. She had asked to come. An interview. It had been a long time since anyone had wanted an interview, thank God. Evelyn always hated them, journalists asking intrusive questions that could only be answered with lies. She'd only agreed that the girl could come because she was Nelli's granddaughter. But which day was it? Evelyn remembered making up a room for her, picking daffodils and putting them in a vase beside the bed. She remembered driving down to Olwyn Moggs's shop to buy a packet of biscuits. She had told Olwyn the girl was visiting and Olwyn had sniffed.

'Imagine Nelli Evans having a journalist for a granddaughter, when Nelli Evans couldn't even make out the letters from the alphabet, let alone read or write.'

Evelyn had wanted to hand back the biscuits and go to Tesco's in Caernarfon instead.

Had that been yesterday?

Evelyn shifted. Her whole body ached now. Stiff and cold and very tired. When had she become an old lady? Surely she was still the girl who used to slide down the bannisters at Wilton Crescent waiting for life to start. In her mind she felt young, though she knew she couldn't get much older. She closed her eyes; maybe this was the day she would stop. She thought of all the people that had gone. Her parents, her brother, Howard and his awful mother, Nelli, Billy, Peter, dear sweet Robert. And Jack.

Jack. Pulling her up from the bed to dance. The wooden boards of the summer house warm beneath her bare feet; dust specks hanging in the air like tiny diamonds as Frank Sinatra's voice crooned from the gramophone on the floor.

You're a wonderful dancer, Evelyn.

'Evelyn.'

So are you, Jack.

'Evelyn.'

When we're old we'll still dance like this, every day.

'Evelyn.'

Do you really believe we'll be together when we're old?

'Evelyn, please.'

Oh yes, it's gonna happen, I promise you.

'Evelyn! Shit, where's the phone?'

I love you, Jack.
And I love you, Evelyn, with all my heart.

'Evelyn, can you open your eyes?'

'Nelli?'

'Oh, thank goodness. Evelyn, tell me where the phone is and I'll get an ambulance.'

Evelyn looked at the girl kneeling beside her. She had a very pretty freckled face and red wavy hair, she looked like Nelli, but somehow different.

The girl stood up. 'I'm going to call an ambulance.'

'No! No ambulance,' Evelyn felt breathless. The effort of speaking was exhausting. 'Tom. Get Tom.'

'Who's Tom?'

'Doctor. My doctor. In the village.'

'Is there a phone in here? My mobile can't get any signal at all.'

'Don't phone,' Evelyn managed. 'Get him. Surgery. White house.' Every word seemed to take more effort.

'I didn't bring a car. I walked up from the station.'

'My car. Keys.' Evelyn tried to gesture towards the door but the pain was agonising.

The girl knelt down beside her again. She was draping something over Evelyn's bare legs. Evelyn couldn't see what it was but she thought it was probably Howard's old hunting jacket that still hung beside the back door. The girl was wearing earrings; little gold swallows. They looked familiar.

'I really think I should get an ambulance,' she said.

'No!' Evelyn kicked out with one leg. The jacket slipped away.

The girl covered Evelyn again and got up to her feet.

'OK. I'll get Tom. Just lie there and be still, I'll be as quick as I can.'

BETHAN

At least the hospital had phone signal. And a Costa Coffee.

Bethan sat in a tub-shaped armchair, took out her phone and started to type.

> Hi Mal, the interview hasn't quite gone to plan. Evelyn has had a fall and broken both her wrists. I'm in the hospital now, waiting for the doctors to make sure it's nothing more serious.
>
> I'm fine and will keep you posted when I can – not much signal round here. Can't wait for my birthday weekend, the hotel in Brighton looks wonderful. Text me. Xxx

Bethan reread the text and added 'I miss you.' She pressed send.

A young couple came and sat down on the leather sofa opposite her. The woman was heavily pregnant; the man put his arm around her and began to rub her back. Bethan stared at her phone. Mal was probably at the gym. He wouldn't be able to answer until he left. She started to type another message.

> Hi Mum, just to let you know that when I got to Evelyn's, I found her lying on the kitchen floor. She has had a fall and now she's in hospital. She's broken both her wrists and having tests to rule out anything else. She's conscious and cross!! I've escaped to Costa where I'm drinking coffee and eating muffins. Evelyn will stay in overnight so I'm just

waiting for a taxi to take me back to the house (been waiting half an hour so far – turns out Bangor is not like Battersea for cabs – or much else, I suspect!). I think I've broken Evelyn's little MG – I haven't dared tell her yet! I'll come back to the hospital in the morning.

Her mother's reply took exactly two minutes.

Poor Evelyn! Please let me know what the doctors say. Bad news about the car – it must be ancient by now. How will you get back to the hospital tomorrow? Will you be OK on your own in that big house? If only the exhibition wasn't so soon I'd come to Wales to look after you both. We're firing the first batch as I type!! Your father will be up all night fretting. Lots of love, Mum xxx

Mum! I'm a grown woman. I will be fine in the house. I'll let you know what they say about E tomorrow, hopefully she'll be a bit less grumpy. Her GP from the village is giving me a lift back here in the morning – he's a bit grumpy himself. Love to Dad – may the kiln gods be kind.

Bethan also sent the picture of the peacock with his tail displayed.

Inspiration xx

Bethan took a sip of her coffee and thought about the grumpy GP. He seemed to have decided she was incompetent and that the car breaking down was due to her inept driving.

'Did you leave the handbrake on? Did you over-rev the engine?'

Of course she hadn't. The little MG had been making the most peculiar noises from the time she set off. It had managed to get half-way down the drive before it completely ground to a halt. Bethan ran the rest of the way to the village just as the rain began again. By the time she saw the sign for the Aberseren Health Centre the rain

24

had become so torrential even her bra and knickers were wet. As she approached the bungalow that housed the health centre the door swung magically open. Bethan stepped into a room with two rows of chairs. An old man sat in one corner, hunched and coughing. Behind the desk a much younger man was on the phone.

'No . . . As big as that . . . Well, it must be horrendous . . . You poor thing . . . I'll make sure I pop you down for an appointment ASAP.' The man looked up at Bethan. 'Oh, hang on, Mrs Griffiths, we've got an emergency just walked in, must go, see you in the morning, nine a.m.'

The man rushed round from behind the desk. He was wearing a bright purple knitted tank top and a green knitted tie.

'Sit down.' He ushered Bethan towards a chair. 'The doctor will be with you in a minute.'

'I need an ambulance,' Bethan was too agitated to sit.

The man put his hand on her arm.

'Is it that bad? What happened? You're soaked to the skin. Have you fallen in the sea?'

'Evelyn Vaughan—'

'Lady Evelyn pushed you in the sea?' The man's eyes opened very wide.

'No! Evelyn Vaughan has had an accident. A fall, or maybe a stroke, or something. She's lying on the floor up at the house. I was too nervous to move her in case I made things worse.'

There were noises coming from somewhere beyond the waiting room; a deep male voice was talking. 'You know you can come and see me any time. Sometimes a good chat can be the best medicine.'

A tired-looking woman walked into the waiting room holding a small baby while a toddler hung onto the back of her coat.

'Thank you, Dr Tom,' the woman said. 'I feel so much better already.'

A tall, ruggedly handsome man followed her through the door; his dishevelled dark hair was threaded with silver, though his face didn't look old enough for him to be going grey.

He stopped when he saw Bethan and indicated back into the corridor behind him.

'You can come straight through. Has Owen taken your details?'

The young man in the tank top hurried back to the other side of the desk and shuffled some papers efficiently.

'It's not her that needs you, Dr Tom,' he nodded towards Bethan. 'She says there's been an incident up at Vaughan Court. Lady Evelyn has collapsed and she's left her lying on the floor.'

'I didn't just leave her!' Bethan protested. 'I tried to get here as fast as possible.'

'Did you call an ambulance?' The doctor's voice was curt.

'I couldn't find a phone and I had no signal on my mobile.'

'No one has any signal round here,' the receptionist said. 'Hashtag-back-of-beyond.'

'She wouldn't tell me where the phone was.' Bethan turned to the doctor. 'She insisted that I come and get you myself in her car. But the car ground to a halt on the drive—'

'Phone the ambulance, Owen,' the doctor interrupted. 'I'll go up there right now.' He reached for a coat from a row of them and then turned back to Bethan. 'Will the ambulance be able to pass the car on the drive?'

'Yes, I think so, I tried to steer it to the side when—'

'I'll give you a lift,' the doctor interrupted her again.

'Thanks.' Bethan gave a smile that wasn't returned. 'I've come to visit Evelyn for the night, she's an old family friend.'

'Well, your visit might not be quite as much fun as you had planned.' Tom shrugged on the coat.

'I wasn't expecting fun.'

'But what about me, Dr Tom?' A fit of coughing emanated from the corner. 'I think it's bronchial pneumatics. I feel it coming on something rotten in my chest tubes.'

'Now, Cled.' The doctor's tone softened. 'I tell you this every week. That cough is nothing that giving up the twenty Embassys a day wouldn't help. But if you can survive a few more hours I'll pop up to the farm after dinner and have a listen to your lungs.'

The doctor nodded goodbye to the old man and hurried out of the door.

'Could you tell Sarah I'll be late,' he called back to the receptionist. 'Tell her I'm sorry, I know she has her book group this evening.'

Bethan followed the doctor outside.

'Come on,' the doctor said, unlocking the door of a mud splattered Volvo parked in a space marked *Dr Rossall*. 'We'd better be quick.'

Bethan pulled open the passenger door; there was a fluffy pink pencil case on the seat and an array of rainbow-coloured gel pens spilled out onto the black leather along with several Love Hearts sweets. The doctor swiftly gathered the pens and sweets together and threw them into the back of the car.

'She's ninety, you know,' he said as he started the engine. 'Hypothermia can set in very quickly.'

'I did cover her with a jacket.'

'She'll need more than a jacket. But I suppose that if you couldn't even find the phone, a blanket would have been too much to ask.'

Bethan mumbled that she had thought getting help was the most important thing but the doctor didn't answer, his handsome face set into an expression that matched the stony silence in the car.

EVELYN

They never let her sleep. All night she was prodded and poked and people stuck things in her ears and wrapped things round her arms. They put a catheter in her hand and attached a drip. They looked into her eyes with a torch and asked her who the prime minister was. She wanted to tell them all to leave her alone. In fact, she knew she had told them to leave her alone, several times, in no uncertain terms.

'Now, now, dear. There's no need for that kind of language. Is it Eve or Evie? Do you need the pan? Take a sip of this. Swallow these. Let's just have a little check of your blood pressure. No, don't try and get out of bed. Come on, Eva, you mustn't make a fuss, think of the other patients, they're trying to sleep.'

Evelyn lay back on the pillows. Every time she moved they made a sort of crackling noise as though they were stuffed with crisp packets. She shifted and felt the sheet slide against the plastic mattress. It was very hot. There were two women in beds opposite; one had purple hair and snored loudly, the other looked as though her days were very much at their end.

Evelyn knew that she didn't want the hospital to be her end. She did not want to die in a noisy, sterile room, staring at the faded green curtains around her bed, wondering why no one bothered to mend the broken rail.

She thought of Howard in the final days. She had pushed his bed into the bay window, looking out towards the sea. He had been bathed in sunlight, cooled by the gentle summer breeze blowing through the open windows. There was no smell of antiseptic; only the scent of roses from the garden and the sound of the peacocks calling to each other across the lawn, even though he couldn't hear them. It had been over twenty-five years ago. Peter had been wonderful, coming every day, helping to relieve the pain, probably helping to hasten the end in a way that Tom would never do.

Evelyn's mind drifted to Robert. He too had been spared the discomforts of a hospital ward; he had simply gone to sleep one night at the age of fifty-five and never woken up. His last words to her had been about going to the beach. She had promised him that the next day they would climb Red Rock and look for pirate ships, and he had clapped his hands with excitement. Evelyn would have liked to say goodbye, to tell him how much he was cherished, how much he had helped. Even as a tiny baby he had saved her from the deep pit of despair – though to tell him the whole story would have been cruel.

The woman with the purple hair shouted out in her sleep.

'I told you, Marlboro Gold not Bensons!'

Evelyn thought she rather fancied a cigarette herself, though she hadn't smoked for decades. She'd started in the war; the American nurses had introduced her to it, sharing their Lucky Strikes with her at break times, showing her how to blow smoke rings.

'So unfeminine,' her mother-in-law would say.

She used to smoke with Jack; they had a heavy glass ashtray in the summer house that he stole from a pub. Evelyn closed her eyes and saw Jack's face. She wondered what suffering had come to meet him at his end. Where had he been? A hospital? A field? A ditch?

A new nurse came to take her temperature. She looked at Evelyn.

'There, there, love. There's no need to cry.'

May 1941

The wisteria was out all over London. A defiant display in the face of the war. Evelyn could smell the flowers – heavy, sickly, much too sweet. But at least the night air was cool on her burning cheeks. She leant against the trunk of a lime tree in the gardens of Wilton Crescent and looked up at the white-stuccoed house in front of her, the biggest and the grandest in the row. Even though the blackout curtains were drawn she knew that they were all in there, dolls in a dolls house, drinking champagne, chattering endlessly about the war and what it was doing for business. Everyone seemed to agree that the motorbike industry was booming.

'I've just signed another contract from the army for ten thousand 16Hs,' her father had been saying when she slipped out of the room to follow Anthony.

Evelyn had been waiting for an opportunity to be alone with him all evening. She was sure she'd seen him look at her several times over dinner, with that look that she interpreted as love.

It was the same way he'd looked at her the time he visited her brother in the Easter holidays from Eton, and all the times he'd come down to Oak Hill to shoot or fish or swim in the lake the previous summer.

He looked so handsome in his new officer's uniform when he'd arrived for her birthday party, transformed from a schoolboy into a man. Evelyn left the sounds of the party behind her and crossed the marble hallway. She found him in the study. She knew he had been waiting for her. She shut the door, leaning against it like she imagined Vivien Leigh might do, languid, seductive in her long pink taffeta dress, then she'd walked across the room.

'You can kiss me if you like.'

Outside in the night air, Evelyn put her hands up to her ears trying to block the memory of her own silly voice. Her words echoed round and round her head. What a fool she'd been.

The siren started to wail. Evelyn stayed where she was. Hitler could do what he liked. She didn't care. In the distance she heard the soft thumps and thuds as the bombers targeted the docks and the factories along the Thames.

She'd thought it was going to be such a wonderful sixteenth

31

birthday party and now it was ruined. Her whole life was ruined. She couldn't get the image out of her mind. Anthony's face, embarrassed, awkward, horribly kind. She could still feel his hands on her shoulders as he'd gently pushed her away. She had turned, her cheeks hot, ready to race from the room but the door was slowly opening and she could hear her sister's giggling voice.

'Darling, I thought I'd never get away from everyone.'

Of course, it made sense; her beautiful eighteen-year-old sister with her lovely figure and Rita Hayworth hair. Evelyn hated her. She hated him. She looked back at the house. She hated them all.

The glossy black front door opened. She could see her mother standing on the step.

'Evelyn, darling, are you out there?'

And then it happened. A strong wind pushed Evelyn back against a tree, then a noise – hammering and shattering – and then a roar that lifted Evelyn off her feet into the air. Debris flew in her face; a slow cascade of stone and glass and masonry. It seemed to go on and on. When it stopped, Evelyn was lying on the grass. There was smoke and little bits of something that looked like petals tumbling and fluttering in the air. She thought of butterflies. She thought of the wisteria. A cloud of dust enveloped her like a shroud. She could taste blood in her mouth.

As the dust cleared she saw the gap. A terrible gap in the crescent.

'Mummy!'

She spent weeks on the children's ward at St Thomas' Hospital, even though she was so much older than the other patients. She didn't know what her injuries were; no one thought to tell her. The nurses changed her dressings with brisk efficiency every day and doctors came and went with pocket watches and grim faces. No one ever looked her directly in the eye.

Sir Nigel Overly had been her only visitor at St Thomas'. A little obsequious man with a narrow moustache, Evelyn had never liked him. As a child she had sometimes encountered him in the narrow corridors of Wilton Crescent and once, at the end of a shooting party at Oak Hill, he had reprimanded her for making a fuss of his spaniel. 'She's a gun dog, not a pet.'

Standing so close to her hospital bed that she could smell the cigar smoke on his breath, he informed her that all the funerals of her family members had been held, and that all the different wills had been read. Then he had smiled and told her, in a tone of voice that suggested she'd be delighted, that she was now 'a very wealthy young lady indeed.'

For all her wealth, when Evelyn was discharged from hospital she had nowhere to go. Everyone had been at her birthday party; her parents, her siblings, her aunt and uncle, her grandparents. Mr James the butler had also been killed along with his wife, who had been their cook. Even her beloved spaniels Gip and Sweep had been obliterated by the incendiary bomb.

Evelyn had gone back to her boarding school in Cheltenham. It was supposed to be her final term but Miss Wyatt had taken pity on her and let her stay for another year. Evelyn had slept in Matron's room because her nightmares had disturbed the other girls.

When she left the school, Evelyn went to stay with one of Miss Wyatt's relations in Hampstead.

The relation suggested the Women's Voluntary Service as something that would keep Evelyn from dwelling on her loss as well as help the war effort. Evelyn was meant to hand out soup and sandwiches to firemen in the East End but every time she heard an air raid siren she froze with fear and was more of a liability than a help.

Evelyn left London and took herself to Oak Hill.

The family country house was empty, echoing with the people who were no longer there. Evelyn spent long, autumnal days walking over the South Downs, but without Gip and Sweep the familiar walks had no purpose. She felt lost in the landscape, disorientated without the dogs. She half-heartedly read the classics in the Oak Hill library and in the evenings, she wrote stories about love and loss and handsome heroes in her old school notebooks. She wrote fairy-tale endings with perfect spring weddings, and young brides wearing beautiful silk and lace dresses, holding cascading bouquets.

She longed for company. Longed for someone still alive that she could love.

It was around this time that Sir Nigel Overly had introduced Evelyn to Howard. Evelyn had gone to London to sign some papers in his office just off the Strand. She had been about to leave when Howard walked in.

'Serendipity' Sir Nigel had described it in the speech he'd made at their wedding.

Howard had been an army captain. His company had been ambushed on their way to the beaches at Dunkirk and one hundred of his men had been massacred by German SS troops. Somehow Howard had got away. Afterwards he had been confined to a desk in Whitehall. He spoke to Evelyn of nerves and battle fatigue; he admitted to nightmares that made him too frightened to sleep.

Even though Howard was twelve years older than Evelyn, she had felt a connection. When he told her his story, she had recognised his description of misery; she imagined his nightmares looked like hers, assumed his disconnection with the real world felt like her own.

Sir Nigel had introduced Howard to Evelyn as 'Lord Vaughan, one of my very good friends.' Later Evelyn discovered they had been business partners, and that Howard owed Sir Nigel a lot of money from a deal that had gone wrong at the outbreak of war. Together with crippling death duties after the death of Howard's father, the Vaughan family were in trouble. They had already sold their Irish estates and much of the land they'd held for generations in Warwickshire and Cumberland. Vaughan Court was all that was left, though it was mortgaged to the hilt and falling into disrepair.

Seventeen-year-old Evelyn had been the perfect solution.

They had married two months later at St James's Piccadilly. Evelyn had worn a jacket and skirt – stiff grey serge that scratched against her wrists all day – and a little pillbox hat. Silk and lace and long dresses had no place in war-ravaged London. There was no bouquet.

34

Howard had worn his captain's uniform; it was the first time Evelyn had seen him out of a suit. He had looked handsome and the anxiety Evelyn had felt for weeks subsided a little. The anxiety returned as soon as they emerged from the church to a dark, sleet-slashed afternoon. Lady Vaughan had insisted that Howard take her arm to lead her down the slippery steps, leaving Evelyn to walk behind them on her own. She heard her new mother-in-law telling Howard that she never imagined the day when a Vaughan would have to marry new money.

'Motorbike factories indeed!'

The wedding reception had been at The Ritz, a small gathering for tea and sandwiches. Howard had told Evelyn she could ask anyone she wanted but she could only think of Miss Wyatt.

When Evelyn had left the gathering to use the ladies' powder room, Miss Wyatt had followed and spoken to her urgently beside the marble wash basins. Her sentences tangled in embarrassment as she realised that Evelyn might not have anyone else to advise her on the intimacies of the night to come.

'He might be a little over-enthusiastic at the start . . . even rough . . . Try to relax . . . Make sympathetic noises . . . It won't last long.'

Evelyn and Howard had gone back to the newly decorated flat on Sloane Street, and Howard had given Evelyn brandy. It had made her choke. They'd undressed in darkness, Evelyn slipping on a satin nightgown that she had found in her sister's room at Oak Hill. She got into the unfamiliar double bed and waited. After several minutes Howard had got into bed on the other side. Evelyn felt the mattress dip towards him and she braced herself for his touch. But he didn't move towards her. Instead they lay very still together side by side until Evelyn heard Howard let out a low snore. After a long time, Evelyn slept, and when she woke in the morning Howard was already up and dressed for the office.

The following night, just as Evelyn had thought that Howard was going to fall to sleep again, he turned to her and placed his hand on one of her breasts, and with the other hand he pulled the nightdress over her

35

thighs. Then she felt him shift and his weight was on top of her, his sharp hipbones grinding against hers, his fingers fumbling hopelessly with something soft. After a few minutes he rolled off her and turned away in silence. Evelyn had the terrible feeling she had failed.

The embarrassment hung between them at the breakfast table the next morning; they scraped butter rations on thin toast and made small talk about the latest war reports on the radio until the car came to take Howard to his office at Whitehall.

When he got back that evening he told Evelyn she was to accompany Lady Vaughan home to Wales.

'It will be so much better for you,' Howard had said. 'You know how your nerves play up at the sound of the sirens, and mother needs to go home. Someone has to supervise the staff.'

It had been a bleak December afternoon when they set off. The day had been short, darkness already descending as the old Bentley wove its way over the never-ending mountain roads of Snowdonia. Evelyn gazed at the alien scenery; endless craggy snow-capped summits, wet black slate and white waterfalls that cascaded furiously down the fractured rocks. Every so often Evelyn glimpsed a desolate farmhouse in the distance; each one looked as cold and empty as she felt.

It had been hours since they'd left London. Evelyn had been desperate for the lavatory but far too terrified of her new mother-in-law to ask if they could stop the car. There hadn't been a building let alone a pub or hotel for miles. At Oak Hill, Evelyn had no qualms about squatting behind a bush if she was caught short on one of the long walks she used to take with the dogs, but Evelyn could tell that Lady Vaughan would be horrified if she asked if she could just pop behind a rock to pee. Instead, she crossed her legs tightly and tried not to wince as every jolt of the car made her feel as though her bladder might burst.

Evelyn had looked out at the barren landscape and hoped that it was all just a bad dream. Soon she would wake up and find herself in the big brass bed in her bedroom in Wilton Crescent; Gip and Sweep on the rug by the fire and her sister wafting in demanding to borrow kirby grips and Nivea cream.

EVELYN

The ward was flooded with grey light as someone pulled back the curtains to reveal a dreary dawn. Tablets were brought round in a little pot, like sweets.

A nurse tipped a plastic cup of water towards Evelyn's mouth. 'There you go, my lovely, swallow them down, have you feeling young again in no time.'

Evelyn's mind was still in the old Bentley, she was still young, still seventeen, looking out of the window at the never-ending mountains. Where had all the years gone? She had never imagined that she would spend over seventy years in that barren landscape. She thought of all the things the mountains had given her; beauty, space to think, to write, inspiration. *Jack*. But they had also brought loneliness, pain and loss. They had no qualms about taking away a life. She thought about poor Billy and felt relief that Tom would never know the story; she knew that Peter had never told his son what happened on that terrible day.

Even after all the years, Evelyn could still see Billy's body lying in the river. She could still feel the initial fear and horror. The realisation that it was all her fault. And lately she had a terrible feeling Billy was back, with his catapult and little stones. Tormenting her in the night, making her remember the things she'd tried so hard to forget.

There was a loud clattering coming from the corridor, the squeak of wheels. Evelyn could smell food.

A young woman wearing baggy blue overalls and a thin plastic apron came into the ward and pulled a table over Evelyn's bed without saying a word. The blue overalls were the most unflattering garments Evelyn had ever seen. Evelyn had hated her own dull brown ward uniform, but at least it had showed off her waist. The young woman disappeared back into the corridor and returned with a plate. She put it in front of Evelyn.

'Toast,' she said and walked away.

Evelyn looked down at her hands. They were both encased in plastic splints that went from her fingers up to her elbows. She no longer had opposable thumbs, but she was extremely hungry.

'Excuse me,' she called after the woman. 'I can't eat this.'

The woman gave a shrug.

'Suit yourself.' She came back and swept the plate of toast away.

'No, I mean I can't pick it up.'

But the woman had already gone through the door.

Evelyn sighed. She hadn't eaten anything since she'd had sardines for her supper two days before.

'You're not missing out, love.' The woman with purple hair was busy chomping through her own piece of toast. 'Tastes like polystyrene.'

BETHAN

Evelyn had done nothing but complain since they arrived. Bethan and the woman with the purple hair exchanged a smile across the ward. The purple-haired woman rolled her eyes slightly as Evelyn protested loudly that a vase on *Cash in the Attic* was obviously worthless tat.

'I think the patient is feeling better,' Tom said, examining the notes on a clipboard at the end of the bed.

Evelyn was definitely looking better than she had done the evening before; her high cheekbones had taken on a rosy tinge and her blue eyes were bright as they darted repeatedly from the large television to the door.

'When are they going to bring some food?'

A nurse rushed in holding a bowl of Rice Krispies.

'I found a box of cereal lurking in the visitors' room.'

'Give the girl the bowl,' Evelyn nodded towards Bethan. 'She'll have to be my hands.'

'Will you be all right with this?' The nurse looked at Bethan and held up a small teaspoon. 'It was all I could find at this time of day, they'll bring the cutlery back at lunch . . .'

'She'll be fine with it,' Evelyn interrupted. 'I'm so hungry she can shovel it in with her hands for all I care.'

Bethan perched on the edge of the bed and carefully scooped up a teaspoonful of cereal. Evelyn leant forward like a hungry bird.

Tom laughed, 'I never thought I'd see the day that Evelyn Vaughan let someone spoon-feed her!'

Evelyn swallowed before she spoke.

'And I never thought I'd see the day that you could practically starve to death in a place that is meant to make you better.' She looked pointedly at the nurse.

'I'm so sorry, Lady Vaughan.' The nurse flushed. 'The orderly thought you didn't want the toast.' The staff had obviously now been briefed on who their elderly patient was.

Evelyn finished her second mouthful.

'Just call me Evelyn, I can't stand being called Lady Vaughan.'

'Sorry,' the nurse stumbled over her words. 'No one realised . . . I mean, we didn't know . . . I mean . . .'

Evelyn opened her mouth and Bethan popped another spoonful of cereal in before Evelyn could respond.

'I read *The Pink Pearl Heiress* a few years ago,' the nurse said. 'It was very good, made me cry. I'm mortified that I didn't recognise your name when you came in.'

Evelyn gave the nurse a sympathetic smile.

'I can see you're all very busy here, and I do understand what it's like, I have some experience of nursing, you know.'

'Really?' The nurse's anxious frown faded.

'In the war; only an auxiliary, I wasn't properly trained like you obviously are. Do you have a diploma?'

'A degree actually.' The young woman straightened her overalls with a smile.

'You seem like a very intelligent woman.'

'Thank you.' The nurse's smile widened. 'I'll just go and see when they're taking you down to get your wrists in plaster.' She walked away with an efficient stride.

'I see you playing the flattery trick.' Tom shook his head. 'There's only so far it will get you on the NHS.'

'Really?' Evelyn sniffed. 'You should give it a try, Tom. Don't think I couldn't hear you yesterday when you came up to the house. You told Bethan I was stubborn as a mule! Your father would never have referred to one of his patients in that way. Peter was a most respectful doctor.' Evelyn sniffed again and turned back to the television.

A middle-aged couple were trying to look grateful for the twenty pounds they had got for the vase.

Evelyn smiled.

'Didn't I say it was worthless!' She opened her mouth for Bethan to feed her another spoonful of Rice Krispies.

'I didn't know you were a nurse, Evelyn,' said Bethan. 'Granny never mentioned it.'

'That was when Vaughan Court was a United States military hospital in World War Two,' Tom said. 'My father used to talk about it sometimes; I think that's what got him interested in medicine. He was an evacuee from a Liverpool slum – the war changed his life.'

'Peter was such a clever boy,' Evelyn said. 'He made a wonderful doctor.'

'I'll never live up to him in Evelyn's eyes.' Tom flashed an unexpected grin in Bethan's direction. Bethan thought it was the first time he'd smiled at her since they'd met. 'If only she'd tell me more about him, I might pick up some tips.'

Evelyn pushed Bethan's next spoonful of cereal away and lay back on the pillows.

'It was all such a long time ago.'

Bethan wanted to ask questions about how a woman who had married into the aristocracy could have ended up working as an auxiliary nurse. It could all be useful for the article, but Evelyn suddenly looked pale and Tom had stressed in the car that Evelyn must not be overexerted.

'She's had a shock; the fall will have affected her more than she thinks.'

Bethan stifled a yawn. She'd had a terrible night's sleep. When she'd got back to Vaughan Court it had been dusk, the empty house submerged in a half-light that cast eerie shadows in the chilly ground-floor rooms.

Bethan had taken her suitcase and gone straight upstairs to look for somewhere to sleep. Numerous rooms lined the long corridors. Most had furniture covered in dust sheets, though some were completely empty, with wallpaper that was peeling off the walls and elaborately plastered ceilings mottled with damp.

One room seemed to have been a child's nursery; a train set on the floor and a large rocking horse in one corner, its glass eyes glinting in the light from the dim bulb. An open window looked towards the dark silhouettes of the mountains; thin muslin curtains billowed on the wind like two ghosts into the room.

Bethan took a deep breath and crossed the room, pulling the window firmly shut. The curtains dropped back into place on each side of the frame as Bethan turned and hurriedly left.

On the other side of an archway a whole new wing of the house revealed itself. It was there that she found what could only have been Evelyn's room, huge and full of books and papers and the smell of Chanel No. 5.

Next door she found an ancient bathroom; a toilet with a high cistern and a cast-iron bath standing in the middle of the room. The sound of a dripping tap echoed around the ceramic-tiled walls, and the light fitting flickered on and off then on again when Bethan pulled on a broken cord by the door.

On the other side of the bathroom, Bethan found a room that seemed to have been prepared for a visitor, with white towels folded on top of the chest of drawers and a little vase of daffodils on the table beside an enormous four-poster bed. A cast-iron fireplace had an ancient electric heater standing in the middle of it. Bethan flicked the heater's switch, and the metal coils started to glow, giving off the aroma of singed dust.

The bed was magnificent – a carved mahogany frame with elaborate silk drapes – but when Bethan slipped between the sheets they were cold and slightly damp. She noticed an antique doll sitting on the dressing table, its dull hair matted and its limbs stiffly arranged. Its face was beautiful, but its open mouth and tiny teeth disturbed Bethan. She wished she'd put it away in the wardrobe before she'd got into bed. Now it was too cold to get back out.

All night the wind had groaned down the fireplace like an old man in pain and a chilly draught kept sleep at bay. The house was full of bumps and creaks, and at some point, when Bethan had actually managed to fall asleep, she'd been woken by what sounded like a shower of pebbles being thrown up at the window. She had lain very still, so frightened that she wasn't sure if the thumping she could hear was her heart or footsteps on the stairs. It had still been dark when the peacocks began calling to each other with their high-pitched cries. Bethan had been relieved – at least it meant she wasn't the only living thing awake.

'We were just wondering how long you're staying?' Tom was looking at her. The nurse was looking at her too and there was a doctor in a white coat who seemed to have materialised like a ghost beside Evelyn's bed.

'Until tomorrow,' Bethan said. 'I'm catching a train after lunch.'

Tom glanced at Evelyn.

'The thing is—' he began.

'The thing is I am not going into a nursing home, even if it is just for a couple of weeks.' Evelyn finished his sentence. Her face had taken on a child-like petulance.

'Now, Evelyn,' Tom continued. 'How are you going to cope on your own back at Vaughan Court? You'll have a bit more movement in your hands once your wrists are in plaster but doing everyday tasks like getting dressed are going to be very difficult.'

'I will manage.' Evelyn glared at Tom.

He turned back to Bethan.

'Do you need to get back to London for work?'

Bethan bit her lip.

'I have the week off but I'm going away with my boyfriend tomorrow evening. To Brighton. It's my birthday treat, there's a vintage clothing fair that I've been really looking forward to.'

Tom stared silently at her for a few seconds before responding.

'Well, we wouldn't want to spoil your plans.'

'Lady Evelyn cannot go back to her home unaccompanied,' the doctor in the white coat said. 'Nurse, can you ring up Ty Gwyn and ask if they have any space?'

'No!' Evelyn almost shouted. 'Not Ty Gwyn. No one ever comes out of there alive.'

'Come, come, Lady Evelyn,' the doctor smiled obsequiously. 'That's a rather sweeping statement, lots of people leave.'

'In coffins!' Evelyn glowered at the doctor.

'She's right, you know,' the woman with the purple hair heckled. 'My mother says you might as well go straight to the mortuary than go to Ty Gwyn. She says it would be kinder.'

The doctor and Tom exchanged a look that suggested Evelyn and the woman with the purple hair's mother might be right.

'Well, what about Lake View?' the doctor continued, smiling at Evelyn. 'I hear they serve high tea every day with macaroons and cucumber sandwiches.'

'I don't want macaroons and cucumber sandwiches!' Evelyn protested. 'And the view is not of a lake, it's a disused slate quarry with a dirty bit of rainwater at the bottom!'

Tom looked at Bethan again.

'Would your mother be able to come to stay?'

'The problem is . . .'

'Oh, that would be splendid,' Evelyn interrupted. 'I would love to see Annie again.'

'The problem is,' Bethan continued, 'Mum and Dad have a big exhibition to get ready for. I don't think she could come before it starts.'

Evelyn's mouth tightened.

'Well, I suppose pots are more important than an old godmother in need.' She looked down at her incapacitated wrists and sighed. 'It looks like there's nothing that can be done. Phone Ty Gwyn and see if they'll take me.' She lay back on the pillows. 'Though I don't suppose I'll ever see Vaughan Court again.'

EVELYN

Evelyn smiled at Bethan.

'Tom says I am manipulative. He says I specialise in emotional exploitation techniques that border on the narcissistic! But I say, what's wrong with a bit of emotional exploitation? It's got me a long way in life. And does he really think I'm going to change my behaviour at my age?'

Bethan laughed. Evelyn began to feel better.

She hadn't meant to make the poor girl feel guilty! She'd said that over and over again. It was the girl's choice if she wanted to stay. And Bethan had seemed quite pleased with the idea of asking her boyfriend to come and stay at Vaughan Court.

'What did you say your young man is called?'

'Mal.'

'I think you and Mal will have a lovely time. It's a beautiful house and I'm sure Snowdonia has just as much to offer as Brighton, as long as the rain isn't too torrential.'

Bethan laughed again, though this time Evelyn detected a hint of uncertainty.

'And then there's the interview,' Evelyn continued. 'It would be very difficult to ask me all those questions in a nursing home. Half the people in there are probably completely ga-ga, they'd be shouting out and interrupting us, and I assume they have strict visiting hours, there wouldn't be enough time to tell you everything. And you only have to stay until Sunday. Tom has promised he will find out about home-help for next week.'

The girl was looking at her phone again. Evelyn thought that she looked at it much more than seemed necessary.

'When will Mal be coming?' Evelyn asked.

Bethan looked up at her.

'Sorry, what did you say?'

'I was wondering when your young man will be able to join you?'

Bethan looked at her phone again.

'I've asked him if he can take a day off and come today, but he hasn't answered yet.'

'It's infuriating that they won't let me out of here until tomorrow. "To be on the safe side!" The safe side of what? I wonder. But at least if your Mal comes today you can have a romantic night on your own without me pestering you for help.'

Bethan was still looking at her phone, finger on the screen as though trying to conjure Mal's answer into life.

'He's probably in a meeting. Or at the gym. He goes at lunchtime sometimes.'

'Ahh, the gym.' Evelyn sniffed. 'All the young men seem to go to the gym. Even Tom likes to use the one at the golf club when Tilly has her swimming lesson there. It seems like a terrible waste of time to me – and energy.'

The girl had stopped listening again. This time she had got up from the chair by the bed and was looking out of the window at the drizzle.

'You look a lot like her, you know?' Evelyn said.

Bethan turned.

'A lot like who?'

'Like your grandmother. You have her wonderful hair. You also have her fabulous figure.'

'You mean big breasts?' The girl sat down again.

'I mean curvaceous,' Evelyn said. 'All the boys liked Nelli.'

Bethan looked more interested.

'Did they? Was this before she went to live in Sussex?'

Evelyn nodded.

'The American airmen in the hospital were always trying to catch a glimpse of her working in the kitchen or cleaning our part of the house – it was a sign that they were in recovery when they'd ask the name of the cute little maid in the frilly white cap.'

'Cute? Really?'

Evelyn nodded.

'These days I think your grandmother would be called "a babe".'

'I can't imagine Granny as a babe!' Bethan laughed. 'She never talked about any boyfriends from her past.'

'She wasn't interested in any of those American flight boys, she only had eyes for her Lloyd.' Evelyn closed her eyes as she remembered Lloyd in his Royal Navy uniform, walking up the path with his sailor's swagger and Nelli running down to meet him, red hair and apron strings flying out behind her, Mrs Moggs shouting at her from the terrace.

'*Dewch yn ôl i chi ferch ddrwg!* Come back here, you naughty girl!'

Nelli and Lloyd had been sweethearts since school. They shared the same laughing eyes, and a passion for the folk stories of their native land. They planned to marry after the war; Lloyd would take over the fleet of fishing trawlers from his father and Nelli was going to have six children, three of each. She used to tell Evelyn what their names would be as she brushed Evelyn's hair at night, though she was forever changing her mind.

'*I've gone off Myfanwy, I like Gwenllian now, but Lloyd likes Olwen after the beautiful daughter of the giant Ysbaddaden who lived on a mountain that's only visible after dark. Do you know that story, Lady Evelyn? Shall I tell it to you?*'

'Who was Lloyd?' Bethan asked.

Evelyn opened her eyes. She didn't suppose Nelli ever mentioned Lloyd to her daughter or her granddaughter; it was probably too painful. She had found such happiness in the end with Michael, and by the time Maggie had been born, Nelli's life in Aberseren had long been in the past.

'Lloyd was just a nice young man,' she said quietly, suddenly exhausted. The morning seemed to have gone on for hours and they still hadn't come to take her to have her wrists put in plaster.

The girl was standing up again. She seemed to find it very hard to sit still. *Have you got ants in your pants?* The phrase came back to Evelyn; it was something that always made Robert giggle.

'I'll go and see if Tom is ready to go back to the village,' Bethan said. 'You look like you need a rest.'

Evelyn nodded.

'A little doze would be rather nice.'

'I'll see you tomorrow.' Bethan touched her shoulder. Evelyn wondered if she was going to bend down and give her a kiss but she didn't. She probably found her a bit formidable. Formidableness was something that had taken years of practice, like her emotional exploitation techniques. Evelyn had needed both when dealing with members of parliament, officious social workers, doctors, and people who thought that the best way to deal with disabilities was to lock what they saw as 'the afflicted' away.

'Shall I pull the curtain?' Bethan already had her hand on the limp green fabric, tugging at it ineffectively where Evelyn knew the rail was broken.

'Bethan?'

The girl stopped pulling the curtain.

'Yes?'

'Is everything all right at Vaughan Court?'

'It's fine. I found some bread for toast for breakfast and the peacocks were gathered around the kitchen door when I got up, they seemed to be expecting food.'

'Did you find a new bag of birdseed on the kitchen windowsill?'

'Yes, I opened that and threw some out into the courtyard for them.'

'And everything else was . . .' She paused. 'Peaceful?'

'Yes.' Did the girl's voice falter? Evelyn thought she was probably imagining it.

'That's good. Let's hope the dashing Mal will be with you tonight to keep you company.'

'I hope so,' Bethan said and waved goodbye. She gave Evelyn a backward glance from the doorway, the briefest of pauses in her step. Evelyn waited for her to say something else but she didn't.

After Bethan had disappeared, Evelyn closed her eyes again. Maybe she should have told the girl to double-check the doors were locked at night. She nearly called her back – but the last thing she wanted to do was scare her away.

BETHAN

Sorry babe, I can't possibly leave London until tomorrow –
full on with new project. Shame about Brighton, another
time eh? X

Hi Darling Girl – you are a star. Thank you so much for
offering to look after Evelyn. I phoned the hospital and
spoke to her, she is so grateful and I am too. It will be lovely
to have Mal there for the weekend – you can show him the
Red Rock and all the places Granny and I used to take you
when you were a little girl. Let's hope for sunshine. Dad
sends you his love. Xx

A photograph of a pile of brightly coloured bowls and vases had followed the message.

The kiln Gods have been kind!

Bethan let her phone fall in to her lap and looked out of the window of the car. She let out a long sigh. She had been looking forward
to Brighton. The seafront hotel had looked lovely; they'd booked a
room with a view of the pier. It would have been just what they
needed, some time together to relax, to talk.
'Bethan?'
Bethan jumped.
'Sorry. I didn't mean to startle you,' Tom said, switching the

windscreen wipers on. 'I just wanted to say that you really didn't need to let her blackmail you into staying.'

'I couldn't bear to see her so upset.'

'She has a way of making us all do what she wants.'

'I can imagine,' said Bethan. 'As a child I was completely in awe of her – terrified but fascinated at the same time. I think she was the first adult I ever heard swear. She was telling my mother and grandmother a story about someone who had been mean to Robert on the beach, she called them a *fucker* – I remember whispering the word over and over when I was on my own.'

Tom laughed and they both fell back into silence as he turned on to the coastal road.

Bethan glanced at his profile. His hair was dishevelled, a far cry from Mal's neatly waxed quiff. He was unshaven and his tie had been at half-mast since he had picked her up from Vaughan Court that morning; earlier Bethan had noticed that one of his navy socks had a line of daisies embroidered on the side.

'Did you grow up in Wales?' Bethan asked.

Tom nodded.

'My father was the GP in Aberseren for over forty years. Dr Peter, as his patients in the village used to call him. Like Evelyn said yesterday, he came here as an evacuee from Liverpool and never left – apart from going to Cardiff to do his medical degree.'

Bethan glanced at Tom again; he didn't seem old enough to have a father who had grown up in the war. Despite his greying hair and the deep frown lines on his forehead she guessed he was probably in his mid-thirties.

'He married very late,' Tom said as though he'd read her mind. 'There was twenty years between him and my mum. They met when she applied to be the receptionist at the surgery.'

'Like Owen.'

Tom gave a brief laugh.

'My mum was not like Owen!'

'I meant Owen's job.'

'Yes, she kept the place running like clockwork for years. She's been a hard act for anyone else to follow – I think my dad would have sacked Owen by now.'

'Did you always want to take over from your father at the surgery?'

'No, not at all. I couldn't wait to leave Aberseren; I couldn't wait to leave Wales. It seemed like the back of beyond.'

Bethan smiled.

'I can't imagine Aberseren has much to offer teenagers.'

'For the kids who liked rock climbing or surfing it held some attraction, but apart from that there was absolutely nothing but the youth club disco once a month.' Tom shook his head. 'They hired an ancient DJ who thought that Abba were still in the charts. At eighteen I escaped to London. Trained at King's College, decided I wanted to be a paediatrician. I spent five years in Bristol Children's Hospital, then back to London for the job I'd always dreamed of at Great Ormond Street, but then . . .' He paused. 'Then I came back.'

Bethan wanted to ask why he'd given up his dream job, why he had come back to live in Wales, but something about the way his grip had tightened on the steering wheel prevented her from asking anything more.

'It must be lovely living with all this,' Bethan said after a while, indicating out of the window; the sea was to the right, the mountains soaring majestically upwards on the left. 'It's stunning, even if it is the back of beyond.'

Tom didn't answer, he seemed lost in his own thoughts and they spent the rest of the journey in silence; the rhythmic thump of the windscreen wipers the only sound in the car.

At last they drove past the sign for Aberseren.

'You'll probably need to stock up on some food.' Tom drew up outside a little shop on the corner of the row of cottages that lined the seafront. It had a sign with the single word *Moggs* painted in red letters. 'Olwyn has most of the basics, but don't ask her for anything like pesto or pine nuts, and whatever you do don't mention hummus.'

He got out of the car and Bethan followed him. She stared at the window display that seemed to be made entirely of boxes of Kellogg's Cornflakes and Persil Automatic

'It looks a bit basic,' Tom said. 'But Olwyn's leek and potato pies are delicious, and her Welsh cakes are the best in the county.'

Inside the shop it was dark. It took some time for Bethan's eyes to adjust but when they did she could see that it wasn't like the corner shops in Battersea. This shop was more like a sitting room, with an electric log-effect fire in the fireplace and a large television mounted on the wall. On the other walls there were shelves, randomly arranged with packets and tins. In the middle of the room a Formica table was covered in cling-film-covered plates. There was also a jar of lollipops and a wicker basket containing a selection of chocolate bars. In one corner a glass-fronted fridge hummed as it showed off rows of milk bottles and packs of cheddar cheese and bacon. At the bottom of the fridge there were three large oranges.

Bethan noticed a peculiar smell; like rotting vegetables, and damp.

'*Duw, duw*! But she looks just like her.'

Bethan turned towards the voice. There was a person sitting in an armchair; a woman with a face as round as the oranges in the fridge and as wrinkled as a prune. She had a pile of knitting on her lap and appeared to be making something ginormous. Tiny eyes peered out from her wizened skin and looked Bethan up and down.

'This is Bethan,' Tom said loudly.

'There's no need to shout, Dr Tom,' the old woman snorted. 'I'm not deaf. And I know who she is. The spit of Nelli Evans. You'd think she'd climbed out of that coffin up at the church and come back from the grave, like one of those zombies I've seen on the late-night films that Owen watches.'

'I don't think she looks that bad, Olwyn.' Tom opened the fridge and took out a bottle of milk.

'Pardon, Doctor?'

Olwyn put her hand to her ear.

'Bethan doesn't look like a zombie.'

'No, she looks like Nelli Evans!'

Bethan smiled at the old woman.

54

'You have a very unusual shop.'

'What did she say?'

'She says you have an unusual shop,' shouted Tom.

'There's nothing unusual about it.' Olwyn pushed her knitting onto the floor and stiffly raised herself from the chair to reveal a figure resembling a ball dressed in a tight purple jumper and an apron. 'It sells good honest food – none of that foreign muck you get in Tesco. I have luxury items too.'

She shuffled to the table and picked up a single box of Milk Tray; it had the remains of what looked like a raffle ticket sellotaped to one corner.

'You like chocolates?' She shook the box in Bethan's direction. 'Eight pounds to you. Special offer.'

The bell above the shop door jangled.

'Daddy!'

A little girl burst into the room and threw her arms around Tom's waist. She had fair hair tied in two long plaits and a very pretty face. Her huge eyes looked up at Tom excitedly.

'I got twenty out of twenty in the maths test. Mrs Mathias gave me a star!'

Tom picked her up and hugged her; Bethan noticed how his features changed in an instant, all the hard lines and rigidity melted into one huge glowing smile.

'Well done, Tilly,' he said to the little girl. 'What about the spelling test?'

Tilly struggled out of her dad's arms.

'I don't want to talk about that.'

'I think we'll just bask in the success of the maths for now,' said a voice from the doorway. Bethan turned to see a blonde woman carrying a pink rucksack and a child's anorak. 'I've promised Tilly a lollipop as a reward.'

'Only one,' said Tom.

Tilly was already unscrewing the top of the lollipop jar.

'Two for three offer today,' said Olwyn. 'An extra one half-price when you buy more than five.'

The woman in the doorway laughed.

'Yesterday it was two for fifty pence and three for a pound.'

'You see why maths is important, Tilly?' Tom was prizing several extra lollipops out of his daughter's hand and dropping them back in the jar.

Olwyn tutted.

'Terrible business up at the Court. Owen told me the news last night. He thought it was a stroke or a heart attack, but he phoned me today to say it was just two broken wrists after a stumble feeding those fancy birds she insists on having around the place.'

Tom frowned.

'Owen isn't meant to be discussing the patients with you.'

'But he's my grandson! He lives here! And I've known Evelyn since I was a child, I've a right to know that she's all right.'

Tom sighed and turned back to the woman at the door.

'I'll be home a bit later than I'd hoped, but I'll be in time to take Tilly to her swimming lesson.'

The woman smiled at him.

'Don't worry, I can do that if you get held up.'

He smiled back, concern in his eyes.

'You're looking tired. You have a rest tonight, I can look after Tilly.'

Bethan realised she was staring at the couple, a stab of envy in her heart; did Mal ever look concerned for her? These days Mal seemed far more concerned with the size of his biceps.

Tilly already had the lollipop in her mouth as the woman began to steer her out of the shop.

'I hope your patients liked your socks today, Daddy,' the little girl called from the pavement outside. 'The one on your right foot is mine.'

The door jangled shut and they were gone.

Tom pulled up his right trouser leg and gave a puzzled frown.

'It's actually the left foot,' said Bethan.

Tom pulled up the other trouser leg.

'Damn!'

Bethan smiled.

'You have a gorgeous daughter.'

Tom smiled back.

'I'm a very lucky man.'

Olwyn gave a loud snort.

'Well, that's not true, is it, Dr Tom?' She shook her head. 'Everybody knows that you are not a very lucky man at all.'

BETHAN

Bethan woke up.

It had definitely been a smash. She was sure of it. A smash, like glass breaking.

She lay very still, hardly daring to breath. She thought she could hear the crunch of gravel beneath her window. She could see through the gap in the heavy damask curtains that it was still dark. Something flashed, an arc of light and then it was dark again. Bethan squeezed her eyes shut and wished that she was back in Battersea with Mal beside her. He'd have an explanation.

'It's just that overactive imagination of yours, Babe. Go back to sleep.'

She sat up and turned on the bedside lamp. The room was flooded with a comforting light, then everything was plunged into darkness again as the bulb burned out. Bethan fumbled on the table for her phone and turned on the torch. She swept the faint beam around the room. Shadows leapt up the walls. The wardrobe door had swung open, and the Victorian doll's face leered out from the shelf she'd hidden it on before getting into bed. Bethan wriggled down the bed so that the sheets and blankets covered her head. Hours passed. The silence pulsed in her ears.

At last the dawn arrived with a grey mist and the high-pitched peacock cries. The paralysing fear subsided. Bethan got up.

She took the quilt from the bed and draped it over her shoulders to try to keep out the cold. She went out into the corridor and padded barefoot along a succession of Persian rugs. The quilt trailed behind her like a cloak and made a rather satisfying swish as she turned the corners.

There were paintings everywhere, generations of Vaughans in heavy gilt frames, and marble busts in alcoves, long-dead family members with laurel wreaths around their heads like Roman emperors. As Bethan descended the staircase the portraits watched her with their almond-shaped eyes and long, well-defined noses. Their mouths were small, pinched into expressions that looked to Bethan like disapproval. She stuck her tongue out at one particularly haughty-looking man in a white wig and scarlet jacket.

On the bottom step she stopped.

There was a stone on the black and white tiles in the hallway. The stone was rough and grey, the size of a cricket ball, just the right size to have broken the windowpane. Glass was everywhere, a myriad of colours from the stained-glass panel at the side of the front door.

Bethan's heart started to pound again. The stone looked so alien in the magnificent surroundings. A piece of the mountains. A piece of the unknown wilderness outside. She peered through the hole it had made in the glass; there was nothing to see but the grey and green of the silent garden. She hadn't had to use the front door, her means of entry and exit had so far only been at the back of the house. She noticed there were at least five bolts on the heavy oak door, some of them looked new.

Bethan glanced down at the stone. She wanted to be back in London, where a broken window could be explained by burglars looking for laptops and jewellery to steal. She thought of running down the drive and getting on the next train, then she remembered Mal was coming. He would have an explanation, he would make a reassuring joke about her fear.

The Vaughans in the paintings seemed to be watching her, as though they were waiting to see what she would do. Bethan forced herself to turn around and go back upstairs to get dressed.

The car appeared as she was taping a flattened Corn Flakes box onto the hole in the window with Sellotape. The first thing Bethan saw was a movement through the remaining stained glass, a flash of red, something sleek and low to the ground. She took her phone out of the back pocket of her jeans to check the time. It couldn't be Tom arriving. It was only just past ten o'clock and he'd told her he'd collect Evelyn from the hospital after morning surgery was finished. Could it be Mal already?

Bethan tried to open the front door; the bolts were stiff and each one hurt her fingers as she struggled to pull them across.

The last bolt came undone just as someone rang the bell. Bethan lifted the latch and heaved. The door swung open and Bethan came face to face with the most enormous bunch of flowers she'd ever seen. A huge bouquet of tulips, daffodils and hyacinths. Their bright abundance looked at odds with the drizzly morning.

The flowers moved to one side and a face appeared; handsome, chiselled, blond hair swept back, skin tanned. It looked like it belonged to a man from an advert for designer aftershave. It was not Mal.

'You must be Lady Evelyn's god-daughter.' The man's voice was deep and smooth and very English.

'Actually, my mother is her god-daughter, I'm just . . .' Bethan paused, trying to think of her exact relationship to Evelyn.

'Her great-god-daughter?' the man suggested. 'Or maybe a god-daughter once removed?'

Bethan glanced over the man's shoulder. She could see a red Porsche behind him. It had a number plate that said DD1.

'God-daughter by proxy?' the man continued, warming to his theme.

'Sorry,' Bethan said. 'Who are you?'

The man held out his hand.

'I'm David Dashwood.'

Bethan took his proffered hand in hers; his grip was firm and warm.

'I own the golf club.' He released her hand and pushed back a strand of hair which had fallen across one of his very blue eyes. 'And the spa and restaurant, and I also have a pheasant shoot.' He indicated towards some distant woodland. 'Just bordering Lady Evelyn's land.' He smiled. Little lines crinkled at the corners of his eyes and made his face look even more handsome. Bethan couldn't help staring at his eyes. They were almost turquoise.

'I've only just found out about poor Evelyn.' David Dashwood's smile disappeared to be replaced with a more concerned expression. 'I had no idea she was in hospital. Awful news. She's usually the picture of good health. I hate to think of her being ill. I wondered if you could take her these when you are visiting.' He held out the beautiful bouquet. Bethan realised she was still holding the roll of Sellotape she'd been using to repair the window. In the intervening seconds since David Dashwood had shaken her hand, she'd managed to wrap some of the tape around her fingers so that they now resembled some sort of hideous plastic wrapped claw.

David Dashwood noticed too.

'I'll hang on to the flowers until you . . .'

'Yes.' Bethan struggled to pull the tape away. She could feel her cheeks flush. 'I don't know how I managed to do that.'

David Dashwood grinned.

As soon as she was free, Bethan took the flowers and buried her face in them as an excuse to hide her embarrassment. The flowers smelled very sweet and very expensive.

'What's happened here?' When Bethan looked up again David was examining the hole in the window.

'A rock came through it in the night.'

'Oh dear! How awful! Are you OK?' David asked, his handsome features now arranged, once again, into a look of concern.

'I'm fine.' Bethan wasn't going to admit that she had been frozen with fear in the night. As the morning had progressed, her terror seemed ridiculous. She couldn't think why she hadn't got up and gone down to the drawing room to phone the police when she heard the smash.

'I'll get one of my men to come up and put a new pane in – not beautiful stained glass of course but at least something a little bit better than cardboard.' He tapped his finger against the flattened cereal packet. It immediately fell onto the ground. 'I'll also get the MG looked at, I heard you had some trouble with the engine on your way to raise the alarm about Evelyn.'

'Who told you that?'

David Dashwood raised one beautifully groomed eyebrow.

'Aberseren is a very small place. Rumour has it that it's the clutch, though some say that you might not have realised that you needed to release the choke.'

He smiled and Bethan felt her cheeks flush all over again.

Later, as she trudged down the drive, Bethan wondered why she'd turned down David's offer of a lift to the village. Had it been her embarrassment about the Sellotape? Or the way he'd looked at her when he'd asked if she was really going to be all right in such a big house all on her own.

'My boyfriend is coming,' she'd replied, and David's expression had changed. Bethan couldn't decide if it was disapproval or disappointment. Though why a man like David Dashwood would be disappointed that she had a boyfriend, Bethan couldn't imagine. What interest could he possibly have in a wild-haired woman with an apparent penchant for wrapping herself in adhesive tape?

She put her head down and pulled her mac tight to stop it billowing out like a gigantic beige balloon. She needed to get some more supplies before Mal's arrival; there seemed to be no coffee in the house and the cupboards were mostly filled with tins of sardines and packets of shortbread biscuits.

She passed the little MG on the side of the drive and peered inside, wondering what David Dashwood had meant about the choke. She was about to set off again, when she saw the small building that she'd noticed the day before. Bethan peered through the twisted bushes and brambles to get a better view.

Long tendrils of ivy snaked their way up the wooden walls and over the slate shingled roof; a single chimney sprouted some sort of plant. Intricately carved wooden weatherboards edged a pointed roofline with a single circular window of stained glass beneath it. There were arched windows on either side of a narrow front door, with steps and a pretty porch with carved details as delicate as lace. A narrow veranda skirted the house with intricate railings and barley-sugar

63

posts, which were entwined with plants; Bethan couldn't tell from a distance if they were roses or brambles. The whole effect was like something from a fairy tale, unexpected amongst the dense damp foliage and bare branches.

Bethan couldn't imagine why it would have been built in that position, halfway down the drive, so far from the big house; but then she noticed the rushes and something glinting, a dark, undulating mirror reflecting the grey sky in watery ripples. She looked further and saw that the water extended for quite some distance. It was a pond, or even a small lake, black as ink and surrounded by thick foliage and over-hanging trees. Bethan could see an old rowing boat half hidden in the reeds, and something that looked like a platform or a jetty, the broken planks of wood slipping below the surface.

She vaguely remembered that there had been a lake somewhere at Vaughan Court, a lake with a little house beside it where Bethan wasn't allowed to play.

There was a screech and when Bethan looked up at the roofline of the summer house she saw that a peacock had appeared. It sat on the ridge as though guarding the building. Its eyes were on Bethan. She had the feeling that if she tried to go inside, it would swoop down and attack her with its pointed beak.

The summer house. A memory came back from a holiday over twenty years before. Evelyn telling her she could play outside with Robert but that they must not go to the summer house beside the lake, as there was a lady who lived there who didn't like children. Of course, as soon as they went outside Bethan had challenged Robert to a race to the summer house; he had become lost in the competition until he had led her to the little house beside the water, delighted that he had been first to arrive, though he refused to go any nearer than a few feet from the veranda. Bethan could remember slowly pushing her way through the nettles and brambles until she reached the dusty window. Robert had called to her repeatedly, 'You are not allowed!' But Bethan had ignored him, wiping away a layer of grime from the glass with her cardigan sleeve to peer inside. She could see closed curtains, but there had been a gap, just wide enough to make out something in the semi-darkness, a shape, a figure and then a face; a face with golden hair and bright red lips. A lady. Bethan had screamed and run back to the house as fast as she could, leaving Robert to catch up with her. She had been so frightened that she hadn't left her mother's side for the rest of the afternoon.

The peacock let out another piercing screech. Bethan took a step back. Could there really have been someone living in there all those years ago? Or had that just been a dream? She shivered; even though the little wooden house looked innocuous now, she was relieved that the rhododendron bushes and brambles blocked her way. She turned around and retraced her steps back to the drive. She didn't have time for exploring. She needed to get to the village and find a signal so she could send the postcode of Vaughan Court to Mal. She'd tried to phone him from the old-fashioned phone in the drawing room but could only reach his answer machine. Without the postcode she was sure it would take Mal hours to find the house; it wouldn't be a good start to their weekend.

As Bethan reached the bottom of the drive she looked back. The peacock was still visible on the roofline of the summer house, its ornate plumage half-hidden in the branches of the trees. Bethan hurried on through the gateposts, but as she started walking down the lane she heard the peacock let out one long reverberating cry.

Bethan trudged through the village checking her phone every few seconds, looking for the elusive bar on the screen, but there was nothing.

She reached the little corner shop on the seafront. Bethan pushed open the door, glad to escape the drizzle and the wind.

Olwyn was sitting just where she had been the previous day, in front of the luminous electric logs, knitting the unidentifiable garment.

'Hi,' Bethan said. 'How are you?'

Olwyn looked up from her knitting with a straight set mouth.

'Ah, Nelli Evans's granddaughter. Back for the oranges, are you?' She indicated towards the fridge with one of her knitting needles. 'Best be quick, there's been a run on them today.'

Bethan looked at the fridge and saw that there was now only one orange left.

'It's that time of year,' Olwyn said. 'Spring is in the air and people's thoughts turn to fruit.'

Bethan certainly hadn't felt spring in the cold drizzle outside.

'It's coffee I'm looking for,' she said.

Olwyn indicated with a knitting needle at the dresser.

Bethan could see four jars of Nescafé Gold Blend set out in a neat row.

'Do you have ground coffee?'

'*Duw, duw*, I wouldn't have that sort of muck here.' Olwyn returned to her knitting, her fingers counting stitches, her mouth muttering numbers in Welsh.

Bethan picked up a jar of Nescafé.

'Do you have granola?' she asked.

'What's that when it's at home,' Olwyn said without looking up.

'Like muesli,' Bethan began to explain. 'Oats and nuts and raisins – toasted.'

Olwyn sighed, pushed her knitting to one side and heaved herself up. She walked slowly over to the window and took a box of corn flakes from the display.

'As I said to my Owen last night –' she handed the box of cereal to Bethan – 'it's only to be expected.'

'What is?' asked Bethan, taking the corn flakes and wondering if almond milk would be too much to ask.

'That Nelli Evans's granddaughter would be like Nelli Evans.'

'Pardon?'

'All airs and graces and eating fancy nonsense.' She gave a snort. 'But at least you're giving me your custom, not like your grandmother. She never set foot in here when she came back for her royal visits. I'd see her walk past.' Olwyn indicated to the window. 'Not good enough for the likes of us any more. There she was with her qualifications and her job in that school of Lady Evelyn's, *and* an English man for a husband.' Evelyn raised a sausage-shaped finger and began to shake it in the air. 'But as I said to Owen, don't think

66

I don't remember where Nelli Evans started; scrubbing carrots at the sink, emptying the chamber pots – I was there, I saw her – useless, she was. She couldn't even read those letters from her sweetheart, depended on Lady Evelyn to tell her what they said. Even as a child I could see it was inappropriate.' Olwyn shuffled to the fridge and took out the lone orange. 'I knew what went on. As I said to Owen last night, they couldn't pull the wool over my eyes.'

'Who?' asked Bethan. 'What went on?'

Olwyn pursed her lips and put the orange into a striped plastic bag. 'Owen will tell you, I'm not one to gossip.'

'I don't need an orange,' Bethan said.

Olwyn ignored her, and taking the coffee and the corn flakes from Bethan's hands she placed them in the bag with the orange.

'That will be twelve pounds, and fifty pence to charity for the bag.' Olwyn held up a jar filled with coins and rattled it.

'Goodness!' Bethan said. 'That's rather a lot.'

'Take it or leave it.'

Bethan thought of Mal. He'd need a cup of coffee as soon as he arrived, and even if they went out for dinner he'd need something for breakfast in the morning. Bethan took a twenty-pound note from her purse and handed it to Evelyn just as the bell on the shop door jangled.

Tom's wife and daughter walked in. The little girl looked like she'd been crying.

'*Bore da*, Sarah, *bore da*, Tilly. Lollipops, is it?' Olwyn said, waddling to the table and unscrewing the lid of the big jar.

'Better not,' said Sarah. 'I've just picked Tilly up from school with a stomach ache. I just need a pint of milk to drop off at the surgery for Tom.'

'Please can I have a lollipop?' said Tilly. 'I feel better now.'

Sarah looked down at the little girl.

'I have a feeling it was spelling-test-induced pain, again.'

Tilly wound the end of one of her plaits around her finger and her pretty rose-bud mouth drooped. Olwyn said something in Welsh to Sarah, Sarah shrugged and put her arm round Tilly's shoulder.

'I'd better go,' Bethan said. 'My boyfriend is on his way from London.'

Olwyn looked Bethan up and down and wordlessly handed her the plastic bag of groceries.

'Do you have my change?' Bethan asked.

With a series of sighs and grunts the old woman shuffled over to a metal tin on a table beside the armchair. She came back with a five-pound note.

'I think it should be seven pounds fifty,' Bethan said. Olwyn grudgingly returned to the tin, came back with the money and started speaking Welsh to Sarah again, looking pointedly at Bethan and shaking her head.

As Bethan left the shop she heard Olwyn say the name *Nelli Evans* and then in English, 'it's not surprising, is it?'

EVELYN

Tom was late. 'As usual,' Evelyn muttered.

He'd said that he'd come to fetch her directly after morning surgery and she knew that finished at midday. The lunchtime news had started on the television in the corner of the ward; surely it couldn't be taking an hour to drive to the hospital from the village?

The woman with the purple hair had been discharged an hour before; a man covered in tattoos had come to pick her up; she'd called him Brick and had asked him if he'd got her ciggies in the car.

'I expect you're desperate for my bed,' Evelyn called to a nurse, who was stripping the sheets from the purple-haired woman's bed. 'Hopefully I'll be gone very soon and you can use it for someone much more deserving of medical attention than me.'

'Don't you worry, Lady Evelyn,' the nurse replied cheerily. 'It's quiet today. You stay as long as you like.'

Evelyn glanced at the door for the hundredth time. Tom was meant to be bringing her clothes. She hoped he hadn't forgotten. She'd told him to ask Bethan to help choose something for her to come home in. She didn't want to be leaving in her dressing gown and nightdress, it was bad enough not having her makeup.

The doors opened and Evelyn sat up, but it was only a ridiculously young doctor in a white coat.

He approached Evelyn without looking directly at her, in the way that reminded her of Howard.

'I have the results of your ECG.' His Adam's apple bobbed up and

69

down as he swallowed. 'You have a slight arrhythmia. It may simply be atrial fibrillation but you need medication.'

'I don't understand a word you're saying,' said Evelyn. 'Don't tell me I have to stay here longer!'

The nurse came across the ward and patted Evelyn's shoulder.

'It's just a bit of a problem with your heart beating irregularly. Don't worry, you can go home today and that nice GP of yours will sort out all the tests and tablets you need to get you feeling better again.'

Evelyn looked at the nurse.

'But I feel as strong as an ox.'

'Good,' the nurse grinned. 'Let's hope we can keep you feeling like an ox for a long time.'

'At your age atrial fibrillation is not surprising,' the doctor said. 'And of course, there are a multitude of other geriatric conditions which may become apparent with further investigative procedures.'

'Thank you very much,' said Evelyn. 'You certainly know how to make a girl feel good.'

The doctor nodded briefly and walked away, the nurse following in his wake.

Evelyn lifted her arm. It felt heavy. Her fingertips protruded from the plaster cast. She placed them on her chest, feeling through her nightdress. There was a beat – faint but steady. It *seemed* normal.

Evelyn remembered the time when she had really thought her heart had broken. The pain had been so intense, she had longed to die. Maybe her heart had been damaged then? Maybe it had been broken all this time. More than seventy years of beating out of time.

BETHAN

When Bethan emerged from Olwyn's shop, she was surprised to find that the sky had turned from gloomy grey to brilliant blue. Standing in the doorway in the sunshine, she had a sudden memory of her grandmother pulling her roughly past a display of brightly coloured beach balls at the same door.

'No! You can't have one, Bethan. Come on, don't stop! Don't even look at them!!'

Bethan had wanted to cry. It was the only time Bethan remembered her grandmother being cross. Mostly she had been full of fun and games, and hugs, and laughter.

Bethan looked towards the beach; the tide was right out and the pink sand stretched in a perfect semicircle around the bay. She could remember her grandmother running with her along the shore.

'First one to Red Rock gets an ice cream from the van.'

Bethan had a sudden urge to run along the beach, just as she had done all those years ago. She crossed the road and scrambled down the grassy bank; there was a soft thump as she jumped down onto the sand. The tideline was littered with shells and little ribbons of seaweed, and beyond it the damp sand was patterned with ripples left by the retreating waves.

At the far end of the beach, Bethan could see Red Rock; a lumpy pink limestone mound crowned with Twr Du, the ruins of the tall watch tower that were supposed to be over a thousand years old. She set off towards it, running, the wind tangling her hair, the sun warm on her cheeks as she clutched the bag of groceries in her arms. On the horizon the sea glinted like a string of diamonds and in the sky, gulls wheeled and called out as though enjoying the change in the weather as much as she was.

At the end of the beach, Bethan scrambled up the path to the top of Red Rock. As she reached the ruins of Twr Du she climbed onto the wide stone ramparts and surveyed the spectacular view. She turned slowly around as she had done as a child, breathing it in, absorbing the beauty. It was then that she heard the sound of an incoming text. She smiled. At last she'd found some signal.

Taking her phone out of her pocket she saw it was from Mal.

Hi Babe, we have a problem with the new project. I'll have to work over the weekend to sort it out so won't be coming to Wales. Sorry. Hope your birthday is a good one. Xxx

All Bethan's happiness drained away. The sun was still shining but it was as though a chilly mist had suddenly blown in. She looked at the text again and wondered whether if they had still been going to Brighton, would he have spent the weekend working? Bethan suddenly remembered that they'd need to cancel the hotel. If Mal was so busy with his project he wouldn't have had time. She found the details on her phone and dialled the number.

'Hello, we have a room reserved,' she said when a woman's voice answered. 'Under the name Malcolm Wright.'

'Is everything to your liking?' the woman asked.

'Pardon?'

'I'm just about to send someone up with your champagne and the hairdryer you asked for. Will you both be joining us for dinner in the restaurant tonight?'

Bethan's heart thudded. It seemed as though time stood still. She didn't hear the seagulls or the waves; she could no longer see any beauty in the landscape or feel any warmth from the sun. She didn't know how much time passed before she pressed the screen to end the call.

She ran down the rocky path and retraced her steps across the beach, through the village and up the hill towards Vaughan Court. It was only when she was halfway up the drive that her brain became clear enough to think of the message she wanted to send to Mal.

With a cry of 'You fucking two-timing bastard, I hate you!' she turned around and ran all the way back to Red Rock to send it.

EVELYN

'Beautiful, isn't it?' It was the first thing Tom had said since they drove away from the hospital.

Evelyn stared through the car window. The mountains looked like crumpled paper, unfolding as the car approached. The sunlight cast shadows in the ravines and valleys and highlighted the peaks and ridges.

'When I first arrived here I thought it looked like another planet,' she said. 'It seemed so unlike London, or Sussex, or anywhere else I had ever been.'

'I can't imagine you anywhere else.' Tom glanced at her with a smile. 'You're as much a part of this landscape as the mountains.'

'Craggy and ancient?' Evelyn raised one eyebrow.

'Are you fishing, Lady Vaughan?'

'Always.'

'Well, in that case, let me tell you that I think you add a touch of refined elegance to the area. A sprinkling of literary allure and aristocratic style amongst these rugged rocks and slatey slopes.'

'Have you been drinking, Doctor?'

Tom laughed.

'Never before afternoon surgery.'

Evelyn smiled and they settled back into silence. Evelyn thought of the first time she had seen Vaughan Court; it had been the last place on earth she had wanted to be.

December 1942

The house had seemed to appear from nowhere as the Bentley finally climbed the tree-lined drive. The car had turned a corner and there it was looming through bare branches: tall twisted chimneys and towering pink walls, ethereal in the fading light.

Evelyn had leant forward, peering out of the car window to get a better look at the house. It seemed to have a pulse. Evelyn could feel its heartbeat. It matched her own, anxious and misplaced. It no more seemed to want to be in the wild and desolate surroundings than she did.

The car stopped outside a portico mounted by a huge stone lion bearing a familiar crest; it had been on all the writing paper that Evelyn had used to thank people for their wedding presents.

A little group of figures stood stiffly on the steps, the remnants of some other time when a whole cast of servants would have welcomed his Lordship's new wife to Vaughan Court.

As Evelyn stepped out of the car, she had noticed Nelli first; a pretty girl with bright hair escaping from a lace cap, her black dress and apron much too thin for the winter air. Beside her stood an old man with a weathered face and a bent back. He seemed uncomfortable in his formal suit, his calloused hands looked like the hands of someone who was used to being in workmen's clothes. There was a young man too, with the soft shadow of a moustache on his upper lip, his jacket too big for his narrow shoulders – Evelyn never could pronounce his complicated Welsh name and he soon left to join The Royal Welch Fusiliers. A child stood in the middle of the group, a solid little girl in a tweed coat with a thin straight mouth and raisin eyes; when Evelyn smiled at her she did not smile back. A tall woman stood slightly apart from the others; her features resembled the child's, but her tall rake-like figure was in no way similar to the little girl's sturdy frame. The woman had black hair, scraped back severely into a bun, and a long dark coat that was buttoned to the throat. Her narrow eyes skimmed Evelyn from top to bottom several times.

'Welcome, Your Ladyship,' she said. Evelyn wasn't sure if she was talking to her or her mother-in-law.

'Good evening,' Evelyn replied.

The woman stepped forward to assist Lady Vaughan from the car.

'She'll have to do, Mrs Moggs,' Evelyn heard Lady Vaughan mutter as she leant heavily on the woman's arm. 'The girl will have to do.'

Evelyn wanted to tell the chauffeur to take her back, all the way to London. She'd do anything, work in a shop, sell beer in a pub, she'd never be frightened of the sirens again. But the chauffeur was already heaving her leather cases from the boot, instructing the young boy to take them inside. And, at that moment, Evelyn's desire to pee was stronger than her desire to run away. She followed Lady Vaughan and Mrs Moggs into the gloomy hallway, her eyes desperately searching for the young maid so that she could ask her where the toilet was.

She heard the boys before she saw them. The noise had woken her the following morning, a thud above her ceiling, then children's laughter which had stopped abruptly before the eerie quietness of the house enveloped her again.

She had got up and walked to the bay window, pulling back the heavy curtains to look outside.

She saw the grey slab of sea in the distance, mountains tumbling through a lowering mist and an endless canopy of twisted trees. She looked directly down and studied the complicated pattern of the flower beds below, trying to trace a way out, like a maze. All paths seemed to lead to the statue in the middle, a cherub spurting frozen water from its mouth.

Evelyn heard the laughter again and saw two little boys running across the lawn, long shorts and Fair Isle jumpers, one with pale blond curls like an angel, a smaller one with glasses and hair that looked like it had practically been shaved.

The blond boy looked up at the window and saw Evelyn. He stopped and waved, she waved back and then the boy with glasses stopped and waved up at her too.

77

Suddenly the tall woman, who Evelyn now knew was Mrs Moggs the housekeeper, appeared. She took both boys by the scruff of their jumpers and dragged them, stumbling, across the lawn and out of sight. It was two days before Evelyn saw the boys again and when she did the blond boy's curls had been shaved off and both of them had bruises on their legs.

She had come across them in one of the greenhouses, when she had been on yet another aimless walk around the grounds. It was the first time she'd been into the walled garden, the first time she'd seen the long line of greenhouses against the far brick wall. The boys had been crouching down beside the bare raised beds. Evelyn had spotted their brightly coloured jumpers through the glass.

'What are you doing?' she'd asked, walking through the rickety wooden door.

'Hiding, miss,' they'd said in unison.

'From who?' she'd asked.

'From Gerry,' the older one said in an accent Evelyn recognised as Liverpudlian. 'There's a boy at school says he saw them land on the beach last night.'

'We've got rifles.' The boy with glasses indicated to the bamboo canes in their hands.

'We're going to ambush them as they pass,' said the older boy.

'Do you need help?' Evelyn asked. 'I used to shoot tin cans with my brother's air rifle, I was very good.'

The older boy solemnly handed Evelyn another bamboo cane and the three of them crouched together until it was nearly dark.

By that time Evelyn knew that they were called Peter and Billy, and that they were eight and nine. They were evacuees from Liverpool and had been living at Vaughan Court for nearly two years.

'She didn't want us,' Billy said, indicating with his head towards the house.

'Lady Vaughan?' Evelyn asked.

Billy shook his head.

'No, Mrs Moggs. The billeting officer made her take us. We were the only ones left.'

78

Evelyn learned that their mother, father and baby sister had been killed in an air raid the year before; a direct hit on the terrace in Bootle.

'Our da was home on leave,' the younger boy explained.

'Meant to be going back to his regiment the next day,' said Billy, the older one.

'We never even met our sister,' Peter said quietly.

Evelyn told them about the bomb that had fallen on Wilton Crescent and about her family, and the dogs.

'Bad luck,' Billy and Peter said together.

Evelyn asked about their haircuts.

'She thinks we've got lice,' Billy said.

'We've not,' said Peter. 'Not since we came.'

'Come on,' Billy said, standing up. 'We'd best get back for dinner or Mrs Moggs will be shouting *bechgyn drug* at us.'

'*Bechgyn drug*?' Evelyn looked at Billy.

'It means naughty boys.' Billy rolled his eyes.

'Don't you speak the lingo?' Peter asked, looking earnestly at Evelyn through his glasses.

'What lingo?'

'Welsh,' said Billy. 'They all speak it round here.'

He and Peter began singing a song in words that Evelyn didn't understand.

Evelyn laughed.

'I'm afraid I don't speak it at all.'

'We'll teach you,' said Billy, pulling his brother up by the arm. 'Tomorrow, after school. Meet us here. We'll do numbers first.'

And so they had taught her, numbers and days of the week and the names of various objects, and Nelli had helped her too, so that by spring Evelyn could hold a simple conversation. She used to talk to Nelli in Welsh as she brushed out her hair at night, asking her about her day, and about her sweetheart, Lloyd, and what they hoped to do when the war ended. Evelyn helped Nelli read the letters she received from Lloyd, sounding out the Welsh words for the girl, even though she often didn't understand what they meant. Nelli would laugh at her pronunciation, and then she'd tell Evelyn how the word should be said and what it meant, though sometimes she would refuse to translate what Evelyn had just read out.

'It's a bit private, Lady Evelyn.'

'I see.' Evelyn would raise her eyebrows, and Nelli would blush, and they'd both end up giggling until it was time for Nelli to go back downstairs to the kitchen to finish her duties.

Nelli told her stories too; ancient Celtic tales of kings and queens, and slaughtered dogs, and mythical birds.

Evelyn's favourite was the story of Branwen, a Welsh princess unhappily married to the king of Ireland. She trained a starling to speak. The starling flew to Wales to tell Branwen's brother, who was a giant, that she was miserable. Her brother waded across the Irish Sea to rescue her and carry her home. Evelyn wished she had a huge brother who would come and rescue her from her misery.

Apart from the times that Evelyn spent with the boys and Nelli, there was nothing to do but shiver in the drawing room with Lady Vaughan, or roam the grounds waiting for the next dismal meal to be served. Sometimes the vicar and his dull little wife came for afternoon tea, but other than that every day was the same.

And it rained. All the time for the first four months. There were a few bright days around Easter and then it rained again until June. Evelyn felt permanently damp and cold. There was never any opportunity to put on a summer dress or go without a jumper. But July had been glorious. She had swum in the sea, diving from the cliffs at the bottom of Red Rock, then she'd lie on the sand soaking up the sun's warm rays. She had encouraged Billy and Peter to come with her and tried to teach them how to swim, with some success.

Then Evelyn had received a letter from Howard in London.

Dearest Evelyn,

Mother is upset. She writes to tell me you have been swimming in the sea with the evacuee boys, and lying on the beach in your bathing suit.

Please refrain from doing so in future. It doesn't do to be seen exhibiting oneself in such a way.

> *Yours,*
> *Howard.*

Evelyn had ripped the letter up into a hundred pieces, but she hadn't gone to the beach again. Instead, she spent the long hot afternoons alone beside the pond that Lady Vaughan called a lake, her bare legs dangling from the jetty, kicking at the murky water, wondering if anything in her life at Vaughan Court was ever going to change.

It was during one of these desultory afternoons that Evelyn had first seen the planes. Two of them passed overhead, huge green dragons sailing across the summer sky.

Evelyn had heard about the airbase; she'd even seen a group of American airmen when she'd visited the dentist in Conway. She'd watched them from the window of the Bentley as it passed the crumbling castle walls. The airmen walked with a swagger, long-legged and lean. Their uniforms had been well pressed, their hair oiled and gleaming. She saw them wave at two girls on the other side of the street. The girls had giggled. Evelyn craned her neck to see what happened next, but the Bentley was already on the bridge, carrying her back to Vaughan Court, too far away to see.

BETHAN

Tom had made a fire. Bethan took off her mac and sat down on the edge of the chintz sofa in front of it.

'Give her a cushion,' Evelyn said to Tom from her seat in the big armchair. 'Something nice and soft to rest against.'

Tom picked up a yellow velvet cushion and handed it to Bethan. His eyes were on her. Bethan wasn't sure if they held embarrassment or pity.

She felt embarrassed. She hated crying in public, she just hadn't been able to help it.

Tom's car had pulled up beside her just as she was going through the gateposts of Vaughan Court. Tom had wound down the window.

'Need a lift?'

Bethan had shaken her head.

'Where's your nice young man?' Evelyn called from the passenger seat.

'He's not nice, he's a wanker,' Bethan blurted out and then she'd covered her face with her hands and started to cry.

'I'll go and get us all a cup of tea,' Tom said in the drawing room.

'Sugar,' Evelyn called as Tom left the room. 'The poor girl has had a terrible shock.'

'I'm fine.' Bethan looked down at the cushion in her hands. 'I've suspected that Mal was seeing someone else for quite a while, I just hadn't admitted it to myself.'

'Tom, bring tissues.' Evelyn was shouting again. 'A loo roll if the box is empty.'

'Don't worry about me,' said Bethan. 'I'm not going to cry any more. Anyway, I'm supposed to be the one looking after you.'

'Bollocks to that.' Evelyn waved one plaster-casted hand. 'Now that I'm home and back in my favourite chair, I'm absolutely right as rain.

'You'll need time to get over this, heartbreak is like grief, it has to take its course. But unlike grief, you have the benefit of realising that your man was a pillock, and that far from losing the love of your life, you've had a lucky escape from shackling yourself to a complete . . . '

'Twat,' Bethan said.

Evelyn frowned.

'I think any word used to describe female anatomy is too good for your horrible man.'

'What do you suggest?'

'Cockwomble!' Evelyn said firmly.

'Cockwomble?'

'Yes, I heard it on the television when someone was talking about the Prime Minister. Isn't it a wonderful word?'

Bethan shrugged.

'It sounds like someone who's a bit stupid.'

'Yes, exactly! Too stupid to see what a beautiful girl he already has!'

Bethan traced her finger across the yellow velvet of the cushion.

'It will hurt,' continued Evelyn. 'But I can tell already that you're going to get through this. If you really loved him you wouldn't be sitting here, upright on the sofa; you'd be prostrate on top of that rock where you found out, unconscious to anything but the agony inside. There would be a terrible searing pain in your heart, and you'd be cursing your cruel body for every breath it keeps taking, because all you'd want to do is die.'

'You sound like you know how it feels.' Bethan glanced at a photograph on top of the mantelpiece. A man in uniform with a long neck and a thin moustache, a girl in a grey suit and a neat little hat. She knew that Evelyn and Howard had been married for a very long time but hadn't imagined that Evelyn had felt so bereft when he had died. She looked back at Evelyn.

The older woman suddenly looked tired, her face very pale. Her body seemed to shake a little as she stared into the fire.

'Are you cold?' Bethan asked. 'Would you like a blanket?'

When Evelyn didn't answer, Bethan got up and fetched a throw from the arm of the sofa and placed it over the old woman's lap, tucking it around her legs and over her feet.

Evelyn looked away from the flames and met her eyes.

'I'd like to tell you to bugger off, and that I'm not so ancient that I need a blanket on my knees, but I am a little chilly.' She smiled.

Bethan dared to touch her shoulder.

'Thank you,' Bethan said. 'Thank you for caring and thank you for your wise words.'

Evelyn laughed.

'Well, I *am* ancient enough to have gained some knowledge about life, and I do know that the gorgeous granddaughter of my best friend Nelli Evans deserves someone so much better than that Mop, or Map, or whatever he was called.'

'Mal,' said Bethan.

'Short for Malcontented, I presume,' sniffed Evelyn.

'Mal the Malcontented Cockwomble.' Bethan started to laugh.

'That's the spirit.' Evelyn grinned at her. 'Who wants a man like that in their life?'

EVELYN

The photograph albums were a wonderful distraction.

'There's no point moping about on the sofa,' Evelyn had said to the girl after Tom left for afternoon surgery. 'We might as well get this interview of yours started. I take it you need to find out more about my life.' Evelyn raised her hand and pointed at a tall bookcase. 'There are some photograph albums over there, bottom shelf, go and get the one that's labelled 1946–1950 and I'll tell you about how I started to write.'

'We don't have to do this now,' Bethan said. 'I expect you're tired.'

'No,' said Evelyn. 'Not at all.'

Bethan walked over to the bookcase. Evelyn watched her as she crouched down to look along a row of leather-bound albums; her blouse was very pretty, Evelyn was fairly sure it was a Biba original.

'They're not in any particular order,' Evelyn called to the girl. Bethan started to read out the embossed gold lettering along the spines.

'The Scilly Isles 1952, Corfu 1970, Oak Hill 1973–1986, Robert's pictures 1978–1980, Royal Wedding Garden Party 1981, Oak Hill Grand Opening 1958 . . . Ah, here it is. Vaughan Court 1946–1950 – it's the thickest one!'

She took it back to Evelyn. Evelyn patted the arm of her chair.

'You can perch here. You'll have to turn the pages.' She held up her plaster-bound hands.

Bethan leant forward and opened the cover to reveal a series of little square pictures: the endless views of the mountains that Howard liked to take with his Box Brownie as she pushed him around the garden in his wheelchair.

Evelyn could smell shampoo on Bethan's hair; the red curls were so like Nelli's and she could see the same scattering of freckles on the girl's nose and high cheekbones. Nelli had been pretty but Bethan was beautiful, though Evelyn doubted that the girl realised that herself. A sudden surge of anger rose in her against the stupid man who was drinking champagne in Brighton with someone else. She remembered long ago how she had felt when she'd discovered the letter; the shock, the pain, the rage and then, ultimately, the resignation.

'Are you OK?' Bethan asked.

Evelyn took a deep breath.

'I'm absolutely fine. Turn the page to something more exciting than these boring views.'

Bethan did as she was instructed.

'Here I am at twenty-one,' said Evelyn. 'I had just finished my first novel and was feeling rather pleased with myself.'

'You look so young.' Bethan peered at the black-and-white studio shot.

'I was young, young enough to write all day and night in those days.'

'You must have been exhausted.'

'At twenty-one, sleep doesn't seem that important, does it?'

'At twenty-one, I can assure you I was far less productive in the early hours.' Bethan laughed and turned another page to reveal a picture of Evelyn sitting on a hay bale beside a pile of hardback books, pen in hand.

'That was taken at the local county show,' Evelyn said. 'I was sitting about three feet away from a prize bull from Harlech. I'd been asked to open the show after my first novel was published.'

'What inspired you to write that first one?'

'Money,' Evelyn replied.

'Really?' Bethan looked surprised.

'You weren't expecting that?'

'Well, I thought,' Bethan indicated around the grand room, 'that you would have had money.'

'No.' Evelyn shook her head. 'By the end of the war there was none left. Howard was a terrible businessman. He was always making bad investments. He lost everything I'd inherited from my family. At the end of the war I found myself with a baby with Down's Syndrome, a husband in a wheelchair, a difficult mother-in-law, a very big house to run and absolutely nothing in the bank. I had to think of something I could do to support us all.'

'What made you think that writing would be the answer?'

'I read an article in *Woman's Journal* about Georgette Heyer. It said she had sold more books than anyone else that year. Women needed a bit of escapism after the war, and a romance set in the Regency period was what they liked best of all – it was very far removed from bombs and rationing and all the horrors that were emerging from the concentration camps in Europe.'

'I can imagine that it was a very grim time,' Bethan said quietly.

'Regency England seemed much more fun.' Evelyn smiled. 'All those bonnets and balls and dashing young men on horseback. It was escapism for me too. I didn't have to face reality while I was writing, I could forget about all my responsibilities, slip into a different world.'

'Surely you must have been tempted to just leave?' Bethan said. 'I mean, if Howard had lost your money, and your mother-in-law was awful. You could have taken Robert and started a new life.'

Evelyn closed her eyes. It was some time before she spoke again.

'They were different times,' she finally said, opening her eyes and straightening her shoulders. 'One didn't simply walk away. Howard's solution to the financial problems was to sell Oak Hill, my family's country house. Even though it was standing empty in Sussex, in my heart it was still my home, my link to the past. Luckily the deeds were in my name and it didn't matter how much pressure he put on me, I would not agree to sell it. And thank goodness I didn't – think of all those children who have benefited from their time there.'

'So instead you wrote books.'

'Yes, and once I'd written one, I found I could write another, then another.' She smiled. 'Too many to count.'

'You've written nearly fifty in seventy years.'

'Good God!' Evelyn said. 'As many as that? I suppose that's according to Wikipuddles or something.' She made a harrumphing noise. Though of course she did know it was nearly fifty. Her publisher was waiting for the fiftieth to be finished by the end of the summer – it was to be marketed as a special anniversary edition along with a reprint of her entire back catalogue in time for Christmas. Evelyn tried not to think about the far-from-finished manuscript upstairs.

'My mother has them all on a special shelf,' said Bethan. 'She inherited all Granny's copies and always buys your latest ones. She keeps them in the order of the years they were published, starting with *The Recalcitrant Duchess* all the way up to last year's *Bequeathed to the Baron*.'

Evelyn's face softened.

'I had no idea Annie bought my books. I would have gladly sent copies to her.' She paused, looking into the flames. 'I always gave your grandmother a signed first edition.'

'Mum says you taught Granny how to read.'

'Yes, I did. Nelli had gone into service without even knowing the alphabet. I think the little school in the village just hadn't bothered to understand her difficulties. These days she'd be diagnosed with dyslexia, but back then she was just labelled a dunce.' Evelyn shook her head sadly, then she brightened. 'But look how well she did in the end, a teaching diploma and a successful career. And I couldn't have started to write any books without her help.'

The flames seemed to conjure up Nelli in Evelyn's memory; her wild red curls, her quick lively movements, a brightness in the way she spoke, the merriment in her glittering green eyes. All that vivacity had been lost when Lloyd had been killed, but it had come back, little Robert had made sure of that.

'How did she help write your books?' Bethan asked.

'Your grandmother looked after Robert, and Howard, and Lady Vaughan, while I locked myself away with my typewriter. She was wonderful, never complained – and my husband and his mother were not easy.'

'Granny loved Robert.'

Evelyn smiled.

'Yes, she did. She treated him like any other baby, with as much right to be loved and cared for as a so-called normal child. Just as she went on to do with all the other children at Oak Hill.' She indicated to Bethan to turn another page and there was a picture of Nelli and Robert, sitting side by side on the lawn. Robert was holding a flower towards Nelli and she was leaning forward to take it. She already wore a daisy chain around her head. 'You can see how well those two got on.'

'Who's this?'

Bethan was peering at the little sepia photograph that had fallen loose from the album. She showed it to Evelyn. A young woman in a floral dress holding a bundle in her arms, something so tiny that could have been a doll.

'It's me, with Robert on his christening day.'

Bethan was staring at it closely.

'Your face looks so sad.'

Evelyn shrugged. She could feel her wrists beginning to ache.

'I was probably worrying about the christening party – butter for the scones, or sugar for the vicar's tea; we were still on rationing even though the war had been over for nearly a year.' Evelyn indicated that Bethan should turn the page. 'It was a very long time ago, I really can't remember.'

But Evelyn did remember. That sunny spring morning in 1946.

It had been the first time for months that she'd tried with her hair or bothered to wear anything other than an old skirt and jumper. She'd had to drag herself out of bed that morning, and drag herself to the church to stand at the font beside Howard in his wheelchair, with Robert still so small and fragile in her arms, despite the fact he was nearly a year old. It had been hard to ignore Lady Vaughan watching with distaste from the family pew, and Mrs Moggs sitting sour-faced just behind, with Olwyn at her side. The little girl had been wearing a white dress; she had looked like a lump of lard.

And then there had been Peter; lovely Peter with his hair neatly combed, socks pulled up to his knees and his glasses mended specially for the day. Nelli had been sitting beside him, sharing a hymn book, trying to follow his finger along the lines of the verses. Earlier she had helped Evelyn dress Robert in the Vaughan family christening gown; vast quantities of lace and satin that had swamped his tiny body. They'd had to roll the sleeves over and over and tie a big ribbon round his middle to stop the gown from falling off. And then, just after they arrived at church, Robert been sick all over it and Nelli had run back to the house to find a romper suit and crocheted shawl. Lady Vaughan had been horrified at the mess the baby had made all over the precious family heirloom.

'Generations of Vaughans have worn that christening gown and now it's ruined,' she complained as they all stood at the entrance to the church. 'Howard looked especially well in it.'

Evelyn had looked down at Howard in his wheelchair and tried to imagine the stern-faced man with the prominent Adam's apple in the frilly dress. She dissolved into a fit of giggles at the thought; she hadn't been able to stop. All the stress and pain of the previous year seemed to tumble out in her hysterical laughter. Howard had reached out and caught her hand.

'Stop it,' he had hissed at her. 'You're making a ridiculous fool of yourself.'

Evelyn had bent down and whispered in his ear.

'I think you'll find that *you* are the ridiculous fool. Don't think I haven't seen the letters from the bank, I know you've squandered all my money.' And then Evelyn had walked into the church, her head a little higher than it had been before.

'I'll sort it out,' she'd whispered to Robert in her arms. 'I'll sort it out for you.'

What an effort that day had been, but somehow it was important. It had been a beginning, a new chapter. She had accepted that no miracle was going to happen. She would have to get on with her life at Vaughan Court and make the best of it. That night she started to write her first novel.

BETHAN

There were so many photographs; like a jigsaw of characters and events. Bethan found herself trying to piece them together to make a picture of life at Vaughan Court in the years that had followed the war.

Lady Vaughan taking tea on the terrace with Howard in his wheelchair. Howard in his chair under the magnolia tree. Evelyn pushing a pram with Robert in it. Evelyn holding Robert up to see the cherub on the fountain. Robert on a blanket at the beach. Robert seemed to get rounder in every photograph; as the pages turned the tiny baby grew into a robust toddler with a beaming smile.

The only picture in which Robert wasn't smiling was one with a severe-looking woman holding his hand.

'Who's that?' asked Bethan, pointing at the woman.

'Mrs Moggs. She was the housekeeper, and during the war she became the cook as well – though she was terrible, made the most appalling food.'

'Was she related to Olwyn Moggs in the shop?'

'She was Olwyn's mother.' Evelyn gave a sniff. 'Never found out what happened to Mr Moggs, I suspect she might have eaten him.'

Bethan looked more closely. She could see a resemblance to Olwyn in the straight set mouth and raisin eyes.

'Let's not dwell on her.' Evelyn motioned to Bethan to turn the page.

There were endless pictures of the garden. Some with Evelyn standing beside newly planted box-hedging, one of a young boy wearing glasses, digging in a flower bed.

'Who's that?' Bethan asked.

'Peter, Tom's father. He was a wonderful help when I began to resurrect the Jacobean knot garden. He and I spent the whole summer of 1947 digging in manure from Home Farm and planting rose bushes.'

'Tom's father was an evacuee, is that right?'

'Yes. When the war ended Peter didn't have a home to go back to, so he stayed here.'

'With his brother?'

'No,' Evelyn said quietly. 'Not with his brother.'

'Goodness!' Bethan broke the silence that followed. 'Is that Dior?' She pointed at a picture of Evelyn standing under the portico wearing a dress with a very full skirt that showed off her tiny waist.

Evelyn brightened.

'Yes, I bought it with my advance from *The Recalcitrant Duchess*. I'd gone up to London to meet my publishers and couldn't resist popping into Harrods for something to celebrate – outrageously indulgent when I think about it, but I needed something to make it all worthwhile.'

Evelyn stroked her fine wool trousers with the fingers that protruded from her cast. 'Wearing nice clothes is important. I ploughed everything I earned into this house and then the school at Oak Hill, but a few quality pieces of clothing a year gave me a little treat.'

Bethan thought of the huge dressing room off Evelyn's bedroom. The evening before, Tom had asked her to help him look for clothes for Evelyn to wear home from the hospital.

'Wow!' Bethan had exclaimed. 'I think I must have died and gone to heaven – this is like my dream vintage shop.'

Tom had given her a look that Bethan interpreted as withering. Unperturbed, Bethan had slowly circled the room, staring wide-eyed at the beautiful clothes.

Dozens of dresses and coats and blouses hung on perfectly spaced hangers along one wall. Bethan had looked at some of the labels: Chanel, Balenciaga, Yves St Laurent, even a Vivian Westwood pair of trousers and an Alexander McQueen jacket. The remaining walls

94

of the room were lined with shelves and drawers. Rows and rows of handbags were as neatly displayed as exhibits in a museum and there was a selection of scarves hanging from a rail like a multi-coloured piece of abstract art. Bethan longed to open the drawers but she didn't want to risk another disapproving look from Tom.

She'd started hunting through the clothes and picked out a gold lamé cat suit with a plunging neckline.

'This would give the nurses something to talk about for weeks if she left in this.'

Tom ignored her and picked out a pair of plain black trousers and a beige cashmere cardigan.

'These will be fine,' he said, and then added a tweed coat with wide enough sleeves to allow for the plaster casts on Evelyn's wrists. Bethan had wondered why he'd bothered asking her to help at all.

The drawing room was warm now; the fire cast a cosy glow around the room. As Bethan turned the pages of the photograph album she recognised some of the clothes she had seen the night before. She suspected Evelyn could still fit into all of them, she didn't look as though she'd put on an ounce of weight since she'd been in her twenties.

In the background of one picture Bethan noticed a circle of feathers.

'You had peacocks even then?'

'That was Perry. He was the first.' Outside a peacock let out a cry, and several other cries followed as if they knew they were being talked about.

'Where did Perry come from?'

Evelyn didn't answer, instead she signalled that Bethan should close the album.

'I've had enough of the past. I want to go to bed now.'

Bethan shut the leather covers of the book and stood up. As she did so the loose photograph of Evelyn on Robert's christening day fluttered to the floor. Bethan bent and picked it up.

'Throw it on the fire,' Evelyn said.

'Sorry?' Bethan thought she must have misunderstood.

95

'Throw the photograph on the fire.' Evelyn's voice was firm. 'I don't want to remember.'

Bethan glanced at the photograph; Evelyn really did look very sad. Could she really have been that worried about the christening tea?

'Please.' Evelyn looked up at Bethan, her eyes imploring.

Bethan gave a little shrug and taking a step towards the fireplace threw the little square into the burning logs in the grate; the edges of the photograph curled and shrivelled, there was a lick of flame and then it was gone.

EVELYN

It was wonderful to be back in her own bed; soft pillows piled high behind her head, the reassuring weight of the satin eiderdown on top of her legs, Egyptian cotton sheets.

Bethan had helped her undress. Earlier Evelyn had been mortified to have to ask Bethan to pull down her trousers and pants so that she could pee, but the girl had been so matter-of-fact about it, that asking her to help her take her clothes off and help her into her nightdress hadn't been too bad at all, though it was infuriating not to even be able to remove her cardigan herself. The girl had looked tired, her face pale, though it was hardly surprising considering all the upset with her boyfriend.

'Stupid man,' Evelyn said out loud.

Outside it was still light. Bethan had offered to draw the curtains but Evelyn had shaken her head.

'Now I'm actually in bed I'm wide awake, so I might as well admire the view.'

The huge bay window faced towards the sea. Through the mullioned glass Evelyn could see the sun beginning to set.

In the garden the peacocks were getting ready to roost. They were crying out as they settled in the branches of the trees.

Last summer Tilly had counted them.

'There are thirty-four,' the little girl had said solemnly. Those were the days when Tilly never smiled at all, not long after they had moved from London.

Tilly was like a different child now, full of chat, in English or

Welsh, brimming with life and fun and laughter.. Evelyn heard her laughing now. It sounded as though she was outside. Someone else was laughing too. Bethan. And Tom. Evelyn wondered what they were all doing; Tom was supposed to be making a meal in the kitchen; he'd arrived with a bag full of ingredients from Olwyn's shop.

'I can see you!' It was Tilly's voice, just below the window.

'I haven't had enough time yet!' said Bethan. Evelyn guessed that Tilly had Bethan playing hide-and-seek already; lately it had been the little girl's favourite activity whenever she came to visit. Even Evelyn had been embroiled into games, squeezing into tiny corners and cupboards, once lying prostrate behind the sofa for half an hour before Tilly found her.

'You have to find a really good place.'

'Hang on, I need a bit longer.'

'*Un, dau, tri.* Coming, ready or not.'

Evelyn shuffled her body towards the edge of the bed. She managed to swing her legs out and stand up without having to put weight on her hands. She walked over to the window and looked out.

Tilly was running through the knot garden, her blonde braids flying out behind her, long legs emerging from the shorts she always wore over brightly coloured stripy tights. She always had on wellington boots too, even on dry days; bright red and glittery. It seemed an odd outfit but Tom had explained that Tilly refused to wear anything else when she wasn't in school. Evelyn had to admire the little girl's individual style.

'Daddy, you're not even hiding properly.'

Tom was crouched down behind the fountain. He stood up and Tilly jumped into his arms.

'Bethan.' Tilly twisted round in her father's embrace. 'I can see you in the arches underneath the terrace.'

'No, you can't.'

'Yes, I can! You're behind the middle arch.'

'I'm afraid the game's up,' Tom called. 'We can see your shadow.'

'Your shadow is making funny shapes now.' Tilly had disentangled herself from her father and was running towards the house. 'Are you dancing?'

Evelyn smiled. Bethan seemed to have forgotten her heartache, or at least she was putting on a good show for the little girl.

Tom followed his daughter towards the terrace. Evelyn couldn't see them any more. The voices and their laughter receded and Evelyn assumed that they had gone inside.

She pressed her forehead against the cool glass of the windowpane. In the garden, Evelyn could see the peacocks in the cedar tree, their long tails hanging down from the branches; opulent in their new spring plumage, waterfalls of shimmering feathers.

It was a whole family tree of peacocks, all of them descendants of the first. She wished that Jack could have seen them.

There was a knock at the door and Tom appeared carrying a tray.

'Your dinner is served; cheesey omelette with a cheesy filling and a bit more cheese sprinkled on the top – it's a medical-student speciality.'

Evelyn turned from the window, aware that the room had become gloomy. She hadn't noticed how much the light outside had faded, how much time had passed. Tom placed the tray on top of the dressing table and switched on the bedside light.

'What are you doing? You're supposed to be resting.'

He took a few steps across the room to try to guide her back to the bed.

'Bugger off.' Evelyn batted at him with her plastered arm. 'I can manage on my own.'

Tom turned away and picked up the plate from the tray.

'And I suppose if I just leave your dinner here you can manage to cut it up and eat it on your own.'

Evelyn scowled and sat down on the edge of the bed.

'I don't think any of the principles of medical ethics include derision. Where's Bethan? I want her to help me.'

Tom sat down beside her and began cutting into the omelette with a fork.

'She's with Tilly downstairs. They're eating their way through a packet of Haribo that they found in your special drawer. Honestly, Evelyn, I think you might be addicted to those sweets.'

'If an old woman can't have some bad habits, what's the point?' Evelyn sniffed. 'I hope they're not eating the fizzy ones; they're my favourites.'

'No, Tilly chose the Starmix. The two of them are deeply engrossed in a debate about whether the raspberry hearts are tastier than the cola bottles, so you can't possibly ask Bethan to come and help you at the moment.'

Evelyn looked down at her hands.

'These bloody plaster casts. I can't bear not being able to do anything.'

'When the swelling goes down you should be able to get some movement back – enough to hold a spoon and a cup, possibly do up buttons, but for now you're going to need help for pretty much everything.'

Tom held out a forkful of omelette.

'It's all right to be vulnerable, you know.'

'Mmm.' Evelyn made a sceptical noise but she let him put the food in her mouth. 'It tastes good.'

'You sound surprised?'

'I thought Sarah did all the cooking in your house.'

'Sarah does all the cooking because she has more time than I do.'

'Mmm.' Evelyn made the sceptical noise again. 'She told me she has more translation work than she can cope with.'

'Don't make me feel guilty. She does know how grateful I am for everything she does.'

'It's because she loves you so much.'

They were silent for a while as Evelyn ate. Within minutes the whole omelette was gone. Tom tried to wipe Evelyn's mouth with a tissue from a box beside the bed. Evelyn flinched and batted him away again. He laughed.

'I think you must be feeling stronger.'

'As I told them in the hospital, I feel as strong as an ox.'

'Good.'

Evelyn looked down at the tips of her protruding fingers. They looked grey against the whiteness of the new plaster.

'But I have been wondering,' she said.

'Yes?'

'About this thing with my heart.'

'The atrial fibrillation?'

'Whatever it's called,' Evelyn tutted. 'I don't care that much about its name or what it means medically, but . . .' She paused, then took a deep breath before starting again. 'All I want to know is do you think it might be . . .' Her voice trailed away.

'Going to kill you?' Tom asked, folding the tissue into a neat square.

'That's rather blunt!'

'Well, I assume that's what you want to know.'

Evelyn lifted her chin.

'Yes. I do want to know. Is it going to kill me?'

'Not today,' he smiled. 'And probably not tomorrow. And hopefully not at all. With the drugs you've been given and careful monitoring it should mean that any risks are minimised, giving you lots more time to die in some other, completely unexpected way.'

Evelyn didn't return his smile.

'But all the same,' she said. 'Maybe it's time I accepted that the end might not be that far away.'

Tom stopped smiling. He folded the tissue into a smaller square.

'The end can come at any time, whatever your age.'

Evelyn sighed and turned to look at him.

'I didn't mean to sound so morose.' She moved her hand towards him across the quilt and winced with pain. 'I know I've had a good innings. More than my fair share of years when others haven't been so lucky. It doesn't seem right that I—'

'I know what you're trying to say,' Tom interrupted her. 'But you don't have to apologise for your age. If I've learned anything in the last few years it's that life is a lottery. People can live to be a hundred and ten, or people can have life snatched pointlessly away when their lives have hardly started. None of it makes any sense.' He stopped, scrunching the folded tissue in his fist. 'And none of it is fair.'

101

'I'm so sorry, Tom.'

Tom straightened his shoulders.

'I'll just say this regarding your diagnosis, if there's anything you want to do – a place you want to visit, a friend you want to see, a new hobby you'd like to take up—'

'A story I'd like to finish.'

Tom nodded.

'Don't put it off.'

BETHAN

Bethan felt sick.

She shook her head as Tilly pushed a small yellow sweet across the kitchen table.

'Don't you like the gummy bears?'

'I couldn't eat another Haribo if you paid me.' Bethan hiccupped slightly.

Tilly laughed and popped the bear into her mouth.

'You've lost your earring.' The little girl touched her own un-pierced ear lobe. Bethan reached up, feeling the little golden swallow.

'Not that side,' said Tilly. 'The other side. When I get my ears pierced I'm going to have earrings that are gold birds too.'

'Oh no!' Bethan felt her other ear. 'They were my granny's.' She stood up and started feeling inside the neckline of her blouse and looking on the floor.

'My mum said I could have my ears pierced when I'm ten, but my dad says I have to be thirteen.' Tilly put both her elbows on the table and rather theatrically put her chin into her hands. 'Now I have to wait five whole years! How old were you when you got your ears pierced?'

Bethan wasn't listening. She was peering at the quarry tiles beside the ancient Aga where she'd helped Tom serve the omelettes, and then she looked around the Belfast sink where she and Tilly had washed the dishes.

'Oh dear,' Bethan sighed. 'I think I might have lost it when we were playing hide-and-seek in the garden.'

She opened the kitchen door. It was nearly dark. She doubted that she'd find the earring now. It was cold and the air felt damp. Bethan hiccupped again, the Haribo aftertaste bitter in her mouth. This was not where she was meant to be tonight. She thought of Mal in the beautiful hotel room and gave another little burp. She stared out at the courtyard, suddenly too miserable to even shut the door. Something brushed against her arm. Looking down, Bethan saw that Tilly was standing beside her.

'This is what Evelyn uses when she goes outside at night to check for slugs,' the little girl said, holding up a torch.

'It's all right, Tilly. I'll look in the morning.'

'I'm a very good finder.' Tilly squeezed past her in the doorway.

'Come back, it's too dark to go out.'

'Don't you want to find it?' Tilly was already in the courtyard.

'Yes, but I don't think now is the time.'

'Let's go on an earring hunt!' The little girl began skipping around the courtyard waving the beam of torchlight across the barn walls and gravelly ground.

'OK, but where's your coat?' Bethan called out to her. 'You'll need it out there.'

'I never feel the cold,' Tilly called back, disappearing around the corner.

Bethan glanced at the coat hooks beside the door and saw an old Barbour jacket. She took it off the hook and slipped it on.

Bethan hurried after Tilly around the side of the house, down the steps from the terrace, onto the lawn and towards the knot garden where their game of hide-and-seek had taken place. Tilly was swinging the torch back and forth, peering at the ground.

'Come on,' Tilly shouted towards Bethan. 'You have to look too.'

Bethan could see that the lawn was in desperate need of cutting; the little earring could have disappeared for good in between the blades of grass.

'This is like looking for a needle in a haystack,' Bethan said as they circled the fountain. Tilly shone the torch around the fountain, focusing the beam on the cherub's weather-worn face. His chubby cheeks were mottled with lichen, his pursed lips distorted with moss. A trail of something slimy hung from the little spout where the water had once spurted out.

'He looks spooky,' said Tilly cheerfully.

Bethan shivered and wrapped the oversized jacket tighter around her body.

'Maybe we should go back inside.'

'Let's look under there.' The little girl pointed to the long walkway underneath the terrace where Bethan had been hiding earlier.

'I'll look under there tomorrow,' said Bethan.

But Tilly was already running across the lawn. There was nothing Bethan could do but follow.

Tilly swept the torch around the vaulted roof. The space seemed like a tunnel. Stalactites hung down like skeletal fingers and everything was painted with limewash, yellowing and peeling away with age.

'Hello,' Tilly shouted.

Hello, hello, hello, her voice echoed through the empty space.

Tilly twirled around so that the torch revealed brief glimpses of piles of dead leaves and foliage that must have blown in during the winter. A single peacock feather lay at Bethan's feet, its rich jewel colours shimmering in the fleeting beam of the torchlight.

Something else glinted as Tilly's torchbeam skimmed across the floor again.

'Here,' cried Bethan. 'Point the torch here.' She crouched down. The tiny swallow was in the groove between two slabs of dark grey slate. Bethan struggled to get it out, but Tilly managed with her little finger. She handed it to Bethan.

'It's lost the bit at the back.'

'It doesn't matter,' said Bethan smiling. 'I can get another butterfly. I'm just relieved it's not lost.' She stood up and dropped it into the pocket of the Barbour jacket.

Tilly had begun kicking at the piles of debris with her boots, spinning around so that the torchbeam caught the dried-up leaves, casting dancing shadows on the walls.

'We'd better get back to the house,' Bethan said. 'Your dad is probably wondering what I've done with you.'

'Have you seen the ghosts?' Tilly stopped spinning.

'What ghosts?'

'These ghosts,' Tilly called. She was already skipping down to the far end of the tunnel.

'Wait.' Bethan was plunged into darkness as the torch beam receded.

'Come on.' Tilly had stopped and was waving the torch at a section of the wall. Bethan joined her. At first she couldn't make out what Tilly was pointing at.

'Look.' Tilly touched the wall with her splayed-out hand. 'Do you see the face?'

Bethan took a step closer. Tilly took her hand away and suddenly Bethan did see the face. It was in profile. A nose, a mouth, a tilting chin, a swan-like neck. There was an eye too, gazing straight in front, blue with very long eyelashes. And there was hair; curls cascading over a shoulder. As Bethan followed the torchlight, she made out the outline of an entire figure, life-size, one knee drawn up, one leg extended. It was very pale, almost as though it was emerging through the white limewash as Bethan stared at it. The figure seemed to be wearing high-heeled shoes.

'There's another one down here.' Tilly walked a little further on and Bethan could see the outline of a kneeling figure; a woman with her arms behind her head, hair swept to one side, a suggestion of a flower behind her ear. Her face was almost too pale to make out, but there was still a smudge of red where the mouth should be and an arch of eyebrow.

'And here.' Tilly was off again. 'But you can really only see her boot and hat.' She swung the torchlight on a short brown boot and a few feet above it what looked like a cowboy hat. 'And this is the last one. She's my favourite.'

The final figure was the clearest of them all. She was sitting down, wearing a red swimsuit and had incredibly long legs, which were stretched in front of her, ending in a pair of strappy sandals, scarlet nail varnish on her toes. Her face was clearer too; full red lips and a perfect nose. She stared straight at Bethan with one big, long-lashed eye; the other eye was closed in a seductive wink.

'Wow!' said Bethan. 'Who painted these?'

'They're not painted,' said Tilly. 'They're ghosts. They are stuck in the wall. They can't get out.'

'Oh.' Bethan looked at Tilly with surprise. The little girl didn't seem at all disturbed by the idea of ghosts stuck in a wall.

'Dad says they've been here since the war hundreds of years ago.'

Bethan walked back along the wall, studying the figures all over again; Tilly followed her with the torch, stopping to illuminate each one. It was hard to tell if they were emerging or disappearing from the wall.

They reminded Bethan of the ancient paintings in the caves she'd seen on holiday in France. They had the same faded ethereal appearance, but the subject matter was very different – these pictures were far more *Playboy* than Palaeolithic.

'But Dad's not right,' Tilly said sombrely.

'He isn't?'

'No,' Tilly shook her head. 'They are dead mothers.'

There was a noise behind them. Bethan jumped and turned to see a figure standing in one of the archways.

Bethan grabbed the torch from Tilly's hand. She pointed it at the archway. Tom stepped forward.

'I've been looking everywhere for you two.'

Bethan's hand was at her chest.

'You gave me a fright!'

'She thought you were another ghost,' Tilly said.

'Not the ghost stories again.' Tom came up to them and put his arm around Tilly's shoulder. 'What are you doing out here? I've been worried.'

'I was helping Bethan find an earring,' said Tilly.

'It was my—' Bethan started to explain, but Tom interrupted.

'It's well past Tilly's bedtime.'

He started to guide Tilly away towards the arches.

'Do you know where the paintings on the wall came from?' Bethan called at his retreating back. 'I don't remember them when I used to come here as a child.'

Tom stopped and turned back to Bethan.

'Evelyn says they were painted by an American airman in the Second World War, when Vaughan Court was used as a US army hospital. They were whitewashed over for years but the whitewash is wearing away so some of the paintings are becoming visible again.'

'They are *not* paintings!' Tilly cried out crossly. 'They *are* ghosts. Evelyn is telling lies.'

'Tilly! You mustn't say that!' Tom shook his head.

Tilly shook her head too, her long plaits swinging from side to side. 'I know she's a liar, a wrinkly old lady liar.'

'Now you're being rude, Tilly.'

Tilly suddenly started to cry.

'I'm not being rude. Evelyn is a liar. And you are a liar too. You never tell me anything. You make everything up because you think I'm too little to understand. You're a big fat liar like Evelyn. And Mummy says you're a big fat liar too!'

'That's enough,' Tom said sharply. He picked his daughter up and turned to look at Bethan; in the torchlight his face seemed as though it were carved out of rock, a frown line making a deep ravine between his eyes. 'I hope you find your earring but you'll have to do it without the help of a little girl who should be in bed, not out here in the freezing cold without her coat on.'

'I did try—'

'And judging by the empty Haribo packet on the kitchen table,' Tom interrupted, 'Tilly has probably eaten far too many sweets as well.'

'She didn't have—'

But Tom didn't stay to hear, he walked briskly away into the darkness, Tilly wriggling and protesting in his arms. Bethan felt the injustice of Tom's sudden angry words as she headed back towards the house behind him, the torch in her hand. She slowed her pace, unwilling to catch up.

The beam of light made shadows of the foliage and trees; branches looked like arms. There was a noise, a cry. A peacock flew down from one of the trees. It perched on the top of a Grecian pillar, feathers cascading down the lichen-stained stone. Bethan hurried past and ran up the stone steps towards the house, taking them two at a time until she reached the terrace.

She could see Tom and Tilly beside Tom's Volvo in front of the portico. Tilly had stopped struggling and was now sobbing against Tom's shoulder. He strapped her into her seat before getting in himself. The headlights came on. After a few seconds the car engine started and the Volvo pulled away. Bethan watched the tail lights as they slowly disappeared down the drive.

She stayed standing very still long after the lights and the sound of the engine had gone. Her legs seemed rooted to the ground and the oversized Barbour jacket felt heavy, the stiff waxed fabric weighing her down.

She pushed her hand into the pocket to check the swallow earring was still there. Instead of the tiny piece of gold she felt something larger; smooth and hard against her fingers. She drew out a slim box. It was made of silver, dulled and tarnished by age; there was a pattern on the lid, fine lines, splaying out into a sun ray. Bethan pushed the catch and the box sprang open. She saw a row of grooves where cigarettes must once have been kept; there was tobacco dust in the corners, it gave off a musty smell. On the inside of the lid there were words engraved in an elaborate, old-fashioned typeface:

To my darling Howard,
Always and forever,
L.D.
Christmas 1944

'L.D.,' Bethan murmured. What did they stand for? A nickname for Evelyn? She couldn't imagine the man in the wedding picture using terms of endearment; Howard looked so stiff and stern, almost Victorian. Would he have had a special name for his young wife? Mal had always called Bethan *Babe*. She'd never liked it. She snapped the lid of the cigarette case closed.

'I'm not your Babe any more!' she shouted out into the darkness.

A peacock let out a cry in reply.

EVELYN

'Good God! Where on earth did those flowers come from?' Evelyn nearly spat out her mouthful of tea. 'They look positively funereal.'

Evelyn was drinking through a straw. Earlier Bethan had put the mug on a pile of books on the bedside table and made an extra-long straw by taping together two bendy plastic ones she'd found in a drawer. All Evelyn needed to do was lean over and suck. At first Evelyn had been horrified but at least it meant she could drink independently and not feel so much like a child.

Bethan was holding a huge display of spring flowers in a vase. She put it on top of the chest of drawers.

'I'm afraid I forgot all about these yesterday,' she said, propping up a drooping tulip against a hyacinth. 'The poor things didn't get any water until last night, but they are reviving a bit now.'

'But where did they come from?' Evelyn asked.

'A man brought them over for you. From the golf club.'

Evelyn lay back on the mound of pillows Bethan had arranged behind her after waking her up with breakfast on a tray.

'Blue eyes, white teeth? Very handsome?'

'He did have blue eyes.' Bethan stood back and seemed to be scrutinising the flower arrangement. 'Beautiful.' Evelyn wasn't sure if Bethan was referring to the flowers or the eyes.

'David Dashwood,' Evelyn said. 'My neighbour.'

'He was very concerned about your health.'

'Good, I like to think that eligible bachelors are concerned for my well-being.'

'Is he an eligible bachelor?' Bethan asked.

'Are you interested?'

'No! I've only just got rid of one man, I don't need another.'

Evelyn smiled.

'Good for you.'

'The golf club looks very smart,' Bethan said. 'Not that I've seen much more than the sign at the entrance.'

'It is smart,' Evelyn said. 'And Mr Dashwood is forever expanding his empire. I sold him the land to build the golf club eight years ago and fifty more acres of woodland last summer for a pheasant shoot. I rather regretted that; from October to January all I could hear was the sound of prosperous businessmen shooting the poor things dead.' Evelyn let out a long sigh and thought about the ancient oak trees that she and Robert used to walk through in the autumn, Robert kicking up the fallen leaves and collecting the shiny acorns. It had been such a peaceful place.

Bethan began tidying up some papers that were strewn along a stool at the end of the bed.

'For goodness sake don't muddle them up!' Evelyn tried not to sound too exasperated.

'Sorry.'

'It's only the first draught but it's all laid out in order.'

'Sorry,' Bethan said again and carefully laid the pages back down where they'd been.

Evelyn wondered if she was trying to decipher her handwriting.

'I'm afraid it's quite illegible, always has been. I used to get rapped over the knuckles for it in school.'

'Oh, I wasn't reading, I wouldn't dare!'

'I wouldn't care if you did. I've never been one of those "I'm not showing it to anyone until its perfect" kind of novelists. But I always write in longhand until I'm happy with each chapter. Then I type it up on the Olivetti.'

'Not on a laptop?'

Evelyn tutted.

'I've had my Olivetti since 1956, why would I need anything else?'

'Research? On the internet.'

Evelyn indicated to a wall lined with shelves. They were piled high with books and files.

'I have everything I need right here.'

Evelyn leant over and sucked up the last of her tea through the straw. 'I seem to have run out. Could you be a dear and get me another cup?'

After Bethan had gone downstairs, Evelyn stared at the papers at the end of the bed. The fiftieth book. *For the Love of Hermione.*

Evelyn groaned. She'd told the publisher it would be ready by the end of the summer. How on earth was she going to get it done with no hands to hold a pen or type? She looked up from the half-finished manuscript towards the view out of the window. The sun sparkled on the distant strip of sea and an idea began to form in her mind.

BETHAN

Evelyn's fingertips tapped noiselessly on the satin quilt.

'It's very simple – I'll dictate and you can write it out.' It was the third time she'd said this since Bethan had returned with the mug of tea.

Bethan readjusted the straw.

'But surely that will take quite a long time?' she said and added another paperback to raise the mug slightly higher.

'About three months.' Evelyn's voice was matter-of-fact.

'But my job?'

'You can write your articles from here.'

'No. My paid job, working in the vegan café.'

'You'd rather serve soya cappuccinos to health-obsessed hippos?'

'I think you mean hipsters,' said Bethan.

'Maybe, but whatever you call them surely it would be better to spend your summer in the idyllic surroundings of Snowdonia?'

Bethan glanced out of the window – it did look more attractive now the sun had come out and sometimes the café customers did drive her mad with their egocentric demands.

Evelyn made a tutting sound.

'And are you really planning to continue to share your flat with the duplicitous Mal?'

'Well, no, I thought . . .' Bethan hadn't really thought at all. She'd been trying very hard not to think about the practicalities of her future living arrangements. In her stronger moments she envisaged going home and throwing all Mal's possessions out of the window of their third-floor flat, but in reality, she knew she could never pay the rent in Battersea on her own.

'Supposing he moves his new girlfriend in?' continued Evelyn. 'How are you going to manage with that?'

Bethan bit her lip. It was hard enough imagining Mal with another woman in a hotel in Brighton let alone imagining him with another woman in their flat. And the flat belonged to Mal. It was his name on the rental agreement; he had taken on the lease after getting an advertising job in London. When they met at a party, Bethan had finished her degree and had been back living with her parents in the flat above the little Battersea pottery studio and shop, just around the corner from Mal's mansion block.

She had moved in unintentionally, gradually, one item at a time, until most of her possessions were distributed somewhere in Mal's flat. Sometimes Bethan thought that their domestic union had been more resignation than invitation on Mal's part, and he had absolutely put his foot down when Bethan had tried to move her cat, Ottis, in. Mal said cats gave him the creeps.

'And of course, I would pay you,' Evelyn said. 'Not very much, but I won't charge you rent.'

Bethan could smell the heavy scent of the hyacinths coming from the flowers on the chest of drawers.

'And I'll pay for all your food,' Evelyn added. 'Providing you don't eat vast quantities of hideously expensive organic pomegranates, or Beluga Caviar for breakfast.'

'Good morning!' Tom's face appeared at the door. He held up a copy of *Vogue* with one hand. Bethan was pleased to see that he had lost the bad-tempered expression of the night before. 'I found this with the post in the hall; knowing you, Evelyn, I thought you'd want to read it as soon as possible.' He glanced from Evelyn to Bethan and back to Evelyn. 'Is everything all right?'

'I'm just bullying Bethan again,' Evelyn said cheerfully. 'I'm doing my very best to manipulate her into staying all summer.'

Tom looked at Bethan.

'Is that what you want to do?'

'Well . . .'

'That's where the bullying comes in,' said Evelyn. 'I'm wearing her down. I think she's almost on the verge of saying yes.'

'I know one little girl who would be very happy to hear you were staying around,' said Tom. 'Tilly talked about you non-stop after we left last night.'

'Did she?' Bethan said, surprised. 'I feel awful that I let her eat so many sweets and let her go out in the cold. And I'm so sorry that she got so upset about the paintings.'

'What paintings?' demanded Evelyn.

'Your ladies under the terrace,' Tom said. 'You know how they fascinate Tilly.'

Evelyn lay back against her mound of pillows and shut her eyes.

'I must get a man in to whitewash over them again. I'll ask David Dashwood if he can spare a groundsman.'

'But surely they're of historical interest,' said Bethan.

'That's what I think,' said Tom. 'Important relics of World War Two.'

'Maybe we could contact a historian?' Bethan suggested. 'The paintings are part of the memories of the war, and the role the house played in it.'

'No.' Evelyn's eyes were open again, her voice scratchy with indignation. 'I do not need historians! And I don't need relics, or memories of World War Two! Why would anyone want to remember that awful time!' She sounded almost as petulant as Tilly the evening before. Bethan and Tom exchanged a glance.

'Go to the golf club.' Evelyn pointed towards Bethan, jabbing the air with a plaster-covered arm. 'Go and tell Mr Dashwood that I need those paintings painted over immediately. Do you understand? I want them gone. I want them all to disappear!'

EVELYN

They had gone downstairs. Tom said he wanted to talk Bethan through her medication but Evelyn knew they would actually be talking about her. She could imagine them, voices lowered.

'I've never seen her get upset like that before.' Tom would probably be shaking his head, face concerned. 'Better keep an eye on her. We don't want her blood pressure to go up any more.'

She glanced at the copy of *Vogue* that Tom had brought up. A beautiful young girl smiled from the cover; glossy hair and impossibly smooth skin. On one side of her head it said *Swirl into spring with a new season dress!*

She gave the magazine a push with the plaster cast and it slid onto the floor with a thud.

Evelyn stared at the door, willing Bethan or Tom to come back; she was ready to shout *Go away and leave me alone* as soon as they did.

No one came. She decided against shouting *Go away*, she would be genial instead. Upset and anger would only lead to more questions about the paintings.

Still no one came.

She tapped her fingers on the quilt. Maybe Bethan was already on her way to the golf club to inform David of the job that needed doing. But she doubted the girl would be so compliant; Bethan had a steely glint in her eyes that reminded Evelyn of Nelli.

Evelyn groaned. It was all so exasperating having to depend on other people to do things for her. Three days before she could have jumped into the MG and gone to see David herself, as simple as anything. Now she had to justify her wishes, argue even. It was her house, they were her paintings. Surely she could do what she liked with them.

She'd painted them over herself before. Frenzied brush strokes, as though she could cover all her rage and grief and pain. But now the pictures were coming back, like the stones at the windows. She'd heard them again in the night; little showers of pebbles tapping on the glass and then a smash. Evelyn shut her eyes, trying to block out thoughts of Billy and his catapult, trying to block out thoughts of Jack.

It was impossible, images of Jack seemed to be re-emerging in her consciousness as vividly as the paintings under the terrace. Evelyn tried to think about her novel: Hermione would meet her suitor at a dance, what would she wear? It would be spring, no need for velvet or fur. But Evelyn's mind refused to concentrate on a Regency ball, instead it drifted back to the afternoon that she had first met Jack Valentine, not at a dance, not in the spring, but on the side of the mountain, on a bleak winter's day.

December 1943

Evelyn lay on her bed; she hadn't even bothered to take her shoes off.

Outside there was a world of nothing. The garden beneath her had completely disappeared into the thick, grey mist, as miserable as the Christmas looming ahead of her. She thought it might even be worse than the last. Lady Vaughan hardly spoke to her these days; she made it very clear that in her opinion Howard had not made a good match despite her fortune. Evelyn longed to tell her mother-in-law what she knew. What she had discovered in the letter, about Loretta Day and Lady Vaughan's precious son.

Loretta. The name made Evelyn feel sick. She could still see the elaborate signature at the bottom of the page, the words seared into her brain.

The letter had arrived after a visit from Howard at Easter. Evelyn had been looking forward to seeing him for weeks. She hoped that things would be different; she had decided things would be different.

She had found a book in the library at Vaughan Court, pushed behind the complete works of Shakespeare. *Dr. Birtwistle's Guide to Marital Relations*, published in 1902. Though its tone had been rather ambiguous, Evelyn had found it most enlightening.

But when Howard arrived from London, he had a heavy cold and asked for a separate bedroom to be made up. Evelyn had been disappointed, but at the end of the week, when he appeared to be much better, she had tiptoed across the corridor at midnight and had very quietly gone into his room.

'I thought you might like some company,' she'd whispered in a voice she hoped was laced with desire as she slipped between the linen sheets.

Howard had given a little cough and turned his back.

'I'm afraid I still feel quite unwell.'

Evelyn lay very still on her back, for a long time, staring into the darkness, before getting out of the bed and returning to her room.

The letter arrived the next day. Howard had already gone back to London on the early train. Evelyn spotted the pale cream envelope on the tiles in the hall on her way to join Lady Vaughan for lunch. Mrs Moggs always collected the post in the morning; she'd take it to Lady Vaughan's study, or if it was for Howard she would readdress it to the Sloane Street flat and Olwyn would be sent to run down to the post office in time for the second collection. Evelyn was surprised that Mrs Moggs would have dropped a letter on the floor; Mrs Moggs was so fastidious in everything she did.

Evelyn stooped to pick it up. The writing on the envelope had so many curls and flourishes it was difficult to read, but Evelyn could see that it was addressed to Howard. She turned the envelope over; there was the merest hint of a lip print and there was also a smell. Evelyn held it to her nose; something sweet and sickly. Violets. She hesitated, looking around to make sure no one was watching, then slipped the envelope inside the pocket of her skirt.

Evelyn could still remember they'd had cheese and lentil savoury for lunch, a recipe that Mrs Moggs said she had followed from a government pamphlet. It had tasted repulsive.

After lunch Evelyn went out. She climbed the mountain path, high up, as far away from the house as she could get. When she read the letter she had vomited little orange lentils all over the rocks.

A week later Evelyn had travelled all the way to London on the pretext of a visit to Miss Wyatt, even though she knew Miss Wyatt had gone to live in Canada months before. She had thought that she would confront Howard in the flat in Sloane Street; instead she found Loretta there, preparing for a show. Evelyn never expected Loretta to be a nightclub singer. It seemed so tawdry, so cheap, so miserably predictable. Evelyn hadn't even bothered to wait for Howard to explain.

Evelyn shivered at the memory as she lay on the cold four-poster bed. She pulled her cardigan tightly around herself and stared up at the swirling plaster patterns on the ceiling. Rain was hammering at the windows now, wind moaning through the frame. The window-panes began to rattle. Evelyn sat up. The wind became a howl, and then a roar, almost deafening. The whole room seemed to shake; she thought the windowpanes might shatter. Then there was a bang, an explosion, not in the house, but somewhere very near. Evelyn leapt up to look out of the window. She tried to crane her neck, but everything was fog. She heard shouting below her. The boys.

'A crash, there's been a crash!'

Without even stopping to think, she wrenched open the bedroom door and ran outside. Ignoring the cold, and her lack of a coat, she ran around the side of the house. The boys were ahead of her, already scrambling up the path that led towards the mountains.

'Peter! Billy!'

She called their names and set off as fast as she could, following them upwards, clambering over rocks and boulders. The smell of smoke was thick on the wind.

The fog was so dense that she and the boys couldn't see where they were going, slipping and sliding on the shale, guided by the orange glow above them, and the smell. Burning rubber, engine oil.

She overtook the boys, splashing through streams, stumbling around the boulders, cheeks stinging from the icy sleet.

'Wait,' they called to her, 'wait for us.'

They caught up then, and she took Peter's hand in hers to help him over the rocks, but Billy ran on ahead.

'It's one of the Yanks' bombers,' he called back. 'And it's crashed on our bloody mountain.'

'Careful,' she shouted out to him. 'Don't fall.'

The fog lifted just as they reached the twisted mass of metal. Evelyn saw cables and glass and one wing, crumpled like a concertina against the rock face.

Billy had already stopped several feet from the wreckage; he'd pulled his jumper over his mouth and nose to protect himself from the smoke and fumes. Evelyn and Peter stood beside him and stared. The plane was huge, a mechanical goliath in the wilderness of the mountain landscape. The wing smashed against the rock face was on fire, flames licking around one of its giant propellers.

'The fuel tanks are going to blow.' Billy had to shout above the wind. Evelyn shielded her eyes from the smoke; the flames were inching towards the smashed nose of the plane. She saw an incongruously glamorous woman painted on one side, and the words *The Lady Bountiful* written in elaborate blue letters. Above the painting she could see the cockpit. She looked away, not wanting to imagine what was inside.

'Look.' Peter let go of her hand to point. 'There's a man.'

Evelyn forced herself to look back. There was a figure, slumped forward against the glass, his head twisted at an alarming angle, blood running down his face, blood smeared up against the window.

'He's a goner,' Billy said.

'There's someone else,' Peter shouted.

Beside the lifeless body there was another figure, slumped down in his seat. They could see little more than his helmet.

'I think he's a goner too,' said Billy.

But as Evelyn peered through the smoke she was sure she saw the second figure move. His head lifted and then one arm slowly raised as though trying to push through the glass window of the cockpit.

'Bloody hell,' said Billy.

'He's alive,' said Peter.

They could hear banging as the airman began to thump at the window.

'Wait there,' Evelyn told the boys.

'I'll help,' said Billy.

'Just wait.' She was already running across the peaty ground.

'What about the fuel tanks?' Peter was shouting. 'Lady Evelyn, don't risk it.'

Evelyn ignored him in the same way she was trying to ignore the heat that threatened to push her back, but she kept on running until she reached the plane. She looked up; she could see the airman through the window, his face was slick with sweat, his eyes wide and full of urgency. He was saying something to her, but she couldn't hear him. His gloved hand banged again and again on the glass.

Evelyn knew she had to get him out. The plane was lying at an angle so it made it easier for her to scramble up onto the wing and clamber past the gigantic propellers. She could see fuel dripping from one of the tanks; the smell was acrid, it caught in her throat and made her wretch. She reached the cockpit; the airman's face was an inch from her own, he was looking straight at her. She could read his lips.

'Get back, get back.' He repeated it over and over. Evelyn ignored him and pulled her cardigan sleeve over her fist and tried to thump at the glass, but it was impossible. She sat back and kicked at it with her feet, but still nothing happened, the glass was much too thick.

'Here, catch this.'

Looking down, Evelyn saw Billy and Peter at the foot of the plane; Billy had a rock in his hand. In a split second he had thrown it towards her, she caught it but was thrown back by its weight, almost falling from the wing. She steadied herself and taking the rock in both hands she bashed it again and again on the glass. She could see the flames advancing on the other side of the cockpit.

'Duck down,' she shouted at the airman, and then, taking a step back, she hurled the rock as hard as she could at the window. There was a crack, then the glass shattered into hundreds of pieces, like diamonds showering all over the airman's helmet and flight suit. The shards glinted in the flickering firelight as the airman sat up again and punched the jagged edges around the window frame.

He started to raise himself up and stopped.

'I'm stuck.' Evelyn could hear his American accent. He was pushing with his hands, trying to heave himself from his seat. Evelyn peered through the broken window. She could see that the second airman was impaled on some part of the machinery and she knew for certain he was dead.

'My leg,' the airman said. 'My leg is trapped.'

Evelyn looked down and saw that the cockpit controls were pinioning his left leg against the crumpled inner wall of the plane.

'Can you move your leg at all?'

The airman pulled off his leather gloves and tried to manoeuvre his leg with his hands; he groaned in pain.

'A little,' he said.

'I'm going to try to pull you,' she said, blinking away the tears from the fumes. 'Try to move your leg away from the wall at the same time. It's going to hurt.'

'Just do it,' the airman said. 'Quick as you can.'

Evelyn heaved. The airman groaned again, but his body didn't budge.

She glanced at the advancing flames; they were licking at the far windows of the cockpit, gaining strength, flicking over the glass window on the roof. Inside the cockpit it was getting very hot.

Evelyn shouted down to Billy and Peter.

'You'll have to help me.'

The boys scrambled up onto the wing and all three of them tried to pull, but it was useless. The airman was stuck fast. Peter climbed inside the cockpit, squeezing down in between the two airmen.

'Be careful,' Evelyn cried.

'I think I can move his leg,' Peter called out. 'I just need to push it this way.'

The man screamed in pain.

'His bone is sticking out.'

125

'Just pull me up,' the airman shouted.

Peter pushed the leg away from the remains of the controls again while Evelyn and Billy held onto one arm each and pulled the airman up and out of the plane in one huge heave. They didn't stop to look at him or his leg as they dragged him over the wing and onto the ground, pulling him as far away as possible from the plane. Peter caught up with them and tried to hold the airman's legs up but the airman let out an agonised cry as the young boy stumbled and dropped them.

'It's OK, kid,' the airman panted as Peter apologised again and again. 'It's OK, kid, just let them drag me.'

Finally, Evelyn decided they were far enough away.

'Stop,' she gasped. One of her feet was in a shallow stream. Icy water gushed around her ankle as she and Billy held the airman between them. He was able to stand on his uninjured leg, though his broken leg looked horribly twisted and the white shaft of bone stuck through the leg of his flight suit in the most horrific way.

Evelyn turned to look back at the wreckage. There was a huge flash of light and the deafening sound of an explosion. The whole plane burst into an inferno of flame, and pieces of metal and glass showered around them, hammering against the rocks, hissing as the molten fragments hit the water in the stream.

'Jesus,' the airman said.

'Jesus,' Billy and Peter said in unison.

'Bloody hell,' whispered Evelyn. 'That was close.'

She staggered slightly under the weight of the airman and felt him wince.

'Sorry.' She looked up at him. He looked back at her with the darkest brown eyes she'd ever seen.

'I think you must be an angel,' he said and promptly crumpled to the ground.

Somehow the three of them managed to get the airman a few more metres away from the burning plane to the other side of the stream, but in his unconscious state he was too heavy to carry.

'Go back to the house,' Evelyn instructed the two boys. 'Get

126

something we can use as a stretcher, like a board, or a ladder, see if Old Dobbs has one in his shed. And tell Mrs Moggs to phone the American airbase. We need an ambulance urgently.'

The boys were anxious about leaving her.

'It's getting dark,' said Peter.

'You'll freeze up here,' said Billy.

'I'll be OK. Just hurry.'

Once they had gone, Evelyn looked around. In the distance she could hear the crackle of the fire and see the wreckage glowing against the mountainside. She knelt down beside the airman, hoping they had done the right thing in lying him on his back. His face looked pale and it was damp with the drizzle that had replaced the sleet. Evelyn touched his cheek. His eyes flickered; he looked as though he was trying to speak.

'Shhh,' Evelyn soothed. 'Help's on its way.'

He mumbled something indecipherable. Evelyn leant closer, her ear turned to his mouth.

'My helmet,' the airman said more clearly, and she could feel his hot breath on her neck.

'Shall I take it off?'

He mumbled something else and Evelyn took it to mean yes. She eased the helmet from his head. His hair was dark, longer than she'd expected; curls blew across his face in the wind. She smoothed them back. He moaned. Even though she was very cold she took off her cardigan and folded it into a pillow under his head.

'You're going to be OK,' she whispered. 'Everything is going to be OK.'

He looked at up her; his eyes reminded her of chocolate. His eyelashes were very long. She smoothed another curl back from his forehead. He smiled at her.

'Thank you,' he whispered, and then he closed his eyes and sank into unconsciousness again.

Time stretched and contracted as Evelyn sat on the damp, cold mountainside.

She took the airman's hand in her own; it felt big and warm through his leather glove. All the time they waited, she talked to him, reassuring him with the most comforting words she could think of, checking that he was still breathing by lowering her cheek to his chest. Once she had touched his lips with her fingers, searching for his breath to make sure he really was alive.

She wondered where he came from, tried to imagine his life in America based on the Hollywood films she'd seen; she doubted that he lived like Fred Astaire or Humphrey Bogart, but maybe he came from a big white clapperboard house. Maybe he had a mother who baked cornbread, and a sweetheart in the house next door like Gene Kelly had in the film she'd been to see a few weeks before.

It was almost dark by the time the boys returned carrying an old pine door between them. Old Dobbs huffed and puffed behind with a roll of thick rope. They lifted the airman's body onto the door and tied him down to stop him slipping off. Evelyn arranged the cardigan under his head again and all four of them carried him, as carefully as they could, down the mountain to the house.

A US Air Force ambulance was coming up the drive as they arrived, followed by a jeep. In a few minutes the airman was transferred onto a more professional-looking stretcher and driven away at speed. The two uniformed lieutenants in the jeep stayed behind to ask Evelyn and the boys some questions about what they'd seen up on the mountain and then they too were gone.

'That's enough excitement for one day.'

Mrs Moggs appeared and bustled the boys away to the kitchen for supper, leaving Evelyn standing on her own on the dark drive. In her hands she held the cardigan. She raised it to her face. She could smell the smoke from the burning plane and leather from the airman's helmet and something else; a memory of the sweets Evelyn had so loved before the war. Sherbet lemons. They'd always been her favourites.

'Lady Evelyn, you must come in now. You'll catch your death out there.'

Nelli was standing at the open front door.

Evelyn turned and as she walked slowly up the stone steps towards the gloomy light of the house, she was filled with a terrible sense of emptiness, as though she'd lost someone she'd known for years.

The boys had become obsessed with the crash site. In the couple of weeks leading up to Christmas they were constantly disappearing up the mountain and coming back down with treasures from the wreckage; nuts and bolts and bits of fuselage.

Mrs Moggs had been furious when they didn't come back until after dark one Sunday. She'd locked them in the cellar for the whole night without their supper or even a blanket to keep out the cold.

When Nelli came up to run Evelyn's bath she told her what had happened to the boys. Evelyn had immediately rushed down to the kitchen where Mrs Moggs had been sitting at the table with Olwyn. They were both polishing the silverware that would be used for the dining table on Christmas Day. Evelyn begged Mrs Moggs to release the boys.

'They've been down there for three hours already in the cold and dark, and they've had nothing to eat since lunchtime.'

Mrs Moggs stoically went on polishing and ignored all Evelyn's pleas. Olwyn smirked at her; the little girl was obviously enjoying her mother's disregard of Evelyn's distress.

Evelyn left the kitchen and went to seek out her mother-in-law in what Lady Vaughan liked to call her *private wing*.

Lady Vaughan was writing at her Chippendale desk, a fine wool shawl draped over her shoulders, a warm fire flickering in the grate of the marble fireplace. She took off her pince-nez and glared at Evelyn for her impudence at entering her territory.

'I know the boys are in the cellar,' she said, turning back to her letter. 'Mrs Moggs informed me after dinner.'

'The temperature is below freezing; they have no way of keeping warm.'

'They have to learn punctuality, Evelyn.'

'But it's so harsh to treat them like this.'

'They are not like us, Evelyn. They are from a Liverpool slum.

Harsh measures are required to teach them that they are not living in that slum now.'

'But—'

'Please leave. I am writing a letter to Howard, the poor man is working so very hard to help the Prime Minister win the war.'

Evelyn wanted to pick up Lady Vaughan's cut-glass inkwell and throw it at her, but instead she went back to her room to hatch a plan with Nelli to get the boys out.

Everything they thought of failed. Mrs Moggs stayed at the kitchen table polishing silver until well after midnight, and she took the key with her when she went to bed.

Evelyn and Nelli had tried forcing the cellar door open but it was firmly locked. Evelyn shouted through the keyhole.

'See if you can find some old potato sacks and wrap them around yourselves to keep warm.'

'Don't you worry, Lady Evelyn,' Billy called back. 'We'll be fine; we've got each other.'

But in the morning Peter had been coughing. By the next day he had a fever. He had to miss the Christmas show at school where he was meant to play a Wise Man, and the village tea party, where there had been real jam in the sandwiches and Olwyn had won a banana in a pass-the-parcel game.

On Christmas morning Evelyn had taken Peter's present up to the little room he shared with Billy, next door to Nelli's, in the attic.

'I've always wanted a diary,' he said with a huge smile as he unwrapped the slim leather-bound notebook.

She'd given Billy a catapult. She knew he'd be far more enamoured with a weapon than a diary. He was already outside aiming stones at the ice on the lake.

'Do you want to hear a secret?' Evelyn asked Peter.

The little boy nodded from beneath the thin grey blanket on his bed.

'The Americans are going to build a hospital.'

'Where?' Peter's eyes widened.

'Here,' whispered Evelyn. 'Right here at Vaughan Court.'

BETHAN

Happy Birthday Darling.

I hope you can try to enjoy your special day. So sorry to get your message about Mal. Dad and I never really thought that he was right for you #nevertrustamanwhodoesntlikecats.

The message was followed by a photograph of Ottis the cat curled up in a fruit bowl with a miniature paper crown on his head.

Bethan sat down on the rough stone wall of the ruins of the tower and looked out across the sea. Even though the sun was trying to push through the clouds, and the view from Red Rock was spectacular, this was not how she had planned to spend her twenty-seventh birthday.

She looked at her phone again. There were some lovely messages on Facebook; her best friend from school had posted a picture of them both at a Spice Girls concert aged ten along with the words: *Friendship never ends. Happy Birthday gorgeous girl – hope Mal is spoiling you rotten in Brighton!*

How was she going to tell everyone what had happened with Mal? Her friends kept joking about the wedding invite; #whentobuythebighat was an in-joke between them. Bethan looked at her Facebook page again. Her profile picture was of her and Mal, faces squidged together, last summer in Corfu. Half her posts were selfies of the two of them looking happy, or at least Bethan looked happy.

She shut her phone cover. How was she going to tell her friends that she wasn't coming back to London? That she'd decided she would stay in Wales and help Evelyn write her book. She looked out across the bay. The mountains soared up from the calm blue sea, sunlight creating brilliant greens on the grassy foothills, dark blues and purples on the craggy summits. Bethan took a photograph and posted it on Instagram.

She wrote #changeofplan and checked in at Snowdonia National Park.

Walking back through town she remembered that she'd promised Evelyn that she'd go to the golf club and leave a message for David Dashwood about whitewashing over the paintings under the terrace.

As she walked up the drive to the golf club the drizzle started again. Three portly men were setting off for the course in a buggy waving furled umbrellas like knights going into battle. On the edge of the drive two skinny boys in matching boiler suits and red caps were deadheading the thick swathe of daffodils that grew on either side of the smooth black tarmac; it was so different to the potholed drive leading up to Vaughan Court.

As Bethan had walked down from the house earlier that morning, she'd wondered how many hundreds of thousands of pounds it would take to return Vaughan Court and the gardens to their former glory. Though it didn't help that someone had been taking potshots at the stone lion on the portico again. Bethan had been woken in the night by the crash. When she'd looked out of the window she couldn't see anything, though just for a second she'd thought there'd been a faint yellow glow dancing across the garden, but then it had disappeared into the gloom.

In the first light of dawn, Bethan had gone down to look for damage and saw that the rest of the lion's crest now lay on the gravel. She didn't want to worry Evelyn but as she walked towards the golf club she did wonder, yet again, if she should inform the police. It seemed that every night a window or a carving was smashed or broken; as if some ethereal vandal was trying to destroy the huge house bit by bit.

The glass doors had *Red Rock Golf Club, Spa and Gourmet Restaurant* etched into them in swirling writing. They slid silently open as

Bethan approached. She was met with a delicious mix of lavender and eucalyptus. Classical music played softly and there were subtly lit cabinets containing a mixture of golfing accessories and expensive-looking beauty products. Bethan crossed the polished slate floor to a long clear sweep of oiled wood that appeared to be the reception desk; the only thing on it was a glass vase containing an orchid. A smooth-faced woman stood behind the desk wearing a turquoise top with a mandarin collar and the kind of makeup that looked out of place in a small Welsh town.

She looked Bethan up and down.

'Can I help you?'

Bethan hastily buttoned up her trench coat to cover the blouse and jeans she'd been wearing for days, but the coat was just as bad with its splatters of mud.

She'd been washing her underwear by hand but her reluctance to interact with Evelyn's ancient washing machine prevented her from washing anything else.

Now she had decided to stay on at Vaughan Court she wasn't sure what to do about her clothes; liaising with Mal and asking him to send a bag of clothes when he got back from Brighton seemed too intimate for someone who had committed such a betrayal.

'I'd like to leave a message for David Dashwood,' Bethan said.

The woman looked her up and down again.

'What is it?'

Bethan noticed that she spoke with an accent more North of England than Welsh.

'It might be easier if I could leave a note?' Bethan said, unwilling to try to explain about the scantily clad ladies and Evelyn's need to cover them up.

'I'll have to get a pen and paper.' The woman turned to a small cupboard behind her.

Bethan supposed it would have made the desk too cluttered to have left pens and paper usefully to hand.

There was a noise on the other side of the foyer. Voices, loud and male.

133

'Of course, I'll look forward to it. Thank you for coming over.'

'A pleasure as always, David.'

Bethan looked in the direction of the voices. David Dashwood was shaking hands with a man who was almost as handsome as he was. They both wore pastel-coloured shirts that accentuated their tanned skin.

'We must play a round sometime.'

'I'd love to.'

'Send my regards to Abby, apologise to her for me taking up your precious Saturday morning with business.'

The glass doors slid open and the man disappeared. David Dashwood turned towards the desk.

'Bethan, what a lovely surprise!'

Bethan was amazed that he remembered her name.

'You look wonderful,' he continued, walking towards her. 'The sea air obviously suits you.' Bethan was sure she didn't look at all wonderful; she hadn't even put any serum on her increasingly frizzing hair. 'And I hear you're staying for the summer.' David Dashwood stopped beside her; she half thought he might be going to give her a welcoming kiss, but instead he leant against the desk. His long legs were clad in very expensive-looking jeans. 'It must be a relief for Evelyn to know she's not going to be all on her own while she recovers from her fall.' Bethan wondered how he knew she was staying, but before she could ask, he leant forward and said, almost conspiratorially, 'Now, tell me Bethan, do you play golf?'

'I'm afraid not.'

'Do you go to the gym?'

'No.'

'Do you go swimming?'

'Sometimes.'

'Then you must join the club and use our pool.'

Bethan hadn't swum for years, but the pool she could glimpse through the smoked-glass window behind reception looked very different to the municipal pool in Battersea. She could see a Jacuzzi at one end that looked rather appealing and imagined the showers that would be so much nicer than the cold enamel bath at Vaughan Court.

'I don't have a swimsuit.'

'No problem.' David indicated a room on the other side of the foyer. 'We have a little shop that sells a selection of swimwear.' He smiled. 'I'm sure we will have one that would be just perfect for you.'

The woman behind the desk gave a little cough. David Dashwood turned to her.

'Chantal, get me a form. We must sign Bethan up.' He flashed another smile at Bethan. 'It's on the house, of course.'

Bethan glanced at Chantal. She was sure she saw the woman's nostrils flare, but she did as David Dashwood said and fetched a form from her cupboard. She put it down on the desk and slid it towards Bethan with the tips of her very long nails.

'Name. Address. Date of birth. Any health issues,' Chantal said flatly as she pushed across a pen.

Bethan picked up the pen and began to write, feeling rather self-conscious with Chantal and David Dashwood so close to her. It wasn't very conducive to revealing any health issues if she did happen to have any.

Bethan started with her name.

'It's very generous of you not to charge me,' she said.

'It's my pleasure,' David replied. 'As you know, I worry about Evelyn, she's such a good neighbour and it's wonderful that you're here to look after her.'

Bethan wrote the first line of her Battersea address then stopped. She drew a firm line through Flat C, 38 Albert Bridge Road and replaced it with Vaughan Court, Aberseren. It felt somehow liberating. A new beginning.

She moved on to date of birth.

'It's your birthday!' David exclaimed. 'How exciting!'

Bethan stopped writing.

'It's not at all exciting. I haven't even told Evelyn.'

'Then I must make it exciting,' David said. 'Let me treat you to dinner tonight. At the restaurant here.'

135

Chantal made a little snuffling noise. Bethan looked at her and noticed that her nostrils had grown even wider.

'I can't leave Evelyn,' Bethan said.

'Surely you don't need to be with her all the time?'

'I need to be with her in the evenings.' Bethan thought about the broken stones and smashed windows. 'I wouldn't leave her on her own after dark.'

'Then I will treat you to afternoon tea,' David said. 'Our pastry chef makes the most amazing cakes.' David's eyes took on a sparkling quality. 'Lemon drizzle. Miniature pavlovas. Little squares of devil's food cake that melt like velvet on your tongue.'

Bethan twisted the pen in between her fingers; it somehow slipped out of her grasp and skittered across the desk.

'You need only be gone for an hour or two.' David reached out and stopped the pen from rolling onto the floor. 'I'll send a car for you at three thirty.' He pushed himself away from the desk. 'Unfortunately, I must go. I have a meeting about sponsoring a sports day for the local children, but I shall look forward to seeing you later.'

Bethan tried not to stare at his retreating back, but Chantal kept her eyes on him until he disappeared through a door marked Chief Executive, then she picked up the pen and looked down at the form on the desk.

'So, no health problems?'

'No.'

'Allergies?'

'No.'

Chantal turned the form over and pointed to some more questions on the back.

'Height. Weight. BMI?'

'I'm not sure,' said Bethan. She wasn't going to tell Chantal what she weighed.

'I'll take a guess then.' Chantal wrote down 5ft 3 and 150 lbs.

'That's not right,' Bethan protested.

A red-faced woman in a towelling robe appeared at the desk. Chantal smiled benignly at Bethan.

'So sorry, but I'm afraid I have another customer to attend to.' She turned to the woman. 'Mrs Davies, I hope you enjoyed the steam room. I'll just tell Tiffany you're ready for your eleven thirty.'

As Chantal turned her back, Bethan picked up the pen and crossed out 5ft 3 and 150 lbs on the form, replacing it with 5ft 5 and 130 lbs. She turned and walked back out through the gliding doors and onto the smoothly tarmacked drive. She heard the doors swish shut behind her. Something made her look back, and she saw that Chantal was standing behind the glass watching her, arms folded, her smooth face set into something that resembled a scowl.

EVELYN

'You forgot to ask him?'

'I'm so sorry.'

Bethan had said she'd been to the golf club. She said she'd signed herself up for the pool and spa. She said she'd seen David Dashwood, but somehow she'd forgotten to ask about painting over the figures on the wall.

'I want that wall whitewashed as soon as possible, I thought I'd made that clear.'

'It's my birthday today,' Bethan blurted. Evelyn wondered if it was meant to be an excuse. She stared at the girl, noticing how pink her cheeks were. There was a little twitch in the corner of one side of her mouth as though she was trying to suppress a smile, or maybe she was about to cry.

Evelyn sighed. She remembered that Bethan was not meant to be spending her birthday looking after an old woman in Wales; she was meant to be having a romantic weekend in Brighton. Evelyn tried to forget about the wall and forced her own mouth into a smile.

'Happy birthday.' Evelyn raised her plaster-cast arms. 'If I wasn't so incapacitated I'd have baked you a cake.' She paused. 'Or I would at least have driven to the nice new patisserie in Caernarfon for one of theirs.'

'It's OK,' said Bethan, turning to adjust the flowers in the vase. 'David Dashwood has offered me afternoon tea at the golf club as a birthday treat.'

'Goodness.' Evelyn raised her eyes. Bethan had her back to her;

she was fiddling with a stem of hyacinth. 'A free tea, you are honoured. I wish I could come with you.'

There was a brisk knock and Tom's head appeared around the bedroom door, followed by Tilly's head just below his.

'We've come to see the patient,' said Tom.

'And Bethan!' Tilly sprang into the room. She had a rainbow on her pale pink jumper and the red glittery wellingtons on her feet.

'It's Bethan's birthday,' Evelyn said.

'Lucky you!' The little girl walked up to Bethan, wrapped her arms around her waist and hugged her. Bethan looked surprised. She glanced at Tom before hugging Tilly back.

'Happy birthday.' Tom gave a brief nod, his tone formal.

'Are you going to have a party?' Tilly asked, looking up at Bethan with her big grey eyes.

'Well, not a party,' Bethan smiled down. 'But I am going to have tea at the golf club.'

Evelyn had an idea.

'We could all go.' She looked at Tom. 'If you drive, we could all go to the golf club and have tea together.'

'Yes!' Tilly started hopping up and down so that the perfume bottles on Evelyn's dressing table tinkled together. 'I'd love to have tea at the golf club. They have those big silver towers with cakes and tarts, and triangle sandwiches with no crusts, and scones, and jam, and little tiny bowls of cream.' She looked imploringly at her father. '*Please* can we go?'

'It would be so nice to get out,' said Evelyn. 'It would do me good to have a little jaunt, and Bethan needs to be cheered up, don't you, Bethan?'

'Well, actually—'

'And they have those long velvet sofas.' Tilly sounded so excited. 'And big lights that hang down from the ceiling like gigantic snowflakes.' She pulled at her father's sleeve. 'And I wouldn't run around or put my feet on the chairs or any of the things you've said I'd do when I've asked to have tea there before.'

Tom looked down at her.

'But I told Mabon Morgan I'd pop over to the farm to take a look at his foot this afternoon. He was going to let you see his lambs.'

'We could go later,' Tilly said. 'I could take the lambs a sandwich.'

'It would be nice to do something to celebrate your birthday,' Evelyn smiled at Bethan. 'Your mother wouldn't want you moping around alone on your own on your special day.'

'I could go to see old Mabon now, I suppose,' said Tom. 'I can pick you both up at about three?' He looked from Evelyn to Bethan, then back to Evelyn. 'Do you think you can manage it, Evelyn?'

'Of course I can.' Evelyn felt a zing of excitement at the thought of choosing something nice to wear. 'Bethan, can you help me put my makeup on?'

'The thing is—' Bethan began.

'Let's ask Sarah,' said Evelyn.

'That would be great,' said Tom. 'She could do with a treat. She's been working her way through a huge stack of translations this morning.'

'And she loves cakes,' Tilly said. 'Chocolate is her favourite.'

'The thing is—' said Bethan, again.

'Of course, David won't be expecting to treat us all,' said Evelyn. 'So I'll pay for the rest of us.'

'No,' protested Tom. 'I'll pay.'

'Don't be silly.' Evelyn waved her plastered arm. 'It's my treat.'

'The thing is—' Bethan said.

'Can I eat the cakes before the sandwiches?' Tilly interrupted.

'No,' Tom said.

'Of course she can,' said Evelyn. 'It's a special day.'

'The thing is . . .' Bethan's voice was suddenly very loud. Evelyn stared at the girl; her cheeks had turned quite pink.

'Whatever is the matter?' Evelyn asked.

'David Dashwood has asked *me* to have tea with *him*.' She paused.

Evelyn watched Tilly's face fall and Tom's harden, as Bethan added, 'Just the two of us – on our own.'

BETHAN

Bethan winced as she waited outside the house for the driver David Dashwood had said he would send. The memory of their faces when she'd said *Just the two of us* was seared into her brain. Evelyn's raised eyebrows, Tilly's downturned mouth, Tom's face with an expression carved into it that Bethan could only interpret as disapproval. The room had been silent for a good few seconds before Tilly had said, 'Like a date?'

'No,' Bethan said quickly. 'Not like a date.'

'But just the two of you,' said Evelyn.

'Yes,' Bethan nodded slowly. 'Just the two of us.'

Now she wondered why she hadn't let them all come. What on earth was she doing going to have tea with staggeringly handsome David Dashwood, on her own. As she'd said to Evelyn the day before, the last thing she wanted was another man.

Bethan peered down the drive.

David Dashwood would probably have been delighted if she'd turned up with hundreds of guests. He was doubtless just as anxious that she would be thinking it was a date when really it was nothing more than a kind gesture.

She shivered and started to do up the buttons of the coat, surprised to feel the warm wool tweed instead of the smooth gabardine of the trench coat. She had momentarily forgotten that she was wearing an entirely new outfit. She touched the silk scarf at her neck and wondered if she really looked as chic as Evelyn had told her she did.

When Tom and Tilly had left, which had been pretty soon after the 'Just the two of us' announcement, Evelyn had looked Bethan up and down and said, 'Well, you can't possibly go on a date looking like that!'

'It's not a date.'

'Well, whatever it is you can't go in those filthy jeans and grimy shirt. Have a rummage in my dressing room and see what you can find to wear.'

'Really?'

Evelyn gestured towards the adjacent room with her plastered arm. 'Try on some things and come and show me.'

Bethan did as Evelyn said but she spent a good ten minutes looking through the rails of beautiful clothes before she had dared pick anything out. The vintage designer pieces seemed much too precious to even think of trying on, let alone wearing out to the golf club. Supposing she ripped a seam or spilled tea on something really special.

In the end Bethan had found an A-line mini skirt made of purple suede with a satin lining and little suede covered buttons that did up on one side. The skirt sat on her waist when it probably was meant to sit on her hips, but she managed to get the buttons done up with room to spare for excess cakes.

She turned to look at her profile, then she turned around again and looked over her shoulder to see the back, she liked the way the soft suede curved over her bottom, flaring out slightly, not too clingy.

Then she chose a soft, black cashmere turtleneck that she hoped didn't suggest that she thought the afternoon tea was in any way a romantic rendezvous.

She pulled it over her head and went back into Evelyn's bedroom.

'I thought a full-length evening gown might be a bit much for the afternoon.' Bethan gave a twirl. 'This seemed more appropriate.'

Evelyn sniffed.

'It's a bit on the chaste side, but where Mr Dashwood is concerned that's probably for the best.'

'I keep telling you, it's not a date.'

Evelyn didn't reply, she was staring at Bethan's feet.

'You can't possibly wear those clodhoppers. Are they all you have?'

Bethan looked at her Dr Martens.

'Yes.'

'What size feet are you?'

'Five,' said Bethan.

'Then you are in luck, I'm also a size five and I believe I have over one hundred and fifty pairs of shoes; Tilly counted them one wet afternoon a few months ago. Go and see what you can find, the mirror has a sliding door at the side; the shoe cupboard is behind it. Choose anything you like.'

Bethan went back into the dressing room and finding a little catch at the side of the mirror slid it back to reveal rows and rows of shoes that were displayed on shelves as lovingly as a collection of Ming vases in a museum. She chose a pair of ankle boots in pale green suede. They fitted like a glove.

Bethan added a pair of black tights and pulled a green Hermès scarf from a rack that must have had over fifty Hermès scarves neatly draped over it. She returned to Evelyn's bedroom.

Evelyn smiled approvingly.

'I bought those little boots in Macy's department store in 1959. I treated myself after a very successful afternoon launching *The Dashing Lieutenant*; the book department was packed, the queue of people who wanted their copies signed went right out of the door and around the block. I remember exactly what I wore that day – a gorgeous Chanel suit, pale blue bouclé, and I had my hair done by Mr Kenneth – the top hairdresser in New York – I looked like the bee's knees!'

'I bet you did!' said Bethan with a smile. 'I've always wanted to go to America. Mal has been several times with work – but he says it's full of arrogant people who think too much of themselves.'

'Mmm,' said Evelyn. 'It takes one to know one.'

Bethan walked to the window and looked out across the garden. A peacock strutted across the lawn, his chest puffed out as he dragged his long-feathered train behind him. It was sunny now. She and Mal could have gone for a long coastal walk. Maybe it had all been a misunderstanding – the hotel receptionist in Brighton could have muddled them up with some other guests. Had she been too quick to react? Maybe Mal was desperately trying to get in touch right now. At least a trip to the golf club would give her a chance to log onto WiFi and check her messages.

'It will be chilly,' Evelyn's voice broke through her thoughts. 'Always is until May. You'll need a coat.'

Bethan turned around.

'I only have my trench coat which is rather dirty.'

'Then you must wear my yellow Balenciaga; I had it made to measure by the man himself in Paris in 1962. I looked extremely chic in it, and so will you.'

Bethan waited in front of the portico wearing the buttercup-coloured coat. It was lovely, with a swing back and batwing sleeves, but it was a little too long for her. Bethan glanced down at the green boots; they were brighter outside. She had an increasing suspicion that, far from looking chic, she looked like an overgrown daffodil.

There was the noise of a car engine coming up the drive. Butterflies started to circle in Bethan's stomach. A dark blue sports car appeared, wheels crunching on the gravel as it steered around a piece of the lion's crest on the ground. Bethan recognised the car as a Maserati – Mal was always looking at them on his phone.

One day, Babe, he would say longingly. *One day.*

The Maserati stopped in front of Bethan. She presumed that the driver that David promised to send would be driving it, but as the tinted-glass window descended David Dashwood himself was at the wheel. He smiled at Bethan.

'You look like the Goddess of Spring.'

EVELYN

The sound of the car engine died away and all that was left was the creaks and groans of the house. It seemed to be increasingly protesting. Maybe it was too old, worn out and aching, like Evelyn was beginning to feel. Bethan had given her painkillers before she left; there were so many pills to take all through the day, pink and blue and ones that looked as though they were full of hundreds and thousands. Bethan had promised to be back in time to give her the next dose. Evelyn had told her not to bother.

'Stay out, have fun, get gloriously drunk and shag David Dashwood all night if you like.'

Bethan had looked shocked.

'I'm only going for a cup of tea and a scone.'

It had made Evelyn laugh.

She lay back against the pillows and wondered if Bethan liked David Dashwood a little more than she was letting on. He was remarkably handsome and very charming; the contemporary version of the perfect hero from one of her novels. Quite a catch.

Evelyn suspected that David Dashwood was thinking of settling down. He'd asked her several times if she'd consider selling him Vaughan Court.

'It would be a wonderful family home,' he'd said.

'It's far too big for modern-day living,' Evelyn had protested. 'Unless you're planning on having about fifty children, and anyway, I have absolutely no intention of leaving here until the day I die.'

It wasn't that she even liked Vaughan Court; for many years she would have said she hated it. But she didn't want to leave. How could she leave? Hope was all she had, hope and memories.

Evelyn gave a little shiver. The memories were also what she was forever trying to push away, but lately they seemed to be coming back, far too vividly for her liking, and hope had worn away to nothing long ago. She picked up the copy of *Vogue* and flicked through to the feature on floral dresses for spring. It had been shot in a desert, somewhere very far away from Wales. The girls were spinning around; kicking up the sand with great big boots that looked like the awful ones Bethan wore. Evelyn wrinkled her nose. The dresses were ill-fitting and the models backcombed hair and smudged eyeliner made them look like vagrants.

Evelyn thought of Bethan in the Balenciaga coat and Hermès scarf; she had looked so lovely, especially when she'd taken off her own awful clumpy boots. She wondered what David would think of her new look. He liked his women glamorous; she'd seen him driving around in his fancy cars with girlfriends who were wearing too much makeup, with their over-blown lips and fake eyelashes. Probably fake breasts too. There was nothing fake about Bethan; she made no attempt to hide the freckles on her nose, and only wore a dash of lip gloss on her naturally full lips, a hint of mascara on her long lashes, and she had wonderful breasts as well. She was as fresh and real and beautiful as her grandmother had been, though like Nelli, Evelyn doubted that Bethan had a clue just how gorgeous she was.

Evelyn wished that Nelli was still alive to see her granddaughter.

She suspected her friend would be turning in her grave to think of the way Mal had treated Bethan.

Nelli had been lucky with her choice of husband. Michael had been such a kind, gentle man, though Evelyn doubted that Nelli had ever felt the passion for him that she'd had for Lloyd. Evelyn could still remember the intense Welsh prose of his letters, vivid descriptions of his love and longing. No wonder Nelli had felt such terrible grief when he died.

The day Lloyd's little brother came up with the telegram his mother had received that morning, Nelli had collapsed on the kitchen floor.

Evelyn had come running from the drawing room when she heard the scream. As she arrived in the kitchen, Mrs Moggs had been poking Nelli with a broom, telling the young girl to pull herself together and continue peeling the parsnips that were in the sink.

Evelyn had wanted to help. She'd let Nelli sleep in her bed for weeks, holding her through the long nights when all Nelli could do was sob. Lady Vaughan and Mrs Moggs would have had a fit if they'd known.

She'd tried to let Nelli talk when she wanted to talk, to hold her when she wanted to be held, just to be there for her, especially in those long dark hours of night.

One night Evelyn had woken to find the space in the bed beside her empty. She knew exactly where Nelli would be; Nelli had been talking about joining Lloyd in the sea for days. As soon as Evelyn reached the beach, she'd seen her in the moonlight, wading into the rough November waves. Evelyn had run in through the crashing breakers and dragged her back, which wasn't easy, as Nelli had filled her pockets with stones. Lying drenched and breathless on the cold, hard sand, Evelyn had wrapped her arms around the girl, and promised that she'd always be there for her.

And when Jack had been lost, Nelli had been there for Evelyn; letting her talk when she wanted to, holding her through the terrible nights.

But Nelli had been lucky. The telegram had made it very clear that Lloyd was never coming back; his ship had been torpedoed, his body found. Nelli had no hope, no glimmer of anticipation. Lloyd wasn't missing, Nelli didn't have to wait. She'd been able to leave Vaughan Court, fly away to make a new life. But Evelyn had been shackled to the stones and glass and twisted chimneys, and now it was too late to escape.

Evelyn touched her face. She was crying, tears running down the deep lines in her face onto the copy of *Vogue*, dripping on the girls in their big boots and floral dresses. The pages had wrinkled, undulating like sand on the beach as the tide goes out.

A peacock screeched, starting off the others; dozens of screeches echoing around the garden. Evelyn remembered how she used to wish the peacocks would take a message, like the starling had done for Branwen in the Welsh legend. If only they could fly across the sea. But peacocks were not good at flying distances, and in all probability, there was no one there to tell.

She took a breath and whispered into the stillness of the room.

'You never came to rescue me, Jack, you never took me home.'

January 1944

The diggers arrived at Vaughan Court on New Year's Day, trundling up the drive, the outriders for the invasion that would shortly follow.

From her bedroom window, Evelyn watched as the Jacobean knot garden was cleared away and the ground flattened. Within a week a whole town had started to appear; over twenty corrugated iron huts, painted green, in neat straight rows, separated by concrete roads. Workmen swarmed all over the site day and night, insulating the buildings, installing lights and wood-burners and all the equipment and furniture a hospital would need.

The medical unit arrived in early February; doctors, nurses, administrators and, before long, an endless stream of ambulances delivering war-damaged bodies in various states of disrepair.

'Best not to look, Lady Evelyn,' Nelli said as she came into Evelyn's room to light the fire one morning. Evelyn was watching a young man being stretchered from the back of a truck. She could hear his agonised screams through the glass, see his face twisted in pain.

'I can't bear it,' she said to Nelli. 'I can't bear to do nothing, I have to help.'

Evelyn started work a week later; Lady Vaughan had been horrified when she discovered Evelyn had applied for a post as an auxiliary nurse.

'We'll see about that.'

There had been the irate phone calls to Howard, but he had been approving of the idea.

'It will give you something to do, my dear,' he had written to Evelyn in his weekly letter.

She had two days of training, along with some other local girls who had volunteered. On the first day they learned how to roll bandages, clean bedpans and make immaculately neat beds. On the second day they were shown around the hospital camp so that they would know where the catering tents, the store cupboards and the laundry were. They were also shown the post office, which contained a little shop selling things Evelyn hadn't seen for years: chocolates, sweets and even stockings for the nurses to buy.

Initially Evelyn was assigned to the head injuries ward, but it was clear that she was ill equipped to cope with the heartbreaking cases of severely injured young men, their faces often half blown away by mines and bullets, their brains so badly damaged that they had little chance of survival, let alone a normal life. After she had been found in tears for the fourth time in a day, she was reassigned to the orthopaedic hut.

The servicemen on orthopaedics were well on the way to recovery; their bones were still broken but their boisterous charm was not. They constantly joked with each other and flirted with the nurses. When they discovered Evelyn lived in the big house, they called her Your Highness, which got affectionately shortened to Queenie as the weeks went by.

The orthopaedic patients were encouraged to get up and dressed each day and they sat in an adjacent recreational tent and played cards or dice games, smoking and listening to swing bands on a big old-fashioned record player. As the weather got warmer, they sat under the terrace to get fresh air and play pool on the two big pool tables that had mysteriously appeared. Even though many of them were in wheelchairs or on crutches it didn't seem to stop their ability to pot the ball. The record player was moved to a spot under the terrace, as were the card tables, and someone found some old armchairs. They strung a line of electric bulbs along the ceiling to have more light in the daytime and the long, vaulted space took on the air of a nightclub; the men called it The Crypt. Evelyn would wheel the most incapacitated patients out to it and wish that she could hang around all day, listening to the music and enjoying mugs of the strong, sweet coffee that the servicemen drank in such vast quantities.

To Evelyn the American nurses seemed like film stars; so confident and assured. They talked about men and sex as freely as they talked about what they'd had for lunch; they swore and smoked and relentlessly teased Evelyn for being so *English* and *prim*. And all of them were gorgeous, with lustrous hair and straight white teeth. The ferocious ward sister, Sister Clifford, looked like Joan Crawford, with perfectly shaped eyebrows and a spectacular bust.

And then there were the patients; they didn't look like British servicemen. They were bigger, broader, as if they'd been fed on a much better diet. Even those on crutches walked with a swagger.

Billy and Peter had been equally entranced by the Americans. The two boys spent as much of their time as possible under the terrace, appearing as soon as school was over. The servicemen gave them chewing gum and chocolate, and showed the boys how to play pool. They also gave them puffs on their cigarettes and taught them dice and card games. Mrs Moggs was furious when Olwyn told her she had seen the boys playing poker for pennies. She banned them from mixing with the servicemen, locking them in the cellar for a whole day to teach them a lesson. But it wasn't long before the boys were back; sometimes Evelyn found them under the terrace when they were meant to be at school.

It was late March when he arrived. It had rained for days and the hospital tents were impossible to keep free of the mud; Evelyn seemed to be constantly mopping the floor. When she'd started work that morning, she'd picked up the mop and bucket on the way, assuming that was what she'd be asked to do. When she arrived, one of the senior nurses had met her with a trolley.

'Can you give the guys their coffee this morning? We're

152

short-staffed with so many nurses off sick. Your damn British weather has given them all the flu. I thought it was meant to be the spring!'

Evelyn had taken the trolley and started pushing it from bed to bed, pouring out the coffee from a big enamel pot into white tin mugs.

'Hey, Queenie, I like it like my women – hot and sweet.'

'Got any whiskey you could put in that for me?'

'Don't forget the new guy in the corner, Queenie; he's only just arrived.'

Evelyn hadn't even glanced at the bed as she poured the last mug of coffee. She turned, the steaming mug in her hand, and stopped. He was staring straight at her with dark brown eyes that looked familiar; he looked as surprised as she must have done. But then he smiled.

'Hi,' he said quietly.

'Hello.' Evelyn found she was smiling too. After what seemed like a very long time she managed to ask, 'How are you?'

He patted his leg and Evelyn noticed the white plaster cast.

'I've had three operations, and a dozen bits of metal are holding me together, but apart from that I'm doing just fine.'

'Good.' Evelyn couldn't think what else to say. There was a long pause; Evelyn could hear the rain drumming on the roof of the hut.

'I've thought about you,' he said.

'I've thought about you too, I mean, I've wondered what happened to you.' Evelyn felt her cheeks beginning to flush.

'After you saved my life?'

'Well, I'm sure I didn't save—'

'You can't argue with it. There's no way I'd have got out of that plane without you.'

There was another long pause. Evelyn noticed that his hair was shorter. She remembered how she had brushed his long dark curls away from his forehead; she remembered how his lips had felt under her fingers.

'Hey, Queenie, are you gonna give the poor guy his coffee or are you gonna just look at him all day,' one of the other men shouted out.

The rest of the ward began to laugh. Evelyn felt herself flush a darker shade of red and she hastily handed over the mug of coffee.

'Is your name really Queenie?'

She shook her head.

'It's Evelyn. Evelyn Vaughan.'

'My name's Jack. Jack Valentine.'

'It's nice to meet you again, Jack Valentine.'

He took a sip of his coffee and looked up at her with his chocolate eyes.

'It's nice to meet you again too, Evelyn Vaughan.'

'Evelyn!' Sister Clifford's loud voice cried out. 'Did you leave this mop and bucket here? Tidy it away immediately, or better still clean the floor, and after that . . .'

Evelyn turned away from Jack and walked across the ward; she wasn't sure if it was the drumming of the rain or the drumming of her heart that was drowning out the rest of Sister Clifford's words.

Luckily the outbreak of flu meant that Evelyn was put on extra shifts in the orthopaedic ward, though she found it very hard to focus on her duties. Sister Clifford reprimanded her again and again for getting things wrong. All Evelyn lived for were the excuses that led her to Jack's bedside.

'Here's your coffee, Lieutenant Valentine.'

'Don't let Sister Clifford bully you.'

'I'll try not to.'

'The guys in here have decided she's related to Hitler. We even think we can see a little moustache; she shaves it off when she plucks her eyebrows.'

Evelyn had laughed.

She found she could talk so easily to Jack. He asked her about things that no one had asked her about for years: her likes, her dislikes, her childhood, her family. Pretty soon she found herself telling him all about her parents and her brother and sister, and the bomb that had dropped on the beautiful house in Wilton Crescent.

'That must have been real sad for you. You must miss your family very much.'

It was the first time anyone had acknowledged that it had been so very hard.

154

Jack told her about his family in Mankato, and the ice-cream parlour his father owned, and his five sisters and all the mischief that they got up to, with boyfriends, and dances, and the pretty dresses that his father said would bankrupt him in the end.

Evelyn imagined Mankato in brilliant colours, like a Hollywood musical. And she imagined the five beautiful sisters, laughing and squabbling in the big sunny kitchen Jack described, with his mother and his grandmother producing endless pots of delicious Italian food at the stove.

Once she asked Jack to list the flavours of all the ice creams that his father served in his ice-cream parlour – there were over twenty-five. That night, Evelyn had repeated the flavours to Nelli when she came up to help her get ready for bed. The two of them had sat on her quilt for hours and tried to decide which flavour they would choose if they were in that ice-cream parlour all those thousands of miles away. Nelli had got into terrible trouble with Mrs Moggs for being late to come back down to the kitchen, but for weeks afterwards, whenever Evelyn and Nelli encountered each other, passing on the stairs, or as Nelli cleared a plate, they would whisper:

'Mint choc chip.'

'Strawberry shortcake.'

'Lemon and lime.'

'Chocolate cookie with toffee sauce.'

Jack told her about the lake he liked to cycle to on his days off.

'I dream of building a house there one day. With a great big window looking out over the water.'

When Evelyn closed her eyes at night she could see it; Jack's house, the lake, the swans he told her returned together year after year to mate.

When Evelyn wasn't on duty, she was dreaming of the next time she would be.

'What's wrong with you, Evelyn?' Lady Vaughan had looked up from the list she was writing and stared at Evelyn over her pince-nez. 'Are you coming down with the influenza those Americans seem to be spreading around the place like wildfire? I think I'll tell Howard that he should forbid you to work in that campsite they call a hospital.'

'No!' Evelyn had almost shouted the word at her mother-in-law. 'Sorry, I mean I'm quite all right, thank you, and they need me in the hospital as so many of the nurses are off sick at the moment.'

Lady Vaughan had stared at her for some time over the tiny glasses, and then went back to her notebook.

'I'll be asking Mrs Moggs to mix you an iron tonic,' Lady Vaughan said. 'I'm writing the recipe out for her and you'll have to take it twice a day. The last thing we need is you catching those nasty American germs and passing them on to me; I'm nearly sixty, you know.'

Evelyn had exchanged a brief smile with Nelli who was standing beside the sideboard ready to clear the table. Mrs Moggs had let it slip in the kitchen that Lady Vaughan's father had died at the Battle of Rorke's Drift. Evelyn had looked up the date. It made it impossible for Lady Vaughan to be younger than sixty-five.

Agreeing to take Lady Vaughan's foul tonic twice a day was worth it to be able to continue with her work in the hospital, though Sister Clifford's demands meant she was rushed off her feet, cleaning the floors and carrying linen to and from the laundry. Sometimes she'd go a whole day and hardly see Jack at all.

He had started spending time with the men under the terrace, playing cards and pool and singing along to Frank Sinatra on the record player. The other men had welcomed him as the newest *Crypt Cripple* – the title they affectionately gave to the patients who spent their time in the increasingly lively space.

Jack had become a great favourite with Billy and Peter; he let them write their names on his plaster cast and taught them a magic trick with a handkerchief and a spoon. They soon found out he was the airman they'd helped to rescue from the mountain and they took on a proprietorial role with him as though he was some long-lost favourite uncle. Jack called them his Superheroes.

'A regular Batman and Robin.'

156

Pretty soon the names stuck with all the men who frequented The Crypt. Billy, being the oldest, was Batman, and Peter was Robin.

'And you're the original Wonder Woman,' Jack had said to Evelyn.

Evelyn and the boys didn't know who Batman and Robin or Wonder Woman were, so Jack sent a message to his friend Walter at the base. Walter turned up one Sunday afternoon with a pile of DC comics for Billy and Peter, and an issue with Wonder Woman on the cover that Jack had presented to Evelyn as a special gift.

'So, you'll always remember the day you saved my life.'

'I don't think I'll ever forget.'

After that, Walter often came over on his days off. He'd sit under the terrace with Jack and the other men, chatting about life on the base, telling them about the latest missions that had been flown, the latest planes that had been lost. One afternoon he'd passed around a photograph of the *Lucky Lill*. The men had been very impressed with the Hula girl painted on the nose of the plane.

'Jack did it,' Walter said.

'She'd sure cheer this place up a bit,' one of the men had said, and that was when the plan had been hatched that Jack should decorate the bare white walls.

Billy and Peter had been only too keen to find the paint.

'There's pots and pots of it in Old Dobbs's shed,' Billy had said to Evelyn when the boys had told her of the plan. 'Will you ask Lady Vaughan if Jack can use it?'

Evelyn had been sceptical.

'She won't want the wall covered in pictures, she's upset enough about her house being turned into a hospital. Anyway, what are these pictures going to be of?'

'Girls,' said Peter.

'Women,' said Billy, indicating breasts with his hands and wiggling his hips before both the boys had dissolved into a giggling fit.

Evelyn had shaken her head.

'Lady Vaughan is never going to agree to that.'

It had been the following week, when Evelyn wheeled a patient out to the terrace, that she had seen the girl in the red swimsuit.

Billy had been playing pool against an airman with his arm in a sling and a bandage over one eye. Billy was whooping with delight each time an airman failed to pot a ball.

'Hey, Batman, it's just not fair,' said the man in a deep Southern accent. 'Can't you see I'm at a disadvantage?'

'What's this?' Evelyn hissed at Peter who was sitting in an armchair writing in the little diary he'd been carrying with him everywhere since New Year. She indicated towards the scantily clad painting on the wall.

'Jack did it,' Peter said. 'We think she's just swell.'

'Swell?' Evelyn couldn't help laughing at the language the boys had recently started to use. She studied the painting. 'You're right, she is swell, but Jack's going to get into trouble if Lady Vaughan sees her.'

'He's a really good artist,' said Billy, coming around the pool table to expertly pot the black.

'I can see that, but let's not tell Lady Vaughan or Mrs Moggs about it and I'm definitely not going to ask where Jack got the paint!'

'It is an act of vandalism,' Lady Vaughan had announced when Mrs Moggs had shown her the wall under the terrace later that week. 'And the girl is practically naked!'

Evelyn had encountered her mother-in-law one evening after her shift.

'Do you know anything about the distasteful painting under the terrace, Evelyn?' Lady Vaughan had turned her elongated nose towards Evelyn, who was still in her auxiliary uniform after a whole day sorting out the linen cupboard and then an extra hour scrubbing the temporary shower block.

'I'm sure I recognise some of the colours,' Lady Vaughan continued. 'I think that obscenely short skirt is painted with the azure blue we used for the drawing room? And the maroon on the brassiere is surely the same paint we used on the kitchen stairs in 1937.' She turned to Mrs Moggs who was hovering beside her. 'It is my belief that someone has been through the paint pots in the shed.'

Both Mrs Moggs and Lady Vaughan turned back to Evelyn.

Evelyn undid the clasp of her cloak. She longed to get upstairs and into a hot bath.

'I don't know anything about the paint. I've been working every day this month. I've hardly had time to eat and sleep before I'm back on the wards.'

Lady Vaughan sniffed.

'That's your choice, Evelyn. You know my feelings on the matter. It is most inappropriate for you to be working at all. Particularly as a nurse.' She sniffed again. 'With soldiers.'

'American soldiers,' added Mrs Moggs from just behind Lady Vaughan's right shoulder.

'It's most unladylike,' continued Lady Vaughan. 'Poor Howard is trying his best to end this awful war back in London and all the while you are washing men's undergarments and spoon-feeding them jello or whatever it is they eat in there.' She indicated with her pince-nez through the hall windows, towards the long rows of huts.

'They are airmen,' said Evelyn, daring to answer back for once. 'They are also trying their best to end the war. They're risking their lives to fly across the channel night after night to bomb our enemies. They see their friends killed, they suffer horrendous injuries. Some of them will never walk again. There's one boy on my ward that has lost both arms and both legs.'

Lady Vaughan raised her eyebrows.

'Please, Evelyn. Spare me the details.' She turned to Mrs Moggs. 'I am going to write to Howard. I shall be instructing him to file an official complaint to the US Army Hospital Board about the lewd cartoons under the terrace.'

'Yes, Lady Vaughan. And shall I ask Old Dobbs if he's noticed any paint go missing from the shed?'

Evelyn's tight regulation lace-ups squeaked as she shifted position. She was sure Old Dobbs would never have noticed the boys taking the paint. He was far too busy bemoaning the loss of his precious roses and grumbling about the fact that the pineapple house had been given over to cabbages and marrows.

Peter and Billy had been very careful, only a couple of paint pots

159

at a time. The large tub of white had been the hardest to remove as it was so heavy; they told Evelyn they'd carried it between them, hiding behind trees and bushes so as not to be seen on their way to the long space under the terrace.

Jack had been delighted with the two evacuee boys' paint-shed pillages.

'They should get a medal for services to the war effort,' he'd joked when Evelyn had found him mixing the colours together. She'd gone down to clear the morning coffee cups away from under the terrace and found Jack painting a new figure on the wall.

She'd been fascinated as she watched Jack create the subtle flesh tones and pastel shades for the dress and boots of a cowgirl. It was just an outline on the whitewashed wall but Evelyn could see the wide-brimmed hat perched at a jaunty angle and what looked like a lasso in her hands.

'Do you work as an artist back at home?' she asked.

He laughed.

'Hell, no! Dad says he didn't come all the way from Italy to have a son who moons away his time with paints and brushes when there's good money to be earned serving ice creams to the population of Mankato.'

'Your friend Walter told me you're a genius.' Evelyn picked up an enamel mug from the floor. 'He says you paint beautiful pictures on the planes, the best in the whole US Air Force.'

'Genius!' Jack laughed. 'Walter is exaggerating; I knew I shouldn't have let him visit me in here. I'm no genius, but I do paint the planes. It's a kinda Air Force tradition. A girl on the nose. Like a good luck charm.' He pulled a piece of coal from his pocket and started to draw the outline of another head on the smooth rendered wall. 'The guys saw my sketchbook back on the training base in Carolina and they asked me to paint a girl on one of the new B-17 bombers. She was my first, *Lucky Lill*. And she is lucky. She's over here, flying missions every night, never a mark on her.'

Jack began to add the outline of a pair of big eyes, a slightly tilted nose, full lips.

'Are all the planes with your girls on lucky?' Evelyn asked.

Jack shook his head.

'The most gorgeous girl I ever painted was on the nose of *The Lady Bountiful* and now she's lying smashed up there on the mountains.' He pointed beyond the arches towards the mountains. 'And my leg is smashed up in here.' He slapped the plaster cast that stretched from his ankle to the top of his thigh. 'Though I suppose she was lucky for me.' He looked at Evelyn and smiled. 'I mean lucky that you found me and got me out of that cockpit. A real-life Wonder Woman come to my rescue.'

Evelyn turned away so that he wouldn't see her blush. She looked at the face on the wall.

'She's very pretty,' she said.

Jack leant on his crutch and turned to Evelyn, pushing back his hair and meeting her eyes with his own. He took a breath as if to speak, stopped and then said so softly that she almost didn't hear him, 'Not as pretty as you.'

It had started just after Easter. It was the last thing Evelyn had been expecting to happen, but it was also the only thing she'd been longing to happen for weeks.

It had been nearly dark. The men were back in their beds, the lights were off all over the camp and the blackout curtains drawn at the house. Evelyn had tentatively walked down the gloomy steps and then crossed over the concrete road to the archway under the terrace, peering to focus in the darker space.

She had gasped when she saw the shadowy figure move against the wall.

'Hey, don't be scared, it's only me.'

'What are you doing here, Lieutenant Valentine?'

'I'm just putting the final touches to this new girl here, a flower in her hair, just like the pretty pink flowers in that little magnolia tree you have out there.'

'But you can hardly see.'

'This is fine for me.' He indicated a glass jar with the stump of

161

a candle burning at the bottom. 'Anyway, what are you doing here?'

Evelyn had stepped forward into the dim light cast by the flame.

'I came to look for Peter's glasses, he left them earlier and Mrs Moggs will get so cross if she finds out he's been here. I've promised Peter I'll find them before she notices.'

'Sounds like an important rescue mission, let me help.'

Jack had picked up the jar containing the candle in one hand and his crutch in the other. He held the light up so that Evelyn could see as she looked under cushions on the armchairs and amongst the magazines and playing cards scattered on the little tables.

Evelyn saw something glint on top of a stack of vinyl records beside the gramophone.

'I see them,' she said and moved towards them.

Evelyn stepped forward, reaching out for the glasses, but she didn't see the small stool at her feet, and she stumbled. Jack caught her arm, dropping the candle as he did so. The glass shattered on the slate flagstones with an echoing crash. The whole space was plunged into darkness. Jack kept hold of Evelyn's arm, he wobbled slightly and Evelyn put her own hand out to steady him.

They said nothing. Seconds seemed like hours. It seemed to happen in slow motion. They found each other's lips as though drawn by an invisible force in the dark. Evelyn had no other thought in her mind than how delicious his mouth felt on hers. He drew her closer to him and she felt his body, warm against her own. The kiss went on and on until, breathless, Evelyn pulled away.

'I'm married,' she whispered.

Jack touched her face.

'I know. But I don't think he makes you happy.'

Evelyn felt tears begin to sting her eyes; she was glad that it was so dark Jack couldn't see her cry.

'I have to go,' she said.

Jack didn't say anything; he gently pulled her towards him again.

This time the kiss had gone on even longer and only the thought of Peter, and his glasses, and the consequences of Mrs Moggs's anger,

162

made Evelyn use all her willpower to disentangle herself from Jack and go back to the house.

'You deserve someone to make you happy.' Nelli whispered the words in her soft Welsh accent, her curls escaping from her lacy cap in the steamy bathroom as she held out the key.

Evelyn had been horrified that she and Jack had been spotted by Nelli, kissing behind one of the pillars on the terrace on her tea break.

'It's not how it seems,' she'd said to the young maid when Nelli came up to run a bath for her after Evelyn had finished her shift. 'Please don't think—'

'It's all right, Lady Evelyn. I'll never tell a soul. You can trust me.'

'I know how it must seem.' Evelyn's voice was hushed too, even though the banging from the plumbing in the ancient bathroom would have prevented anyone outside the door from hearing.

'It seems like the most understandable thing in the world,' Nelli said.

'Really?'

Nelli nodded.

'He's a lovely man, Lady Evelyn. Handsome too. Like Errol Flynn with a cheeky grin. If you don't mind me saying.'

Evelyn had smiled.

'He is handsome, isn't he? And he's kind, and funny, and he's got so much talent.'

'He certainly has a way with a paintbrush.' Nelli added bath salts to the running tap. 'Those girls he's painted under the terrace are like something from a magazine – though Mrs Moggs says they are nothing but smut.' She rolled up her sleeve and swirled the water, and the smell of lavender filled the air.

'She hasn't found out where Jack got the paint, has she?' Evelyn slipped off the lace-ups she detested so much and began to roll down her thick brown stockings.

Nelli turned back from the bath and shook her head.

'She asked Billy and Peter if they knew anything about the paint, but they looked like butter wouldn't melt. I don't think she suspects them at all.'

'That's good.' Evelyn began to unbutton her uniform. 'It would be awful if the boys got into trouble.'

'It would be awful if you got into trouble too.' Nelli took a key out of her apron pocket; the key was small and rusty, a faded label was attached to it with garden twine. 'It's the key to the little summer house by the lake. No one ever goes down there, apart from me and my Lloyd sometimes, but he's away at sea, not due back for months.' Nelli took Evelyn's hand and pressed the key into it. 'You could have the whole place to yourselves. There's a bed in there, an old wrought-iron one – Lloyd found a mattress for it and I've put rugs on the floor, curtains at the windows, it's really nice and cosy.'

'Nelli! I can't—'

'Take it, Lady Evelyn. You deserve someone to make you happy.'

It had been wonderful. Six whole months of wonderful. At first, Evelyn and Jack had met just for a few hours a week, snatched hours in between Evelyn's shifts. Jack had excused himself from the ward by persuading the doctor that long walks down to the sea were helping his leg get stronger after the plaster cast was removed. The doctor wasn't there to see that before he reached the bottom of the drive, Jack would veer off towards the little wooden building hidden amongst the bushes. The weather that early summer had been unsettled so few of the other recuperating airmen ventured away from the hospital buildings; they preferred to sit under the terrace and play cards or pool with a brazier going to warm the space. Lady Vaughan was confined to bed with shingles for many weeks and Mrs Moggs was called upon to be at her beck and call. It was perfect. No one seemed to notice Evelyn or Jack or where they went or what they were doing.

Evelyn had never imagined that making love would be so enjoyable; *Dr. Birtwistle's Guide to Marital Relations* had made it sound like a mechanical act, but with Jack it had been as easy and delicious as eating candy floss at a fair. He was kind and considerate, enjoying her pleasure as much as his own, taking his time, waiting until her hunger for him would consume them both.

Afterwards they'd lie entwined, and talk, and laugh, or simply stare into each other's eyes. The few hours they had together seemed to slip away so fast. It was always a wrench when they'd realise it was time for Jack to go back to the hospital and Evelyn to go back to the house.

Evelyn found an ancient wind-up gramophone in the attic of Vaughan Court and brought it to the summer house. Jack sneaked some records from The Crypt; Frank Sinatra and Ella Fitzgerald were their favourites.

Sometimes they would dance, cheek to cheek, across the wooden boards, their naked bodies pressed together, lost in the music, lost in each other.

It had been Jack's idea that he should paint her.

'You're so damn gorgeous,' he'd said as he gazed at her body, stretched out on the bed as he got dressed. 'I'd love to paint you.'

Evelyn laughed.

'What a shame you don't have a canvas.'

Jack smiled and gestured to the walls.

'What about these?' he said. 'The best canvas there is.'

Evelyn had looked around.

'Suppose someone sees the painting.'

'No one can come in. You have the key, and Nelli's Lloyd will be at sea for months, so they won't be coming here – anyway, we could paint the walls white again before he comes back.'

Evelyn looked uncertain.

'Are you sure you'd want to paint me?'

'I've never been so sure of anything. I'll bring some pots of paint tomorrow, and you can wear your best pearls.'

It had taken weeks for Jack to paint the first one. It was hard for him to concentrate before he'd be so consumed with longing that he'd have to put down his dripping brushes and tear off his clothes. More than once Evelyn had ended up with multi-coloured finger-prints on her breasts or thighs.

When the painting was finished Evelyn had stared at it in wonder.

'I never thought I was beautiful before.'

All too soon Jack was deemed fit enough to return to active service. Lots of the airmen were being given a clean bill of health, even those that clearly still hadn't quite recovered. The D-Day landings had taken place in June and as many servicemen as possible were needed to help push the Germans back through France.

'I'm frightened for you,' Evelyn whispered against Jack's bare chest as they lay on the old wrought-iron bed. Ella Fitzgerald crooned softly from the gramophone and shadows from a single candle on the floor played on the reclining figure Jack had just finished painting on the wall. 'I'm frightened for us.'

'There's no need to be frightened.' Jack had pushed a lock of Evelyn's hair behind her ear. 'If I can survive your mountain trying to kill me, I can survive a few Germans trying to shoot me down.'

'Oh, Jack, please, I don't even want to think about what could happen.'

Jack stroked her neck.

'They don't call our planes "Flying Fortresses" for nothing.' His fingers trailed down her bare back. 'Walter says we've got a brand new one. Just flown over. They've already asked me to paint the nose as soon as I get back to base.' He let one finger linger on the dip at the base of her spine, making delicious little circles on her skin.

'Have you agreed?' Evelyn murmured, beginning to kiss his chest.

'Sure I've agreed. On one condition.'

'Which is?'

'I get to name her.'

Evelyn looked up at him, one eyebrow arched.

'You want to know the name?'

Evelyn nodded.

'The Lady Evie,' Jack said with a grin.

'Oh, Jack! No!'

'The guys love it.'

'They'll think you're naming the plane after me.'

'Yeah, I've told them that.'

Evelyn sat up, pulling the red-and-white checked blanket around her.

'But they'll guess, about us.'

Jack laughed.

'The guys don't suspect a thing. They think it's because you saved my life, rescued me from that plane and then nursed me back to health.' He pulled her gently back down towards him. 'They know I've probably got a bit of a crush on you, who wouldn't have a crush on a girl that looks like that?' He gestured towards the painting on the wall. 'But you're married to a Lord and you live in a stately home, and you look like a princess.' He kissed her mouth. She pulled away from him.

'I do not look like a princess!'

'You sure do, more like a princess than your Princess Elizabeth. You're much more beautiful, and a whole lot sexier by far.'

'I could get you sent to the Tower for that sort of talk, Lieutenant Valentine.'

Evelyn gave him a playful shove and let him kiss her again.

'Are you certain the boys at the base don't suspect?' she said after a while.

Jack smiled.

'No one would ever dream you'd be interested in some Italian Joe from Mankato, who only knows how to serve a mean Knickerbocker Glory and paint cute ladies with very little clothing on.' He glanced back at the painting; the blonde figure was completely naked apart from a single string of pearls. 'What could you possibly want with a boy like me?'

Evelyn smiled back at him.

'I know what I want with a boy like you.'

Jack laughed.

'You're getting brazen, Lady Evelyn.' Then suddenly he was serious. 'You know this isn't some cheap fling for me.' He stroked her cheek; his brown eyes seemed to melt into her own. 'I want to find a way for us to be together. I want to find a way to take you home, make you my very own wartime bride.'

Evelyn started to shake her head.

'It's impossible, Jack.'

'It's not impossible. I will find a way. I promise you.' He kissed her again. 'I don't ever want to be without you.'

Evelyn ran her hand through his thick dark hair.

'I don't want to be without you either.'

She pushed her finger into one of the curls that fell over Jack's forehead; it fitted like a ring.

'I will find a way,' Jack repeated. 'I'll move heaven and earth, just give me time to figure it all out. I promise you, when this war is over, I'll be taking you home with me.'

BETHAN

Bethan eased the magazine from under Evelyn's hand.

In her sleep the old woman mumbled something incoherent, the lines between her closed eyes deepening into furrows. Her mouth twitched and Bethan distinctly heard the word *home*.

Bethan reached out and touched Evelyn's cheek; the skin was soft despite its papery appearance, but she did look very pale.

Should she have stayed? Resisted the birthday tea? Forgone the cakes and the miniature pavlovas, the three glasses of champagne and the enjoyable conversation with the exquisitely handsome David Dashwood?

Bethan thought about David Dashwood's concern for his elderly neighbour; at least half their conversation had been about her.

They had talked about Evelyn's strength of character, her spirit, her talent, her style. Mostly they had talked about their mutual admiration for the way she fended for herself despite her age. David told a story about finding Evelyn clearing snow from the drive with a shovel so that she could get out in her car to attend a New Year's Day drinks party.

'She'd made it halfway down the hill by the time I arrived! She had a cocktail dress under her fur coat, full makeup, hair coifed, it was practically dark. She said she wasn't going to let a few inches of snow spoil her fun.'

Bethan had laughed.

'That sounds like Evelyn.'

'What was her husband like?' David asked, leaning forward to top up Bethan's glass with more champagne.

'Lord Vaughan?' Bethan took a sip. 'I don't know, he died before I was born.'

'Did your grandmother ever talk about him?'

'I don't remember her saying anything. He looks a little stern in the photographs I've seen.'

'He must have been handsome once,' David said. 'To make a match with a glamour-puss like Evelyn.'

Bethan thought about the wedding photograph on the mantelpiece.

'I suppose a uniform can make most men look attractive.'

'Do you think so?' David Dashwood arched one eyebrow, but before Bethan could formulate an answer he turned the silver cake stand around and indicated some tiny squares of fruitcake. 'You must try the bara brith, it's Chef's speciality.'

It had been at that point that Bethan had realised that Olwyn Moggs and Owen were sitting on one of the long velvet sofas on the other side of the room. Owen wore a tight red-and-purple-striped jumper that stretched across his rounded stomach like a Christmas bauble. Olwyn appeared to be wearing a knitted skirt and cardigan that matched Owen's jumper. She sat up very straight, a teacup in one hand, the saucer in the other. Her feet didn't quite touch the floor and Bethan could see that she was wearing her slippers. Owen raised a hand in what Bethan presumed to be a wave in her direction.

'I didn't expect to see Olwyn Moggs here,' Bethan said, waving back.

'Owen brings his grandmother for tea every week.' David lowered his voice. 'I don't know why, she always finds something to complain about.'

As though on cue Bethan heard Olwyn calling over a waiter.

'Call this bara brith? It's nothing more than soggy sponge with a few currants in it. I wouldn't give it shelf-room in my shop.'

Bethan and David exchanged a smile.

'She reminds me of my own grandmother,' David said. 'Nothing's ever quite as good as it should be.' He paused. 'Don't get me wrong, my grandma Margaret is lovely, a sweetheart underneath her steely exterior. She just has high standards. Aspirations, you might say.'

'Where does Grandma Margaret live?' asked Bethan, taking another sip of her champagne.

'She ran a little bed and breakfast in Disley for over fifty years, but she's in a home in Chester now.' David looked down at his glass. 'I wish I could do more for her, she was so good to me when I was a child, brought me up when my mother decided that chasing her dreams of being the next Celine Dion round the working men's clubs of Britain was more exciting than raising a child.'

Bethan waited for him to expand; instead he leant back in his chair and smiled.

'I make sure she gets the best care possible. I go to see her every week. She's still bright as a button, wants to know everything that goes on here.'

'She must be proud of what you've achieved.'

David's shoulders gave a little shrug.

'She will be. One day.'

'David . . . I mean Mr Dashwood, there's a gentleman at reception who wants to see you.'

Chantal towered above them in patent stilettoes. She beamed at David and then shot a narrowed glance at Bethan.

David stood up with a sigh.

'I'm so sorry, Bethan, I knew I was enjoying myself too much for it to last.'

Chantal folded her arms, making her breasts look even more enormous than they already were. Bethan looked down at her own and realised she had crumbs cascading down the black cashmere. She tried, ineffectually, to brush the crumbs away; they seemed to have embedded themselves into the dense wool. When she looked back up Chantal was staring at her, a little smile playing on her inflated lips.

'I must go anyway,' Bethan said. 'Evelyn will be wondering where I am.'

'I'm afraid I've kept you from her for too long.' David leant down and kissed her lightly on the cheek; he smelled of sandalwood and lemons. She had to try very hard not to noticeably inhale.

He straightened and turned to Chantal.

'Could you ask Paul to drive Bethan back up to Vaughan Court, please?' He turned back to Bethan. 'I do hope you've enjoyed your birthday tea.'

'Oh yes, it's been lovely.'

David held her gaze for a few seconds; his piercing blue eyes seemed to be studying her face intently. He smiled.

'Yes, it really has been lovely, hasn't it?'

Then he walked away, striding through the room with his wonderfully long legs, sweeping back his thick blond hair with one hand, waving at someone he knew with the other. Bethan noticed women's heads turning, lingering until he disappeared through the double doors. It was only then that Bethan realised she'd completely forgotten to check her phone for messages all afternoon.

There was nothing from Mal. Bethan quickly scanned through her texts and Facebook, ignoring the birthday messages from friends, and the dozens of WhatsApp notifications from her mother. She even checked her emails. Nothing from Mal at all, not even any new posts on Instagram. She waited for the emotion to come, the tears to spring, her heart to ache but she felt surprisingly fine, even happy.

'You've got jam,' Chantal said.

Bethan looked up from her phone, she had no idea the woman was still there.

'Pardon?'

'On your chin.' Chantal pointed at her own beautifully smooth chin.

Bethan reached up and felt the sticky blob of strawberry jam that must have come from a scone.

Chantal handed Bethan a napkin.

'I'll go and tell Paul you're ready to leave.'

In Evelyn's bedroom, Bethan shuddered at the memory of the jam. How long had it been there?

There was the noise of gravel from outside the bedroom window. For a few delicious seconds, Bethan thought it might be David Dashwood.

I've come to tell you that even though you had crumbs on your breasts and jam on your chin you are still the most beautiful woman I've ever seen.

But when Bethan looked out of the window she saw a small, slightly battered hatchback that definitely didn't look like it would belong to David Dashwood. The passenger door opened and a small figure sprang out holding something that, even at a distance in fading light, Bethan could see was a bright pink cake covered in candles.

'Tilly was determined to make you a cake,' Sarah said, taking out the last of the many candles that Bethan had taken four puffs to blow out.

'It was so sweet of her.' Bethan smiled towards the kitchen staircase that Tilly had just run up to see if Evelyn had woken up. 'And it was very kind of you.' She turned to Sarah sitting at the big pine table. 'I'm sure you had better things to do with your Saturday afternoon.'

'When Tom went to see old Mabon Morgan about his foot, he found the old man could hardly walk, so he's ended up taking Mabon to hospital himself. Knowing Tom, he'll stay there until he knows he's getting the right treatment, it could be hours. Baking seemed like a good way to fill the afternoon.'

'I suppose that's the downside of being married to a doctor.' Bethan opened a cluttered dresser drawer looking for a knife big enough to cut through the cake. 'You must get used to being suddenly abandoned for sick people.'

'Well, I suppose I would get used to it, if I *was* married to a doctor, but luckily history teachers rarely have to tend to the sick.'

Bethan stopped searching for the knife and looked at the pretty blonde woman at the table who was putting all the candles into a very neat row.

'But I thought—'

'You thought I was married to Tom?' Sarah interrupted.

'Well, I presumed – not that you have to be married to live together and have a child.'

'Tilly's not my child.'

173

'Oh.'

'She's my niece.'

'Oh.'

'And Tom is not my husband, he's my brother.'

'I seem to have got it all wrong. I thought you were her mother with you living together.'

'We don't live together. I have a cottage a few miles up the road. I live there with my partner Gwen.'

'Oh,' Bethan said again.

'I thought Evelyn would have told you.' Sarah picked up one of the spent candles, twisting it between her fingers.

'Told me what?'

'About Tom's wife.'

Bethan shook her head.

'She hasn't said anything.'

'Tom's wife died, so I spend a lot of time helping Tom look after Tilly.' She put the candle down and folded her arms. 'Though I've never been the motherly type, poor Tilly, I'm far too fussy. Our own mother died ten years ago. If only she was still alive, she'd make a much better job of looking after Tilly than me.'

Bethan sat down, questions swirling round her brain, but none of them quite forming into a sentence.

'When Tom came back from London,' Sarah continued. 'I gave up my job teaching Welsh in the local secondary school to look after Tilly.' She smiled. 'Though sometimes I think Tom needs just as much looking after as his daughter. I still do a bit of translation work to pay my share of the bills at home, and Gwen is very understanding. She's trying to write a book about Celtic women's history, so she's often locked away in the study at weekends, which means I'm around if Tom and Tilly need me.'

'How did Tom's wife die?' Bethan asked.

Sarah picked up the candle again and let out a long sigh.

'A van ploughed into a group of pedestrians waiting at a crossing one Sunday morning in Wimbledon. Alice and the baby were on their way to the swimming pool.'

Bethan gasped. 'I remember hearing about it on the news. It was horrendous, a terrorist attack, wasn't it?'

Sarah nodded.

'Six people died. Luckily Tilly was at a sleepover so she wasn't there. Alice took the full force as the van mounted the pavement. She died instantly.'

'And the baby?' Bethan said quietly. 'What happened to the baby?'

'She died in hospital eight hours later.'

'That's so sad. Poor Tom.'

'He doesn't talk about it,' Sarah sighed. 'And he hasn't told Tilly what really happened, just that it was an accident when her mum was trying to cross the road.'

'Evelyn's awake.' They heard Tilly's cry before the clatter of her wellington boots on the wooden stair treads. Both women turned. 'And she wants cake.'

EVELYN

She dreamed of the flat on Sloane Street. The smell of the gas, the woman's body slumped on the kitchen floor, the sound coming from the bedroom, more like a kitten than a baby. Outside she could hear the crowds on the street, hundreds of people pouring towards the palace, whoops and cheers; soldiers, sailors and civilians. It had taken Evelyn ages to push through them all to get from the Tube.

In her dream, Evelyn reached for the cooker to turn the gas off but the knob came away in her hand. A man appeared – Howard – he was taking a cigarette from a silver case, he lit a match.

Evelyn woke up, her heart pounding in her chest. She tried to raise her hand to ease the hammering, but her arm felt heavy, weighed down. When she looked, she saw the plaster cast and remembered it was no longer VE day, and she had turned the gas off and that, of course, Howard hadn't been there. No one had lit a match, but it had still been too late to save Loretta.

It was very dark. She reached out for the lamp beside the bed. The cast made it impossible to turn it on. She tried again but the lamp tipped over, rolling off the table with a crash as the nineteenth-century Dresden base broke into pieces.

'Bugger,' Evelyn said, lying back against the pillows. 'Bugger, bugger, bugger.'

Her mouth felt dry, her lips cracked and painful. She tried to lick them and tasted a fine sprinkling of crumbs.

She remembered the cake. Bethan had fed it to her of course;

popping little slices of it into her mouth. Tilly had laughed and said Evelyn was like a baby bird.

The cake had three layers of intensely green sponge sandwiched together with chocolate spread, the icing on top was a lurid pink with what looked like breakfast cereal scattered over as decoration.

'Tilly insisted on using all the food colouring we had,' said Sarah, pulling on one of Tilly's plaits affectionately as the little tea party had taken place around Evelyn's bed. 'She tipped the entire bottle of green into the mixture.'

'It's meant to be a rainbow cake,' said Tilly, perched on the edge of Evelyn's bed chomping her way through her second slice. 'But we didn't have yellow, or blue, and we didn't have enough butter for the butter icing so we had to use Nutella, and we didn't have hundreds and thousands so we used Cheerios instead.'

'We did try to buy more ingredients from Moggs's shop,' said Sarah. 'But it was shut.'

'That's because she was at the golf club.' Bethan spoke through her own mouthful of cake. 'Complaining about the bara brith.'

'That sounds like Olwyn. Always complaining, even as a child,' said Evelyn.

'Olwyn Moggs used to be a child!' Tilly sounded incredulous.

Evelyn laughed.

'I know it seems hard to believe. Mind you, she seemed like a little old lady even when she was your age. She didn't play with the other children who lived here, she much preferred skulking about, listening to conversations she shouldn't have been listening to, reporting back to her mother, getting people into trouble.'

'What kind of trouble?' Tilly had stopped eating, her slice of cake halfway between her plate and her mouth.

Evelyn pursed her lips.

'Big trouble,' she said. *Very big trouble indeed*, she thought.

'Did she get you into trouble?' Tilly's eyes were round. 'Did she get Grandfather Peter and his brother, Uncle what's-his-name, into trouble?'

'Great Uncle Billy,' prompted Sarah.

'Yes, Great Uncle Billy.' Tilly took a big bite from the cake. 'Dad told me they came to live here a long time ago because they were refuge trees.'

'Refugees,' corrected Sarah. 'And don't eat with your mouth full.'

Tilly wiped her mouth with the back of her hand.

'We did about refuge trees at school. Children came from big cities with labels round their necks, and people who lived in the countryside had to choose which ones they wanted to sleep in their attics or under their stairs. It was because of the war, in the 1980s when no one had an iPad and Queen Victoria was in charge.'

Evelyn burst out laughing, nearly choking on the little piece of cake that Bethan had just put into her mouth.

'I think I need Gwen to give you a history lesson,' said Sarah.

Tilly ignored her aunt. Instead she turned to Evelyn, leaning towards her on the bed, her eyes even wider.

'Do you know what happened to him?'

Evelyn swallowed the cake.

'To who?'

'Great Uncle Billy. Dad says he died when he was a boy. He says Grandfather Peter didn't ever want to talk about it.'

'It was many years ago.' Evelyn indicated to the plate in Bethan's hand. 'Your cake is really very good, Tilly, I'm impressed. And I've always wanted to try a Cheerio, I've seen them for sale in Tesco, often wondered what they taste like.'

'Was it a mystery?'

'The taste of Cheerios?'

'No,' Tilly giggled. 'I mean when Uncle Billy died.'

Evelyn leant back on the pillows.

'I'm not sure I can remember that long ago.'

'Was it because of the war?'

Evelyn closed her eyes.

'Was it an accident? Was it a bomb?'

She heard Sarah whisper, 'That's enough now, Tilly.'

There was a pause, more whispering, the sound of tea being

179

poured from the teapot. Evelyn kept her eyes closed. She felt Tilly slip off the bed.

'I'm going to go and see the ghosts. I want to ask them about Great Uncle Billy.'

'No, Tilly,' Sarah said. 'We'd better go home, I think you've worn poor Evelyn out.'

'Please,' Tilly pleaded. 'Please, please, *please*.'

'Tilly!' Sarah's voice sounded sharp. 'I said we have to go, but first we need to clear this mess up, the bed is covered in your crumbs.' Sarah began sweeping at the eiderdown. Evelyn wished she would stop.

'I just want to see them.' Tilly wasn't giving up.

'I'll go down to the garden with you.' Bethan's voice was cajoling. 'Maybe we could play a game of hide-and-seek, like we did before. Are you OK with that, Sarah?'

'That's fine.' Sarah sounded relieved. 'Hide-and-seek would be much better than looking at those silly old paintings under the terrace, and I can tidy up the tea things.'

'They're not silly old paintings,' Tilly began.

'Come on,' said Bethan. 'I'll race you to the knot garden.'

Evelyn heard the bedroom door opening, footsteps running down the corridor, Tilly giggling. Evelyn kept her eyes closed. Sarah was moving around the room, teacups and plates clinking as she gathered them together. After a few moments the noises stopped.

Evelyn opened her eyes. Sarah was standing by the window staring out towards the sea.

'I wonder if you'd do something for me,' Evelyn said quietly. Sarah turned around.

'Of course.'

Evelyn must have fallen into a deep sleep. Now it was the middle of the night and she was wide awake. She thought of her request to Sarah, wishing she could cover up all the memories so easily, paint over all the faces that kept emerging from the past.

In the darkness she could see Billy. His cheeky grin and big, bright eyes; very like Tilly's, so full of life and fun despite the loss of his mother and father. He had been by far the more confident of the two brothers, always the one with the ideas, the one who had a practical solution for every problem. Peter would have done anything for him, followed him to the end of the world – if he'd been fast enough to keep up. Evelyn tried and failed not to think of the last time she'd seen Billy. His eyes had stared up at her from the water; as soon as she looked down into the ravine she'd known he was dead.

The sound of shattering glass was almost a welcoming distraction. Was it Billy? Billy with the catapult she'd given him for Christmas, come back to haunt her. Maybe he was trying to punish her. Trying to frighten her to death.

BETHAN

Under the covers she shivered, remnants of the dream she'd been having floating back into her mind. Women, ghostly women, flying round and round a room that seemed to be full of fog. She'd been trying to get out but she couldn't find a door. The women were flying too close to her, looming through the mist, their high-heeled shoes tangling in her hair, their smudged lips grinning as she tried to bat them away. Her hand hit out hard; the woman shattered, a thousand tinkling pieces falling on the floor.

Bethan woke up. She was pretty sure the noise had been real. Another window breaking. She thought about the conversation she'd had with David Dashwood during tea at the golf club.

'It seems as though vandals are targeting the house,' she told him. 'I'm trying to persuade Evelyn to tell the police.'

'Evelyn won't want the police.' David ran his hand through his hair. 'She's probably worried they'll tell her she shouldn't be living on her own, or that the social services will get involved and make her move to an old people's home.'

'I can't imagine anyone telling Evelyn what to do.' Bethan had been piling jam onto a miniature scone.

'No,' mused David. 'She's certainly determined to do what she wants, especially when it comes to that house.'

In the darkness Bethan decided that in the morning she would phone the police, whether Evelyn liked it or not.

She shivered again, listening out for every creak and groan. She thought she heard a muffled voice but it turned into the moan of the wind. Her dream kept coming back to her, mixing with reality until she wasn't sure what was the nightmare and what she had seen under the terrace.

Tilly had insisted that they went to see the paintings, despite Bethan's attempts to engage the little girl in hide-and-seek.

'I think she's the prettiest,' Tilly had said, pointing at the reclining figure in the red swimsuit. 'Then this one with the flower, then this one with the curly hair.' Tilly skipped along the passageway under the terrace. 'But this one hasn't really got a face at all.'

Bethan peered at the painting of the cowgirl; she seemed to have more of a face than she'd had a few days previously, the suggestion of a mouth, the arch of an eyebrow. Bethan stepped back; the others looked clearer too. It was as if they were emerging from their stone canvas, developing like the old Polaroid photographs her granny Nelli used to take. The cowgirl seemed to be materialising in front of her; she could see fingers, a palm held up as though pushing through the peeling paint. Bethan rubbed her eyes to get rid of the terrible impression that the figure was trying to get out.

'I think they're trying to get out,' said Tilly, as though reading her mind. Tilly reached up and touched the hand of the reclining figure. 'I think she wants to find her little girl.'

Bethan looked at Tilly. It was gloomy under the terrace; she found it hard to see the child's expression.

'What do you mean?'

'I told you. I think they are the ghosts of mothers. They've lost their children. They are trying to get out to find them.'

Bethan glanced behind her; the late-afternoon sun was filling the garden with a golden glow.

'Come on, let's play hide-and-seek again, this time I'll hide.' She tried to steer Tilly's shoulders towards the light, but the little girl shrugged her away.

'This one might be Uncle Billy's mummy.'

'Or shall we feed the peacocks? I'm sure it's time for their tea.'

'And this one with the flower is the mummy of a little boy who drowned in a pond. I heard about it on the news on the car radio.'

184

'I think I can hear Sarah calling you.'

'And this one has told me that she knows where my mummy is. She says my mummy will come, from here.' Tilly ran down the passageway and splayed her arms along a blank bit of the wall, leaning against it, her cheek pressed against the dank whitewash, as though trying to hug the stone. 'She'll come out of here and she'll bring my little sister with her.'

'Tilly!' It was Sarah's voice. 'What are you doing? You'll get your jumper filthy.'

Tilly stepped away from the wall as her aunt rushed towards her.

'You've got bits of paint all over you.' Sarah knelt down and started trying to brush the flakes of whitewash from Tilly's rainbow jumper. She picked a bit of paint from the little girl's plaits. 'It's even in your hair. We'll have to go home and wash it.'

Bethan watched Tilly's face, looking for the tears she'd seen a few nights before; but Tilly wasn't crying, she didn't even look upset at Sarah's harsh tone. She was staring at the wall.

'I can see her,' she said. 'I can see my mummy coming.'

'Don't be silly,' said Sarah. 'We have to go.' She pulled at Tilly's hand, but Tilly stayed firmly rooted to the spot.

'I see her,' Tilly repeated. 'I see her face.'

Tilly stretched out her hand and tried to touch the wall, Sarah pulled her back.

'If you won't come, I'll have to carry you.'

Sarah hoisted Tilly up into her arms, staggering slightly under the weight of the child.

'Mummy,' Tilly cried out as Sarah started to walk away.

'Sorry,' Sarah said to Bethan over her shoulder. 'She gets like this when she's tired.'

'Mummy,' Tilly was shouting now as Sarah carried her across the garden. 'I can see my mummy.'

Bethan heard Sarah's raised voice telling Tilly that she needed a bath and an early bedtime. Tilly kept on shouting *Mummy*, the echo from the mountains shouting *Mummy* back. Gradually Sarah's voice and Tilly's shouting faded.

185

Bethan turned back to the wall; the fragile paint was peeling off where Tilly had leant against it. Bethan blinked. She could see something; the faint outline of a nose, an eye. She took a step closer, peering in the gloomy light. It was a woman's face. A fragment of paint dislodged itself and drifted gently to the ground like a feather. Bethan stared at the place where the piece of paint had been, a smudge of red smeared on the stone. Another flake fell on to the flagstones and Bethan could see the slight trace of a smile.

EVELYN

A shaft of morning sunlight came through the curtains. Evelyn was waiting for Bethan to come. She seemed to have been waiting for hours. The girl had appeared earlier with a glass of water and her tablets. It had been much too early. And she'd been saying something ridiculous about phoning the police. Evelyn had sent her away and told her to come back at a more sociable hour.

Now Evelyn was wide awake and longing for a cup of tea and some toast. She hoped the girl wasn't really going to phone the police; it was probably some silly boys from the village. Before her fall she'd have gone down and fetched the shotgun. Twice she had actually gone out and pointed it into the darkness.

Evelyn pursed her lips. She didn't want the police to come. What could they do? Sergeant Williams from the village police station looked as though he'd only just left school. He'd already been up to talk about security last summer. He'd interrupted her while she'd been trying to prune the roses.

'Hello, Your Ladyship,' he'd enunciated much too loudly, taking off his hat and smoothing back his immaculately groomed hair. 'It's Elderly in the Community Week and I'm doing a little survey, popping round to old people's houses, making sure their windows have mortice locks and that their doors have chains. Can you tell me about your security provisions?'

Evelyn had laughed and pointed up at the mullioned windows of the house.

'Do you think these windows have mortice locks? They are fifteenth century, you know.'

Then he'd had the nerve to ask her if she was all right 'up here in this big house all alone.'

She'd sent him away with a flea in his ear, but she'd spent the next six weeks worrying that some busybody with a name badge would be sent up to suggest that it was time to move. Evelyn had enough trouble with Tom telling her she ought to get herself a little cottage in the village, and David Dashwood had even given her some estate agents details about bungalows. Evelyn shuddered at the memory. She'd chucked them straight in the bin and told David Dashwood to bugger off.

Evelyn plucked at the eiderdown; it didn't hurt so much to move her fingers now. She tentatively touched her thumb with her forefinger; she might even be able to hold a slice of toast. She hoped that Bethan remembered that she liked the marmalade in the nice hexagonal jar, not the awful stuff Evelyn had bought from Olwyn Moggs in an attempt to shop locally at Christmas.

Outside the peacocks were calling to each other. Some people hated the noise they made but to Evelyn it was always a comforting sound. It reminded her of Jack. She remembered him sitting in the jeep at the side of the house, so handsome in his leather jacket. It had been such a relief to see him. It had been over a week since he'd been back at the base and Evelyn had missed him dreadfully.

September 1944

Jack jumped down onto the gravel as he saw Evelyn coming towards him.

'I was worried that you didn't get my note.'

'Billy and Peter were very efficient postmen.' Evelyn had smiled. 'But why did you want to meet here? Isn't it a bit risky?'

'We're OK. I've just seen the Bentley going down the drive. Lady

V was with that housekeeper woman, noses stuck up in the air. They didn't even look my way when I pulled over to let them pass, and no one from the hospital can see from here.'

'I thought we were meeting at the summer house tonight?'

'We are,' Jack grinned. 'But just you wait until you see what I've got you for a Christmas present!'

He indicated with his head towards the jeep.

'Christmas is three months away.'

'Well, it's an early present, just in case I'm not here then.'

'Oh, Jack, don't say that.' Evelyn noticed dark shadows under his eyes. 'How did last night go?'

'It went just fine, for us,' he said quietly, his expression suddenly grave. 'But we lost another one. The crew were from Ohio, youngest was just eighteen years old.'

'Don't tell me.' Evelyn had covered her ears. 'I can't bear to think of losing you.'

'I know, I'm sorry.' Jack stepped forward and put his arms around her. 'You know I'm like a cat with nine lives. By my reckoning I've still got eight left.'

Evelyn bit her lip.

'It doesn't seem enough.'

'Let's not talk about it any more. Let's talk about what I've got you as a present.' His voice grew exuberant again and he let her go and turned back to the jeep. 'This'll look mighty fine on your English lawn.'

'How many times? We are in Wales; it's a Welsh lawn.'

'Whatever you say, Wonder Woman.' Jack laughed and pulled back a heavy tarpaulin. Something large flew out with a piercing squawk.

Evelyn cried out.

'Oh my goodness, what on earth . . .'

The thing settled on the ground and ruffled a magnificent array of blue and green feathers. It was a peacock.

'One of the boys won him in a game of poker, from some local man with a big house near the base.' Jack took a piece of bread from his pocket and approached the bird. The peacock craned his neck

189

forward and snatched the bread, gobbling it down in an instant. 'He's called Perry. Like Perry Como, do you know him?'

Evelyn shook her head.

'He's a singer. A handsome guy – very like me.' Jack winked at Evelyn. 'Italian family too. I'll bring you one of his records.'

Jack edged closer with another piece of bread. Perry snatched it again, swallowed and gave himself a shake. He looked from Jack to Evelyn then lifted his long tail and opened it up to reveal a spectacular display of feathers.

'Isn't that just the most beautiful thing?' Jack came to stand beside Evelyn. He had taken her hand in his.

Evelyn looked up into his handsome face.

'How am I going to explain him to my mother-in-law?'

'Just say he flew in.'

'Like you did?' Evelyn raised an eyebrow.

'Yeah.' Jack grinned. 'Like I did.'

'I didn't understand how one peacock could possibly just fly in,' Lady Vaughan said, looking out of the window. 'But for another one to appear is positively bizarre.'

Mrs Moggs poured more tea into Lady Vaughan's china cup.

'Do you think they might be some sort of Nazi spies? I've heard that they use pigeons.'

Evelyn looked down at her porridge and tried not to laugh.

Billy and Peter had come to find Evelyn after her shift the day before. It was early October, just a couple of weeks after Perry had arrived.

'Jack's waiting for you.' They'd both been so excited as they took her hands and pulled her towards the stable block. 'He's got another present.'

Laughing at the two boy's exuberance, she let them lead her towards the ramshackle collection of buildings where the horses had once been kept. They turned the corner to find Jack leaning against the wall watching Perry putting on a magnificent display for a rather dowdy-looking brown bird of a similar size.

'A fellow shouldn't be without someone to show off his tail feathers to,' Jack said with a grin.

'Where on earth did you get her?' Evelyn couldn't help smiling herself.

'Same place as Perry.'

'Did your friend win another poker game?'

'No, I drove over to the guy who'd lost Perry, asked him if he had any peahens. He sold me Penelope, said she'd been pining for Perry ever since he left. Turns out they've been lovers for years. Perry and Penelope, a perfect pair. Like Romeo and Juliet.' He looked at Evelyn and lowered his voice. 'Like us.'

Evelyn had glanced at the two boys. She could feel her cheeks colouring. She folded her arms and tried to look exasperated.

'And how am I going to explain where she came from to my mother-in-law?'

Jack shrugged.

'You can say she must have been sent from heaven for Perry, like you were sent for me.'

Evelyn rolled her eyes.

'I think you've spent far too much time in the cinema, Jack Valentine. You do come up with some very tawdry lines.'

He took a step towards her.

'Like, I want to see you later? Like, I can't wait to hold you in my arms? Like, I love you?'

She glanced at the two boys again; they were watching the birds, laughing at Perry's huge fan of quivering feathers, trying to touch them as Perry paraded in front of his avian sweetheart.

She looked at Jack with a smile.

'Do you?'

Jack raised an eyebrow.

'Do I what?'

'Do you love me?'

'Oh yes, Evelyn, I do.'

EVELYN

The peacocks were very loud outside; they often were much more vocal in the spring. Lying in bed, Evelyn thought of Howard, and how lucky she had been that he hadn't been able to hear the birds.

By the time Howard had come back to Vaughan Court, Perry and Penelope had produced three chicks; straggly brown adolescents scurrying around the garden making a terrible racket with little tufts of feathers sticking up from their heads like Mohicans.

'Where did all these bloody birds come from?' Howard had said as Evelyn helped him into the wheelchair from the Bentley. She wheeled him over the gravel towards the kitchen door.

'This is the tradesman's entrance,' he'd complained.

'Well, I'll never get the wheelchair up the steps to the front door.'

'What did you say?' Howard had cupped his hand to his ear.

'I'll never get the wheelchair up the front steps,' Evelyn shouted.

'Speak louder, woman,' Howard said. 'Bloody explosion has ruined my ears.'

It was true: the V2 bomb had ruined his ears. It had dropped in the path of the government car as he'd been driven home from Whitehall to the flat on Sloane Street. The driver had been killed instantly, several pedestrians too. Howard had been lucky, if losing your legs and half of your hearing could be called lucky. It had been one of the last bombs to be dropped on London. If Howard had left the office two minutes later he would have missed it and Evelyn's future might have been very different. She tried not to dwell on this, but sometimes it was impossible not to feel furious.

A clattering of mugs and plates heralded Bethan's arrival with the breakfast.

'Sorry I've been so long,' she said. 'I've been talking to our local policeman on the phone. Sergeant Williams, I think he said his name was, he sounded very nice.'

'Don't get your hopes up,' Evelyn sniffed. 'He and young Owen at the surgery have been stepping out for over a year – but don't tell Olwyn, she thinks Sergeant Williams is just teaching Owen to drive.'

Bethan flushed.

'I wasn't getting my hopes up. As I've said, I don't want another boyfriend.'

'But what about your date with the dashing Mr Dashwood? You haven't told me how it went?'

Bethan poured the tea into a striped mug.

'It wasn't a date.'

Evelyn laughed.

'I'm only teasing you. Now, I hope that Sergeant Williams told you not to worry about the broken windows. I'm sure half the residents of Aberseren get tormented by delinquent boys.' She leant over and took a sip of tea from the long straw that Bethan had put into the mug.

Bethan sat down on the edge of the bed with a plate of toast on her knee.

'He didn't say that at all. He was actually quite worried. He said he was concerned about you up here on your own.'

'How ridiculous! I've been up here on my own for decades.' Evelyn batted Bethan's hand with the toast away from her mouth. 'I'm going to try and eat that myself.' She slowly pressed her thumb and finger until she'd grasped the slice and took it from Bethan. She managed to manoeuvre it towards her lips, but then, just as she'd opened her mouth, the toast fell, marmalade side down, onto the satin quilt.

'For fuck's sake!' Evelyn exploded. 'All I want to do is eat some food myself!'

'Don't worry.' Bethan was up and wiping at the quilt with tissues. 'I think you just need more practice. Maybe start with something less sticky.' She looked around, and then opened a drawer in the bedside table. 'This old postcard might be good to exercise your pincer movements.'

Evelyn took the postcard, managing to keep her grip, though her hand was infuriatingly shaky. While Bethan fussed around with the quilt Evelyn looked at the familiar picture on the front. Red Rock rising up from the sand, a scattering of beach umbrellas at its base. The postcard was hand-tinted, the pastel colours immediately suggesting the past. With great difficulty, Evelyn rotated her wrist to turn the postcard over, even though she'd looked at it a thousand times before.

Evelyn had been on a book tour around Britain for her eleventh book, *The Unsuitable Earl*. It had taken her away from home for weeks. The postcard had been waiting for her at The Caledonian in Edinburgh.

Deer Mummy,
  I am having a nice time with Nelli. Today we went to the beach.
We climbed Red Roc. I miss you.
    Love
    Robert
    Xxx

Most of the writing was in Nelli's neat hand, with her customary spelling mistakes that always made Evelyn smile. But the name at the bottom wasn't in Nelli's handwriting. The letters were large and wobbly, laboriously written. Robert had been fifteen; all Nelli's years of trying to teach him to write his name had paid off.

'Sergeant Williams is on a training course for the next few days.' Evelyn realised Bethan had been speaking for a while, and that she hadn't been listening. 'But he says he'll come on Wednesday.'

'We don't need him to come,' Evelyn protested. 'They are just juvenile delinquents. They'll soon grow up and get tired of their silly games.'

'It's vandalism.' Bethan sat down on the bed again, the plate of the remaining toast back in her hand. 'And trespass.'

'What's Sergeant Williams going to do? Hold an overnight stake-out? Bring Owen for a hot date in the panda car at the bottom of the drive?'

'He's going to have a look around.'

'I don't want him traipsing about the place in his big policeman's boots.'

'It's for your own good, and mine. I get freaked out in the middle of the night.'

'Don't be such a mouse! I'm sure you get worse things outside your window in London. Phone Sergeant Williams back and tell him not to come. It will just be a waste of his time. I don't need his help—' Her sentence ended abruptly as Bethan shoved a piece of toast into Evelyn's mouth.

'Just eat your breakfast and leave it to me.'

BETHAN

The sun was very bright. Bethan wished she'd remembered to bring her sunglasses from London. She wondered if Evelyn had some she'd let her borrow; a fabulous 1950s pair with sweeping tortoiseshell cat-eyes, or 1960s oversized frames with tinted orange lenses, or maybe some Chanel originals with diamanté adornments; they would have looked very stylish with the pale blue cashmere jumper she'd borrowed from Evelyn's wardrobe along with the pink silk scarf that Evelyn insisted looked *just the thing* that morning. Bethan looked down at her feet as she trudged up the mountain path. Evelyn's green wellington boots didn't exactly complete the stylish outfit and Howard's old hunting jacket was much too big for her. When she'd set out it had been raining, but now the sun had unexpectedly appeared and the sky turned from grey to blue in minutes.

It was good to get out of the house. Two whole days had been spent in Evelyn's bedroom, writing and writing until Bethan's wrists and fingers ached. She had hoped that she'd get some time to start on the article for *Frank* in the evenings, but Evelyn had kept her hard at the manuscript with only the briefest breaks for making meals and cups of tea.

They had started on Sunday morning when Evelyn had outlined the plot of *For the Love of Hermione*. Then she'd read out extracts of the chapters she'd already written, which turned out to be not as many chapters as Bethan had hoped.

'I can't help noticing that there's a bit of a formula to your plot lines,' Bethan said as she sat on the edge of the bed, ready for Evelyn to start dictation.

'Yes,' Evelyn nodded in agreement. 'Vulnerable young girl meets handsome young man; invariably there is a difference of class.'

'And invariably girl is already involved with some kind of dodgy bloke,' added Bethan.

'A rogue.' Evelyn said the word with a satisfying roll of the R. 'He's usually after her virtue, or her money.'

'Then the handsome young man saves the girl from a perilous situation.'

'That's right. Anything from an out-of-control horse to marrying said rogue.'

'Then the girl reveals, or discovers, her true identity.'

'Orphaned ladies' companion is really a duchess, impoverished governess finds out she's a Russian princess, or in the case of this one,' Evelyn tapped the A4 sheets she'd been reading from, 'the little heart-shaped birthmark on Hermione's neck proves that she is really a member of the aristocracy.'

Bethan smiled.

'I wondered how she was ever going to get out of becoming the mistress of that evil Lord Melksham and be able to marry the prince.'

'Sometimes it's the other way around,' said Evelyn. 'Sometimes it's the man who finds out he's really an aristocrat, or that he's about to come into an inheritance, or that the little machine he's invented makes him his fortune, etcetera, etcetera. Then they both realise they really can be together.'

'And it all ends with a lovely wedding.'

'Of course!'

'You must have loved Howard very much.'

Evelyn had looked at her, eyebrows raised.

'Why do you say that?'

'The way you write. Your books are full of passion. Surely that must come from experience.'

Evelyn put down the manuscript.

'I do have an imagination, you know! Next you'll be saying that I must be older than I look because I write about the Regency period so well!'

Bethan pursed her lips.

'Now you say it!'

Evelyn tutted and gestured towards the shelves of books.

'I told you, everything I need to know is here.'

'I'd love to write a novel,' said Bethan. 'I just find it hard to come up with ideas for plots.'

'It's easy,' Evelyn said. 'Just start with a boy and a girl who are in love, tear them apart, and then write seventy thousand words finding a way that brings them together again, with a few villains and some life-or-death situations thrown in for excitement.'

'Sounds so simple when you put it like that.' Bethan smiled.

'Write down what I tell you.' Evelyn nodded towards the pen and note pad in Bethan's hand. 'See if you can pick up some tips from me.'

Two days later it was such a relief to be outside in the spring sunshine. Bethan flexed her fingers and rotated her stiff wrists. Evelyn had dictated at great speed, the words flowing out of her while Bethan had struggled to keep up. If only she'd brought her laptop with her from London to type it all up. She dreaded trying to master the Olivetti. She'd already jammed the keys up practising and made a terrible mess of the ribbon.

When Evelyn had suggested a morning off, Bethan had been delighted, and even more delighted when she realised how beautiful the weather had become. She undid the buttons on Howard's jacket and followed the path through a copse of pine trees. The air smelled of the musty forest floor and wild garlic, somewhere in the distance there was the sound of water bubbling in a stream. Bethan climbed higher, coming out of the trees and onto steep moorland.

The path had disappeared so she followed a route that looked like it had been made by sheep; it rose steeply, the route increasingly strewn with boulders. The mountains spread out in front of her as far as she could see, craggy ridges and jagged peaks soared up into the sky, beneath them lakes and rivers shimmered in the sunlight and swathes of purple heather and yellow gorse were like artists' brushstrokes on the illusory view.

After a few more minutes Bethan felt breathless and her thighs were aching from the climb. She stopped and took in a deep breath, raising her arms above her head in a full body stretch.

Deep in the pocket of the jacket something buzzed. Bethan drew out her phone and squinted at the two messages on the screen.

The first was from Jessica, the editor of *Frank*.

How's it going? Deadline fast approaching.

The other was from Bethan's mother.

Hello my Darling, Dad and I wondered if you managed to enjoy your birthday. I know it wasn't what you'd planned, but we were thinking of you all day, hoping that you and Evelyn had some fun, or at least a few glasses of sherry. Very busy with the exhibition. Only three days until the private view. Let me know how you are. Xx

Bethan replied to Jessica.

I'll get the article to you by the end of the week.

Then she lifted her phone and took a selfie to send to her mother.

I've escaped into the mountains. Heading for a summit!

She glanced at the photograph before pressing send; it was then that she noticed what was in the background. Twisted hunks of metal against the rocks behind her. She turned to see what looked like wreckage; rusted and skeletal from weather and age. Grass and ferns were growing through the remains. Huge slices of ancient steel, rivets still visible; numbers, words, and bright paint, a picture on its buckled surface. Bethan took a few more steps towards the debris, feet slipping on the mossy rocks. She could see something that looked like a propeller half buried in a peaty trench. There was a wheel too, and bits of metal wiring coming out of what must have been an engine. Even though it was smashed into many pieces, it was unmistakably a plane.

EVELYN

Where was the girl? The carpet was scratchy against her cheek and her heart was racing at an alarming rate. Evelyn knew from her experience a few days previously that trying to raise herself from the floor with her arms would be absolutely futile.

'Bugger,' she hissed through the pain as she decided to give it a try anyway.

'Evelyn!' A man's voice. Tom.

'Thank God,' Evelyn said. 'About bloody time someone came.'

Tom was at her side in a second, taking her pulse, covering her up with a blanket from the bed.

'What on earth happened?'

Evelyn lifted her head slightly. It hurt from where it had hit the edge of the chest of drawers as she fell.

'All I wanted was to get my clothes on.'

'Where's Bethan? She should be here to help you.'

'She's gone out.'

Tom made a little huffing noise. Evelyn couldn't see his face but she suspected a frown.

'She said she needed fresh air,' she explained. 'I think I wore her out with dictation.'

'Can you lift your head a little more? It looks like you've got a bit of a cut there.'

'She calls herself a journalist.' Evelyn let Tom turn her face towards him. 'She can't even do shorthand. This book is going to take years to get down on paper.' She winced as Tom examined the cut.

'Look at me.' He shone the torch from his phone into her eyes. 'Mmm, I think I need to get you back into that bed.'

'Bloody bed! I hate it! It's so boring.'

'Come on.' Tom began to ease her gently off the floor.

'I've been in bed for nearly a week.'

'Lean on me, that's the way.'

'All I wanted was to get dressed; I can't live in a nightdress for ever. I managed the loo just now so I was pretty sure I could ease myself into some slacks and a loose silk shirt.'

'Well, it looks as though you were wrong.'

'There's no need for facetiousness, Tom.' Evelyn stuck her tongue out at him as he sat her down on the side of the bed. 'Your father was always the model of respectfulness when it came to his patients.'

Tom lifted her legs onto the mattress and pulled the covers over them.

'Well, I'm not my father and from what I remember his patients were always very respectful of him.' He plumped up the pillows and gently pushed Evelyn back so that she was lying against them. 'I don't think they would have dreamed of making childish faces at Dr Peter.'

Evelyn poked her tongue out again but Tom already had his back to her, heading for the door.

'Where are you going?' she called.

'I'm going to get my bag from the car. I need to take your blood pressure. And I'll get a dressing for the cut, I'm afraid it may need a couple of stitches.'

'If you send me back to that hospital,' Evelyn raised her voice as he disappeared, 'I'll, I'll . . .' She couldn't think what she would do. Instead she let her head sink into the pillows. 'I'll be very cross indeed.'

BETHAN

Her aim of reaching the summit was long gone. All she could think of was getting down the mountain as fast as possible; she needed to look at the paintings underneath the terrace again. She hurried down the path, slipping and sliding as she descended, the wellington boots slapping her calves. She turned her ankle more than once but the adrenalin acted as excellent pain relief. She skidded down the last bit of shingle path before finding herself at the stile leading onto the footpath that crossed the boundary of Vaughan Court. As she climbed over the wooden step she could hear the peacocks' piercing cries; something was setting them off.

She ran through a copse of rhododendron bushes and across the top lawn, making her way towards the house. She was hot in the heavy coat but she was in far too much of a hurry to take it off. At the corner of the stable block she took a shortcut through some dilapidated glass houses until she was on the terrace looking down across the knot garden. Amongst the noise of the peacocks, she heard a dog bark. She stopped and looked over the stone balustrade. Below the terrace a black Labrador was pulling on a leash – it was desperate to get to a peacock that was perched on the branch of a nearby magnolia tree. The bird's jewel-like colours were heightened by the pale pink buds and it seemed to be goading the dog, craning its long blue neck and edging its way along the branch as though daring the dog to try to attack.

Bethan couldn't see who was on the other end of the leash but she could see a bucket and a wooden brush lying on the paving slabs below. A loud male voice interrupted the barking.

'Jasper! Stop it!'

Jasper immediately stopped and turned towards the voice, the leash slackening as he obediently sat down.

Bethan could hear other voices coming from underneath the terrace.

'Good job, boys,' the male voice said. 'Lady Evelyn will be pleased.'

Bethan leant further over the balustrade. A piece of coping stone dislodged itself and fell onto the slabs ten feet below just as the figure on the other end of the dog lead stepped into view.

'Hey!' The figure looked up. 'Are you trying to kill me?'

Bethan recognised David Dashwood's handsome features underneath a tweed cap. He put his hand to his eyes and peered upwards.

'Bethan? Is that you?'

Bethan pushed her hair back, trying to smooth it down at the same time, her fingers catching in the tangled curls. She wished she wasn't wearing the wellington boots and was acutely aware that the Barbour jacket David Dashwood was wearing was very different from the outsized filthy jacket of Howard's that she had on. Under the jacket she was bathed in sweat and she was sure her face must be the colour of a tomato.

'Come down,' David beckoned. 'Come and see what the boys have done. They've smartened up this wall no end.'

At the mention of the wall, Bethan forgot all about her shabby outfit and scarlet face. She ran quickly down the stone steps at the side of the terrace.

'Oh no!' Bethan cried out as she arrived at the arches.

'What is it?' David asked. 'Don't you like it?' He looked at Bethan, his expression concerned. 'I think the boys have done a very good job.' He nodded towards two skinny boys in matching white overalls, they both wore caps bearing the Red Rock Golf Club logo.

'The paintings!'

'I know,' David smiled. 'You can't see them at all, can you? Just like Evelyn asked for.'

'But when did she ask you?' Bethan couldn't stop staring at the long expanse of white. 'I was meant to ask you on Saturday but I completely forgot.'

'Sarah left a message with Chantal at reception. Apparently Lady Evelyn asked for the wall to be whitewashed as soon as possible. Sarah was very specific that Evelyn had said that the paintings had to disappear completely.' He smiled as he stepped backwards. 'I must say, I can see that it makes a difference. Nothing like a lick of paint for smartening a place up.'

'We've been at it all afternoon,' one of the boys said.

'Haven't even stopped for a smoke,' said the other.

'What's the matter, Bethan?' David looked at her. 'You look upset, has something happened?'

'No.' Bethan caught her breath; she had run down the mountain so fast she was almost panting. 'I just wanted to look at the paint-ings,' she began. 'I wanted to compare them to the painting on the plane wreck that I found up on the . . .' Her voice trailed away along with her energy. What was the point? The paintings had gone, she felt suddenly too tired to explain why she was so disappointed, espe-cially in front of the two youths who were both staring at her as though they'd never seen a sweaty, dishevelled woman before.

'If you want to see the paintings I took some pictures before the boys got started.' David Dashwood took his phone from the pocket of his jacket. 'I thought they might be of some interest to someone one day. Oh dear.' He looked up from the screen. 'Out of charge.' He put the phone away. 'I'll text them to you later, I can get your num-ber from the club.'

Bethan took another deep breath; she supposed that was better than nothing. At least she could compare David's photographs with the painting on the piece of the plane. The winking blonde had been pockmarked with weather and crumpled by the force of the crash, but it was clear that she was very similar to the figures underneath the terrace. She had the same pretty face, the same flowing hair and long shapely legs. She was dressed in a tight red, white and blue swimsuit and standing to attention beside what looked like the remains of some wording which had almost completely weathered away.

Bethan crouched down to pat the dog sitting obediently at David's side.

'Meet Jasper,' David said.

Jasper lurched towards Bethan and licked her face with a large wet tongue. Bethan laughed and stood up, wiping her face with the back of her hand.

'I'm so sorry,' David Dashwood laughed too. 'It's a sign he likes you.'

He took a white cotton handkerchief from his pocket and started to dab Bethan's cheek.

She laughed again and took the handkerchief.

'It's OK, I can do it.'

'Bethan!' The voice was sharp and came from above. Bethan and David both looked up.

'Ah, Dr Tom,' said David. 'So nice to see you. Is everything all right?'

'It is now, but only because I happened to call round in time.'

'Is Evelyn OK?' Bethan called up to Tom on the terrace above.

'She's had another fall,' Tom said.

In a second Bethan was hurrying up the steps.

'She's all right,' Tom said as Bethan arrived at his side. 'I've tucked her up in bed and checked her over.' He looked Bethan up and down. 'You could have phoned me to tell me that you were going out for a dog walk with Mr Dashwood.' He indicated with his thumb over the stone balustrade. Bethan glanced down; from this angle the two handymen weren't visible at all. All she could see was David and Jasper.

'It wasn't a dog walk—' she began.

'It doesn't matter what it was, I don't think Evelyn should be left for long periods of time until she's fully recovered.'

'I was only gone for an hour or so . . .'

'She has a gash on her head,' Tom continued, running his hand through his dishevelled hair. 'I've put a couple of butterfly stitches in to close it up, but if Evelyn gets dizzy or feels sick, call me immediately. I have to go as I'm now very late for Tilly's parents' evening at the school, and I still have calls to make.'

Bethan nodded dumbly.

'I'll be off now,' David Dashwood called up from below. 'I'll text you later, Bethan.' The dog barked once. 'Jasper says goodbye, he's looking forward to seeing you again soon.'

Tom's face stiffened; there was a slight movement in his jaw, he opened his mouth as though he had more to say, but instead he turned around and walked away, his footsteps crunching on the gravel.

'Tom,' Bethan called after him.

'Evelyn will need her afternoon medication,' he shouted as he got into his car. 'And remember, if you need to go out on a date, let me know and I'll arrange for someone else to look after Evelyn for as long as you need.'

EVELYN

The girl was very quiet, though she had told Evelyn that Tom had told her about the fall.

'It wasn't a fall,' Evelyn grumbled. 'It was more of a totter which got intercepted by the chest of drawers, which led to the bang on my head, which then required a little lie-down on the carpet.'

Bethan nodded as though she wasn't really listening and hadn't even had a sip of her tea.

Evelyn sipped her own, holding the teacup with both her hands. It was so nice not needing the straw. The straw had made her feel like a child.

'Did you have a nice walk?' she asked.

Bethan looked at her sharply.

'I was on my own.'

'Of course you were, I wasn't expecting you to join in with the ramblers.'

Bethan tucked a stray strand of hair behind one ear and sighed.

'It was good to be outside.'

'Did you meet David Dashwood?'

'Is that what Tom told you?' the girl's eyes flashed.

'No!'

'Sorry, of course, he was leaving then.'

'When?'

Bethan sighed again; Evelyn wished she wasn't looking so miserable.

211

'Oh, it was just I found David Dashwood under the terrace with his handymen.'

'Yes, I saw the young men arrive from the window. That's when I decided to get dressed. I thought I might go down and tell them to help themselves to tea and biscuits from the kitchen. Then I heard David's voice after Tom had confined me back to bed, I think that black dog of his was upsetting the peacocks.'

'The men have completely painted over the paintings under the terrace.'

Evelyn took another sip of tea.

'Good.'

'I think it's a shame, because I had just discovered something.' Bethan suddenly looked more animated; she put her mug down so hard she splashed tea on the tray. 'Look what I found on the mountain.'

'The mountain! I'd imagined you'd gone down to the beach in this lovely weather.'

Bethan didn't seem to be listening; she was standing up now, wiggling her phone out of the pocket of her jeans.

'I took a photo.'

The girl walked over to the bed and held the phone in front of Evelyn's face. Evelyn squinted. It looked like a load of metal and grass. Bethan swiped her finger across the screen and another picture appeared. Evelyn recognised it immediately. She looked away.

'You shouldn't have gone up the mountain on your own! It's dangerous, all sorts of hidden gullies and sheer drops.'

'Don't you think the remains of that painting looks like the paintings underneath the terrace?' Bethan was tapping at the screen, making the image bigger, trying to make Evelyn look at it.

Evelyn shut her eyes.

'I can't see what you were showing me on that confounded tiny screen, I'd need my glasses.'

'Shall I get them for you?'

'No! I can imagine it.'

'It looks like one of those saucy ladies under the terrace. I think it's the same artist.'

'I don't know why you're so interested in the paintings, Bethan.'

'It just seems such a coincidence, that the plane wreck on the mountain has a painting on it in exactly the same kind of style as the paintings on the wall.'

'It's what the Americans did, they painted those women on the noses of their bombers to bring them luck, except that one didn't end up being so lucky.'

'So, you know about the plane?'

'Well, I know it's up there.'

'Did it crash in the war? Were you living here then?'

'Enough.' Evelyn raised one hand to the dressing on her forehead. 'I'm beginning to feel quite ill, my head is spinning.'

Bethan looked concerned.

'Sick and dizzy?'

'Yes, very sick and dizzy.'

'I'd better go down and phone for Tom.'

'There's no need for that.'

'He said to phone immediately if you had those symptoms.'

'They're not symptoms, they're just a reaction to all your silly questions.'

But Bethan was off, disappearing through the door.

'We need to get on with the novel,' Evelyn called out. 'I think I might change the chapter where Lord Melksham finds Hermione picking snowdrops in the hedgerow.'

There was no answer.

'Bugger,' Evelyn muttered. She didn't want Tom to come all the way back to see her. He'd mentioned Tilly had a parents' evening, it would be terrible if he missed it on her account. 'Bugger,' she muttered again. If only the girl hadn't gone up the mountain. Evelyn wished she'd thought to put her off before – she could have told her how slippery the rocks were, how deceptively steep it was, how professional climbing equipment was really a necessity – she could have invented a beast, some big cat creature or an old tyrant living in a cave.

And it was unlucky that she'd found the plane. The last time

Evelyn had seen it, it had been almost completely obscured by bracken. But that had been high summer, years ago.

Now the bracken would only just be pushing through the soil, little unfurled shoots that would do little to hide the wreckage.

BETHAN

Tilly looked like she'd been crying. Her head hung down and one of her plaits had come undone.

Bethan had an urge to take her in her arms and hug her but the expression on Tom's face made her feel that he would disapprove.

'Let's take a look at the patient then.' He walked briskly to the bed where Evelyn was looking embarrassingly perky.

'I told her I don't need to see you.' Evelyn waved her arm towards Bethan. 'She's making too much fuss.'

'You did say you were feeling sick and dizzy.' Bethan wished that Evelyn's cheeks weren't quite so pink and healthy; maybe she had overreacted when she'd called the surgery and asked if Tom could come up and see Evelyn as soon as possible.

'Can't be too careful with bumps on the head.' Tom put his bag down on the bedside table and started rummaging in it. He looked almost as despondent as his daughter; there were dark shadows underneath his eyes, his tie hung down at half-mast.

'I do hope I haven't dragged you away from Tilly's parents' meeting,' Evelyn said.

'No, we've finished with that, haven't we, Tilly?' He glanced up at his daughter.

Tilly didn't answer; she was standing by the door, sucking at the end of her untied plait.

'What's the matter?' Evelyn asked. 'Did your teacher tell your father that you're the naughtiest girl in the class?'

A large tear rolled down Tilly's cheek.

'Tilly, stop,' Tom sighed as he produced a torch from his bag. 'Just because your teacher is worried about your reading doesn't mean you need to be upset.'

'And my spelling,' Tilly said quietly.

'But you're such a whizz at maths,' Evelyn said, smiling at the little girl. 'Not like me. My teacher at school didn't even bother teaching me things like fractions or long division – not that I can see that my life has suffered much for it.'

Another tear rolled down Tilly's cheek.

'She said I was stupid.' The little girl's voice was a whisper.

'She did not say you were stupid.' Tom looked stern. 'She said you were slower than the others in the class – that does not make you stupid.'

'She said I might be dys-something.'

'Dyslexic,' Tom said.

'I don't want to be dys-something,' Tilly said.

Tom gave another sigh.

'I bought some sausage rolls from Olwyn earlier, maybe after I've checked Evelyn over we could climb up Red Rock and eat them, and then we'll have a chat about the kind of tests your teacher said that she might do.'

'Shall we go downstairs?' Bethan suggested to Tilly. 'It's nearly time to feed the peacocks, I think I can hear them shouting for their supper at the kitchen door.'

She glanced at Tom; he nodded as though he thought that going downstairs would be a good idea.

In the kitchen Bethan took the bag of bird seed from out of the cupboard.

'I've learned the trick is not to open the back door until you have some bird seed in your hand.'

But it was too late; Tilly had already opened the door. In an instant the peacocks were trying to get inside, pushing past Tilly, craning their long necks towards Bethan and the bag of seed.

'Get back, you beasts,' Bethan cried, trying to shoo the huge birds away with her hand.

Tilly laughed as Bethan threw handfuls of seed over the peacock's heads into the courtyard; the peacocks tried to turn around, their long tails getting stuck in the narrow doorway.

Tilly scattered some more seed on the ground and then she and Bethan stood back to watch. It really was quite a sight; so many birds gathered together, their beautiful feathers shimmering in the early-evening sunlight.

'You know, dyslexia isn't a bad thing,' said Bethan, as the peacocks began to strut away from the courtyard, trailing their long tails across the gravel. 'Walt Disney had dyslexia and look how successful he became.'

'But I don't want to be Walt Disney.'

'I think my granny Nelli was dyslexic.'

Tilly glanced up at Bethan.

'Nelli who used to work here?'

Bethan nodded.

'She never learnt to read or write at school.'

'But I want to learn to read and write.'

Huge tears welled up in Tilly's eyes. Bethan crouched down beside her and wiped the tears away with the sleeve of her jumper.

'That was a very long time ago. When teachers didn't understand how to teach children who needed to learn in a different way. Now they have lots of things to help with dyslexia.'

'Did your granny Nelli never learn to read?'

'She did learn,' Bethan smiled. 'Evelyn taught her to read and to write, and then Nelli taught Evelyn's son Robert to read and write, and helped lots of other children too when she worked at Oak Hill, even though her spelling was always a bit hit and miss.'

'What's Oak Hill?'

'It used to be Evelyn's family's house in the South of England. She inherited it and no one lived there for ages. Then Evelyn decided to make it into a school for children like her son Robert who had Down's syndrome, to give them the opportunities to learn like other children. Nelli went to work there. That's where she met my grandfather, he was the art teacher.'

'So Nelli became a teacher?'

'Yes.'

'I want to be a teacher. Like Sarah and Gwen.'

Bethan smiled.

'There's nothing to stop you.'

Tilly smiled back at her.

'Let's play hide-and-seek.'

In an instant Tilly was off, her long legs in their stripy tights and wellington boots running across the courtyard. 'I'll hide first,' she called behind her.

Bethan counted loudly to twenty.

'Coming, ready or not.' She set off in the direction Tilly had gone, round the corner of the house, then down the stone steps towards the knot garden. Bethan heard a noise and turned to look towards the arches under the terrace. Tilly was standing, staring at the wall.

'Tilly,' she shouted and started to run towards the arches. When she reached her, Tilly didn't say anything. Bethan put her hand on the little girl's shoulder.

'The mothers,' Tilly whispered. 'The mothers have all gone.'

'Oh Tilly, I should have told you. Evelyn wanted them to be painted over.'

'But why?'

Tilly walked forward and put her hand onto the wall.

'They're still there,' Bethan said. 'They're still under the paint.'

Tilly moved her hand across the smooth white surface.

'But I think my mummy has gone.' She turned to Bethan. 'She won't come back now, will she?'

Bethan bit her lip; she could see Tilly's chin begin to quiver.

Bethan went towards her and wrapped her arms around the little girl, hugging her tightly, rocking her back and forth. Tilly was crying now, big shuddering sobs.

'I miss her, I miss my mummy, and I miss my baby sister Megan.'

Bethan looked at Tilly's face and wiped the tears away again with the sleeve of her jumper.

'I'm sure you do.'

'What's going on?' Bethan looked up to find Tom walking towards them.

'Tilly is upset about the wall being painted over.'

Tom looked at the wall. He didn't speak. Instead he put his arms out to his daughter and lifted her up into an embrace.

Bethan stood up.

'She's upset about her mum as well.'

Tom shut his eyes, holding Tilly tighter.

'Ahh, there you are, Bethan.' David Dashwood was striding towards them. 'Admiring the handiwork? I just came down to make sure the boys had tidied up the tools.'

Tom stared at David but remained silent.

'Sorry, am I interrupting something?'

When no one answered he carried on.

'Also, I was going to send you that text, Bethan, then I realised that you have no signal up here so I've printed out the pictures for you. Then I thought you and Evelyn might like a little treat.' He held up a wicker picnic basket. 'I asked Chef to make a special dinner. It's all in here in foil boxes; seared tranche of salmon with crushed new potatoes in a pesto and lime sauce, plus . . .' He paused for effect. 'Chef's famous sticky toffee pudding with banoffee chocolate sauce.'

'Oh.' Bethan glanced at Tom's frowning face. 'Sounds delicious.'

'And a lovely bottle of Chardonnay that I chose myself from our wine list,' David continued. He looked towards Tom and Tilly. 'If I'd known you were here, I'd have asked Chef to make us more, but I'm afraid there's only enough for three.'

'You're having dinner with us, David?' asked Bethan.

'Of course, I thought it would be a lovely opportunity to catch up with Evelyn.'

'She's still in bed,' said Tom.

'I thought she would be,' David said cheerfully. 'It will be fun, a picnic in a bedroom.' He flashed a smile at Bethan. 'Nothing better.'

'I'm more of a picnic on a beach kind of man,' Tom said, still holding Tilly in his arms. 'And talking of which, my daughter and I have some sausage rolls to eat on top of Red Rock.'

Tom pushed in between David and Bethan and walked away.

David watched him go.

'Is something wrong?' he turned to Bethan.

'Tilly was a bit upset that the paintings have disappeared. She was fascinated by them.'

David shrugged.

'It's what Evelyn wanted.'

'It's just that they were so interesting, part of the history of the house.'

David smiled.

'There are the other ones. No one's asked me to paint over them.'

EVELYN

'I thought you were meant to be choosing something sensible to wear.' Evelyn frowned at Bethan.

'I just wanted to try it on, it's so pretty and it fits almost – the waist is just a tiny bit tight.'

Evelyn smiled as Bethan performed another spin in the full-skirted pink silk dress; it twirled out to reveal an embroidered net petticoat underneath.

'It looks gorgeous,' Evelyn said. 'Princess Margaret had the exact same one – Pierre Balmain, 1955.'

Bethan twirled again and stumbled against the stool; she sat down heavily on the end of the bed and laughed.

'I think I'm still a little tipsy from that wine last night. When David said he'd chosen a nice bottle of Chardonnay, I didn't realise he meant a nice bottle each!'

'He was very generous,' said Evelyn. Her own head felt a little muzzy. She wasn't sure if it was the bang on her forehead the day before or a hangover. Whichever it was, she was pretty sure Tom wouldn't have approved of the four glasses of wine she'd had with dinner.

Bethan took a deep breath.

'The waist on this dress is getting tighter by the minute. I don't think I'll be able to take dictation without passing out.'

'Then you'd better change into something else, we have a lot to get through this morning. What about a little pinafore? I'm sure there's a very nice Mary Quant in the dressing room, or a Zandra Rhodes kaftan?'

Evelyn watched Bethan disappear into the adjoining room; she could hear her humming a tune as she flicked through the hangers of clothes. The girl seemed surprisingly cheerful; *high-spirited* were the words that Evelyn's mother would have used.

Evelyn thought about the evening before; there had been a lot of laughing. David had regaled them with stories of his college days working in a pizza restaurant in Manchester to fund his way through a business studies degree.

'I had to wear a straw hat and a stripy blue-and-white T-shirt, and learn to spin the pizza dough on one finger.'

'I'm always so impressed when I see that being done,' Bethan had said through a forkful of salmon.

'I'm afraid I wasn't very good. One night the dough spun right off my finger, across the restaurant and straight onto the head of this poor girl celebrating her twentieth birthday – she was gorgeous – I'd been secretly eyeing her all night, so you can imagine how mortified I was.'

'What happened?' Bethan asked.

David had grinned.

'I was sacked on the spot by my manager, had to give back the stripy T-shirt and the hat immediately.'

'What about the girl?'

'I waited outside for her to leave so that I could apologise.'

'Did she forgive you?'

'I think so. We went out together for three years, and I worked for her father's hotel chain after I left college. It was her father who introduced me to golf. The flying pizza was quite fortuitous really, she'd never have agreed to go out with me on that first date if I'd still been wearing the ridiculous hat and T-shirt.'

'Where is she now?'

'Happily living in a former vicarage in Berkshire, with a very nice stockbroker, four beautiful children and a golden retriever called Gordon. I'm godfather to her eldest daughter.'

'You stayed on good terms then?'

'Of course. I always stay on good terms with my exes.'

Bethan had sighed.

'I can't see me and Mal staying on good terms.'

'That is because he is obviously a fool.' David had topped up Bethan and Evelyn's glasses again. 'Who didn't deserve you in the first place. Don't you agree, Evelyn?'

'I certainly do.' Evelyn had raised her glass, very carefully holding the stem between her thumb and finger. 'I propose a toast – to the beautiful Bethan and good riddance to the malcontented Mal.' She tried to suppress a little hiccup and failed, causing the wine to slosh onto the quilt.

'Damn these bloody broken wrists,' she'd said as Bethan attempted to mop up the spillage.

'It puts a whole new meaning to the phrase *being plastered*,' David had said with a smile, and they had all laughed, a lot. Then David had poured more wine, and told a very funny story about his grandmother Margaret and a gin-tasting evening he had organised in her old people's home.

Bethan now returned, still wearing the Balmain frock but holding out an olive-green cape hanging over a brown-and-white striped dress.

'I found this pushed to the back of the rail. Is it your nurse's uniform from the war?'

'Good God – don't show me.' Evelyn looked away. 'It's hideous! Norman Hartnell designed the British military nurse's uniforms, but whoever designed the American ones didn't quite have his flair.'

Bethan held it away from herself and looked it up and down.

'It does look a bit drab. Why didn't you wear the British one?'

'It was a US military hospital that set up camp here, so I had to wear their uniform.' Bethan sat down on the end of the bed.

'You must have seen some awful things when you worked on the wards.'

'It was a convalescing hospital, so the soldiers and airmen had already been patched up and treated. They came here to recover and to be assessed to see if they got sent home or sent out to fight again. Some of them just had broken ankles or broken ribs. But some of them had lost limbs or their sight or hearing, or were badly burned,

223

or all of those things. Quite a few of them were suffering with what today we'd call post-traumatic stress.'

'Poor things,' said Bethan. 'But I bet you cheered them up. You must have seemed so glamorous.'

Evelyn nodded towards the cape and dress in Bethan's hand.

'Not in that outfit! I also had to wear the most awful brown lace-ups, they creaked when I walked and were the shape of potatoes.'

Bethan laughed.

'But it must have been very strange, having Americans swarming all over Vaughan Court.'

'They weren't exactly swarming all over it, my mother-in-law made sure of that. They requisitioned the east wing as office space and accommodation for the senior doctors, but the patients were in Nissan huts in the garden. Rows and rows of them – quite a little town.'

Bethan left the uniform on the end of the bed and walked to the window.

'It's hard to imagine, it's so quiet and peaceful down there now.'

Evelyn smiled.

'The Americans seemed to burst into our lives, exotic creatures, so loud and animated, not like the stiff-upper-lipped British at all. It was as if a boring black-and-white film had suddenly turned into a tech-nicolour musical. It was a terrible shock when it all disappeared.'

'Disappeared?' Bethan turned around.

'The hospital was packed up overnight, the patients were moved to another hospital and the entire medical unit was sent to Belgium; as the allies advanced, they needed a field hospital closer to the fighting. One minute there were hundreds of people everywhere, the next it had turned into a ghost town. All those empty huts, all the silence; it was eerie looking down on it all from my window, especially at night.' Evelyn shuddered.

Outside there was the sound of a car coming up the drive.

Bethan looked back through the window.

'It's the police! I'd completely forgotten about Sergeant Williams coming this morning, now I'll have to go down and talk to him looking like I'm going to a school prom.'

Evelyn laughed.

'Trust me. If there's one thing I know about Sergeant Williams, it's that he'll love that dress.'

Evelyn stared at the nurse's uniform Bethan had left on the end of the bed. *Glamorous.* Evelyn thought about the word Bethan had used to describe her. She had definitely not been glamorous. It had been the American nurses who had been glamorous; so confident and worldly-wise. Evelyn felt shy and prudish in their company. They talked about what they got up to with their boyfriends in lurid detail that made Evelyn blush. Evelyn knew they thought she was very prim and proper, and even the nurses had ended up calling her Queenie.

Evelyn had longed to tell them about Jack, and all the un-prim-and-proper things that they got up to in the summer house, but nurses having relationships with patients was strictly prohibited, especially married nurses, and especially married nurses who were married to the lord of the manor.

If Evelyn had been able to have talked to the nurses, she might have learned how to be more careful. When she thought back to those days, she knew that it was inevitable that she would become pregnant. It was as if, in the war, taking risks had just become a way of life.

December 1944

It had been very cold the day she realised she was carrying Jack's baby. They'd woken up to snow. The nurses' rest station was just beside the fountain; Lady Vaughan had put her foot down when it had come to removing the Italianate fountain to make way for the field hospital. Howard had put in a special request that it should remain. It had been turned off, of course. No more water spurted from the cherub's mouth and the rainwater in its shallow pool had turned green with algae months before. That freezing December day, Evelyn had noticed how the sludgy liquid had turned to ice.

She was standing, smoking a Lucky Strike, warming her hands in front of the brazier that had been set up outside the nurses' tent.

A group of nurses stood gossiping beside her.

'She thought he'd got her into trouble, but thank God it was a false alarm.'

'Sweet Jesus, can you imagine if she'd had to marry him?'

The girls laughed.

'That doctor's married anyway,' one of them said.

'Gee, his wife would have been in for a surprise if he'd taken her back home.'

'There's going to be a lot of surprises by the time all this is over.'

Evelyn took a drag of her cigarette. The nurse's talk had moved on to a film that was going to be shown in the officers' mess tent that night, but Evelyn was still thinking of the previous conversation.

She was trying to count in her head. How many weeks since her last period? Five? Maybe six? She realised it had been nearly two months. Her stomach was hidden beneath the large regulation cape, impossible to tell if anything was showing, but Jack had already commented on her swelling breasts. The last time he'd painted her he'd said that she was becoming buxom. Said he'd liked it.

She'd have to tell him.

Jack was spending more and more time at the base. They were preparing for a big push after New Year; pretty much carpet-bombing Germany, Jack said. Surely Hitler would surrender very soon.

Evelyn threw her cigarette butt into the fire and lit another.

'Go easy on those things,' one of the nurses said to her. 'Don't you know there's a war on?'

The other nurses laughed and then they all moved away to go back to their duties. Evelyn touched her stomach. The thick wool of the cape scratched against her fingers. She knew that she was right. There was a baby, Jack's baby, growing inside her. Despite how desperate the situation was, her heart felt warm. Jack had promised that he'd find a way for them to be together, a way for him to take her back to Mankato. She imagined his mother and his grandmother, and all his sisters, sitting in their sunny kitchen passing round the baby, telling her that Jack was so lucky to have found her and to have brought her home.

Evelyn started walking back to the orthopaedic ward; in her mind she made a plan. When her shift was over, she'd write a letter to Jack and arrange to meet him at the summer house as soon as he had time off. She'd get the boys to post it in the morning. Everything would be all right.

BETHAN

'Are those sequins on the neckline or bugle beads?' Sergeant Williams looked as though he wanted to get as close as possible to the dress.

'I think they're beads,' said Bethan. 'And if you look at the petticoat, the hem is embroidered with daisies with a cluster of beads in the centre of every flower.'

'Oh my God, I just love it.' Sergeant Williams delicately stroked the petticoat with beautifully manicured fingers. 'Would you mind if I take a photo? My boyfriend Owen would adore it. Just look at the way those beads sparkle in the sunshine, and that magnolia bush in the background complements it perfectly.' Sergeant Williams began clicking, snapping pictures of the dress at different angles, with the camera he had been using to photograph the damage to the lion on the portico.

'I've met Owen,' said Bethan, trying to back away slightly. 'At the surgery; he has an interesting selection of knitwear.'

Sergeant Williams stopped taking photographs and pursed his lips.

'His grandma Olwyn makes him wear those awful woolly outfits. Poor man. She has no idea what he wears when he sneaks out clubbing with me in Bangor on a Saturday night.' He laughed and slipped his camera into his uniform pocket. 'Anyway, I can't stand around chatting about clothes all day. I have to catch these criminals who've been terrorising you and Lady Vaughan. It's so exciting!'

'It can't be that exciting,' said Bethan. 'It's probably just some local youths.'

'Well, it's the biggest crime since we had a spate of tax discs cut out of car windscreens, which as you can imagine, given that tax discs have been out of service for some years now, was well before my time.'

Bethan tried to suppress a laugh.

'I'm glad you're taking it so seriously,' she said.

'I am going to do my very best to solve this and bring these wicked perpetrators to justice. Don't you worry about a thing.' Sergeant Williams got into the car and wound down his window. 'I am on the case and justice will be done!' With a spray of gravel he lurched forward, stalled and then after restarting the car started down the drive at considerable speed, his blue light flashing as he went. Bethan watched him come to a sudden stop to let a silver sports car pass a few yards down the drive.

The sports car stopped in front of Bethan, she noticed it was a Mercedes this time.

David Dashwood stepped out and looked Bethan up and down.

'You never told me you were going to a ball.'

'Don't start,' said Bethan. 'I've just had to take part in a photo-shoot with Sergeant Williams.'

David grinned.

'I shall ask no more about the ravishing dress or why our local policeman was taking pictures of you. Though it's photos I've come to see you about. I was having such a lovely time last night that I completely forgot to give you these.' He held out a clear plastic wallet. 'The photos of the ladies on the wall.'

'Thank you,' Bethan said. 'I want to compare them to the painting on the crashed plane on the mountain.'

David turned back to his car and took out another wallet, this time pink.

'I also printed out a set for Tilly. I would have given them to her myself when she comes for her next swimming lesson, but Tom has seemed so off with me lately it's probably best you give them to Tilly.'

'That's so kind of you to do that for her.' Bethan took the second wallet and smiled. 'Actually, I wanted to ask you something yesterday evening, but I didn't want to ask in front of Evelyn.'

'Oh yes?' David arched one eyebrow.

'Well, you said yesterday that there are other paintings?'

'There are. I was thinking of suggesting that you take Tilly to see them, but on second thoughts I think they may be a bit racy for a little girl to see.'

'Racy? The others were quite racy.'

'Well, these ones go a little further.' David grinned again. 'In every picture the girl is nude.'

'Goodness,' said Bethan.

'With what I would describe as a *come-hither* expression on her face. I'm sure you can imagine.'

Bethan tried not to imagine in case her face took on the same expression.

'Where are they?' she said.

'In a hidden place, I don't think anyone has been there for years. If you hop in the car we can go now.' He looked Bethan up and down again. 'Though I think I'm going to have to ask you to take off that dress.'

'Really?' Bethan felt her cheeks beginning to flush.

'I mean, you may need to go in and change into your jeans and that old Barbour jacket you had on yesterday, the place is a little bit *off-road.*'

'I have to take dictation for Evelyn now, I'm already late starting, but Tom is coming over at five o'clock to see her. I could go with you then.'

David smiled.

'Perfect. If you fancy stretching your legs instead of getting a lift, I'll meet you at the bottom of the drive.'

He jumped back into his car and started the engine. Before he pulled away he leant out of the window.

'It might be better not to mention our little expedition to your new friend Sergeant Williams. Some breaking and entering will be involved.'

Bethan watched the Mercedes disappear down the drive. She had a sudden urge to spin around and around like she'd tried to do in Evelyn's bedroom earlier.

Instead she opened one of the wallets and began to look through the photographs. A breeze began to blow, rustling the petticoats of her dress as she looked at each painting in turn. The breeze turned into a gust, whipping the sheaf of photographs from Bethan's hand. Bethan had to run to catch them. The last photograph blew against the stone steps of the portico, then just as Bethan reached it, the photograph sailed up the steps and landed by the door, fluttering against the ancient wood like a butterfly trapped at a window. Bethan picked it up and stared. She didn't recognise this painting. A woman bending forward, her long blonde hair falling over one shoulder, one finger raised towards her lips as though to suggest a secret. The woman was smiling. Bethan recognised the smile. It was the face that had barely been more than a few smudges a few nights before; the face that Tilly had said was her mother.

EVELYN

It was very hard to focus on Hermione. Evelyn kept losing track of who the girl was meant to be dancing with at The Pump Room in Bath.

'Shall we start the chapter again?' Bethan asked. 'There are so many crossings-out I'm not sure I'll be able to read what I've written so far.'

Evelyn lay back on the pillows and stared up at the ceiling.

'I don't know what's wrong with me today, I just can't seem to get my brain into gear.'

'Maybe it was the bump on your head yesterday,' suggested Bethan.

'Or Mr Dashwood's Chardonnay,' said Evelyn, though really all she could think about was Jack. Ever since Bethan had appeared with the uniform it was as though she was reliving the emotions. They'd been so confusing at the time; confusing and frightening and wonderful. Evelyn could feel the tightness in her stomach and the flutter in her heart. She felt as though she was back there, back in that cold December of 1944.

'He'll have to agree to a divorce,' Jack had said as they lay back against the pillows. 'You know your husband's been unfaithful. You still have the letter from his mistress, don't you?'

'Yes, hidden under my mattress. But if he finds out about us, Jack? If he finds out about the baby? What will he do? He could have you court-martialled. I'm scared, Jack, I really am.'

'Hey, Wonder Woman.' Jack leant on one elbow and looked into her eyes. 'You don't need to be frightened. You have your super-powers and I have a plan.'

'But . . .' Jack put a finger to her lips.

'Don't worry. The word is this war is nearly over, we're dropping so many bombs on those Germans every night, there can't be much of the country left. They say they'll surrender by Christmas, and then we can sort everything out.'

'But how, Jack? I can't see how?'

'It's easy. As soon as peace is declared you just pack a bag and head for Liverpool. You can get a ship to New York from there, and head over to Mankato on a train. I'll write to my mother and tell her to expect my fiancée. Then it won't be long before I'll be demobbed and home, and we can start building that wooden house out by the lake for the three of us.'

Jack put a hand on her stomach.

'But what about sorting out the divorce? And what will your mother say if she finds out I'm already married, and how will I get to Liverpool? Oh Jack, there just seems so much to sort out.'

Jack kissed her.

'Don't worry about a thing. I've got one more mission to fly before I'm owed a few days' leave. Maybe I could hole up here and you could spend all night with me? That way we can really get the plan sorted out. I'll send a letter with the date I'm coming. Tell the boys to look out for it.'

The boys had looked out for it, but the letter had never come. Evelyn had felt more and more desperate as each day passed. She'd spent long sleepless nights wondering what to do, and when she did sleep she had terrible nightmares about the plane crash on the mountain; Jack's face at the cockpit window, his fist thumping at the glass, and the plane exploding before Evelyn could get him out.

'Tom's here to see how you are.'

Evelyn opened her eyes; Bethan's hand was on her shoulder gently shaking it. Evelyn looked around.

'Have I been asleep?'

234

'For a few hours. I didn't want to wake you up, you looked so peaceful.'

'But we had so much work to do. We were going to start again on chapter fifteen.'

'It doesn't matter. We can start it tomorrow. Besides, it gave me time to write the article about you for *Frank*.'

Evelyn pushed herself up into a seated position.

'I didn't think you'd finished your interview with me.'

'I've got everything I needed just from spending time with you – your life story and the inspiration for your work.'

'I'd imagine it's an impressive read.' Tom came in with his doctor's bag. 'Novelist, campaigner, the most stylish woman in North Wales, not to mention a wonderful mother and caring wife.'

Evelyn scowled at him. She wanted to ask him what the bloody hell he knew? Nothing. He knew nothing of the truth of who she was, what she'd done.

His father had known. His father had known it all. She looked at Bethan. Her grandmother had known it all too. But neither Nelli nor Peter had ever told a soul. They didn't mention it to Evelyn either. All those years of friendship and they never talked about the events in the war that, in the end, had shaped all their lives. She glanced from Tom to Bethan; it had shaped their lives too, ricocheting down the generations, starting with that first illicit kiss under the terrace in the dark.

'I think I ought to check your blood pressure.' Tom had his bag open at the bottom of the bed.

'It's absolutely fine,' Evelyn tutted.

'You look a bit flushed.' Tom was already unfolding the fabric cuff. 'And I also need to change the dressing on that cut. Any headaches today?'

'Only a hangover.'

'I hope you weren't drinking wine last night with your takeaway from the golf club,' Tom said, but he was smiling at Evelyn too.

'Gallons of it, I was drunk as a skunk!'

'She only had a couple of glasses,' laughed Bethan.

'You're lucky I'm not getting drunk every night,' Evelyn sighed. 'It's so boring in this bed, it's not good for my mind, I can't focus.'

'Maybe you could get up tomorrow.' Tom fitted the cuff around the top of Evelyn's arm. 'If Bethan helps you get dressed you could even go outside and sit in the sun, it would be good for you to get some fresh air.'

'Freedom at last!'

'That's all right with you, isn't it, Bethan?' Tom looked at the girl; Evelyn wished he wouldn't frown every time he spoke to her. 'Or did you have other plans?'

'No plans tomorrow,' Bethan replied. 'But actually, would you mind if I just popped out for an hour or so now? There's something I have to do.'

'Another date?' Tom started to press the pump on the blood pressure monitor.

'No,' Bethan said. 'I am meeting David, but it's not a date.'

'Ow!' Evelyn protested. 'You're crushing my arm with your pumping, Tom.'

'Sorry.' Tom released the pressure on the cuff and glanced at Bethan with a barely concealed scowl. 'I'll stay here and look after Evelyn while you enjoy your *not a date.*'

'I don't need looking after,' Evelyn muttered as Bethan left the room. 'And why do you have to talk to Bethan like that?'

'You do need looking after, yesterday's fall rather proved that point, and what do you mean about the way I talk to Bethan?'

'You sound like you're talking to a wayward teenager. It's as if you disapprove of her.'

Tom shook his head.

'I have no idea what you're talking about.'

Evelyn sighed.

'It is all right to find other women attractive, you know.'

'I don't find other women attractive.'

'Well, perhaps you should! How long has it been?'

'Evelyn, please. I don't want to talk about it. I want you to be very still and quiet while I take this dressing off.' Tom pushed her back against the pillows.

Evelyn winced as Tom removed the tape from her forehead.

'You're not nearly as gentle as your father.'

'You've told me that before.' Tom dabbed something stinging on Evelyn's wound. 'Oh, I nearly forgot to tell you, Tilly and I were looking through an old box of my father's things last night.'

'Really? I wouldn't think old things would hold much interest for a little girl.'

'Tilly is obsessed with finding out what happened to my Uncle Billy.'

Evelyn stiffened.

'There's not much to know, it was just an accident on the mountain.'

'She wants to know what it was like for him and my father living here as evacuees. She was upset last night about the ladies under the terrace being painted over, and I knew there was a box labelled "school days" in the attic, so I got it down to distract her. I thought it might have some clues in it, you know my father never talked about the war.'

Evelyn's head began to ache.

'There wasn't much in the box,' Tom continued. 'Just exercise books and some bits of old machinery and wire. But in the bottom we found a diary. I haven't read it properly yet, but the date on the front is 1944.'

BETHAN

David Dashwood was already waiting at the bottom of the drive. He was wearing expensive-looking walking boots, thick leather gloves and holding a pair of secateurs in one hand.

'For breaking and entering?' Bethan asked.

'For brambles,' David replied with a brief snip of the secateurs; the blades glinted in the afternoon sunlight. 'I'm glad to see you've got that old jacket on, I'd hate it if you ripped something pretty.'

Bethan looked down at Howard's Barbour.

'I'm afraid it's a bit hideous, and far too big for me.'

David smiled.

'On you, I think it has a certain charm.'

Bethan tucked a stray strand of hair behind her ear.

'Where are we going anyway?'

'Not far.' David was already walking back up the drive. Bethan followed him. After a few minutes David turned off down the little track that led to the summer house.

'I came here last week,' said Bethan. 'Then I had a memory from childhood. Something in there frightened me when I looked through the window a long time ago.'

David turned back to her with a grin.

'I told you it wasn't suitable for little girls.'

He started to cut through the brambles that had grown even thicker than the week before.

He let the branches fall to the ground and then trampled them with his boots so that Bethan could pass.

There was a noise ahead of them, a flap, a flash. A peacock flew up onto the roof. In the sunlight the effect was more spectacular than spectral.

'There's always a peacock here,' said David.

'You come here often?'

David snapped off a rhododendron branch.

'When I bought the woodland behind, I assumed this building came with it, so I came to have a look through the window a couple of times. But when we sat down with our solicitors Evelyn made it very clear that the summer house was not part of the sale. She got quite het up, I didn't dare tell her I'd actually been inside.'

He cut through the last of the brambles blocking their path until they were standing by the steps to the front door.

'Is it locked?' asked Bethan.

'We have to get in this way.' David indicated the arched window to his right. Bethan could see curtains half drawn at the window, she remembered peering through them all those years before, reaching up on tiptoes to see.

David stepped through the broken railings onto the veranda and took a small crowbar from the pocket of his jacket as though it was the most normal thing in the world to be carrying around. He pushed it in between the window and the rotten wooden frame. He began to push and pull, back and forth.

'It doesn't look like it's going to budge,' Bethan said.

'The frame is just swollen from the rain.' David gave one more pull and with a judder the window swung back, nearly knocking David off his feet. He regained his balance and grinned down at Bethan. 'Are you coming?' He took off his glove and held out a hand.

Bethan let David pull her up beside him.

'Ladies first.' He gestured to the open window.

'I think I'd rather follow you.'

'Coward,' David laughed and disappeared through the long dusty curtains like an actor going on stage.

'Come on,' he called from inside. 'I'm sure it's not as scary as you remember.'

From the roofline the peacock let out a cry.

Bethan was aware that the bird was watching her. She inched her way along the rickety veranda until she was standing in front of the window. She peered through the gap between the curtains. Inside it looked gloomy, though she could just see David standing in the middle of the room.

'Come on,' David repeated, and Bethan stepped through, trying not to shudder at the ancient spider webs that traced their way over the surface of the faded velvet. She could see mummified insects; she was sure she had some caught in her hair. David held his hand out to help her down from the narrow sill.

Bethan found herself standing in the semi-darkness. She could just make out a wrought-iron bed on one side of the room and a fireplace on the other. On the fireplace she could see a row of glass jars containing candle stumps. Above her she could see the circular stained-glass window; its intricate pattern threw jewel-like colours on the floor at her feet. She noticed there was a rug by the bed and an upturned crate. There was a heavy glass ashtray on the crate and another candle stump in a jar. Next to the crate there was an old-fashioned gramophone, complete with a vinyl record, thick with dust. On the bed there were pillows and a traditional red-and-white Welsh blanket. It looked as though someone had just got up and thrown the blanket to one side; only the layers of spider's webs that covered the woven wool suggested that it had been many years since anyone had lain there.

'I'll just draw the curtains.' David walked over to the window on the other side of the front door. Sunlight flooded into the room. David walked back to the window they'd come through and pulled the curtains apart with a puff of dust and dead flies.

Bethan blinked; the air around her was thick, moving slowly in the light as though disturbed from a long sleep.

'Look,' said David. He was standing in the middle of the room, his arms outstretched, gazing around the walls. Bethan looked.

There were three of them. Three beautiful portraits of the same blonde woman. She was reclining in different poses, staring directly at the viewer, and completely naked apart from a single string of pearls.

'Wow!' Bethan looked from one to the other and back again. 'She's so beautiful.'

'She's certainly a stunner,' David said with a smile.

'She's lying on a blanket just like this one.' Bethan pointed to the blanket on the bed. 'I think she lay here and posed for the paintings.'

David came to stand beside her.

'I wonder who she was.'

Bethan looked at him.

'Don't you recognise her?'

He shook his head.

'It's Evelyn,' Bethan whispered. 'They're paintings of Evelyn, a very long time ago.'

EVELYN

The sun was very bright through the window. Evelyn wished that Tom would hurry up and come back with the tea. She'd ask him to close the curtains. Maybe that would help. Block out the light. Block out the memories.

She hadn't thought about the diary for over seventy years, but now she could think of nothing else. The slim green notebook Evelyn had given to Peter for Christmas. He'd loved that diary. He'd kept it in the top pocket of his school blazer throughout that whole year of 1944.

Billy used to tease him. He called him the professor.

'You're always writing things down.'

'I'm keeping a record,' Peter would say, pushing his glasses up on his nose.

'A record of what?'

'Of the weather, and important events, and the things we've done.'

'Like what?'

'Our errands.'

Errands. That was what they'd called them.

'Would you run an errand for me, boys?'

'We've been on an errand for Jack.'

'Got any errands you need running today?'

Hundreds of notes, back and forth. The boys had been like postmen. They'd loved it. The secrecy, the illicit excitement of the intricately folded pieces of paper, so small the boys could slip them into their pockets with ease, transfer them into a palm with the deftness of a magician.

Evelyn and Jack depended on them: times, places, expressions of their growing love, especially after Nelli gave Evelyn the key to the summer house. They hardly needed to speak to each other in public at all.

After Jack was transferred back to the base, they depended on the errands even more. Jack would send a letter addressed to the boys.

'From our old auntie on Anglesey,' Billy would say if Mrs Moggs quizzed them. 'She likes to keep in touch, with us being orphans and everything.'

They'd pass the letter on to Evelyn, slipping it under the door of her bedroom in between the pages of an exercise book. After breakfast she'd come down to the kitchen and give them back the book.

'I've checked your homework, Billy. You need to keep practising your spelling.'

'Nine out of ten for your maths, Peter, but you need to show your workings.'

'Well done, your essay about the dolphins in the bay was charming.'

The boys then posted her letter in the postbox on their way to school.

'What would we do without our Batman and Robin?' Evelyn would say as Jack arrived at the door of the summer house.

Jack would step inside and immediately take Evelyn into his arms.

'And what would I do without my Wonder Woman.'

Evelyn had never thought of the diary. If she had she would have assumed that Peter had thrown it away years before. Besides, even at the time, she'd hardly given a thought to what might be written inside.

As Evelyn squinted against the afternoon sun, she tried very hard not to think of all the things Peter might have written. All those days and weeks and months that had seemed such bliss to her but had ultimately led to tragedy for them all.

BETHAN

She heard the kettle whistling on the Aga as she walked into the kitchen. Through a haze of steam she could see Tom picking it up and pouring water into a teapot on a tray.

He looked at her.

'You're early.'

'It took less time than I thought.'

'Good date? Or should I say non-date.'

Bethan opened her mouth to start to protest but she really couldn't be bothered. Besides, she could still feel the tingle of David Dashwood's lips on hers, the weight of his body; all the confused thoughts were still whirling through her head in the most disconcerting way.

The discovery of the paintings had been amazing. They were so intimate, so beautifully executed. In the sunlight the skin tones had glowed with warmth and vitality. The young Evelyn stared straight at the viewer, eyes sparkling with life.

'She must have been looking straight at the artist as he painted her,' Bethan said to David as she walked around the walls examining each figure.

'Do you see what I meant about the come-hither look?' David smiled. 'She does have a rather seductive expression on her face.'

'It's more than that.' Bethan came back to the centre of the room to stand beside him. 'It's more than desire, I think it's love.'

David had been silent then. Bethan had glanced up at him. He looked sad, as though his thoughts were very far away. Bethan touched his arm and that was when it had happened. In her memory it was a blur; somehow his face had come down to meet hers, his lips softly parting her own, his hands were on her waist, then underneath the jacket, then unbuttoning her blouse. She'd momentarily pulled away, thoughts of Mal filling her head.

David's hands had fallen to his sides and he'd taken a step back.

'I'm so sorry. I don't know what came over me,' he said.

Bethan had taken a breath.

'I think it must be this cottage, the paintings . . .'

'Or you, Bethan.'

David took another step towards her and then Bethan's mouth was reaching up for his again, her hands pulling at his shirt, feeling the taut smooth muscles of his back beneath her fingertips. Together they stumbled backwards, falling onto the bed. Bethan could smell the musty sheets and blanket, but she could smell David too, the sandalwood and lemons she'd noticed before. He undid the rest of the buttons of her blouse, and expertly undid her bra, his mouth was on her nipple. She gasped and succumbed to pleasure, all thoughts of Mal abandoned, as she started to unzip David's jeans.

Afterwards Bethan realised she was still wearing Howard's jacket, though her jeans and underwear lay on the floor.

'How did you get my bra off?' she asked.

'It's a trick I learned at a very young age.' David grinned down at her as her head nestled in the crook of his arm.

'I don't usually do that sort of thing,' Bethan said.

'Let men take your bra off?'

She laughed.

'Exactly. I've never been the sort of girl that has one-night stands.'

'I think it's technically a one-afternoon stand.' David's smile grew wider. 'What do you think?'

'Well, yes. I suppose it is.' Bethan wanted to say she'd like it to become another afternoon stand, many afternoon stands in fact. But she didn't want to appear too eager. 'Just a one-afternoon stand.'

There was a pause, she looked up and saw that David's smile had faded. He shifted his body so that he could look at his watch. 'You'd better get back to Evelyn,' he'd said. 'I don't want you to be late.'

Bethan had hesitated.

'I still have some time, I said I'd be an hour or so and I'm sure I've been less than . . .' Her voice trailed away as she saw that David was already sitting up, doing up his jeans, reaching over to pick up her own jeans and underwear from the wooden floor. He handed them to her and got off the bed. Bethan stuffed the bra into the pocket of the jacket and did up the buttons of her blouse, her heart beginning to sink at the rapidity of David's change of mood. It was as if a spell had been cast on both of them and now it was broken.

When Bethan had finished getting dressed, David picked up the crowbar and climbed back through the window. Bethan followed him. Outside he took her hand to help her jump down from the veranda but then he quickly let it go to push the window firmly shut.

Silently Bethan retraced their earlier steps, back through the bushes and down the track. She could hear David behind her.

'Thank you for showing me the paintings.' She turned to face him when they reached the drive.

'At least I know who the girl was now.' David shook his head. 'Lady Evelyn Vaughan, who'd have thought it! No wonder she didn't want to sell me the summer house.'

'I wonder who painted them?' Bethan said.

'Her husband, I'd imagine. A way of adding a little spark into their marriage maybe?'

David raised his eyebrows and looked down at Bethan. She thought he was about to say something else, but instead he had given her a small smile and walked away. Bethan watched him, waiting for him to turn around, or even just to raise one hand to wave, but he had gone on walking towards the gateposts without looking back.

Bethan had trudged up the drive towards the house, her mind a whirr of confused emotions. It was obvious that David had regretted what had just happened between them.

The air was chilly despite the sunshine and Bethan pushed her hands into the pockets of Howard's old jacket. Her fingers found the bra in one pocket and the silver cigarette case in the other. She had

247

forgotten all about the cigarette case since the night, a week ago, that she had discovered it. She stopped walking, opened the lid and read the inscription again.

To my darling Howard,
Always and forever,
L.D.
Christmas 1944

She snapped the cigarette case shut. Had Evelyn and Howard's marriage been more passionate than it seemed? What had gone on all those years ago? She looked up towards the twisted chimneys pushing through the trees ahead of her. What secrets did Vaughan Court hold behind its inscrutable mullioned windows and pink stone walls? And what had gone on in that summer house? Then and now? It was as if the small room and the paintings had had some sort of bewitching effect.

'You know he wants this house,' Tom said.

'Pardon?' Bethan was hanging Howard's jacket back on the hook by the kitchen door, hoping that Tom hadn't noticed the dust and cobwebs that were covering the back of it.

'David Dashwood. He wants Evelyn to sell him Vaughan Court so he can turn it into a hotel.'

Bethan walked over to the dresser and took down a mug.

'How do you know?' she asked.

'It's obvious. He's already asked Evelyn several times if he can buy it. He's told her he wants it as a home for him and some mythical family he's planning on having in the future, but I'm pretty sure a luxury hotel will be next on his empire-building agenda in Aberseren.'

Bethan opened the cupboard and took out a jar of coffee. She slowly unscrewed the lid and turned to face Tom.

'Would that be such a bad idea? You've said yourself that Evelyn might be better living somewhere smaller. And maybe a luxury

248

hotel would be just what Aberseren needs? It would provide jobs and the tourists would bring money to the village.'

Tom looked at her, his expression incredulous.

'This house has been in the Vaughan family for centuries.'

Bethan shrugged.

'Evelyn is ninety. She has no heirs. I don't even know who she'd plan to leave the house to in her will.'

'So, you think David Dashwood should buy it and rip it to pieces, putting in en suite bathrooms and fire doors and probably a colour scheme to match the golf club – what do you call that shade? Some sort of taupe?'

Tom was opening a packet of shortbread biscuits with unnecessary force.

'I think you mean teal,' said Bethan.

'Whatever.' The packet burst open. Several biscuits scattered on the table. 'Evelyn doesn't want to sell it to him, she's made that very clear.'

'Maybe it's just that you don't like David Dashwood,' Bethan said. She took the kettle from the Aga and poured water into her mug. 'You make that very clear.'

'I don't like him using you.'

'Using me? What do you mean?'

'I think he has designs on you.'

'Designs? That's the sort of word that Evelyn would use in her novels. The evil David Dashwood had designs on poor innocent Bethan, so the chivalrous Doctor has to ride in on his steed of a Volvo and put an end to Mr Dashwood's villainous duplicity and heroically reveal the golf club mogul for the money-grabbing rake that he truly is.'

'Evelyn would write that much better,' Tom said, picking up the tray and turning to the stairs. He paused on the bottom step. 'I'm just saying that he might be trying to befriend you to influence Evelyn. You've just split up with your boyfriend, you're vulnerable, you must feel—'

'You don't know anything about how I feel,' Bethan interrupted, spooning sugar into her coffee; she spilled some on the table as she realised she'd put four teaspoonfuls in by mistake. 'Maybe David Dashwood likes me, which is more than I can say for you. You seem to find me incompetent, irritating and incapable of looking after Evelyn properly.' Bethan grabbed a dishcloth from the sink and wiped away the sugar. 'But I'm a grown woman and I can look after myself, and Evelyn.'

Tom sighed and started to mount the wooden stairs.

'It's not that I don't like you, Bethan, it's that I don't want to see you get hurt.'

EVELYN

The morning sky was a bright azure blue. It was better to be outside, and better to be wearing some proper clothes and makeup at last. Though Bethan hadn't been very competent at applying the mascara and lipstick, there had been a lot of apologies and wiping with tissues. Evelyn would have liked foundation and blusher but it had seemed too much to ask, but Bethan had brushed her hair quite nicely and agreed to put her diamond earrings in.

Evelyn looked at the garden in front of her. All around her the leaves were bursting from bare branches, fresh and brilliant green, like a Liberty lawn shirt that she'd bought in the seventies. It had been one of Robert's favourites. Evelyn raised her face to the sun and closed her eyes.

She could see Robert's happy smiling face.

'I like your shirt, Mum.'

'Thank you, Robert. And I like yours.'

Robert had always liked to look smart. From the age of ten he'd insisted that he wanted to wear a shirt and tie.

'Like Dad,' he'd used to say. Maybe it had been an attempt at getting Howard to acknowledge him. It had been many years until Howard had stopped looking at Robert with reproach, and stopped muttering to Evelyn, 'There are places that he could go to, places that would know how to look after him.'

Lady Vaughan had been worse.

'The baby is a Mongol; he belongs in a home or hospital, not at Vaughan Court.'

Evelyn heard a car coming up the drive and knew it would be Tom. She kept her eyes closed but her heart began to race, as it had done intermittently ever since she'd asked Bethan to phone him first thing that morning. Evelyn had told Bethan to ask him to bring the diary when he came to check on her, after morning surgery.

She'd told Bethan they were going to have a day off from dictation, but in reality, her imagination was incapable of summoning up Hermione or Regency Bath; all that she could think of was the slim green notebook and the year of 1944.

She'd lain awake all night. By dawn she had decided that by far the best thing would be to see the diary for herself, hopefully before Tom had a chance to look through it. And then maybe, if it were accidently lost or mistakenly thrown away, Tom would forget all about it. What interest could the diary entries of a nine-year-old boy possibly hold for him, even if Peter had been his father.

She heard the car come to a halt, the engine stop, the crunch of feet on gravel. Then Bethan's voice, then Tom's; greetings, short and curt. Footsteps coming down the stone steps from the terrace.

'It's nice to see you sitting out here,' said Tom. 'And you've picked the loveliest day we've had so far this month.'

Evelyn opened her eyes.

She smiled.

'Yes, it is lovely.'

'The knot garden is coming back to life.' Tom indicated towards the intricate pattern of flower beds and hedges in front of her.

'I can't help noticing that it's in a bit of a state,' Evelyn said. 'It's quite overrun by brambles and the box is looking decidedly shaggy.'

'Get those young lads of David Dashwood's to come up, they'd have it tidied up in no time, and they could mow the lawns for you too.'

'I'm sure David's workmen have better things to do.'

Tom sat down in the chair beside Evelyn with a sigh.

'And I'm sure David Dashwood would like any excuse to get into

252

your good books. He was only too pleased to paint that wall for you, and he brought you that ridiculously oversized bunch of flowers, and dinner the other night. If you call him, he'll have those boys up here with hedge trimmers and a couple of strimmers in no time, he'll probably bring up one of those great big golf course ride-ons and mow the grass for you himself.'

Evelyn glanced at Tom. The evening before he'd been berating David Dashwood for monopolising Bethan's time, now he seemed to be accusing him of wheedling into her own affections. He really was becoming quite paranoid about the man. But she didn't have time today for conversations about David Dashwood.

'Did Bethan mention the diary to you on the phone?'

'She did, but I was in such a rush this morning I'm not sure if I remembered it; the school wanted Tilly to go in early for some tests. They're hoping to get her on a waiting list to see an educational psychologist who'll be able to make a proper dyslexia diagnosis.' Tom patted his jacket pockets.

'Damn, I think I left it behind.'

'Maybe you put it in your bag?'

'I don't think so, but I'll have a look.'

Tom squatted and rummaged through his bag of instruments. Evelyn noticed that he needed a good haircut and that the collar of his shirt was slightly frayed. She wondered how he'd react if she suggested he should take some styling tips from David Dashwood.

'No, it's not in here.' He sat down again. 'I must have left it on the kitchen table. Sorry, Evelyn. I'll bring it over tomorrow.'

'No!' Evelyn realised she had shouted. 'I mean, do you think you could possibly go back and get it now?'

Tom looked at her.

'Is it really that important?'

'Yes. I wanted to check something,' she said, thinking fast. 'A date. Something that happened during the war.'

'What was it?'

Evelyn smoothed her hair with the fingers that protruded from the cast.

'Just a party.' She tried to look nonchalant. 'Just a party that was held for the servicemen who were convalescing here.'

Tom sat back in the chair and surveyed the garden.

'It's hard to think of all this being covered in army hospital huts.'

'Yes, it is, but do you think you could go home and get the diary?'

Tom didn't seem to hear her.

'I can't imagine my dad running around amongst it all. I'd never realised he'd been so friendly with the patients.'

Evelyn looked at him.

'What do you mean?'

'I was reading the diary last night to Tilly. It seems that Peter and Billy were constantly running errands for this American fellow called Jack.'

'Errands?'

'Notes, back and forth to someone my dad refers to as WW in the diary. They sound like love letters. I think she must have been a nurse; she seems to have been living here, in the house itself. Maybe you remember her?'

Evelyn swallowed.

'WW you say?'

'Maybe she was a Wendy, or Willa, or Wanda? She could have had a surname like Williams?'

Evelyn stiffened. *Wonder Woman.*

'I don't recall anyone with those names.'

'What about Jack?'

'There were so many servicemen, I really can't remember them individually.'

'Jack was an airman. The notes seem to have gone on in the form of letters after he went back to his base on Anglesey in the September. My dad refers to posting a letter from WW to Jack in the village post-box on his way to school, and then delivering post to WW from Jack by slipping it under her door.'

Evelyn could feel her heart beating fast. She was glad that Bethan had insisted that she wore her leopard coat to keep out the breeze, otherwise she was sure Tom would hear it.

254

'Did you read the entire thing?'

'No, we got to October, but by then it was way past Tilly's bed-time so we had to stop. We'd just reached the day that Nelli finds out her fiancé Lloyd has been killed. His battleship was torpedoed in the Atlantic. Dad goes into quite a lot of detail about it, he says that Nelli cried all through supper.'

'Poor Nelli,' Evelyn mumbled.

'The boys were obviously fascinated with the war. Dad lists all the developments: the Siege of Leningrad, the Battle of Cisterna, D-Day, the progress of the allies through Europe. And he goes into great detail about the injuries of the servicemen in the hospital. Maybe it's where he got his interest in medicine.'

'I can't wait to read all about it,' Evelyn said.

'But the funny thing is,' Tom laughed, 'Dad and Billy seem to have been forever searching for paint.'

'How peculiar.' Evelyn smoothed the fur of her coat with her fingertips. 'Are you going home for lunch?'

Tom sat back and stretched out his legs.

'I've picked up a cheese and leek pasty from Olwyn's.' He laughed again. 'The diary mentions Olwyn quite a bit. It seems she was the bane of Dad and Billy's lives, always telling tales on them. Olwyn's mother dealt out regular beatings to both the boys for things that Olwyn told her that they'd done. Am I right in thinking Olwyn's mother was the housekeeper here?'

'Yes, she was. But it would be fascinating for me to actually see the diary myself.'

Tom seemed lost in his own thoughts. He shook his head.

'When I think about it, that woman was abusive. Those poor boys. They'd lost their home, their parents, they'd been uprooted from their community, come to live here . . .'

'It was a different time,' Evelyn interrupted.

'I really feel for them,' Tom continued. 'I mean, where was any love?'

'I loved them.' Evelyn blurted out the words without thinking. 'I'd lost everything as well. I'd been uprooted. The boys were like my family. Nelli too. I tried my best to protect them from Mrs Moggs, I tried, I tried so very hard.' She took a breath, gulping back unexpected tears. 'I wanted to look after them.'

Tom stared at her in silence for a few moments, then he said quietly, 'That's good to know, but the strange thing is the diary doesn't mention you at all.'

BETHAN

The sardines had a sell-by date of 2013. Bethan tentatively opened the tin and sniffed.

It was all there was for lunch. Food stocks were seriously depleted in the house and Olwyn's seemed to be rather limited in healthy dietary options, as well as being expensive. Bethan put two slices of dried-up bread into the toaster.

The little MG had been towed away to some specialist garage in Cheshire; it seemed its problems were far more serious than the clutch or the choke. Bethan wondered if Tom might be willing to take her to Tesco in Caernarfon but the thought of a car journey with Tom felt daunting. He'd hardly said two words to her when he arrived to see Evelyn earlier, and when she'd phoned him at half past seven that morning he'd been positively rude.

'Do you know what time it is?'

Bethan had stammered out Evelyn's request for some diary he'd mentioned to her the evening before and put down the phone as quickly as possible.

Maybe David would take her to the supermarket?

Bethan bit her lip. That seemed just as daunting. He might think she was trying to find an excuse for them to be alone together again, though she hoped that David Dashwood would realise that she didn't think the Tesco aisles would be the best venue for a repeat of what had happened in the summer house.

Bethan began buttering the toast. She could hear the television in the drawing room; it seemed to be getting louder. It was as though

Evelyn was putting the sound up a bit more every few minutes. Bethan wondered if Evelyn was going deaf.

She was worried about her. Evelyn had hardly eaten anything for breakfast and hadn't touched the shortbread biscuits that Bethan had given her with her cup of tea in the garden.

Bethan wanted to ask her about the paintings in the summer house, but after Tom left, Evelyn had seemed agitated; asking Bethan to help her inside, then to fetch her writing things. Bethan had thought she wanted to resume work on the novel, but when she brought the A4 notebook and a biro from upstairs, Evelyn had shouted at her and said she wanted proper notepaper and a fountain pen.

'For a letter. Though you young people probably don't even know what letters are.'

'Shall I write it out it for you?' Bethan had asked, returning with the Vaughan Court headed paper and a silver pen that Evelyn had instructed her to fetch from a writing desk in another room.

'I'm perfectly capable of writing my own letters,' Evelyn had snapped. Then she'd looked down at her hands as though she had forgotten they were encased in plaster. 'For fuck's sake! Why is everything so difficult.' Then she had said, in a much quieter tone of voice. 'But what's the point of trying to explain after all these years.'

She'd suddenly looked very old to Bethan; her skin more deeply lined, her eyes watery and pale.

Bethan thought about the paintings in the summer house. Evelyn had been so young, so fresh and bursting with life, like the new leaves outside. It had been her spring. It had been a very long time ago.

While Tom had been with Evelyn in the garden, Bethan had taken the opportunity to go back to the summer house to take photographs. She'd been much too flustered to think of taking photos the day before.

She'd taken a poker from the fire in the drawing room; it was the closest thing she could think of to a crowbar, and it worked a treat. In a few seconds she'd managed to pull the summer house window back and climb inside.

Bethan began to snap away with her phone, trying to ignore the bed, and her memories of what had happened on it the day before.

She noticed some objects piled in one corner. She walked over and saw that they were paint pots, lots of paint pots; different sizes and colours. She squatted down to look. The lids were rusty and encrusted with hardened lumps of paint. They had paper labels on the front that disintegrated at Bethan's touch. There was a jar beside them; it was streaked with drips of dried-up colour and full of brushes. Bethan picked one of the brushes up; its bristles were fused together, hard as rock. She wondered whose hand had held it last; could it really have been Howard's?

Standing up, she walked over to one of the paintings. She held the paintbrush up to the wall and turned her head to look at the bed, trying to imagine Evelyn lying on the blanket.

That was when she'd seen the peacock. It was in the room, feathers trailing over the dusty floor. It seemed to have materialised from nowhere. Bethan gripped the brush in her hand, as though it might protect her from the bird if it came too close. The peacock stared at her, she stared back. Minutes passed. Somewhere in the distance another peacock called. With a swish, the peacock turned, hopped onto the window ledge and left, its long tail slipping through the window as fluidly as silk. Bethan looked back to the painting on the wall. That was when she'd noticed what Evelyn was holding; a peacock's feather, spectacularly long and ornately coloured. Evelyn looked as though she were teasing the artist with it, her eyes playful, intimately comfortable with the artist who was paying homage to her body with his brush.

'Who was he?' Bethan whispered to the painting. 'Who was the man who painted you?'

'Bethan!' Evelyn was calling to her from the drawing room. 'Bethan, come here!'

Bethan hastily stopped spooning sardines over the toast and rushed up the back stairs.

'Are you OK?' She was almost breathless as she arrived in the drawing room. The one o'clock news was turned up very loud.

259

'The letter,' Evelyn said, and then she added something Bethan couldn't hear above the television.

'Sorry?' Bethan found the remote control on the arm of Evelyn's chair and turned the sound down.

'The letter,' Evelyn repeated. 'I've decided I do want you to write it out me after all.'

'Well, lunch is ready now, shall we do it after we've eaten?' Bethan turned to go back down to the kitchen.

'I don't want lunch.'

Bethan ignored her and came back up with their two plates of food. But after half an hour of coaxing Evelyn to eat hers, Bethan gave up and disappeared to fetch a large packet of Haribo from the special drawer.

Evelyn pursed her lips.

'I'm not a child, Bethan.'

Bethan left Evelyn with an episode of *Friends* and went back to the kitchen to throw away the uneaten sardines, wash up the dishes and eat half the packet of Haribo herself.

'Can we start the letter now?' Evelyn said when Bethan had re-appeared in the drawing room.

Bethan turned off the television and sat down on the sofa. She picked up the notepaper and pen.

'OK, what do you want to say?'

Evelyn took a deep breath.

'Dear Tom, there is something I feel I must explain . . .' Evelyn stopped. 'No, start again on a new sheet.'

Bethan took another piece of headed paper.

'Dearest Tom, as you know, your father meant so very much to me. He was a kind and honourable man, and a wonderful doctor to my family for many years. As you also know, I knew him from an early age and of course I also knew his brother Billy . . .'

Evelyn's voice trailed away. She let out a long sigh.

'Dispose of that, Bethan, start again.'

Bethan had only brought two sheets of writing paper from the desk, so she had to leave the room and go and fetch some more.

When she returned she sat down, closer to Evelyn, perching on the coffee table in front of her.

'OK, Evelyn, are you ready?'

Evelyn took another, deeper breath.

'My dear Tom, I think when you read the rest of the diary you will find out that I owe you a sincere apology for the circumstances that led up to . . .'

Evelyn paused and then she shook her head. 'This is very hard.'

'What is it that you're trying to say?'

'I don't know!' Evelyn thumped the arm of her chair with a plastered hand. 'I can't find the words.'

'Maybe if you explained it to me first?'

Evelyn shook her head vehemently.

'Just go and fetch me a cup of tea and put the television on again. As loudly as you can, please, I need to drown out all the noise.'

'My goodness, I can hear Monica berating Chandler from outside.'

Bethan jumped at the sound the voice. She turned from the tea tray she'd been setting on the kitchen table to see the tall figure of David Dashwood silhouetted against the sunlight at the back door.

'Hi,' she said as nonchalantly as she could, while at the same time fumbling with the foil on the top of a milk bottle.

'Here, let me help you with that.' David stepped into the room and expertly removed the lid. 'You're obviously not used to our old-fashioned milk dispensers.' He poured some milk into a little flowered jug. 'I just wanted to apologise. For yesterday.' David paused and leant back against the kitchen table. Bethan wasn't looking at him, but she had the distinct feeling that he was looking at her.

She put a cup and saucer on the tray, it rattled in her hand.

'There's really no need. It was my fault, I'm sure I made the first move; I realised afterwards that it was the last thing you'd probably wanted to do—'

'It wasn't the last thing by any means,' David interrupted. He stepped towards her.

It took Bethan a few moments to realise that his hand was on her

261

shoulder, and then a few milliseconds to notice his hand was lifting her chin and his face was coming down to hers.

'It really was rather wonderful,' David murmured, pulling her towards him. 'And now I'd like to do it again some time. If that's all right with you?'

'Yes,' Bethan whispered. 'I'd like that.'

She closed her eyes and felt David's lips make contact with her own.

Somewhere in the background she could hear Joey making a noisy entrance and then canned laughter. Chandler made a wise-crack about Joey's shirt and the laughter grew louder. And all the time, David was kissing her, passionately, deliciously; Bethan felt as though she never wanted it to end.

'Hello, anybody home?'

Bethan opened her eyes. The voice had not been Chandler's or Joey's.

'Hello,' the voice called again.

Bethan hastily disentangled herself from David. She turned to the back door just as a figure stepped into the frame. Against the bright sunlight was impossible to see clearly, but Bethan recognised the wide sloping shoulders and the burly set of the legs.

'Oh my God,' she whispered.

The figure stepped into the kitchen, dropping a canvass holdall on the flagstones.

'Who the hell are you?' David asked, protectively stepping in front of Bethan.

'It's all right, David,' Bethan said. 'This is Mal.'

262

EVELYN

The man sitting on the sofa had a beard the consistency of a dirty Brillo pad. It was at odds with his neat shiny hair, which was styled into the sort of quiff that Teddy Boys had sported in the 1950s. She wondered if it would feel firm to touch, though she had no actual desire to touch this young man's hair.

What she really wanted to do was reach out and slap his face.

He was drinking tea out of one of her bone china teacups, thick fingers grappling with the tiny handle. He was complaining that the muddy Welsh roads had made his new Nissan dirty; on and on he went, as though it was Bethan's fault.

Bethan offered him a shortbread biscuit. He stopped complaining about his car and stared at Bethan as though she'd offered him a plate of worms.

'You know I don't eat biscuits, Babe.'

He had the same accent as a man that used to sell brushes door to door when Evelyn had been a child. She could remember sitting at the kitchen table in Wilton Crescent while he gave a demonstration. He had all the different brushes his company sold represented in miniature. He carried them in a brown leather case. Of course, Evelyn wasn't meant to be watching the demonstration, but she'd been in the kitchen helping Cook make jam when he arrived. She'd found the man's accent and his tiny cleaning utensils fascinating and repelling at the same time. Evelyn wondered if the man in front of her had any tiny brooms in the bag that he had at his feet.

'So, Malcolm, did you have a nice time on your recent trip to

263

Brighton?' Evelyn asked. She ignored the furious look Bethan was shooting her across the room. Evelyn had no intention of stopping. 'Such a lively town, so many hotels. It used to have quite a reputation for adulterous liaisons.' She could see Bethan giving her a firm shake of her head. 'Did you enjoy it, Malcolm?'

'It's Mal, not Malcolm,' the man said in his brush-salesman voice.

'Mal and I need to talk,' said Bethan hastily. She was perched on the edge of the sofa beside the man. Evelyn noticed that the girl hadn't bothered with a cup of tea for herself.

'Yeah,' said Malcolm. 'I've got some explaining to do.' He gave Bethan a smile and Evelyn saw his hand reach out to touch Bethan's knee. With relief she saw Bethan move her knee out of reach.

'Talk away.' Evelyn took a sip of her own tea. 'Don't mind me. And Bethan, could you be a dear and pass me one of those biscuits, it seems a shame to let them go to waste. Though I do understand, Malcolm, that you probably need to watch that little paunch.'

Mal looked down at his stomach. Evelyn saw him breathing in.

'I think we should go for a walk,' Bethan said, looking at Mal.

'Or for a drink?' Mal suggested.

'You could go to the golf club,' Evelyn smiled. 'The owner is very welcoming, and such a successful businessman. He has a wonderful array of beautiful cars, and he's very sporty; tennis, golf, skiing, it's what keeps him so lithe and lean. Remarkably handsome too.' She smiled at Bethan. 'You must introduce Malcolm to David Dashwood, they might get on.'

Mal looked at Bethan.

'Wasn't that the name of that bloke in the kitchen?'

Bethan stood up.

'Yes, it was. But I don't think the golf club is really your scene.'

'Isn't there a pub or something round here?'

'No.' Evelyn shook her head sadly. 'We don't have a pub in Aberseren, though the Baptist chapel will be hosting its whist drive this afternoon. Great fun!'

'Not my scene either,' Mal muttered and turned to Bethan. 'OK, let's go for a walk, but not too far, I've strained my groin.'

264

'Really?' Evelyn tried to look concerned. 'Over-exerting yourself in Brighton, I expect. The pebbles on the beach can be very difficult to negotiate.'

'It's a gym injury.' Mal handed his cup and saucer to Bethan and stood up as well.

'We could just walk around the garden,' Bethan said.

Outside, one of the peacocks let out a high-pitched cry.

'What's that racket?' Mal peered towards the window.

'A peacock,' said Bethan.

'I thought it was the locals murdering someone.' Mal laughed, a silly laugh, that reminded Evelyn of a donkey.

'Well, it's true, the locals don't like English people very much.' Evelyn snapped her biscuit into two perfect halves.

Mal laughed again, a little less enthusiastically.

'Where can I put my bag?' He turned to Bethan and indicated the holdall at his feet.

'Oh, are you staying?' Evelyn asked.

Mal looked incredulously at Evelyn.

'I have just driven all the way from London, it's taken hours.' Mal turned back to Bethan. 'Shall I put my bag in your room, Babe?'

'Let's go outside and have a walk first,' said Bethan.

'Go as far as you like,' said Evelyn. 'Tom's coming back later, he'll miss seeing you, Bethan, but I'm sure I'll be fine in his capable hands.'

'Tom?' Mal asked, looking from Evelyn to Bethan and back again.

'Tom is my physician. Extremely well qualified and such a lovely man.' Evelyn lowered her voice. 'Between you and me, Malcolm, Tom has quite a crush on Bethan.'

'Evelyn!' Bethan hissed.

'You may be too modest to see it, darling, but it's as plain as day to me.' Evelyn turned her head back to Mal. 'Tom is another one of our eligible bachelors. Then there's the gorgeous medical administrator Owen Moggs, and our dashing policeman Sergeant Williams. All these handsome men have been practically tripping over themselves since Bethan arrived.'

Bethan sighed.

'Come on, Mal.' She started to walk towards the door. 'Let's go outside.'

'Maybe you'd like to pop a sweater on, Malcolm?' Evelyn called after them. 'There's a brisk wind coming in from the sea, and that shirt is gaping a little, you don't want to catch a chill.'

It was very quiet in the drawing room after they'd gone. Mal had left his bag beside the sofa. Evelyn wrinkled her nose. She was sure that she could smell sweat and cheap aftershave emanating from it.

She felt nauseous. Now the stupid man had arrived, Bethan would have no time to help her with the letter to Tom. Evelyn put the television on, then she turned it off again. She hadn't been subtle enough with Tom earlier. Her own determination to see the diary would have peaked Tom's curiosity. He'd probably go home to read it as soon as he could. She had hoped that presenting him with the letter would prevent her having to say the words out loud, but that wasn't going to happen now.

Evelyn pushed herself up out of the armchair and walked stiffly across to the window. She could see Bethan and Mal standing amongst the hedges of the knot garden. They seemed to be having an intense discussion, though it looked from where Evelyn was standing that Mal was doing most of the talking. She tutted.

'Evelyn.'

Evelyn turned from the window to find Sarah standing in the middle of the drawing room.

'What a nice surprise.' Evelyn smiled. 'What brings you here in the middle of the afternoon?' She glanced at the carriage clock on the mantelpiece. 'I thought you'd be picking up Tilly?'

'Tom's picking her up,' Sarah said. 'Her teacher wanted to have a word with him after school.'

'So, you're off duty today?'

Sarah shook her head.

'I thought I'd use the extra time to tidy up Tom's house while he and Tilly weren't there. You know how messy he lets it get.' She shook her head. 'Papers everywhere, clothes left lying around. I've been at it for hours; a proper spring clean. I was sorting out the kitchen and found this on the table, under a pile of letters from school.' Sarah took something from the pocket of her coat. Evelyn recognised it immediately.

Sarah held the diary in both her hands as though it were something very precious.

'I've read and reread it several times. I wondered if I could ask you some questions about what happened to our uncle Billy?'

BETHAN

Mal's car was disappearing much too fast down the drive. Bethan turned back to the house and started to walk briskly across the gravel. It was his fault if he had an accident, she really didn't care what happened to him.

She stopped.

She *really* didn't care.

For five years all she'd seemed to do was care about Mal; what he'd like to eat, what he'd like to do, how he'd like her to behave. Constantly tidying up so he wouldn't call her messy, trying to lose weight so he wouldn't call her fat. She'd turned down the chance to do an MA in creative writing in Manchester because of him. She kicked at the gravel.

'Twat!'

She didn't realise how loud she'd shouted till she heard the echo. It made her want to laugh. She gazed at the view: the sea, the hills, the mountains, all bathed in the warm sunlight of the late afternoon. A feeling swept through her; the word *euphoric* sprang to mind.

She wanted to run and jump and skip through the garden, just as she'd done all those years before when she was a child. She peered over the stone balustrade of the terrace. She would always remember that exact spot, beside the fountain, where she had finally realised that Mal was not the man that she wanted to spend the rest of her life with, where she'd finally realised what he really was.

It hadn't been his half-baked excuses; his supposed moment of weakness at the gym Christmas party that had led to so many more moments of weakness, 'because after all, Babe, I'm just a man.'

It hadn't been his explanation that he'd fallen for the woman's long blond hair and cosmetically enhanced breasts because of a bump on the head putting up their Christmas decorations.

'I think I had concussion, like a serious brain injury, Babe.'

It hadn't been his comment that the sex with the woman was great, but he had come to realise that he had little in common with her intellectually.

'She was a bimbo, not like you, Babe, at least you read real books.'

It hadn't even been when he'd tried to blame his mother for not giving him enough love as a child, or his father for forcing him to go to Scouts, or when he'd started to cry.

It had been his comment about Evelyn.

'She's a bit batty, isn't she?'

'Pardon?'

'The old bird.' He nodded towards the house. 'A bit senile, talking nonsense. She doesn't seem to have a clue what she's saying, all those men she says fancy you, her snide comments about my weight.' He put his hand out to Bethan and touched her shoulder. 'I'll help you find an old people's home for her, we could go and see some over the next few days. Then you can come back to London, back to our flat.'

'You've always said it was your flat,' Bethan said.

'Of course it's ours, Babe. And I've been thinking about our future, I've been thinking about us getting a bigger place together, somewhere we can start a family.' He gestured towards the house. 'Surely you'll be getting a share of this when it's sold?'

Something in Bethan had snapped.

'Fuck off,' she'd said quietly.

'Sorry, what did you say?'

Bethan shrugged his hand from her shoulder.

'I said fuck off.'

'Fuck off?'

'That's right. Get back in your fucking car, go back to your fucking pretentious flat in London, to your fucking avaricious advertising

270

job, your fucking overpriced gym and your fucking gym bimbo, who is probably not a bimbo at all but a nice, intelligent woman who has had the bad luck to fall for a selfish, shallow cockwomble like you!'

'Cockwomble?'

'You heard me. Now fuck off out of my life. For ever.'

'But, Babe . . .'

'Just go, Malcolm.'

'Malcolm? Only my mum, my boss, and now that old bag up there ever call me Malcolm.' He nodded towards the house again.

'I presume that's because those people don't like you. And I've just realised that I don't like you either, and that I would very much like you to leave.'

She'd turned around and gone up the steps, with Mal following behind muttering about all the miles he'd driven, and the cost of the petrol, and the time he'd taken off work.

'Talk about selfish!' he'd shouted as he stomped back into the house to collect his bag. 'I come to give you a bit of support and this is how you treat me!'

Bethan had waited beside his car and scratched, I am a Cockwomble called Malcolm, into the dirt on the back window.

Mal had come back with his bag and had thrown it onto the passenger seat.

'What about if I took you away for a late birthday treat? Not Brighton, Babe, obviously. But Paris, or maybe Amsterdam?'

Bethan had silently shaken her head and opened the driver's door, with a sweep of her hand that suggested Mal should get in. Reluctantly he obeyed.

'We've always talked about going to Marrakech, haven't we?' His puppy-dog eyes stared up at Bethan with well-practised despondency. 'Let me book the tickets, we could be there by the weekend.'

Bethan slammed the car door firmly. After a brief pause, Mal had started the engine and, with a skid of wheels on the gravel, he had driven away.

Bethan felt the wind pick up. She turned and leant back against the balustrade to let it blow through her hair. She had a feeling that Evelyn would be very pleased with her. It was then that she noticed Sarah's little orange hatchback parked just around the corner by the side of the house. She wondered if she had time to go to town while Sarah was visiting. She could send the finished article for *Frank* from the golf club, and she could even see if David was free.

She owed him an explanation about Mal. David had been very accommodating when Mal had appeared in the kitchen. He had immediately made his excuses and left, but not before asking if Bethan was going to be all right and whispering, 'You know where I am,' as she saw him to the door.

'He seems a bit full of himself,' Mal had commented when Bethan had returned. Bethan had looked away, wondering if she looked as though she had just been kissed in a far more enjoyable way than she had ever been kissed by Mal.

Bethan went into the house through the front door. She couldn't wait to tell Evelyn what she'd written on Mal's car. As she crossed the hallway, she could see the drawing-room door was ajar, and hear Sarah; her tone sounded gentle and calm, like a teacher talking to a child.

'So, he was trying to run away?'

'Yes, they both were.' Evelyn's voice sounded shaky, as though she might be on the verge of tears.

Bethan pushed open the door and walked into the room.

'Is everything all right?' she asked.

'Evelyn is just telling me—' Sarah started, but Evelyn cut her off.

'We are quite all right, thank you, Bethan.'

Bethan glanced at Sarah. She was holding a small green book in her hands.

'I was going to pop down to the village,' Bethan said. 'Would that be OK?'

'Yes, yes. You go.' Evelyn waved one hand dismissively. 'You're not needed here.'

Bethan glanced at Sarah again. Sarah nodded.

'I'll stay here until you come back,' she said. 'And I think Tom is coming as soon as he's finished talking to Tilly's teacher at the school. I phoned to tell him about what I'd read in the diary before I left.'

'No!' Evelyn's voice had been almost a wail.

'It's all right,' said Sarah softly. 'No one is blaming you. We just want to understand.'

'What's going on?' asked Bethan.

'Nothing.' Evelyn's voice sounded harsh.

'I think you should just leave us for now,' Sarah said to Bethan with an apologetic smile.

Bethan had shrugged and left, quietly closing the door behind her. The last thing she heard Evelyn say was, 'If I hadn't slipped on the ice, we might have reached him in time.'

The sun was warm on Bethan's face as she walked down the drive. Her curiosity about Evelyn and Sarah's conversation soon faded as she felt overwhelmed by the beauty of the countryside around her. She noticed that the celandines were coming out in carpets of yellow around the bottom of the trees that lined the drive. She remembered, long ago, her grandmother taking her to Oak Hill to show her where she used to work. It had been during the Easter holidays so there hadn't been any children, but what Bethan remembered most vividly were the flowers. The spring flowers had been everywhere and Nelli had taken her on a walk through the grounds, telling Bethan the names and letting her pick some to take home to press between the leaves of a book.

Bethan had been wearing a frilly party dress that she'd persuaded her mother to let her wear, it had spun out as she twirled around her grandmother.

'The prettiest flower of them all,' Nelli had said and Bethan had hugged her and noticed that she could feel her grandmother's bones through her coat.

That summer Nelli had died.

Bethan stopped and picked a violet. It smelled sweet. She decided to find a big book in the Vaughan Court library and press it; she'd

273

make it into a card for her mother. She slipped the flower into her pocket and carried on down the drive, glancing towards the summer house as she passed. She let herself enjoy the memories now, David's hands on her body, the sensation of his lips.

She hurried on, hardly able to contain her excitement at seeing him again.

As she approached the entrance of the golf club, she was surprised not to see any cars in the customer car park. She checked her phone. Four thirty. It didn't seem likely that on such a beautiful day no one was playing golf or sitting outside in the rattan chairs on the decking having tea.

As she got nearer she found that the glass doors were already open, half ajar. She walked through into the reception; there was no relaxing piped music playing, and no one behind the desk.

Bethan peered through the smoked glass towards the swimming pool; it was eerily empty. She could see the Jacuzzi bubbling all by itself.

'Hello,' she called.

There was no answer.

'Is there anybody here?'

Again, no answer.

Bethan walked towards the door marked Chief Executive and knocked.

'David?'

There was no reply. She wandered into the lounge. There was no one sitting on the big velvet sofas, and no staff serving afternoon tea. The bar was also empty, and as Bethan looked out of the big window she couldn't see anyone playing on the rolling greens of the golf course.

Bethan heard a noise. A sort of whining, snuffling noise, like a small animal in distress. It was coming from behind a set of double doors that Bethan presumed led into the kitchen. Warily she approached the doors, standing on tiptoes to look through a circular glass window.

She could see a woman in a turquoise top sitting on a stool beside a stainless-steel work surface. The woman was eating chocolate

274

profiteroles from a large Tupperware box, shovelling them in with an oversized spoon, intermittently wiping her eyes with what looked like a tea towel.

Bethan pushed open one of the doors.

'Chantal, is that you?'

Chantal looked up, her cheeks were streaked with mascara and her eyes were very red. Bethan noticed that she had a blob of chocolate on her top lip. Chantal wiped her mouth with the back of her hand, and the chocolate smeared into a little moustache.

'What's happened?' Bethan asked.

'It's David.' Chantal dropped the spoon into the Tupperware box and buried her face in her hands.

'Oh my God.' Bethan stepped forward. 'Has he been in an accident?'

Chantal took her hands away from her face and looked up at Bethan, her face twisting as she let out a sob.

'No. He's, he's been . . . I can hardly bear to say it.'

'He's been what?' Bethan tried to resist the urge to shake Chantal.

Chantal took a deep, gulping breath, before blurting out the words.

'He's been arrested!'

EVELYN

It felt like an interrogation.

Sarah on one side of the sofa, Tom on the other. They both kept telling her not to be so upset.

'But I am upset,' Evelyn protested. 'I've been upset for seventy years.'

'It wasn't your fault,' Tom said gently.

'How could it *not* have been my fault? I used the boys.'

'When I read the diary, I worked out that you were WW almost immediately,' Sarah said with a smile.

'Which was more than I did,' said Tom.

'And that Dad and Billy were happy to run errands for you,' Sarah continued. 'They loved you. You were the only adult in the house who was really looking after them.'

'It was that awful woman Mrs Moggs that made Dad and Billy want to run away,' said Tom. He stood up and walked to the window to watch Tilly playing in the garden. Evelyn could see the child going round and round in circles on a pink plastic scooter.

'If only Mrs Moggs hadn't seen the letter,' Evelyn said, picking at the plaster around her thumb with her fingers. She noticed how grubby the white cast had become, stained with tea and jam and now mascara from her tears. 'I was clumsy, I usually hid the letters in their school books, but that morning I was so desperate to see Jack, to tell him to meet me. I was thinking of the baby, of the plan Jack had promised that we'd make.'

277

Evelyn's brain was a whir; nine days had passed since she'd last seen Jack. He'd said he only had one more mission to fly before he had leave. Surely he must have flown the mission by now. But there had been no word from him; she'd asked the boys every day if there had been a letter addressed to them in the post.

Evelyn woke very early that morning. She got up immediately and started to write.

> *Darling Jack,*
>
> *I haven't heard from you for so long. Is everything all right? Have you flown your last mission? I'm desperate to see you again, we need to make plans. I think I'm beginning to show, I couldn't do up my skirt last night, my beastly mother-in-law is sure to notice soon. I'm worried, darling, I'm worried that something has happened. Please write to me and tell me when I can see you. I love you, I always will.*
>
> *Your angel, your Wonder Woman, your Evelyn. Xxx*

Evelyn put the letter into an envelope, addressed it to Jack at the airbase. After she had dressed in her uniform, she hurried downstairs, hoping she'd catch the boys before they left for school.

When she reached the kitchen, she could see the two satchels were on the floor beside the door, waiting for the boys to finish their breakfast. They were sitting at the table with bowls of the horrible thin porridge Mrs Moggs made them eat, more water than oats. Olwyn sat opposite the boys eating her porridge with a spoonful of jam on top. Mrs Moggs had her back to the door. She was putting Olwyn's hair in plaits, tying the ends with ribbons, speaking softly to the girl in Welsh.

The radio was on. The news announcer was talking about the Battle of the Bulge. The boys were riveted by the reports of fighting in the forests of Belgium.

No one seemed to have noticed Evelyn coming into the room,

but Nelli. She smiled at Evelyn from the sink, though she didn't speak, as if she knew it was better not to attract attention.

Evelyn tried to catch Billy's eye, to signal to him that she was going to put the letter in his satchel. Olwyn looked up from her porridge.

'Lady Evelyn has a letter, Mam.' She said it in Welsh, but Evelyn could understand enough of what she said. 'She's trying to put it in Billy's bag.'

'What's this?' Mrs Moggs stopped tying the ribbon in her daughter's hair. 'If you have a letter, Lady Evelyn, you know you can leave it in the hall and Olwyn will take it to the postbox for you.'

'I know,' said Evelyn. 'But the boys will take it for me on their way to school, I thought it might make the early collection.'

'I wonder if there is a special reason your letter needs to make the early collection?'

Evelyn hesitated.

'Well, no, it's just . . .' she stammered.

Mrs Moggs stepped forward and snatched the letter from her hand, reading the address out, like she was a serving girl, instead of the lady of the house.

'Who's this? Jack Valentine?'

She ripped the envelope open, silently reading all of Evelyn's words.

Olwyn said something else in Welsh, much too quickly for Evelyn to follow fully. The little girl seemed to be talking for ages, breathless and excited, on and on while Mrs Moggs's tiny eyes widened in surprise.

Evelyn couldn't move. She felt paralysed with horror, fear, embarrassment, she couldn't understand all of what Olwyn was saying but she understood enough to know that she was telling her mother that the boys were always posting letters for Evelyn, and that Jack Valentine had been the man who painted the pictures, and that she knew the boys had stolen the paint.

'I'll be showing this to Lady Vaughan.' Mrs Moggs put the letter in her apron pocket. 'But first you boys need to be taught a lesson.'

279

She pulled them both up from their seats by their jumpers, hoisting their shirts up, so that their bare backs were exposed.

'Put the poker in the fire, Olwyn,' she said in English.

'Please, no.' Evelyn rushed forward but she stumbled against a chair, knocking it over onto the slate flagstones with an echoing crash, then falling on top of it. A pain shot through Evelyn's stomach as Nelli helped her up from the floor. Mrs Moggs already had hold of the boys before the hearth.

'Please,' Evelyn gasped. 'Don't hurt them.'

'They are naughty boys who must be taught a lesson,' Mrs Moggs replied.

Nelli spoke up, her arm still supporting Evelyn, pleading with Mrs Moggs in Welsh.

Mrs Moggs didn't take any notice.

'Is the poker ready, Olwyn?'

Olwyn pulled the poker out of the coals; it was a glowing orange, white at the tip. The boys began to writhe, Billy was swearing, but that just made it worse. Mrs Moggs had a firm hold of their jumpers. She dragged them nearer to the hearth.

'It's all my fault,' Evelyn was shouting. 'You mustn't punish the boys.'

'Three stokes each,' Mrs Moggs instructed her daughter.

'I forbid you to do this.' Evelyn rushed forward and tried to pull the woman's hands away from the boys' jumpers. 'You must stop right now.'

'I don't take orders from you,' Mrs Moggs hissed. 'You're a wicked, wicked girl. A harlot.'

Then she spat in Evelyn's face, momentarily causing Evelyn to step back.

Olwyn raised the poker and brought it down hard on Peter's bare back, hesitating for a second so the hot metal could sear into the skin. Then she raised it again and brought it down on Billy's. Both boys were screaming.

'No!' Evelyn shouted.

'Again,' Mrs Moggs said.

There was a thwack, the smell of burning flesh. Another jolt of searing pain shot through Evelyn's stomach. She grasped the edge of the table. Nelli rushed to Evelyn's side, stopping her from falling to the floor again.

'I'll tell Lord Vaughan,' Evelyn gasped. 'I'll telephone him in London as soon as he gets to his office. I'll have you dismissed for this.'

Mrs Moggs ignored Evelyn; she nodded at her daughter.

'Olwyn, strike the boys again.'

Olwyn brought the poker down a third time, the boy's screams got louder.

Then the servants bell began to jangle on the wall, Lady Vaughan was calling from the breakfast room. Mrs Moggs dropped the boys to the floor, where they fell into a heap.

Peter was crying, but Billy was standing up, pulling down his shirt and jumper.

'You're a witch,' he shouted at Mrs Moggs as she started to smooth down her apron and climb the back stairs. 'A bloody witch.'

Mrs Moggs stopped on the second step.

'When I come back down you'll both be going in the cellar.' She looked at Evelyn and smiled. 'I'll be showing this to Lady Vaughan right now.' She took the letter from her pocket. 'I daresay she'll be telephoning Lord Vaughan to tell him what you've been up to. You won't be so high and mighty then.'

She started up the stairs again.

'You're evil,' Evelyn shouted behind her. 'Evil and cruel and . . .' Her voice trailed away as Mrs Moggs disappeared.

For a few seconds everyone was silent. In the background the news announcer on the radio still droned on.

'I'm so sorry . . .' Evelyn began.

But Billy was pulling Peter up from the floor.

'Come on,' he said. 'We're going home.'

Peter stood up.

'I won't let her lock you in the cellar,' Evelyn said. 'I will forbid it.'

Olwyn laughed.

'Like my mam will listen to you.'

'Olwyn Moggs, how dare you talk to Lady Evelyn like that,' Nelli scolded.

'Olwyn's right,' Billy said as he picked up his satchel, wincing from the wounds on his back. 'She'll never listen to you, Lady Evelyn.' He emptied out his school books on the floor, the catapult skittered out across the flagstones. Billy grabbed the loaf of bread from the table, he shoved it into his bag, and snatching up the catapult he opened the back door.

'Come on, Peter.' He was already outside in the icy air. His breath rose in puffs like smoke.

'Billy, don't go,' Evelyn begged. 'Peter, stay here.'

Neither of the boys looked at her as they left.

'Billy! Peter!' Evelyn shouted from the door, Nelli beside her. She was shouting at the boys too, but they were walking into the distance very fast. Evelyn and Nelli followed them across the courtyard. They turned towards the terrace and the lawn beyond the hospital instead of the drive.

'They're heading for the mountains,' Nelli said.

'Come on, we have to stop them.' Evelyn started to run, calling all the time.

Billy looked back and then the boys started to run. Evelyn and Nelli followed them down the steps and along the edge of the hospital camp, pushing past groups of nurses heading for their morning shifts and doctors about to start their rounds.

The boys disappeared so quickly but Evelyn knew they'd be heading for the mountain path. She and Nelli ran across the lawn and through the bare bushes. It didn't take them long to spot the boys, Billy was wearing a blue jumper, Peter a red one. They were dots of colour in the freezing mist. The two women scrambled upwards, Evelyn in her nurse's uniform, Nelli in her thin black dress and apron; neither of them were in appropriate clothing for the mountains. Soon they gave up shouting; their voices were hoarse. Instead they concentrated on keeping their footing on the icy rocks. Evelyn had on her hospital shoes; they had no grip on the slabs of slate that she and Nelli were trying to make their way across. The boys didn't stick to the path. They passed the crash site of the plane and then veered off the path, a way that Evelyn had never been before.

She saw Peter ahead, lagging behind Billy.

She started to shout again, calling his name. Peter looked back.

That was when Evelyn slipped, tumbling down the rock face, her hands grasping at the gorse bushes, landing at the bottom of a gully with a tremendous thump. As she stood up she felt the pain. There was blood too. Blood running down her legs and over her shoes and onto the icy rocks. She knew it was the baby.

Peter and Nelli rushed to help her.

'What about Billy?' she gasped. 'You have to find Billy.'

'He'll follow us,' Peter said. 'When he sees I'm not behind him, he'll come back.'

They had helped Evelyn back to the house. She could hardly walk with the pain, but all the time she begged them to go on after Billy. But Peter insisted his brother would be back.

Nelli put Evelyn to bed and fetched a doctor from the hospital. He knew what was happening, said there was nothing that could be done. Evelyn begged him to get some help to go after Billy; she told him that a ten-year-old boy was trying to make it to Liverpool over the mountains.

He telephoned the police and a search party was sent out. Some of the doctors and nurses from the hospital helped too, and the teacher from the village school came out to search with some of the older boys when the lessons ended.

The weather worsened, there was thick fog; the police called off the search when it got dark.

The next day Evelyn got up, very early in the morning. She was still bleeding but she couldn't go on lying in the bed, waiting to hear news.

She tried not to think about the baby, she couldn't think about the baby. She could only think of Billy.

She pushed her feet into the hideous brown shoes, ignoring the pain as she stooped to tie the laces. She threw her nurses' cloak over her nightdress and wrenched open the bedroom door. As quickly as she could she walked down the long corridor, down the stairs and through the heavy oak front door.

The outside air was icy. The rain had stopped, but the mist was freezing, swirling around her, enveloping her in cold. She hurried around the east wing of the house and picked up speed as she skirted the hospital camp. She nearly ran straight into a group of nurses heading for their morning shift. One of them called out her name but Evelyn ran on, across the lawn, past the glasshouses; she thought of nothing but finding Billy. She would bring him back, warm him by the fire in her room, wrap him in her eiderdown, feed him bread thick with jam and Nelli would bring sweet tea. Peter would be so pleased to see his big brother back safe and sound and Evelyn would never ask the boys to run errands for her again.

She raced on over the damp grass, her cloak billowing behind her like wings as the wind picked up. She pushed through the bare branches of the rhododendrons and started to scramble up the mountain path, concentrating on keeping her footing on the shifting shale.

The weather seemed to be clearing, the mist lifting to reveal a lowering sky. As she climbed higher, Snowdonia spread out in front of her, a million different shades of grey.

Evelyn recognised the point she'd slipped the day before, the gorse bush uprooted where she'd tried to catch it as she fell. She looked upwards at the craggy ridge and climbed on, ignoring the pain, ignoring the blood she could feel trickling down her inner thighs. Her breath came out in gasps, her heart a hammer against her chest. She clambered over boulders, slipping and sliding on rivulets of water that had turned to ice. She only stopped when the path petered out. There was nothing but the sheer rock face on one side and a jagged ledge on the other; beyond it a sheer drop.

Evelyn crouched on all fours and very slowly inched her way forward to peer over the ledge. Far beneath she saw a stream; a silver ribbon threading through the stones.

Billy lay looking up with unseeing eyes, his thin body twisted in the water, his red jumper unbearably bright against the harsh grey rocks and decaying mountain bracken. The catapult was still clenched in his lifeless hand, as if it was the most important thing in all the world.

EVELYN

'It was all my fault.' Evelyn's mouth felt dry from all the talking, her head ached, her heart was racing much too fast.

'It wasn't your fault,' Sarah said. 'A terrible accident, but not your fault.'

'But if I hadn't written the letter. If I hadn't gone down to the kitchen that morning. If I hadn't slipped on the rocks . . .' Evelyn paused. 'If I hadn't been having an affair.' She raised her hands to her face then. 'What must you think of me?'

Bethan was at her side now. Evelyn hadn't even realised she'd been in the room. She was sitting on the arm of the chair, her arm around Evelyn's shoulders.

'We don't think badly of you at all.'

'I always remember what Mrs Moggs said: *Harlot.* I was a harlot and poor Billy paid the price.'

'What happened to Jack?' Tom asked.

Evelyn found she couldn't speak any more. She swallowed, her throat felt tight. Bethan was stroking her hair. It reminded her of Nelli and how she used to soothe her all those years ago.

'Did he crash on the mountain?' Bethan asked. 'Is the wreckage up there the plane that Jack was killed in?'

'No.' Evelyn shook her head. 'He didn't die up there.'

'Where did he die?' asked Sarah gently.

'*The Lady Evie* came down over Germany.' Evelyn stared blankly into the empty grate of the fire. 'The night after I found Billy, I paid one of the ambulance drivers to give me a lift to the base. They told me

287

Jack was missing in action, presumed dead. It had happened a whole week before. I have no recollection of being driven back to Vaughan Court, or Billy's funeral, or Christmas, or all the days that followed till well into January.' Evelyn patted Bethan's hand. 'I don't know what I would have done without your grandmother.' She looked at Sarah and Tom. 'And your poor father. He was just a little boy, but he was so kind to me, even though he'd lost Billy. We were all grieving in our different ways, me and Nelli and Peter. All mourning the ones we'd loved best of all. We stuck together after that. We always stuck together.'

'And Lady Vaughan?' Sarah asked. 'What did she do when Mrs Moggs showed her the letter?'

Evelyn sighed.

'She had a stroke. The first of several over the next six years. The first was only mild, and by the time she recovered I was strong enough to tell her that I knew the real reason Howard stayed in London all through the war.'

'Which was?' asked Tom.

There was a knock at the door.

Sergeant Williams walked in.

'I'm so sorry to interrupt,' he said, looking around the room at each of them in turn. 'I have an update on the case.'

Evelyn wanted to tell him to go away and come back later, but Tom was standing up and telling him it was quite all right to come into the room.

'What case?' Sarah asked.

'Trespass and the wilful damage of property, here at Vaughan Court,' Sergeant Williams said, his eyes wide with excitement. His voice had taken on the tone of a detective in an amateur dramatics play. 'I'm happy to say that following an extensive investigation, I have apprehended the culprits red-handed.' He looked around the room at each of them again. 'I presently have them in custody. Two local lads. They are this minute locked up in a cell.'

Evelyn could feel Bethan shifting on the arm of the chair.

'But I have also arrested another suspect.' Sergeant Williams looked around the room yet again.

'For goodness sake, get on with it,' said Evelyn. 'Tell us who the hell has been throwing the rocks, and then maybe Bethan would go and get us all a cup of tea, though I think I'd rather have a stiff whisky.'

Sergeant Williams raised himself up on his toes. His shiny shoes creaked. 'The third suspect is someone I like to call, "The Ringmaster".' He made little quotation marks with his fingers, and then produced his notebook from his pocket with a flourish. 'The Ringmaster is not denying what he's done.' He paused. 'But he has a rather peculiar story and I wondered if you could verify it for me, Lady Evelyn?'

BETHAN

Tom shook his head as Bethan came to stand beside him at the door.

'It's certainly quite a story,' he said.

'It explains this.' Bethan had fetched the silver cigarette case from the pocket of the Barbour jacket while Tom had been saying good-bye to Sergeant Williams. She handed the case to Tom.

'Look at the inscription inside.'

'L.D.' Tom read out the initials. 'That must be Loretta Day, Howard's mistress.'

'And David's grandma Margaret's mother.' Bethan took the case back from Tom. 'Turns out you were wrong about the luxury hotel.'

Tom made a harrumphing noise.

'But I knew he wanted the house for some reason. I don't understand why he had to send his two gormless workmen to try to frighten Evelyn into selling it.'

Bethan shrugged.

'I suppose he was desperate. His grandma is getting old, and he'd promised her since he was a little boy that he'd find a way for them both to live at Vaughan Court.'

'Lord Dashwood. Sounds like something out of one of Evelyn's novels.'

'He's Lord Vaughan,' corrected Bethan.

'Illegitimately,' Tom muttered.

'I'm sure he really does want to get Margaret out of the old people's home in Chester so he can care for her.'

'He and Chantal,' said Tom.

'Mm,' Bethan said. 'It does seem from what Chantal said to me that she was under the impression she'd get to be the lady of the manor.' Bethan sighed. 'You were right about him using me.'

Tom turned to face her.

'I'm sure he genuinely did like you.'

In silence they watched Tilly walking slowly across the lawn, her scooter now discarded on the drive.

'Is she OK?' asked Bethan. 'She doesn't seem herself.'

'She's been having nightmares the last two nights,' Tom sighed. 'Since the pictures under the terrace were painted over. And now her teacher's worried about her. She's stopped playing with the other children and she's been saying that she misses her mum.'

'Sarah told me what happened,' said Bethan, still watching Tilly. 'To your wife and baby daughter.' Tom didn't answer. 'I'm so sorry. What a terrible tragedy for you and Tilly.'

Tom shifted. He took a breath as though he might speak, then changed his mind.

'We'd better check on Evelyn and Sarah,' he said after a long pause. 'Evelyn's had a shock, not just the news about David, but reliving that horrific story about Billy and Jack and losing the baby.'

'I think I'll go and get Evelyn a cup of tea,' said Bethan.

'Coffee with a dash of brandy might be a good idea,' Tom called as he started to walk back to the drawing room. 'In fact, get one for all of us.'

Bethan went down to the kitchen and came back with four cups of coffee and an ancient bottle of Hennessy that she had found in the larder.

'I wasn't sure if you were being serious,' Bethan said to Tom as she put down the tray.

'I was being very serious.' Tom started to add a slug of brandy to each mug. 'Doctor's orders.'

'That's the best thing you've ever prescribed me.' Evelyn's laugh sounded breathless.

'Are you OK?' Bethan asked. Evelyn did look very pale as she took the mug from Bethan with shaking hands.

292

'Yes.' Evelyn nodded. 'I know it's silly to get upset about the things that happened in the past.'

'It's not silly at all,' Sarah said. 'You've lived with all that pain locked up inside you for decades. You should really have had counselling to help you process it.'

'I never needed counselling!' Evelyn waved her hands so that a slug of coffee sloshed onto her plaster cast. 'Waste of time and money.'

Bethan took the mug from her and put it down on a small table.

'I know what you're thinking,' Evelyn continued. 'Because of that stiff upper lip approach, the effects are still being felt today. Like David Dashwood. He was only trying to put right the injustices of seventy years ago.'

'The man was trying to drive you out of your home, Evelyn,' said Tom.

'Only so that he could keep his promise to his grandmother.' Evelyn shook her head. 'I thought Billy was haunting me, smashing windows with the catapult I gave him, trying to make me pay for my mistakes by terrorising me at night.'

Bethan shuddered.

'I had begun to imagine it was ghosts too. I never thought that David would be the one to blame.'

Evelyn shook her head. 'I can't get over the fact that David's grandma Margaret was Loretta and Howard's daughter.'

'Did you ever meet Loretta?'

'I met her once. After I read a letter she sent to Howard. I went up to London. I was so upset; I wanted to confront Howard, get some sort of an explanation – I thought he'd tell me it was nothing, just a fling. Or he'd tell me it was all my fault. I'd driven him into the arms of another woman, with my undesirability.'

'You can't have thought you were undesirable?' Bethan looked incredulous.

'I did,' Evelyn said quietly.

'But you were gorgeous,' said Sarah.

'Howard didn't seem to think so. I definitely didn't seem to *turn him on* as you young people say. And no one had ever told me I was pretty, or beautiful, or desirable. Until I met Jack.'

Bethan came back to sit on the arm of Evelyn's chair. She put her arm around her shoulder and hugged her. Evelyn patted Bethan's hand.

'Maybe, in some strange way, I thought if I confronted Howard with the affair, it might bring us closer together. I went to the flat on Sloane Street. It was early so I was going to wait until Howard came back from Whitehall, but she was there.' Evelyn closed her eyes, the scene still vivid in her mind. 'Loretta opened the door in a dressing gown. Her hair was in rollers. She looked ancient to me, and very much as if the flat was her home. I didn't know what to say. She was kind, invited me in, gave me a drink – sherry, I think. I remember my hands were shaking, like they are now.' Evelyn raised one trembling arm. 'Loretta said she was sorry, and that she loved Howard and he loved her. She said he'd made it clear divorce was out of the question, but all she wanted was to be with him. I left as soon as I could. Came back here . . .' Evelyn's voice trailed away.

'Why didn't you just leave then?' said Bethan.

'I had no family, no friends. There was a war on. Where could I have gone? Anyway, I blamed myself. I had failed as a wife. But I realise now that Loretta probably gave Howard all the love and affection he never got from his mother. He was a sensitive soul really. He could be morose and grumpy, and he had a fierce temper, but underneath he was still the frightened little boy whose mother used to shower him with adoration one minute and reject him the next. What was it Philip Larkin said?'

'They fuck you up, your mum and dad.' Tom sighed.

'Well, Lady Vaughan well and truly fucked Howard up,' said Evelyn. 'His father probably had a hand in it too. Howard had been messed up by the war as well; he couldn't forgive himself for what happened to his men in France. Loretta Day may only have been a nightclub singer in Soho, but somehow Howard was able to find comfort with her. He could love Loretta in a way he could never love his actual wife. He could never have fathered a child with me.'

'But you and Howard had a baby in the end. You had Robert,' said Bethan.

Evelyn looked up at Bethan and shook her head.

'Robert wasn't mine. He was their son.'

Bethan's eyes widened.

'Howard and Loretta's? They had a son as well as Margaret?'

Evelyn nodded.

'Robert was born a month after Howard's accident. Howard was still in hospital. He had gangrene in the wounds on his legs. It was touch and go whether he'd survive. I got a telegram from Loretta. She asked me to come to London. I don't think she even realised it was VE day. She must have been in such a dark place at that time.'

Evelyn paused, staring into the fireplace.

'So you went to London?' Bethan prompted.

'Yes. I went to the flat. It was the evening by the time I got there. The lights were going on all over London – for the first time in six years. It was extraordinary. All those lit-up windows, you could see straight into the rooms. A party going on in every one. But there were no lights on in the flat. Everything was dark. I found Loretta in the kitchen. I can still smell the gas. She had a letter in her hand addressed to me. She said a doctor had told her she was very ill, she'd never cope with the responsibility of looking after Howard with his injuries. She asked me to look after him for her, but she never mentioned the baby.'

'Where was he?' asked Sarah.

'He was there, in the flat. I often wonder what would have happened if I hadn't heard him. I suppose the police would have taken him somewhere, to some hospital or institution. He was lying in the middle of the big double bed, swaddled in a blanket, making little noises, more like a kitten mewing than a baby.'

'Poor thing,' whispered Bethan.

'So you brought him back here then?' asked Tom.

'Yes, I brought him back to Wales on an overnight train jammed with demob-happy soldiers. I cradled him in my arms for the entire journey, protecting his tiny body from all the jostling people. Nine hours, and he never even cried. I had to coax him to take milk from a bottle. I think I fell in love with him on that journey. When I brought him back here your grandmother Nelli and Peter fell in love with him too. I often thought he was our baby. He belonged to the three of us. We all helped to bring him up, and he helped us all to heal.'

'But Margaret? Where did she fit in?' Bethan asked.

'I don't know. I need to talk to David myself. I need to find out more about his grandmother.'

'Well, you'll have to wait until Sergeant Williams releases him.' Tom stood up. 'I must go and see where Tilly has got to.'

'I'll make her a hot chocolate,' Bethan said. 'And I'll make you another coffee, Evelyn. I think you spilled most of that one.'

'I haven't asked you where Malcolm is,' Evelyn said as Bethan walked towards the door. 'We noticed him fetch his bag from the room, didn't we, Sarah?'

'He looked a bit cross.' Sarah gave a grimace.

'If I were writing it in a novel I'd say *he had a face like thunder*,' added Evelyn.

Bethan smiled.

'I shall tell you the story when I come back with your coffee. I think it will cheer you up, Evelyn.'

It was as Bethan went back down to the kitchen that she noticed the water. A trail of it from the sink to the back door, bubbly splashes all over the flagstones. She was sure the floor had been dry when she had been in the kitchen earlier.

Bethan opened the back door. A few peacocks were still searching for the last of the bird seed she had thrown them for their dinner; amongst their swishing tails she could see a dark line across the gravel, and occasional bubbles, like rainbow marbles sparkling in the late-afternoon sun. Bethan followed the trail, around the corner and onto the terrace. There were bigger splashes going down the steps. She could hear something. A scraping, scrubbing sound; rhythmic, unrelenting. There was another sound as well, little gasps and sniffing. Bethan went down the steps and peered through the arches underneath the terrace. That was when she'd seen her. Tilly. She had a scrubbing brush and bucket, and she was trying her very hardest to clean the whitewash off the wall.

BETHAN

The morning sun was glorious. A warm spring breeze had replaced the initial chill of the day.

Bethan sat down on the wall of Twr Du and looked out across the bay. The tide was far out and there was a party of schoolchildren on the beach, with two teachers helping them to make a giant picture in the sand. They had little rakes and sticks and from the top of Red Rock it was easy to see they were drawing a dragon.

She heard a noise, someone coming up behind her. She turned and found herself face to face with Tom.

'What are you doing here?' she asked.

'I could ask you the same.'

Bethan sighed.

'I'm trying to decide what to do with the article about Evelyn that I've written. I told the editor I'd send it today, but now it doesn't feel quite right. I'm not sure that a lot of it is really true.' She looked at Tom and gave a little shrug. 'Or maybe I should say, "correct" rather than "true".'

Tom sighed.

'Everything is certainly a bit different. Evelyn wasn't the happily married woman we all thought she was, tirelessly caring for Howard out of love.'

'And she wasn't the mother of a child with a learning disability,' added Bethan.

'But it is true that she successfully campaigned for disability rights, set up Oak Hill School and wrote many bestselling novels.'

'I know that.' Bethan pushed her hair from her eyes as a gust of wind blew from the sea. 'I just feel her story is so much more interesting than what I've written. My article feels a bit banal in light of everything we've found out in the last twenty-four hours.'

'Do you think Evelyn would want you to write about all that?'

'I don't know.'

'You could ask her?'

Bethan stared out at the beach, watching the children running back and forth. 'Sarah's with her now, helping her get dressed for her meeting with David Dashwood. I'm supposed to be getting milk so I thought I'd take the opportunity to send the article from up here.'

'I'd wait and see what Evelyn says after she's talked to David.' Tom looked down onto the sand and smiled. 'I came up to spy on Tilly before I set off for my house calls. I wanted to make sure she was happier at school today.' Bethan could see Tilly amongst the children, her plaits flying out behind her as she drew a long line for the dragon's tail.

'Is Tilly OK about the pictures now?' Bethan asked. 'It was heartbreaking to see her trying to scrub away the paint.'

'I think she finally understands that they were just paintings done by an American airman in the war,' said Tom. 'Having those photographs that David took helps. Thank goodness you had those to give her yesterday.'

'At least she can still see the pictures,' said Bethan. 'And I hope she understands that they were part of local history rather than anything more ethereal.'

'I think she finally does. Now she wants to know all about the Americans.' Tom smiled. 'She's fascinated with the idea that they gave chocolate and chewing gum to the local children when they'd had nothing like that for years.'

'I wonder if there's anything on the internet about the airbase?'

'There must be something,' said Tom. 'I should have a look sometime.'

'No time like the present.' Bethan held up her phone. 'What shall I try?'

'What about US Air Force Squadrons – UK – World War Two?'

Tom had one eye on the beach, watching Tilly running back and forth with a stick, making patterns on the dragon's wings.

After some time pouring down lists of British airbases, Bethan found the name of a US Air Force unit based near to Aberseren on Anglesey.

'I'm going to put in the name of the unit and aircraft crashes in Snowdonia,' she said, shifting to a more comfortable position on the rough stone wall. 'There might be something about *The Lady Bountiful*, there might even be something about Jack.'

Very quickly a picture of the crash site on the mountain appeared and various articles describing a crash in bad weather in December 1943. It seemed that two airmen were flying the plane to another US airbase in England. The pilot had misjudged the height of the mountain in the fog. There was no mention of who the pilot and co-pilot had been, though one article did say that the co-pilot had survived.

'Now try the unit name and a list of aircraft crashes over Europe in World War Two,' Tom suggested. 'They might mention Jack's plane going down.'

The list of lost planes seemed endless.

'So many planes,' said Bethan sadly. 'So many lives.'

'Add 1944.'

Again the list was very long.

'What about if I try typing in *The Lady Evie*?' Bethan typed the name into her phone. 'Bingo!' She smiled at Tom and began to read out loud, '*The Lady Evie* was a Boeing B-17G Flying Fortress in World War Two. She came down over Belgium on 17 December 1944.' Bethan bit her lip. 'That's all it says. Hang on – let's look at images. Someone might have taken a picture of the plane.'

Tom didn't answer; he was looking down at the beach. The schoolchildren were lining up, getting ready to go back to the school.

'Look at this.' Bethan shuffled along the wall so that she was closer to Tom. 'It's *The Lady Evie* having her nose painted!' She pointed at the screen. 'And look who it says the man who's doing the painting is.'

Tom took the phone from Bethan's hand.

'Lieutenant Giacomo Valentine. Giacomo?'

'Didn't Evelyn say Jack's family was Italian. I bet that Jack is short for Giacomo.' Bethan took back the phone. 'He's so handsome. Look at that smile!'

'Let's put Giacomo Valentine into a list of US airmen killed in the war,' said Tom.

After a few minutes of searching Bethan shook her head.

'I can't see his name coming up.'

'Put in Jack Valentine.'

Bethan typed in the name then scrolled down the list of results.

'Anything?' Tom asked.

Bethan blinked. She checked she'd spelled his name correctly. Her mouth fell open.

'What is it?'

Bethan handed Tom the phone.

'You'd better see this for yourself.'

EVELYN

David Dashwood looked terrible. He hadn't shaved. His eyes were bloodshot and smudged with dark shadows; his skin had a yellow tinge instead of its usual golden glow.

'I don't know what to say.' His voice was low. 'I feel ashamed.'

Evelyn looked at him from across the garden table that Bethan and Sarah had set out underneath the magnolia tree. There was a peacock perched on one of the branches, its beady eyes were on David's face, as though it were sitting on a jury, waiting for the accused to start his defence.

Evelyn stared at his face too. For the first time she noticed that his features bore a similarity to the portraits of the Vaughan's that lined the stairs and corridors in the house. The long line of his nose, the almond-shaped eyes. But the genes of other families had diluted David's features. Maybe Loretta had given him the high cheek-bones and the beguiling smile. Maybe David's grandfather had gifted him those startling blue eyes, and his own father could have given him the thick blond hair and athletic physique. Somewhere along the way, David had acquired an abundance of charm, more than was usual for a boy whose mother had deserted him as a tod-dler and left him with his grandmother. Maybe the charm was in his genes as well.

Looking at him hunched in his chair, it seemed the charm had deserted him for the moment.

'I've fucked up,' he said. 'There's no other way to describe it, is there?'

Evelyn didn't answer. The peacock shifted on his branch, its feathers rustling amongst the pale pink flowers.

'Thank you for agreeing to see me,' David continued. 'And thank you for not bringing charges against me, or the boys.' His head hung low, his hair looked dull and ashen. After a few moments he looked up at Evelyn. 'I expect you have questions you want to ask.'

There were so many questions she wanted to ask but none of them would form properly in her head.

'It's such a shame about the lion,' she said.

David looked up towards the house, even though from where they sat it was impossible to see the portico.

'I know, the boys went too far. I told them just to throw gravel at the windows. I always meant to get the lion repaired, and the windows.'

'When the house became yours?' Evelyn raised her eyebrows.

David ran his hands through his hair.

'I'm so sorry. I know I should never have tried to frighten you into selling Vaughan Court.'

'You should have known that not much frightens me, especially not a couple of youths with a good aim. And you of all people should understand that is no way to conduct business.'

'I have no excuses.'

'You have your grandmother,' Evelyn said.

David nodded.

'It's true I wanted the house for her, it was what she'd always wanted.'

'I can't really imagine why anyone would want such a draughty old pile. Do you have any idea how much it costs to heat, let alone maintain?'

'It was what it symbolises. To Grandma, it's her inheritance.'

'Your inheritance too? The last male Vaughan? The rightful heir? I suppose that's how she sees it.'

Bethan appeared with a tray of tea. She put it down on the table and started distributing the cups and saucers.

'I see Bethan doesn't deem you worthy of a biscuit,' Evelyn said, looking pointedly at David.

'Sorry, Evelyn, shall I get the shortbread?' Bethan said as she poured the tea into the cups.

'No, no. This is quite adequate.' Evelyn picked up a teaspoon and began to stir her tea. 'Are you joining us, Bethan?'

The girl shook her head.

'I have things to do.'

Evelyn noticed that she didn't look at David.

'You led her on, I even suspect you seduced her,' Evelyn said as Bethan disappeared back up the steps. 'That, to my mind, is worse than the stones.'

David shook his head.

'I really did like her. I do like her. She's a lovely girl.'

'Well, by all accounts you have your hands full with Chantal, and I suspect Bethan is already over you in the same way she seems to be over that other awful man, Malcolm.'

David was silent. Evelyn picked up her teacup and sipped her tea.

'Tell me more about your grandmother,' she said. 'Start with her age so I can figure out just when the affair between Loretta and my husband started.'

David looked up into the magnolia tree as though he were counting in his head.

'Let me think, she was seventy-eight on her birthday last month. So she was born in 1938.'

1938. The date kept repeating in Evelyn's mind, long after David had gone. 1938. Four years before Evelyn had met Howard in 1942. Before he had joined up, before Dunkirk, before the business dealings with Sir Nigel Overly had gone so wrong. Evelyn tried to take it in. When she had married Howard, he already had a mistress and a child. She closed her eyes, trying to contain the fury that had bubbled inside her. Why hadn't Howard just married Loretta?

Evelyn knew the answer. Lady Vaughan would never have let her son marry a nightclub singer, even if that woman had born Lady Vaughan her first grandchild.

David had told Evelyn that when the war started, Margaret had been sent to Loretta's sister in the Peak District. Her aunt used to tell the little girl all about the big house in Wales, by the sea. She'd told Margaret that it really should be her house, that Howard should have married Loretta and made her a Lady, and that Margaret should be living in the beautiful rooms with a large garden to play in, and servants bringing her everything she could ever want.

After the war her aunt had brought Margaret to Aberseren on the train. They had climbed the hill and looked up the long drive. Margaret had told David she had seen the twisting chimneys through the trees and thought that they looked like the sort of chimneys that would belong to a princess's palace.

Evelyn sat in the garden for a long time, thinking about Margaret.

A lifetime of longing, a lifetime of feeling you were entitled to someone else's life.

David had told Evelyn that his grandmother had scrapbooks, full of articles about Evelyn and her life. Sometimes magazines printed pictures of Vaughan Court; more than once it had appeared in *Homes & Gardens*. Margaret had it all, neatly pasted onto sugar paper pages. David said that she looked at the scrapbooks every day.

'It keeps her alive,' he'd said. 'It's the only connection she has with her past. Her aunt died when she was fifteen. After that she had no family. No mother, no siblings. Only a father who never replied to the letters she sent him.'

Margaret hadn't known she had a brother. She hadn't known about Robert.

Her aunt had told her that there had been a baby who had been stillborn and that Loretta had died a few days later as a result of complications with the birth.

Evelyn wondered what Margaret's aunt had known. She must have been told about the suicide, but maybe she really hadn't known the baby had lived. Evelyn had scooped him up and brought him back to Vaughan Court that evening of VE Day. It would have been up to Howard to inform Loretta's sister of the baby's whereabouts.

Evelyn looked across the knot garden at the low maze of hedges, the fountain, the flowers, the lawn and trees beyond. It *had* been Loretta's child who had enjoyed Vaughan Court. For fifty years

Robert had loved it all; always the child in the big garden, never growing up.

Evelyn closed her eyes. So many secrets; it was as though a dam had burst. Decades of them cascading out. All her fears. Evelyn had always imagined that her secrets would pour into a raging river of anger and resentment. Instead it seemed as if they were tumbling into a clear, calm pool of truth.

She heard a noise beside her and opened her eyes.

'I thought you were asleep,' Bethan said.

'Of course I wasn't,' Evelyn tutted. 'Merely resting my eyes.'

'I think you need to come inside.' Bethan's voice was gentle. 'Tom and Tilly are coming to see us. And Tom and I have something very important we want to tell you.'

BETHAN

As Bethan helped Evelyn slowly back up the steps towards the house, she felt a knot of nervousness building in her stomach. She hoped what she and Tom had discovered wasn't going to be too much for the elderly woman to take in.

Tom had phoned to say he'd already had an answer to the email he'd sent at lunchtime.

Bethan and Tom had talked for over half an hour, until Owen had reminded Tom that the afternoon surgery was about to start. But by that point they had decided what would have to happen. They had decided that Evelyn really had to know.

'What's up with you?' Evelyn asked as they reached the terrace. 'Not moping over Mal, I hope? Or David Dashwood? Scoundrels, the both of them!'

'No,' Bethan said firmly. 'I'm not moping. I'm definitely not moping over Cockwomble Malcolm.'

'A little bit over Mr Dashwood?'

Bethan made a face.

'I can't help thinking it's like one of your novels,' she said. 'Born the grandson of a humble B&B landlady yet turns out to be a Lord. What would happen next if you were writing it?'

'He'd scoop you up and marry you, I suppose, though in theory he is the rogue, so you should be scooped up by someone much more reputable. I'm afraid in my experience reality has always been more complicated than fiction. Stick to fantasy – that's always been my policy. Forget real-life romance, it's much too messy.'

'Don't worry,' Bethan said. 'I don't think I'm going to let myself be swept off my feet by David Dashwood again.'

'He is a surprisingly handsome man,' said Evelyn. 'For a Vaughan. Though a little on the dishevelled side today.'

'He had just come from a police cell.'

Evelyn stopped to catch her breath. She leant against the balustrade.

'Do you think Sergeant Williams will ever forgive me for asking him to drop the charges?'

'I felt sorry for him,' sighed Bethan. 'He'd worked so hard on the investigation, and he was so pleased with his midnight stakeout success. "I apprehended the culprits red-handed,"' Bethan mimicked Sergeant Williams' serious voice. 'When I phoned this morning to say you didn't want David to be prosecuted, I thought he was going to cry. He told me he thought it was going to be his career-defining case!'

'Well, he'll just have to wait for some mafia gang to set up their headquarters in Aberseren, or for Olwyn to decide to start a marijuana farm in the back of her shop.'

Bethan laughed. 'I love that idea, I bet Olwyn would be great at getting a good price for her stash. Maybe she would give up trying to con children like Tilly with her lollipos.'

'Poor little Tilly.' Evelyn glanced over the balustrade towards the arches below. 'Imagine trying to scrub off all that paint, I do hope she's feeling better today.'

'Much better. You can see for yourself, I think I can hear her and Tom coming.'

Both women turned towards the sound of the Volvo coming up the drive.

Evelyn straightened.

'What is this important thing that you and Tom want to tell me?'

'It's something rather wonderful.' Bethan linked her arm through Evelyn's. 'In fact, it's not just wonderful – it's a miracle.'

310

EVELYN

They'd sat her down in the drawing room, fussing over her with a blanket and a cup of tea. Tom had a sheaf of papers in his hand.

'We've got something that we want to tell you.' Bethan had come to sit on the arm of her chair.

'Yes, you've said that already.' Evelyn had waved her arm. 'Just get on with it.'

Bethan and Tom had exchanged a glance, they had serious expressions on their faces, neither of them seemed to know how to start. In the end it had been Tilly who had blurted it out.

'The man who painted the ladies on the wall is alive.'

Evelyn hadn't heard anything else for quite some time. She was aware of voices, of Tom and Bethan talking, of Tilly being told to go outside to play. Then she was aware of Tom laying out pictures on the coffee table. Paintings, lots of paintings, of people, some of the people she recognised. Actors and politicians, a man that had walked on the moon. But everything was distorted. She was listening under water, seeing through a murky pool.

'Sorry,' she said. 'I just don't understand.'

'Jack painted these,' said Tom, gesturing to the pictures.

'He's a very famous portrait painter in the United States,' added Bethan.

'Jack,' Evelyn said. 'Jack who?'

Bethan had put her arm around her.

'Haven't you heard what we've been saying?'

'No,' said Evelyn. 'You'll have to tell me everything again.'

Jack was alive.

Bethan had said it was a miracle.

'I don't believe in bloody miracles,' Evelyn muttered to herself as she lay in bed trying to remember what they'd told her. 'I don't believe in miracles at all.'

Jack hadn't died when his plane crashed that December night; he'd been taken captive. Marched for hundreds of miles and put into a camp, half starved, beaten for trying to dig a tunnel.

When the allies found him, he'd been very ill. He'd been in hospital for a year.

When he recovered he hadn't gone to serve ice creams in Mankato, he'd made a career as a painter. For decades he'd been alive; breathing, sleeping, eating, drinking, working, walking, driving, watching seasons change. Without her.

Evelyn took a deep breath as the pain seared through her.

Why had he never got in touch?

Why had he left her here?

'Why didn't you come?'

Evelyn said the words into the dark room for the hundredth time. 'Why didn't you come?'

She could see a thin sliver of light between the curtains. She didn't think she'd slept all night.

Tom would be arriving at ten o'clock. They'd be going to the bungalow next door to the surgery. Evelyn hadn't been there since Peter had been dying. She'd gone every day then. Taking him little treats, Fry's Chocolate Cream had been his favourite. She'd sat with him for hours while Sarah was at work. Only once they talked about the past.

'Do you ever think of him?' Peter had asked. 'Do you ever think of Jack?'

Evelyn had been startled. She had stood up and straightened the covers on the bed.

'It was all such a long time ago,' she'd said.

'It seems like yesterday,' Peter had replied, and Evelyn had sat down at his side again and admitted that it seemed like yesterday to her as well.

312

'He's always there,' she'd said. 'I try to push him away, but he's always with me in my mind.'

Now he was going to be there. Alive. In that bungalow, on some confounded screen.

'No, no, no,' Evelyn shouted. 'I can't do it. I don't want to.'

'What is it?'

The door opened and Bethan rushed in.

'I don't want to see him.' Evelyn was struggling to sit up. 'I don't want to see Jack Valentine.'

'It's OK,' Bethan soothed. 'It's just a little video his niece made. Tom says it's very touching. On his big computer screen you'll be able to see it properly. Tom says you'll be delighted.'

'Delighted?' Evelyn sat up straight. 'How can I be delighted? All these years! All these bloody wasted years!! You don't understand! You don't understand at all!'

Bethan came to sit on the edge of the bed. In the gloomy darkness she took Evelyn's hand.

'I know it must be a surprise.'

'Surprise! That's a bloody understatement! Why did you go poking around – like a couple of amateur detectives? It must have taken you ages; surely Tom, at least, has better things to do.'

'It was quite easy on the internet.'

'But I didn't ask you to find him.' Evelyn was determined not to start crying.

'But when we did find him we thought you ought to know the truth.'

Evelyn could feel the tears slipping down her cheeks.

'To know that all these years I've been locked up in this house, he's been out there, in the world, alive. As free as a bird.'

'Oh, Evelyn. You haven't been locked up here.'

'I have. I could never leave. I had Howard, and Robert, and my writing, and the charity and the school and all the bills. And I had my hope that one day he'd appear.' Evelyn brushed away a tear with the tips of her fingers. 'I never wanted to give that up.'

Bethan got up and drew the curtains. The soft light of the early morning flooded the room. Bethan fetched a tissue from a box beside the bed and gently wiped Evelyn's cheeks.

'Would you rather think that Jack was dead?'

'Yes.' Evelyn swallowed. 'Yes, I would. Now he is old, and I am old.' She put her hands to her wrinkled face. 'I'm not the girl he fell in love with. He can't be the man I knew.'

Bethan had left then.

'You'll feel better after some breakfast,' she'd said. 'I'll go and get you some.'

Evelyn put her head back against the pillows. As if a bit of toast and marmalade would help.

After Bethan had gone, Evelyn sat up and swung her legs out of the bed. With a racing heart she found the clothes she'd worn the night before and put them on, cursing at the buttons she couldn't do up without Bethan, the cardigan sleeve that refused to fit over her cast.

'What are you doing?' Bethan stood in the doorway with a breakfast tray.

'I want to go to Tom's,' Evelyn said, picking up a brush. 'I want to go immediately.'

'But it's half past six in the morning. He and Tilly will be fast asleep.'

'Phone him, wake him up.' Evelyn was trying to pull the brush through her hair. 'Tell him to come with his car.'

'But, Evelyn—'

'I have to see the film right now.' The brush fell out of Evelyn's hand onto the carpet. 'I have to see Jack Valentine.'

BETHAN

It was the first time she'd been inside Tom's bungalow. Bethan doubted it had been touched since his parents had built it as an extension of the surgery in the 1960s. It still seemed to be full of all the original furniture and fittings; a primary-coloured three-piece suite, large floral patterns on the curtains, geometric wallpaper. Everything was very bright.

The orange kitchen units were especially bright in the early-morning sunlight. The sun lit up the red and yellow wall tiles and glinted off the large starburst clock on the wall. There was a picture window overlooking a big garden and, in the distance, Bethan could just see the sea.

'I love your kitchen,' she said to Tilly, as the little girl showed her where to find coffee and sugar. In the living room, Tom was settling Evelyn in the Parker Knoll chair in front of the computer screen.

Tilly stood on a stool.

'This is where Daddy hides the biscuits.' She opened up a red-and-white-striped tin hidden in a top cupboard. 'Chocolate Hobnobs or custard creams?'

'I think Evelyn might need some chocolate,' said Bethan.

'Good,' said Tilly. 'Hobnobs are my favourite.'

The little girl was wearing pink gingham pyjamas; her hair was a river of golden waves where she had taken out her plaits. She carefully arranged the biscuits in a circle around a black-and-white plate, and then she sat down on the stool and started to eat one herself.

'Should you really be eating a Hobnob before breakfast?' Bethan asked.

Tilly put her finger to her lips.

'Don't tell my dad.'

'Don't tell me what?' Tom appeared in the doorway.

Bethan and Tilly exchanged a glance.

'That I've just spilt coffee all over your kitchen,' said Bethan.

It was true; she had just managed to drop a spoonful of ground coffee onto the Formica work surface as she aimed for the cafetière.

'Don't worry about that,' said Tom. 'As you can see it's not the tidiest of places.'

Bethan had already noticed the many piles that littered the surfaces. Piles of papers, piles of clothes, piles of Tilly's reading books, piles of Tilly's drawings which looked very good for an eight-year-old.

Tom opened a cupboard and took out a box of Weetabix. He handed it to Tilly.

'Cereal first, then a chocolate biscuit.'

Tilly rolled her eyes and slipped down from the stool to fetch a bowl.

'I think we're nearly ready.' Tom picked up the tray of coffee things. 'I've got it all set up. Evelyn is a bit nervous.'

'I know,' Bethan said. 'I thought she was going to refuse to watch it at all.'

'We've given her a shock,' Tom said.

'She's spent so many years pushing the past away, blaming herself for things that were not her fault.' Bethan started to follow Tom through the door.

'Hopefully Jack's words will help her get some sort of closure.'

After Tom and Bethan had discovered Jack was still alive it had been so easy to find out more. On Wikipedia they read that Jack had gone to Art College in Minnesota, and after graduating he'd spent years living in an artists' community in Upstate New York. This was where he'd honed his skills and started to gain a reputation as a portrait painter. He'd moved back to Minnesota in the 1980s and lived

316

in a cedar-clad house, which also served as his studio. The house was by a lake. They had found a picture of it, but they couldn't find a way of contacting Jack.

'Wikipedia said his father had owned an ice-cream parlour in Mankato and that it was still in the family. They had googled 'ice-cream parlour Mankato' and sent a long and rambling message from Tom's phone to the contact page of the first one on the list.

'I expect they were amazed.' Bethan held the old Bakelite receiver to her ear when Tom had phoned her later to tell her that he'd had a reply. 'They probably usually get orders for knickerbocker glories or banana splits.'

Tom laughed.

'Yes, but a woman called Mary says she's Tom's great-niece and that he's just celebrated his ninety-third birthday!'

'Wow!' Bethan exclaimed. 'It's amazing that he and Evelyn are both still alive.'

'Mary said she was going to drive over immediately to tell him about my message. She said that she, or one of his other nieces or great-nieces, visit him every day.'

'No children of his own then?'

'She didn't mention them. She implied that he lives by himself. *He's a tough old cookie*, that's the line she used.'

'He and Evelyn both!' Bethan laughed.

Mary had sent another email that afternoon with a short video attached.

'I think Evelyn will be delighted,' Tom said. 'After all these years she can finally see him again.'

Evelyn had forgotten her glasses. She insisted that there was absolutely no point in her looking at the video if she couldn't see the screen properly.

Tom drove back to the house to get the glasses while Evelyn, Bethan and Tilly waited in the living room. Bethan and Tilly sat on the sofa while Evelyn sat at the desk. Evelyn swivelled round to face Bethan.

'I've changed my mind,' she said. 'When Tom comes back I'm going to ask him to take me home.'

'Don't you want to see Jack?' Tilly asked. She was scraping the bottom of her cereal bowl with her spoon.

'No,' Evelyn said. 'I don't want to see him. In my mind he has been dead for seventy years. It will be like being confronted with a ghost.'

'Like the ladies coming out of the wall,' said Tilly.

'Yes, exactly.' Evelyn tapped her fingers against the edge of Tom's desk. 'He has materialised through time. And I don't want to see him again.'

'You want to paint him over?' Tilly asked the question while at the same time adding a spoonful of sugar from the sugar basin to her bowl. 'Like you painted over his ladies.'

Evelyn stopped tapping her fingers.

'That is an excellent analogy, Tilly. I want to paint him over. Like he never existed.'

'Maybe you need more time,' Bethan said gently. 'We could do this later. It could wait until tomorrow, even next week?'

'I don't need more time.' Evelyn stood up. 'I've decided. It's a ridiculous idea and I will not watch the silly film.'

'Well, I think that's sad.' Tilly put down her empty bowl. 'Because he looks like a nice man.'

'You've seen him?' Evelyn asked suspiciously. 'On this?' She gestured towards the large computer screen.

Tilly nodded and reached for a Hobnob.

'He has really smiley eyes, and white hair that is messy, and millions of wrinkles, and he says he's never stopped thinking about you, Evelyn, not even for one day.'

EVELYN

It was not Jack. It was an old man.

Evelyn peered a little closer at the screen. An old man frozen in time, one hand raised, his mouth slightly open. She knew that the old man was about to speak, if only Tom could make his confoundedly complicated machine work.

'Maybe the internet needs a reboot?' said Bethan.

'I've downloaded the video from Mary's email.' Tom was pressing lots of buttons on a keyboard in front of Evelyn. There was a little arrow that kept sliding around. 'It should just play.'

Evelyn studied the face in front of her. Tilly had been right, there were a million wrinkles. His face was very brown, as though he spent a lot of time outside beside the big lake she could see through the window behind him. And his hair was white, a dandelion fuzz that looked in need of a good cut, or maybe just a good comb. He had a neat grey beard that appeared to have far more attention paid to it than the hair, and he wore a crumpled denim shirt. Evelyn could see splodges of colour on the dark blue fabric; there were splodges of colour on his hands as well. She remembered that Jack's hands were always covered in paint. She tilted her head; this man's hands were gnarled and veined, age spots amongst the paint stains. How could they be Jack's?

'If I just try this,' Tom said, leaning across her and pressing some more buttons all at the same time.

Evelyn returned her gaze to the man's face.

His eyes were heavily lidded, but Tilly had been right – they

319

were smiley; they seemed to twinkle out at her. Evelyn felt a tiny glimmer of recognition.

'Why don't you do this, Daddy?' Tilly was beside Tom.

It was as though the features on the man's face were starting to shift in her mind, if not on the screen.

'It's OK, darling, leave it to me.'

Evelyn could see him. She could suddenly see him. There he was. Jack. It was as if all the years had fallen away and she could see the young man in the burning plane, the young man in the hospital bed, the young man in the candle-lit summer house.

'But, Daddy, look, if I do this . . .' Tilly was reaching across Evelyn now. And then Jack was moving. His hand lifted into a wave.

'Hi, Evelyn.' Jack's voice was so clear and strong. 'I never thought I'd ever get the chance to speak to you again, but here it is, here's my chance and I can't think of a darn thing to say.' He smiled and gave a little shrug. 'All I can do is tell you that I've never stopped thinking of you, not even for one day. You were the love of my life, Evelyn, my angel, my Wonder Woman.' He looked away and rubbed his hand across his eyes.

'Shall I stop filming, Uncle Jack?' It was a woman's voice.

'It's OK, Mary.' Jack looked back at the camera. 'Evelyn, I'd love to hear from you. I'd love to hear how you are, and what you're doing. Do you remember how we used to dance to Frank Sinatra and Perry Como? Do you still like to dance, Evelyn? Though, if you're like me you're probably a bit creakier than you used to be. I know you write books. Please write to me.' He paused. 'I've missed you.' He looked away again. 'You can stop filming now, Mary.'

The screen went blank.

'Do you want to send a reply?' asked Tom.

Evelyn looked at him. A reply? Her heart was beating very fast; she felt a stab of pain. Maybe this was it. The end. Killed off by Jack Valentine and his meaningless words.

'You probably need a bit of time to think about what you want to say,' said Bethan.

Evelyn took her glasses off.

'I know what I want to say,' she said.

'OK.' Tom was crouching down beside her, fingers hovering over the keyboard. 'I can put it in an email to Mary.'

Evelyn shifted in the seat. The leather creaked. Tilly surreptitiously took another Hobnob from the plate.

'Hang on,' Tom said, standing up. 'Maybe if I write it all down on paper first, it might be easier than trying to type across you.'

'It won't be a long message,' said Evelyn. 'Just one sentence.'

'Only one,' said Bethan. 'Are you sure?'

Evelyn sniffed.

'It may technically be two. But I only have one thing to say to him.'

'OK,' said Tom hesitantly. 'What is it?'

'Why did you never come back? You fucking bastard.'

BETHAN

'Well, I sent it.' Tom leant against the Aga holding a mug of tea in his hands. 'Goodness knows what Mary will think, let alone Jack.'

'It was such a lovely message that he sent to Evelyn,' said Bethan, sitting down at the kitchen table with her own mug. 'I don't know if that will be the response he was expecting, though I can see why Evelyn is upset.' Bethan took a sip of her tea. 'All those years when they could have been together; no wonder she feels angry.'

'Tilly has been saying "fucking bastard" under her breath all day.' Tom gave a grim smile. 'I've had to tell her that it's not appropriate language, even if Lady Evelyn Vaughan did say it.'

'Where's Tilly now?'

'She and Sarah have gone to Caernarfon to look for sandals. Tilly needs some for the summer.'

'I've only ever seen her in wellington boots.'

Tom rolled his eyes.

'She'd sleep in them if I let her. She's been mad about them ever since she learned to walk. Alice and I used to call her the Wellington Boot Kid.'

Bethan glanced at Tom. It was the first time she'd heard him mention his wife's name.

'Have you heard from David Dashwood?' Tom asked before Bethan could say anything else.

Bethan shook her head.

'Nothing. But Evelyn asked me to take him a picture of Robert so that he could show his grandmother the brother she never knew.

I think I'll just post it through the letterbox of the golf club instead of having to talk to him myself. I'm not sure I can face his apologies or smarmy excuses, he can save them for Chantal.'

'Are you upset?'

Bethan shook her head again.

'It was nothing much anyway. Just a silly fling.'

'What about your boyfriend in London?'

'I'm completely over him. In fact, I think I'm completely over all men.'

'Good,' Tom said. He raised his mug, then stopped. 'I mean, that sounds sensible. To take a break from men.' He put his mug down on the Aga.

'And you?' Bethan began tentatively. 'Are you taking a break?'

'From men?' Tom raised his eyebrows. 'I leave that sort of thing to Owen and Sergeant Williams. There's only so many gay men one Welsh village has room for.'

Bethan laughed.

'I mean from women.'

Tom looked down at his feet; there was a long pause.

'I think I've turned into one of those grumpy middle-aged men before my time.' Tom drained his mug, and shrugged. 'I don't think I'd be much good to any woman.'

Bethan stood up to pour more tea for both of them. 'Do you think your wife would have wanted you to be on your own for ever?'

Tom sighed as he held his mug out to Bethan.

'I don't know what she'd want, the last conversation we had she told me I was selfish, more committed to my work than to her or the girls.'

'Oh.' Bethan sat back down. 'That's hard.'

'It wasn't really a conversation, it was more of an argument, and I think she had a point; I was . . .' Tom paused.

'You don't have to tell me.' Bethan cradled her mug.

'I want to tell you. I never talk about it to anyone. I was a work-aholic in those days. I didn't prioritise my family, and now I feel responsible for Alice and Megan's deaths.'

'How could it be your fault? It was a terrorist attack.'

Tom ran his hands through his hair.

'Usually we all went swimming on a Sunday morning, I always drove Alice and the girls to the leisure centre. It was a family thing. I helped Tilly practise her swimming while Alice played in the baby pool with Megan, then we all went to Pizza Express for lunch. But that day I'd arranged to go into the hospital. I had a research paper to finish, I wanted to make my name as an expert in paediatric brain injuries. At that time, I was thinking of nothing else. Tilly had been at a sleepover, I knew Alice could manage with Megan at the pool on her own, I saw it as my opportunity to go into work. Alice was furious. I'd promised her we'd be going swimming as usual. We had an argument the night before. We went to bed in a rage with each other and I left the house at dawn, drove in early to avoid the traffic. I didn't even text Alice to apologise.'

'Oh Tom, I don't think you should blame yourself.'

'But I do. I should have been with Alice and Megan. They should never have been on that pavement when the van mounted the kerb. I should at least have left the car so that Alice could drive to the swimming pool.' Tom sighed. 'I never finished that paper, I gave up my job at Great Ormond Street, I couldn't bear to be in our house in Wimbledon. I just kept remembering our argument, my selfish behaviour.'

'Is that why you came back here?' Bethan said softly.

Tom nodded.

'I figured it would be the best thing. To take over my father's General Practice and look after Tilly as well as I could, though God knows what Alice would think of my attempts at that.'

'It seems to me that you're doing a great job,' Bethan smiled. 'You make time for her, you help her with her problems at school. Anyone can see how much you love her.'

'Love doesn't bring her mother or her sister back. And I can never tell her what really happened. She thinks her mum got knocked down accidentally, I don't want her to know how evil someone could be.'

'Maybe you should tell her,' Bethan said softly. 'I think she suspects you're not telling her everything.'

325

Tom took a step away from the Aga, abruptly changing the subject.

'I'm going to check on Evelyn. And then I'm going home to make the dinner for Tilly. Sarah will be bringing her back from Caernarfon soon.'

'You shouldn't be so hard on yourself.' Bethan watched him cross the kitchen.

'I've probably burdened you with far too much.' Tom was already at the foot of the stairs. 'The last thing you need to hear is my sob story.'

'No, not at all,' Bethan replied, but Tom had disappeared, taking the steps two at a time as though he couldn't wait to escape from the heart-breaking words that still seemed to fill the air.

'It's so sad,' said Bethan, handing Evelyn a fork. 'To lose your wife is bad enough, but your baby daughter too.' Bethan put a plate on Evelyn's lap.

Evelyn started prodding at the little bits of cut-up salmon.

'Where did this come from?'

'I found it in the freezer.'

'I can't eat it.'

'Oh dear,' Bethan grimaced. 'Has it been in the freezer for decades?'

'No. I'm feeling ill.'

Bethan put her plate down on the coffee table.

'What is it? Is it your head again?'

'No. It's my heart. It's painful. I think it's the condition they told me that I have at the hospital.'

'The atrial fibrillation?' Bethan asked.

'Yes, that's it. It's getting worse.'

Bethan stood up.

'I'd better phone Tom.'

'There's nothing he can do. I know I'm dying.' Evelyn let the fork fall onto the plate. 'The pain has been getting worse all day.'

'Then I'd better phone an ambulance.' Bethan's finger was already inserted into the number 9 on the circular dial.

Evelyn picked up the fork again.

'Don't you dare.' She started gesticulating with the fork at Bethan. 'Or I shall throw this at you.'

Bethan stopped dialling the emergency number.

'If you have pains in your chest you need to go to hospital.'

'I'm not going back there, and I'm definitely not going to die there!'

Bethan pursed her lips.

'So, what shall I do? Sit back down and finish my supper?'

'Yes, and I shall sit here and expire. You can put the television on if you don't want to watch me.'

Bethan almost laughed.

'I'm going to phone Tom.' She turned back to the phone. 'He can phone the ambulance if he thinks it's necessary.'

After a brief conversation, Bethan put the receiver down and walked back across the drawing room to Evelyn.

'He says he's coming to see you. He'll just wait for Sarah to look after Tilly and then he'll be here.'

Bethan took the plate from Evelyn's lap and put it down on the coffee table beside her own unfinished meal.

They sat in silence for a while.

Evelyn picked at a bit of fluff on her trousers. Her legs were crossed and one foot tapped impatiently in the air.

'Would you like a glass of water?' Bethan asked.

'No.'

'Tea?'

'A little medicinal brandy would be nice,' said Evelyn.

'I'll leave that for Tom to prescribe.'

They fell back into silence.

Bethan noticed that Evelyn's cheeks were pink, her eyes looked bright; she didn't look like a woman who was about to die.

'Is the pain getting worse?' asked Bethan.

327

'Yes.'

'Would you like to lie down?'

'No.'

'Shall I get you a blanket?'

'No.'

'Maybe you should be in bed?'

'Stop treating me like a bloody child, Bethan. Shut up and let me die in peace.' Evelyn shifted in her seat. 'If you want to do something you can get me some Haribo. Not the plain ones, I want the fizzy ones that are coated in sugar. They're my favourites.'

Tom walked into the kitchen with his doctor's bag as Bethan was rummaging in Evelyn's special drawer.

'How is the patient?' he asked.

'Self-medicating on Tangfastics,' said Bethan, putting a handful of the sweets into a porcelain bowl. 'I can't help thinking she looks very well for someone who claims to be at death's door.'

Tom headed for the stairs.

'I'll check her over and if she is fine, I've got some news that I think might be a cure.'

EVELYN

Tom had printed out the email. He handed it to Evelyn.

'Whatever it is, I don't want it.' She pushed the piece of paper away; it floated silently onto the carpet at her feet.

'I think it might help those pains in your chest.' He was putting his instruments back into his bag, shutting the catches with a click.

'I told you. I am very ill.'

'I've conducted a thorough examination and unless you let me take you to hospital for further tests, as far as I can see you're in good health. Blood pressure, pulse, heart rate, breathing – all excellent. I'd say the medication is working and you're on fine form for your age.'

'But I have a pain. Right here.'

Evelyn touched her chest.

Tom crouched down in front of her and picked up the sheet of paper.

'I think this might be the way to ease it.'

Evelyn took the piece of A4 paper and held it in her hands. There was writing on both sides. Without her glasses it was just a sheet of blurry lines, like the thin black caterpillars that ate her nasturtium leaves in the summer.

'It's an email from Jack,' Tom said.

'I expect you want these.' Bethan was hovering beside the chair with her glasses.

'No, I don't. Take this thing away.' Evelyn waved the piece of paper at Bethan. 'Throw it in the fire and get rid of it.'

'If you do that I will go home and print out another one,' said Tom. He sat down on the sofa.

Bethan took the paper out of Evelyn's hand and sat down beside him.

'I'll read it out to you,' she said. 'I really think it's something you should hear.'

'You've read it?' Evelyn said.

'I had a skim through it while Tom was checking you over.'

'How dare you read my correspondence.' Evelyn raised her voice. 'Jack wrote those words for me.'

Bethan and Tom both nodded.

'Yes, he did,' said Tom.

'So, you should read them.' Bethan offered the piece of paper and the glasses back to Evelyn.

Evelyn waved her hand towards Bethan.

'You might as well read it out, seeing as you already know what it says. Anyway, I can't think of an explanation of his that will make me feel better at all!'

My Dear Evelyn,

Shall I take fucking bastard as a term of endearment? I'd like to.

Maybe there is no point in raking all this up after so many years but I want you to know what happened. I want you to know that I fought with every bit of strength I possessed to come back all those years ago.

That December night in 1944, The Lady Evie came under fire somewhere over the German border. She was hit in both engines and coming down fast. We had to bail out. I knew I had to get out of that plane as quickly as I could, for you, for us. I parachuted into a field. It was dark – I couldn't find the other guys. I set off on my own. There was only one place I was headed and that was back to you.

I spent a week walking – through forests, over endless frozen fields. I slept in barns and garden sheds by day and walked all night. One day I slept in a tree. It was so cold my eyes froze shut. I ate raw turnips

330

that I found in a pile on a road – that was all I had to survive, turnips and my love for you.

On day seven I walked slap-bang into a German encampment having their breakfast. I was taken prisoner and put on a cattle truck and sent to a camp near Austria. It wasn't too bad; at least there was some food, of sorts. I was there for three months. I thought you'd know where I was; I thought you'd have found out that I was a prisoner of war.

In February 1945 the Russians were coming from one side, the British from the other. The Germans evacuated us from the camp and forced us to march west – three hundred miles. My boots fell apart. I marched one hundred miles with bare feet in the snow. Anyone who grew too tired or lagged behind got shot. I knew I had to keep going, I had to keep walking. Every time I thought of giving up, I remembered your beautiful face, your embrace, your kisses, our little summer house.

Eventually we were put in another camp. I was weak by the time we got there – we'd hardly eaten on the march. I got typhoid. I was very ill. I don't remember the camp being liberated and I only have hazy memories of being taken back to the US on a troop ship.

When I got home to Mankato, I weighed 112 lbs. My mother and my sisters nursed me. I couldn't even walk to the bathroom without help. It was Christmas before I could walk down the street. I wrote to you, Evelyn. As soon as I could, I wrote you letters. Did you get them?

It was in the April of 1946 that I came back to England – I know I should say Wales. My family said I still wasn't strong enough but I had to see you, I had to know why you hadn't answered my letters.

I wrote to you to tell you I was coming. I thought you might be there to meet me at the train station. When you didn't come, I headed up to the house. It was when I passed the church that I saw you all. You, and that awful mother-in-law of yours, and the man in a wheelchair, and the baby in the christening gown. I watched from behind a yew tree at the gateway. I saw how tiny your baby was, knew that he wasn't mine. I saw you tenderly tucking the blanket around your husband's knees, and then you were laughing. Your husband took your hand and you bent to whisper something in his ear. You were smiling, the way you used to smile at me.

331

When the girl passed by I called to her. She didn't recognise me at first, God knows, I hardly recognised myself in those days. I told her my name and I could see she remembered me then. I asked after you and she told me you were looking after your injured husband. She said through nursing him back to health you'd found real love together. You'd had a baby. You were very happy. She said you had told her I was a wartime fling – a mistake, that it had meant nothing, just a way to pass the time.

I turned around and headed back down to the station. Six hours I waited on that platform for the next train. It was agony. The journey back to the US was numbed by whisky.

By the time I got back to Mankato I was determined to forget you.

I went to art college – then I moved to Upstate New York, helped set up an artists' commune. I suppose I became a bit of a hippie, before hippies were a thing. I started painting portraits, got quite good at it. Painted a president once – it's hanging in the White House.

I never married. Turns out forgetting you was harder than I thought. There were women, I can't deny that, but no one that I wanted to share my life with in the way I'd wanted to share my life with you, Evelyn. No one who touched my heart the way you did.

I never stopped dreaming – never stopped hoping that one day you would walk back into my life.

I saw you in a magazine, a whole article about your books. I found out that you'd be visiting New York. I went to the bookstore where you were signing copies. I bought your book – I queued up so you could sign it. It was a long queue. I had plenty of time to look at you. You were so beautiful, so perfect in a pale blue suit, your hair all done up. You'd grown into this sophisticated woman. I looked down at my paint-spattered hands, my shirt cuffs were frayed. There were two people ahead of me when I decided to leave. I still have the book. I treasure it.

I hope you've had a happy life. I hope what that girl told me was right – that you did find love with your husband, that you've been happy in that great big house.

I don't know what more to say. I had to let you know that I had come back to get you. I didn't forget, I've never forgotten.

Always and forever yours,

Jack Valentine.

P.S. Whatever happened to Perry and Penelope? Please write back, if only to tell me that?

Afterwards, Evelyn sipped the brandy Tom had finally allowed Bethan to give her, fury mounting inside. Only the fact that it was so late prevented her from telling Tom to take her to Olwyn's immediately, and if she had seen Olwyn she knew she would have had to be physically restrained from battering the old woman to death with her plaster casts.

Instead, Evelyn tried very hard to remember back to the day of Robert's christening. She'd never noticed anyone else in the churchyard, never noticed anyone watching as they gathered outside the church door waiting to go in for the service.

Robert had been fretful tied up in the long silk dress, and Howard had been exasperated by all the fuss. He had almost refused to go inside the church at all.

'Bloody waste of time.'

Evelyn had had to soothe him, tucking his blanket round his knees when he complained of the cold.

Lady Vaughan had been anxious about the tea.

'Have we got enough jam for vicar's scones? Did Nelli set out the best porcelain?'

Mrs Moggs had patted Lady Vaughan's hand.

'Don't worry, Your Ladyship. I haven't let you down.'

Evelyn remembered that Robert had been sick all over the christening gown. Lady Vaughan had been outraged and Nelli had run back to the house to fetch more clothes for him. Evelyn had started to laugh, she hadn't been able to stop. Howard had snatched her hand in his and reprimanded her; he'd said she was behaving like a ridiculous fool, and she had bent and whispered in his ear, standing up for herself for the very first time. Was that the tender scene Jack thought he saw?

And Olwyn? Where had Olwyn been? Watching with those little raisin eyes. Of course she would have been the one to notice a stranger.

Evelyn swallowed back her rage along with the brandy and, putting on her glasses, read the email one more time.

BETHAN

Bethan wondered for the hundredth time if this really was a good idea. She glanced back at Tom. He was helping Evelyn from the car.

'Knock on the door, Bethan,' Evelyn called as she shrugged away Tom's offer of a supportive arm. As she crossed the road she looked like a film star, in her long leopard coat and huge sunglasses.

Bethan tentatively knocked on the glass door of the shop. Evelyn and Tom came to stand beside her and Evelyn knocked herself, rapping with her plaster cast so hard that Bethan thought the glass might crack.

'Keep your hair on.' The voice on the other side of the door sounded husky.

There was the sound of a bolt being drawn back, a chain rattled; the door opened. Owen was standing in a short knitted dressing gown.

He looked at each of them in turn and rubbed his eyes.

'We've come to see your grandma,' said Tom. 'I know it's rather early for a Sunday.'

Owen glanced behind him.

'She's doing her online Bingo. Got her headphones on so I don't think she could hear the knocking.'

He turned around and took a few steps back into the shop.

'Mamgu,' he called as he disappeared into the musty darkness. 'Mamgu, you have visitors.'

After a few moments he returned to the door.

'She says can you come back later? She's on a live link and she thinks she might be just about to get a line.'

'For goodness sake!' Evelyn stepped over the threshold and took her sunglasses off, looking around the room.

'She's in the kitchen,' Owen said, nodding towards the back of the shop. 'But she doesn't like to be disturbed while she's playing.'

They could see Olwyn's broad back hunched over the work surface in front of the window; she was wearing a pair of ginormous headphones. Her legs dangled down from the high stool, thick brown stockings sagging round her ankles.

'Olwyn,' Tom called. 'I've brought someone to see you.'

There was no response from Olwyn.

'Mamgu,' Owen said as loudly as he could. 'Lady Evelyn is here.'

Still no response.

'This is ridiculous.' Evelyn reached over and pulled the headphones from Olwyn's head.

'Get away, Owen.' Olwyn batted her hands in the air. 'I was just about to win that game.' She turned around. 'Good God! Lady Evelyn, what are you doing here?'

'I've come to ask you why you thought you had the right to ruin my life.'

Olwyn slowly lowered herself from the stool and stood in front of Evelyn with her arms folded.

'If you've come to complain about the Glamorgan sausages I sold Nelli Evans's granddaughter last week,' she nodded at Bethan, 'I have a disclaimer by the door that any food poisoning is nothing to do with me.'

'I am not talking about the Glamorgan sausages! I am talking about Jack Valentine!'

'Jack Valentine?' Olwyn raised her pale eyebrows. '*Duw, duw,* now there's a blast from the past.'

'I think it's getting a bit crowded in here,' Tom said. 'Maybe we should move next door.'

Bethan nodded in agreement. The five of them were squeezed into the narrow galley kitchen, like sardines in a tin.

'Shall I go and flick the fire on, Mamgu?' Owen tried unsuccessfully to squeeze past Olwyn. 'We could offer Lady Evelyn the armchair to sit in?'

'That would be more comfortable, wouldn't it, Evelyn?' said Bethan.

But neither Evelyn nor Olwyn were listening.

'Why did you tell him those lies when you saw him at Robert's christening?' Evelyn's voice was raised. 'Why did you tell him I was happy? Why did you tell him that I'd said our affair was a mistake, a wartime fling?'

'Can someone explain what's going on,' Owen said. 'Who is this Jack Valentine?'

'He was the love of my life,' said Evelyn. 'And your grandmother sent him away. Though she'll probably say she can't remember.'

Olwyn raised herself up as far as her small height allowed, then she grabbed the earphones from Evelyn's hand and glared at her.

'Of course I remember.' Her voice sounded deliberately unhurried. 'I remember the christening like it was yesterday. My mother made the tea before we went to church; she let me cut the scones out myself. It was sunny, a day like today.' Olwyn gestured through the window into the garden, a tiny strip of blue sky was visible above a dilapidated fence. 'I remember that Robert got sick on the family christening gown and Nelli ran back up to the house to get a change of clothes. That was when I saw Jack Valentine; lurking in the shadows, snooping around, I reckoned he'd been watching for a while.'

'And then you decided to speak to him,' Evelyn said, her voice venomous. 'Tell him all those lies.'

Olwyn shook her head.

'I didn't say a word.'

'He says a girl spoke to him. Who else could it have been but you?'

'I've told you, Lady Evelyn, I didn't speak to him, but I saw who did.' She turned and jabbed a podgy finger towards Bethan. 'It was her grandmother, the high and mighty Nelli Evans herself.'

'Nelli?'

'Yes.' Olwyn nodded, a smug smile spread across her face. 'Jack Valentine stopped her as she went through the gate. Caught her by the arm. I could tell that even though he looked thinner she recognised him as well as I did. She looked shocked at first, and then she started talking. I couldn't hear what she was saying, but I do remember that whatever it was made him look like he'd been slapped across the face.'

Bethan sat beside Evelyn in the garden, the afternoon sun shone on the lush green hedging and Bethan noticed that tulips were coming out in the flower beds, their heads a myriad of pinks and purples.

The bundle of letters sat on Bethan's lap. It had taken Evelyn over two hours to read them all. Bethan sat quietly beside her, taking each letter from the old woman's hand as she finished it, slipping it back into its envelope and putting it to the bottom of the pile. Every now and then, Evelyn would read a sentence out loud or show her a sketch that Jack had added to the letter. Sometimes they were of his mother, or his sisters, or the bedroom he'd been confined to for months, but usually they were of Evelyn. Accurately drawn from memory, beautiful portraits of the girl he was begging to write back to him. More than once a tear had slipped down Evelyn's cheek and Bethan had reached over with a tissue to gently wipe it away.

There were over thirty letters. Olwyn had taken them from a drawer in the kitchen.

'I suppose you might as well have these.' She had thrust the bundle at Evelyn; they were tied together with a piece of wool. 'I found them in my mother's desk after she died. Don't know why I kept them.' She shrugged. 'I liked the American stamps more than anything.'

'It's so terribly sad,' Evelyn said as she handed the last letter to Bethan. 'I should have known that Mrs Moggs would have intercepted any post.'

Bethan looked down at the letter. It had been sent from London.

I'll be arriving at Aberseren station on the two o'clock train. I can't wait to see you, my darling, to tell you how much I still love you, how I want to spend my life with you, how I still believe we can find a way to be together. I have a hunch you may not be getting my letters. If I'm right, you won't get this one, but when I come I can explain everything.

*I long to take you in my arms and dance you away with me – into the
sunset, into our happy ever after.*

Bethan let the letter fall into her lap.

'Why did Granny do it? Why did she tell him you were happy
when she was the one person who knew how terribly unhappy you
really were?'

Evelyn pushed her glasses up onto her head and sighed.

'I've been thinking about that and I think I might know.'

Bethan looked at her.

'Can you tell me?'

'Nelli had been so devastated when Lloyd was killed; she'd
wanted to die herself. I had to stop her drowning herself.'

Bethan gasped.

'She was heartbroken,' Evelyn continued. 'When I thought that
Jack had died, I wanted to die too, and Nelli was the one to look
after me. We grew very close. I don't know what I would have done
without her and she often said she didn't know what she would have
done without me. We both cared for Peter, who was missing poor
Billy so very much, and when I found Robert and brought him here
we both shared the care of him. She was just as much a mother to
Robert as I was when he was little. He gave her purpose, a reason to
live. I think Nelli only let me teach her how to read so that she could
read stories to Robert. In that year after the war we became such
good friends, more like sisters. We shared everything. Our grief,
our pain, our joy at every little development Robert made. We also
had Howard to look after – we did that together too, which wasn't
easy – he was a very irritable invalid.

'I think when Nelli saw Jack at the church gate she must have
been frightened. She must have thought he'd take me far away from
her, and take Robert too, even Peter – she knew how much Peter
adored Jack. Then where would she have been? All by herself.
She was only semi-literate then, what kind of job could she have
got? She'd have had to stay on at Vaughan Court, with Mrs Moggs
in charge. She'd have been looking after Howard on her own,

attending to Lady Vaughan and her diminishing health.' Evelyn shook her head. 'How miserable she must have imagined her life would be.'

'So you think she was afraid Jack would take you, Robert and Peter away to the States and leave her behind?'

Evelyn nodded.

'She was protecting herself.'

Bethan was silent for a long time.

'If only she'd told you,' she said eventually. 'How different your life could have been.'

Evelyn reached out and patted Bethan's hand with the tips of her fingers.

'Look at all the things that have happened because she *didn't* tell me.' She smiled. 'My books, Oak Hill, Peter's career as a doctor, Tom, Tilly. You.'

Bethan smiled.

'That's a very generous way of looking at it.'

Evelyn tapped the pile of letters on Bethan's lap with her index finger.

'Think of all those years these were sitting in a drawer in that beastly little shop. It wasn't only Nelli's fault I didn't get to have a different life.'

'Maybe Nelli could have gone with you to America? She still could have learned to read and had an education. She could have married a man from Mankato, had children and grandchildren with him. Maybe there would have been an American version of me over there, a taller version, with lovely straight hair.'

Evelyn laughed. 'You are perfect just the way you are, you silly girl. But yes, she could have come with us, I've been thinking just the same, I would never have wanted to leave her behind.'

Bethan touched one of the little swallow earrings and thought about the hazy memories she had of her grandmother; her kindness and empathy, her warmth and compassion for everyone she met.

'I wonder if Granny felt guilty,' she said quietly. 'I wonder if she ever thought about telling you what she did?'

340

'We shall never know,' Evelyn sighed.

The two women fell into silence. In the distance the peacocks were calling to each other.

'Would you help me do something?' Evelyn said, turning to Bethan. 'Would you help me make a film?'

'A film?'

'Yes, on that phone thing of yours. Can you make a film of the peacocks that I can send to Jack? Show him all the offspring of Perry and Penelope.'

'Of course I can,' Bethan said. 'But what about you? Can I film you sending Jack a message?'

Evelyn put one hand up to her face.

'Oh, I don't think he'll want to see me. I'm not the lovely young woman he has in his mind.'

'Did he look old to you?' Bethan asked. 'When you saw him on the video?'

'At first, he looked ancient. But then, as I looked at him, the years began to fall away until all I could see was the incredibly handsome young man I used to know.'

'Well, there you are then. Don't you think it will be the same for Jack?'

'Maybe.' Evelyn pursed her lips. 'But I'll need time to prepare. I'll have to make an appointment at the hairdressers and get my nails painted.' She turned to Bethan. 'And will you do my makeup? And help me choose something really beautiful to wear? And could you use one of those clever filter things on the camera, that will make my wrinkles disappear?'

'I don't think you should try too hard.' Bethan watched a peacock stop in front of a small brown peahen and open up his tail into a shimmering fan. 'Remember how Jack was scared off when he saw you in the bookshop in New York; you were too glamorous, too polished. I think you should just be yourself, like you are now.'

'This isn't me!' Evelyn protested. 'I haven't even got my lipstick on.'

Bethan watched the peahen walk away with hardly a glance at the peacock's magnificent display.

341

'Maybe your clothes, and makeup, and perfect hair are like a suit of armour, protection against all the pain you've had in your life.'

'Bollocks!' Evelyn waved her hand dismissively. 'I like to look beautiful.'

'But you do look beautiful, Evelyn, just as you are.'

EVELYN

It was gone. Sent. It would be there already.

Bethan had sprinkled bird seed around Evelyn's chair so that the peacocks flocked together, delighted with their early dinner. Then Bethan had taken out her phone. She'd started with the view, panning across the bay, up to the mountain and then across the knot garden in front of them, before turning to the peacocks, lingering over their colourful feathers and elegant tails and then she had pointed the camera at Evelyn.

'OK,' she'd whispered. 'You can start now.'

Evelyn had looked straight at the top corner of the phone like Bethan had told her to do.

'Hello, Jack. You wanted to know what happened to Perry and Penelope? Well, as you can see, there are many peacocks now, all descendants of our original pair.' She stopped and looked away.

'Is that all you want to say?' Bethan asked.

'No, no. I want to tell him what happened.' Evelyn looked back at the camera again. 'I have so much I want to tell you, Jack, so many things I want to explain. I didn't know you were alive until two days ago. I didn't know you had survived the war. And I didn't realise you came back to find me and I didn't know anything about these.' Evelyn touched the letters in her lap. 'I've just read them, Jack. I've just read every one.' Evelyn paused and took a breath. 'I've spent so many years trying to push the memories away.' She paused again. 'I felt guilty. I felt ashamed. Billy died. He died on the mountain because Mrs Moggs found a letter I'd written to you. She found out the boys had been

343

acting as our postmen. She punished them and they ran away. Billy fell. It was all my fault. I lost our baby – I thought it was my punishment. And then I heard your plane had come down and I'd lost you too. Another punishment.' Evelyn took another breath and looked out towards the sea.

'Are you OK?' Bethan whispered.

Evelyn nodded and looked back at the phone.

'I have spent seventy years here, Jack, in this house that has never felt like my home. It was the only connection I had to that wonderful love we shared. So many years have passed. The war seems like another world. It's hard to imagine it now. This is where the hospital used to be.' Evelyn gestured around her. 'I restored the garden on the site when they pulled down the huts. There are roses where the wards were. Crimson Glory where your bed was, Jack, I've always given that rose extra care.'

Evelyn signalled to Bethan to turn the camera off.

'No goodbye?' asked Bethan.

Evelyn shook her head. She couldn't speak, she couldn't say any more.

Bethan had phoned Tom, and he and Tilly had driven up to the house and taken Evelyn and Bethan back to their bungalow so that they could email the video to Jack.

Evelyn had protested all the way down the drive.

'I wish you'd let me put my lipstick on, Bethan. I'm sure I look a terrible fright on the film.'

'You look beautiful,' Bethan said from the back of the car.

'You never told me I still had my bloody reading glasses on my head.'

'I didn't even notice, Evelyn, and I'm sure Jack won't care.'

'I don't like what I said,' Evelyn continued. 'I should have written the words down first.'

'You said it from the heart,' said Tom. 'It's much better that way.'

'I don't want you to send it. I'll do the film again, tomorrow.'

'The video is perfect,' Bethan said. 'The sooner it's sent, the sooner Jack gets a chance to answer.'

344

'That's what worries me,' muttered Evelyn. 'I think I'd rather have a bit more time before hearing his response.'

'Like another seventy years?' asked Tilly cheerfully. Tom and Bethan laughed.

'Yes, Tilly,' Evelyn said. 'Like another seventy years.'

Tom and Bethan were in the kitchen making a cup of tea and Tilly was trying to show Evelyn how to dress a unicorn as a fairy on the computer.

'You can have any of these wings.' Tilly leant across her to push her finger around the little square beneath the keypad. 'But not these, because they cost money and Daddy won't pay for them.'

'I see,' said Evelyn. She was trying to hear what Bethan and Tom were saying in the kitchen.

She could hear their low voices.

'I wonder what he'll say.'

'At least they both know that they never stopped thinking about each other.'

'Which ones?' asked Tilly. 'The sparkly blue ones or the golden ones that flash on and off?'

'Umm? The golden ones.'

'And what about a tiara? The pearly one or the diamonds?'

Something pinged on the computer screen. A rectangle appeared in the right-hand corner with the words 'Jack Valentine' and a picture of a postage stamp.

Evelyn let out a gasp.

'Shall I open it?' Tilly was moving the little arrow towards Jack's name.

'No, don't.' Evelyn's heart was beating fast. 'Just leave it until later.'

But it was too late, Tilly was already clicking on the email tab.

There were lots and lots of words. Evelyn no longer had her glasses on her head; she'd taken them off in horror when she'd realised she'd been wearing them in the video. She'd left them in the drawing room while she and Bethan had waited for Tom.

345

'What does he say?' she asked Tilly.

'I don't know,' said Tilly. 'I'm no good at reading.'

They both stared at the screen in silence.

'Can you try?' Evelyn said after a few moments.

Tilly shook her head.

'I don't think so.'

'What about just the first three words?'

Tilly shook her head again.

'Maybe for a packet of gummy bears when I next get to the shops?' Evelyn suggested.

Tilly let out a big sigh, but she stretched out her arm and put her finger on the first word in the screen.

'M . . . y . . .' she began to spell each letter out very slowly. 'D . . . a . . . r . . . l . . .'

'My darling?' prompted Evelyn.

'Yes, that's right,' Tilly nodded. 'My darling Ev . . .'

'Evelyn.'

'My darling Evelyn.'

'Well done, Tilly, that was very good. What about the next line?'

'You . . . look . . . so . . . be . . . tif . . .'

'Beautiful.'

'Beautiful,' Tilly repeated. 'Y . . . yo . . . you still l . . . oo . . . k just the sam . . .'

'You still look just the same.'

'Yes – you still look just the same.'

'You're doing so well, Tilly, can you try the next line?'

Tilly let out another sigh but she carried on.

'And s . . . e . . . see . . .'

'Seeing . . .'

'And seeing yo . . . you I rel . . . rel . . . is . . .'

'I realise.'

'I realise I still lo . . . v . . .'

'I realise I still love you.'

'Wit . . . th, with all . . . my h . . . e . . . art, heart! With all my heart.'

Tilly looked up from the screen with a huge smile. 'I read that bit on my own!' She stopped smiling. 'Why are you crying?'

Evelyn wiped her eyes with the tips of her fingers.

'I don't know, Tilly, they are just such lovely words and you've read them so very, very well. Thank you.'

A noise behind them made Evelyn turn her head. Tom and Bethan stood in the doorway watching. They were both smiling.

'Wonderful reading, Tilly,' said Bethan.

'I'm exhausted now!' Tilly flopped back in her chair.

'I'll print the email out in large print,' Tom said. 'And you can read the rest of it yourself, Evelyn, while we all have a cup of tea.'

Evelyn read the email for the hundredth time and finally let it fall back onto the quilt. Outside she could hear the peacocks calling even though it had been dark for at least two hours. It was as though the events of the day were keeping them awake, as though they were just as filled with excitement as Evelyn was.

Jack was coming. He was actually coming. He'd sent another email to say that Mary was coming too. They'd bought their tickets and would be here in a week.

Bethan opened the bedroom door.

'Have you got over the shock yet?'

Evelyn shook her head.

'I still can't believe it. Jack Valentine, coming here – my poor old brain is addled at the thought, and my heart is leaping around in my chest like a frog – I'm not sure if it's atrial fibrillation or anticipation.'

Bethan sat down on the edge of the bed.

'I expect you're a bit nervous.'

'I am, and I don't care what you say, I'm getting my hair done before he comes! And I'll be booking a facial and a manicure – Sarah will have to drive me to Caernarfon, and I've seen a rather lovely kimono-style jacket in *Vogue*, could you phone up the shop and order it, please? It will cover up these awful things.' Evelyn held up her plaster casts. 'If only they were going to be off by the time Jack comes, they make me feel so inelegant!'

347

'I'll order the jacket tomorrow,' Bethan said. 'And I'll ask Sarah when she's free and then I'll book the hairdresser and the beautician. And when Jack comes I'll do your makeup just as you want it, and I promise to tell you if you've left your glasses on your head.'

Evelyn reached out and touched Bethan's hand.

'You're a wonderful girl, Nelli would be so proud of you.'

Bethan smiled, then her face took on a serious expression.

'I've got something to tell you, Evelyn. Something that will make you rather sad.'

Evelyn frowned.

'Don't tell me you've realised Malcolm is the man to fulfil all your emotional needs and you've forgiven him and are returning to London post-haste?'

Bethan rolled her eyes.

'No!'

'Thank goodness for that. What is it then?'

'David Dashwood phoned, I've been talking to him.'

'And you've decided *he's* the man to fulfil your emotional needs – when he's not fulfilling Chantal's or using vandalism to acquire houses for which he has illegitimate claims?'

Bethan shook her head.

'No, surprisingly I've not decided that either.'

'So, what is it?'

'David and Chantal went to visit Margaret today in the care home.'

'Did they take the picture of Robert?'

'Yes, they took her the picture. David said Margaret was amazed to find she had a brother, but pleased, and she was glad to hear that he'd had a lovely life with you, in this house – it seemed to bring her comfort. For the first time in years she didn't mention how unfair it was that she had never been able to live at Vaughan Court.'

'I can send her more pictures, maybe David would bring her over one day for tea and I can tell her all about Robert? I have so many stories about him, and albums full of photographs, as you know.'

'Unfortunately, she won't be able to come for tea.' Bethan paused and bit her lip. 'David had a phone call when he got back from the visit. Margaret passed away this evening. The staff found her in her armchair in her room before dinner. She was holding the picture of Robert in her hand.'

BETHAN

Bethan cycled down the drive in the bright sunshine. Sarah had given her an old bicycle that she and Gwen had inherited with their cottage. It had Happy Shopper written on the side and a wicker basket on the front.

Bethan filled the basket with cleaning things; dusters, cloths, wood polish, a dustpan and brush, and a box of candles. She'd also put in some secateurs to cut back more of the brambles and rhododendron branches.

She stopped the bike with a gentle jolt and dismounted beside the path that led up to the summer house.

She took the secateurs out first, cutting through the undergrowth as she made her way towards the door. The lock was rusty. Bethan had to push the key and turn it with all her might. The hinges squeaked as the door finally opened; a shaft of sunlight spread out across the dusty floorboards as she walked inside.

'I think you should know I've seen the paintings in the summer house,' Bethan had said as she'd brought Evelyn her tablets the night before.

'The summer house!' Evelyn cried out. 'No one is meant to go there! That's why I've kept it locked up for over seventy years. I haven't been back there since the last night I spent there with Jack . . .' Evelyn's voice faltered. 'Sometimes I've thought I should get it torn down,' she went on quietly. 'But while the summer house was there I suppose I felt as though a little piece of Jack was still alive. Though I have always looked away as I pass it on the drive. I

351

didn't want to think of all that happiness, all that love. Everything that I'd lost.'

'David Dashwood showed me inside. I know we shouldn't have broken in.'

'No, you shouldn't!' Evelyn made a petulant face. 'That bloody man! I'll get in touch with Sergeant Williams and say I've changed my mind about the trespassing charge!'

Bethan took out her phone. 'I took some pictures,' she said gently and sat down on the edge of the bed. 'I presume the paintings on the wall were done by Jack.'

'I don't want to see them,' said Evelyn, but she was already reaching for the phone.

She took it from Bethan's hand and started to jab at the screen.

'How does this confounded thing work?'

Bethan leant over and showed her how to swipe her fingertip to see the photos.

Evelyn was silent as she peered closely at each picture in turn.

'It's just the same,' she said after a few minutes of swiping back and forth. 'Nothing has changed, it's just as we left it, I'm sure that record on the gramophone is Perry Como. And look at me.' She let out a laugh. 'Quite the blonde bombshell!'

'You were very beautiful.'

'I think I've been waiting,' Evelyn said. 'I've been waiting on those walls.'

'Like Tilly's ghosts under the terrace,' said Bethan.

Evelyn nodded.

'Would you like to see those paintings again? See that room?'

Evelyn handed Bethan back the phone.

'I think I would.' She let her head fall against the mound of pillows behind her. 'But I'll wait until Jack comes and then we'll go back there together.'

Bethan returned to the bike and fetched the cleaning things. She wished she'd been able to bring a vacuum cleaner but she doubted there was electricity and she knew she'd never have managed to carry Evelyn's ancient Electrolux all the way down the drive.

After she finished cleaning, she planned to go to the golf club. She had a card that Evelyn had dictated to her for David, words of condolence and a request to attend Margaret's funeral if David didn't mind.

While she was at the golf club, Bethan would use the WiFi to send an email to the editor of *Frank*, explain to her why the article about Evelyn was late, explain to her why she wasn't now going to send the article at all. And she also wanted to message her mother. She knew her mother would be delighted with Evelyn's suggestion, but Bethan still wasn't sure she'd be able to do it. A knot of anxiety twisted in her stomach but her heart skipped with excitement and her brain whirred with a hundred ideas for how to start.

Evelyn and Bethan had spoken over breakfast on the terrace. There was a chill in the morning air despite the sunshine, but Evelyn had insisted that they should have their tea and toast outside.

'If I have one more meal in bed I shall scream!'

Evelyn wore her long kimono dressing gown, with a woollen shawl draped over her shoulders and sheepskin boots.

Bethan had worn Evelyn's leopard coat and a floppy-brimmed felt hat.

'What do you want to do today?' she asked after they had finished their slices of toast and marmalade. 'Shall we get on with *For the Love of Hermione*? It's been days since we've worked on that.'

Evelyn took a sip of her tea and looked out towards the sea.

'You know, I've been thinking about *For the Love of Hermione*. I'm just not sure it's working.'

'The plot?' asked Bethan.

Evelyn made a face.

'The characters?' Bethan continued. 'That bit at the dance?'

'The whole bloody thing really.' Evelyn sighed. 'I'm just not sure it's really working for me.'

'I don't understand?'

'I'd thought that all these years of writing were about making money, but I've begun to realise that the writing was also fulfilling something else. I lived vicariously through all those duchesses and viscounts and lady's maids. I gave them my dreams and my desires so that I didn't have to pursue those things myself.'

'And now that has changed,' Bethan said. 'Now Jack is coming you don't need to escape into a made-up story, you have a real-life romance to experience yourself.'

Evelyn raised her eyebrows.

'Well, I wouldn't go that far.'

'You can't deny that he's travelling four thousand miles to see you—'

'Let's not get ahead of ourselves,' Evelyn interrupted. 'Jack and I are both extremely old, far too old for the giddiness and passion we experienced all those years ago.'

Bethan poured them both some more tea.

'Well, I think I could see a twinkle in Jack's eyes on that video.'

'I do not wish to speculate on the twinkliness in Jack's eyes, it might be a complication of cataracts, for all we know.' Evelyn sat back in the wicker chair and held the steaming cup between her fingertips. 'I'm simply saying that I'm finding it hard to focus on Hermione and Lord Melksham at the moment.'

Bethan stirred sugar into her tea.

'What about if you wrote a different story?'

'You mean start again with a new novel?'

'Yes.'

Evelyn shook her head.

'I really can't be bothered to come up with another storyline. And to be quite honest, I'm tired of all those muslin dresses, and ribbon-trimmed bonnets, and men galloping around the country-side on steaming horses. In my head I've been living in Regency England for far too long, I think it's time to start living in my own world before it's too late.'

'Exactly.' Bethan sipped her tea. 'You could write about *your* world. You could write *your* story.'

354

'I don't want to write a biography, Bethan, that sort of thing always strikes me as terribly vain.'

'Not a biography. I mean a novel. A romantic novel, about you and Jack. You could write about how you met, and how you fell in love against the backdrop of the war. You can write about your life as a young bride at Vaughan Court, and your unloving husband and your awful mother-in-law, and what happened when they built the military hospital, and what it was like when the Americans arrived. You could write about how you saved Jack from the burning plane, and how you met again when you were working as a nurse, and how you fell in love, and then how you thought he had died and you threw yourself into years of work and caring for another woman's child, and then how you discovered Jack was alive all these years later, and then . . .' Bethan stopped, breathless.

'And then what?' Evelyn raised her eyebrows.

'Well, we don't know what happens next, but by the time you get to the future you'll have finished with writing about the past.'

Bethan watched Evelyn as she gazed out across the view. She seemed to be focused on a large ship on the horizon, it was moving steadily across the sea.

Evelyn turned her attention back to Bethan.

'I don't want to write that story.' She put her cup down in the saucer with a clink.

'That's fair enough,' said Bethan. 'It's very personal. I can understand you don't want to share something so private.'

Bethan popped a final crumb of toast into her mouth.

'But you could,' said Evelyn.

Bethan looked up from the plate.

'I could what?'

'You could write that story,' Evelyn continued. 'You could write our story as a novel.'

'You think I could write your story?' Bethan shook her head. 'But I'm not, I can't . . . I don't think I could do that.' She stumbled over her words. 'I'm not a good enough writer, and how would I know what really happened?'

'You only need to base it on our story, you don't even need to use our real names. You can continue interviewing me as you did for the article – only now I have nothing to hide, so I promise to be more honest, and when Jack comes maybe he'd let you interview him too.'

Now it was Bethan's turn to stare out to sea. The ship had vanished; there was a little sailing boat skimming over the waves.

'I could give it a try, write a plan, maybe a few chapters.' She turned back to Evelyn. 'You could read them and see if you think it's worth me carrying on. It is the most romantic story I've ever heard.'

'That's what your grandmother said when Jack and I met again after I rescued him from the plane crash.' Evelyn reached out and patted Bethan's hand. 'And I think she would be very proud if she knew that her granddaughter was the one who was going to put it into words.'

Bethan stretched up with the feather duster to remove the last of the cobwebs from the corner of the room. She took a step back and gazed around her. It was so much cleaner than a few hours before; the layer of dust had vanished and the dead flies and spiders were all swept away. She hoped the room looked as though no time had passed since Evelyn and Jack had last been there.

She straightened the blanket on the bed, trying not to remember the moments of passion with David Dashwood. She still wondered if the summer house had cast some sort of seductive spell.

'Hello.'

Bethan jumped at the sound of the man's voice.

She turned to see Tom framed in the doorway.

'I saw the bike and thought you might be in here.' Tom took a step inside the room and looked around. 'I've always wondered what it's like in this cottage.' He stared at the walls. 'These paintings are amazing.'

'Evelyn wants to come back here when Jack arrives next week. I thought I'd give it a bit of a clean for them.' Bethan turned and brushed away a cobweb that she'd missed with the duster.

356

'Such a beautiful woman,' Tom said. Bethan turned back to him.

'I meant Evelyn.' Tom nodded towards the painting of Evelyn with the peacock feather.

'I didn't think you meant me.' Bethan gave a little laugh.

Tom looked at his watch.

'I was just on my way up to the house, to check on Evelyn's blood pressure after all the excitement.'

Bethan started to swipe the feather duster along the little mantelpiece, even though she'd already wiped it ten minutes before.

'Evelyn is in a very good mood today. Sarah's with her organising appointments with the hairdresser and the beautician in Caernarfon. And Evelyn has a pile of catalogues, she's determined to find a new pair of high-heeled shoes.'

'I'll go and join them.' Tom took a few steps back and stopped. Bethan glanced at him. He was wearing a pale blue linen jacket she hadn't seen before. She noticed how it complimented the threads of grey in his hair.

'Nice jacket,' she said.

Tom stroked the sleeve.

'Sarah and Tilly bought it for me on their shopping trip on Saturday. They tell me I need smartening up.'

'That's good,' said Bethan.

'You think I need smartening up?'

'Maybe a little.'

'I'll ask Sarah to book me in to the beautician as well,' Tom laughed. 'And what about some new high heels?'

He looked down at his scuffed leather brogues.

'Maybe just some socks that match?' Bethan suggested.

Tom looked at his watch again.

'I'd better go now.'

'OK,' Bethan said. 'Bye, Tom.'

'Bye.' Tom raised his hand in a wave.

Bethan bent down to start to gather up the cleaning things. It was a few more seconds before she heard Tom's footsteps on the wooden floor as he walked away. The room became very quiet, only a faint rustling came from outside. Bethan wasn't sure if it was Tom pushing his way through overhanging branches as he made his way down the path, or the peacock she knew wouldn't be far away.

Bethan was about to stand up when she saw something underneath the wrought-iron bed. She reached out and picked up a peacock feather, faded blue and green and gold. She wondered if it could be the same one that Evelyn was holding in the painting. She stood up and placed it gently on the blanket on the bed.

She heard more footsteps. Tom was back in the room.

'Look, Bethan. I'm not very good at these things.' Tom ran one hand through his hair. 'I didn't mean that you're not beautiful. When I said about the painting earlier.' He gestured to the wall again. 'Obviously I meant Evelyn, but . . .'

'It's OK.' Bethan stood up with the armful of polish and cloths. 'You don't need to explain.'

'But I think you are beautiful,' Tom said quietly. 'Very beautiful.'

There was an echoing clatter as Bethan lost her grip on a can of Mr Sheen. It rolled towards Tom, stopping at his feet.

Tom bent to pick it up. He straightened and looked directly at her.

'When I first saw you, standing in reception at the surgery, splattered with mud, soaked to the skin, panicking about Evelyn, I was blown away with how beautiful you looked.'

Bethan held the armful of cleaning cloths closer to her chest, she could feel the beating of her heart. She wondered again if the summer house really did cast some sort of spell on people.

'I haven't thought that about another woman for a very long time,' Tom continued. 'Not since . . .' He stopped. He took a breath. 'Not since my wife died.' He looked down at the can of polish in his hand. 'I felt disloyal to Alice. I think maybe that's why I came across as a little . . .'

'Rude?'

'I was going to say terse.'

'Maybe taciturn is a better word?'

'Well, whatever the word is, I'm sorry.' Tom appeared to be

studying the little white nozzle on the can of polish, twisting it in his fingers. 'It was only because I felt . . .'

'I understand,' said Bethan.

'You do?' He looked up at her.

Bethan nodded. There was a hissing sound and a puff of waxy polish atomised over Tom's jacket.

'Damn!' He looked down at the mark it had left. 'Sarah and Tilly will be furious.'

'Let me wipe it.' Bethan stepped towards him and started to rub at the linen with a cloth.

'Thank you,' Tom said.

'Don't thank me yet.' Bethan rubbed a little harder. 'I'm afraid it's not going to come off without going to the dry cleaners.'

'I don't mean for trying to clean my jacket.' Tom put his hand over hers. 'I mean thank you for everything you've done, for me.'

Bethan looked up at him, struck by how handsome his face was, just as she had been the first time she'd seen him.

'I haven't done anything.'

There was a noise behind them. They both turned to see a peacock standing in the doorway watching them. It took a step over the threshold.

Tom's hand was still on Bethan's. It felt strong and warm. He smiled down at her.

'I think Evelyn and Jack have helped to restore the faith I'd lost with the world. Good things do happen.'

'I never had you down as such a romantic, Dr Tom,' Bethan laughed.

'I'm not, I mean, I'm not usually romantic, or sentimental, or . . .' He paused.

'Lost for words?' Bethan suggested.

'No, I'm not usually lost for words at all.' He pressed her hand against his chest. 'But when I'm with you I . . .' He paused again. 'It's just that every time I'm with you all I want to do is . . .'

'Is it something like this?' Bethan asked. She reached up and gently kissed his mouth.

'Yes,' Tom whispered. 'It's exactly that.'

He pulled her closer to him, kissing her back, holding her against him. The smell of wax polish filled the air; Bethan's head spun. She wondered again about the little wooden house and its power to enchant. She succumbed to the feelings she realised had been there for days. Tom's arms felt strong around her, the touch of his hands seemed to be melting her heart.

The peacock let out a cry. They pulled away from each other to see the peacock's tail had become a shimmering fan, almost filling half the room.

'I think he approves,' Tom said with a smile.

'What about Tilly?' Bethan looked up into Tom's dark eyes. 'Will she approve?'

'She adores you, Bethan.' Tom stroked Bethan's face. 'And I took your advice.'

'My advice?'

'I told her the whole story. I told her what really happened to her mother and sister.'

'How did she take it?'

'She was pragmatic, thoughtful, sad that human beings could do that to other human beings. But she was relieved to finally understand what happened. And she hasn't had any nightmares since, which I think means it was the right thing to tell her the truth.'

'If there's one thing I've learnt in the last few weeks,' Bethan said, 'it's that the truth can make all the difference between a happy or an unhappy life.'

Tom put his arms around Bethan, drawing her back towards him.

'That's why I wanted to be honest with you. Honest about my feelings. I didn't want to waste any time pretending that I don't like you, very, very much.'

Tom bent to kiss Bethan again. The peacock let out another long cry, but this time Tom and Bethan didn't pull away from each other; they didn't even notice.

Three years later

Bethan took the dress off the hanger, relieved to see that the creases had fallen out over the course of the night. It had been one of Evelyn's favourites, pale pink Dior. It had been altered so that the hem wasn't quite so long and there was a little bit of extra fabric added to the back so that Bethan wouldn't have to breath in for the entire day. Evelyn had requested that everyone look colourful, so Bethan had a fuchsia peony made of silk to pin onto the dress, and a turquoise shawl.

'Are you sure this tie isn't too gaudy?' Tom appeared in the bathroom doorway. He was in the process of tying a pink and purple spotted tie.

'Evelyn said as cheerful as possible.' Bethan smiled. 'Tilly chose that for you herself, she said she reckoned it was just the sort of cheerfulness Evelyn meant.'

Tom sighed.

'It's just not very traditional. I'm used to these sorts of occasions being a bit more formal.'

'I don't think today is going to be very traditional, or formal.' Bethan walked over to Tom and adjusted the tie. 'But it will be a very special day. More about celebration than formality.' She reached up on her toes and kissed Tom, letting him pull her towards him, forgetting all about how easily the dress might crease again.

The door to the hotel room opened, and Tilly walked into the room.

'Do you two ever stop?' she said.

'You should learn to knock, young lady.' Tom reluctantly let Bethan step away from him.

'You look lovely.' Bethan smiled at Tilly.

'I didn't think black was allowed,' said Tom.

'I like black,' said Tilly, flopping down on the bed. 'And I'm going to wear my red suede jacket when we go to the church.'

Bethan sat down beside Tilly.

'Do you want me to do something with your hair?'

'I think I'll leave it loose.'

Tilly shook her head so that her hair fell in one wave down her back.

'I could put it in plaits,' Tom offered.

'I'm nearly twelve, Dad! I do not want my hair in plaits, I haven't had plaits for years.'

Bethan and Tom exchanged a smile. Tilly was growing up so fast. She was tall too, taller than Bethan already. Since she'd started at her new school, her confidence had grown as well. She had the advantage on the other pupils as she knew the building so well, even though many changes had been made to accommodate the class-rooms and the technological resources that were so vital to helping the children with their individual ways of learning.

Bethan loved driving Tilly up the long drive every morning and dropping her off in front of the portico. It looked so smart now. David Dashwood had wanted to get an exact replica made of the stone lion, but Evelyn had wanted something different; a peacock, with its tail fully fanned out in a magnificently carved display.

'After all, the house isn't Vaughan Court any more,' Evelyn had said in her speech at the opening ceremony. 'It's Peacock House School now, and it's appropriate that a peacock should welcome the pupils into the building every morning.'

There were one hundred pupils, sixty boarders and forty day pupils. The school had been Evelyn's idea.

'Somewhere where a bright child like Tilly can get all the help they need to thrive academically and gain their full potential.'

Bethan and Tom had helped to find an existing school in England that was looking to establish another branch in Wales. The governors thought Vaughan Court was the perfect place, with space in the grounds for sports fields, and lots of opportunities for outdoor education with the mountains and the sea so close at hand. The peacocks were still there. The children loved feeding them and collecting up their feathers from the grass.

Evelyn had only been back once.

'Do you miss it, Lady Evelyn?' the headmaster had asked, as Evelyn and Bethan sat in what had been the drawing room and was now the headmaster's study.

'No.' Evelyn had smiled and accepted the cup of tea the headmaster's secretary had offered her. 'It never felt like my home. It was always the Vaughan's.' She nodded towards the portraits on the walls that were still there as part of the heritage of the house.

'So, you feel at home in America?' the headmaster asked.

Evelyn nodded.

'Oh yes, Jack's house by the lake feels just as much mine as his.' Her face crinkled into a smile. Her skin was brown from the weather and her cheeks were flushed with a permanent pink, from health rather than makeup. 'It's much smaller, of course, but we don't need much space. We spend most of the time in the summer sitting on the veranda looking out across the lake, and most of the winter sitting in front of the fire. Jack's nieces are such lovely girls, they check on us every day, but really we're just happy with each other.'

'Sounds idyllic,' the headmaster said.

'It is,' Evelyn said. 'It really is.'

There was a knock on the hotel room door. Tilly sprang up to answer it.

'Hello, darling.' Bethan's mother threw her arms around Tilly as she walked in the room. 'My goodness, I swear you get taller every time I see you.'

'How was your journey?' Bethan stepped towards her father and gave him a hug.

'Long,' said her father. 'The plane was late leaving Heathrow and then the transfer at Chicago was delayed taking off.'

'But we're here now.' Bethan's mother gave Bethan and then Tom a hug. 'All together for today, and that's the most important thing.'

'I think a lot of people will have made the effort to come,' said Bethan.

'I almost forgot to tell you, Bethan.' Tom was shrugging on his jacket. 'You'll never guess who Tilly and I saw in the lobby this morning, when we went down for breakfast.'

'Who?' asked Bethan.

'David Dashwood and Chantal.'

'I didn't expect them to be here,' said Bethan's mother. 'But I suppose Evelyn kept in touch with David after he sold the golf club. I think she always had a soft spot for him despite what he did.'

'I heard Chantal was going to have a baby a couple of years ago,' Bethan said.

'It wasn't just the one baby,' Tom laughed. 'It was twins! One of them was careering around all over the foyer at high speed; David was trying to catch him by bribing him with an enormous bar of chocolate. Chantal was trying to stop the other one from grabbing all the complementary peppermints on the desk.'

'She doesn't have those fake nails any more,' Tilly said. 'And David's practically bald.'

'I wouldn't go that far,' Tom grinned. 'Noticeably receding might be a more accurate description.'

'Poor David.' Bethan shook her head as she peered into the mirror trying to pin on the silk flower. 'I bet those fancy cars of his have had to go too.'

'Let me do that.' Bethan's mother took the flower from Bethan's hand. 'It's such a gorgeous dress. I'm so pleased that you've kept so many of Evelyn's clothes.'

'Any news about the film?' Bethan's father asked.

'The production company is still in negotiation with my publisher.'

'All our fingers and toes are crossed for you, darling.' Bethan's mother stood back to check the angle of the flower. 'But it really doesn't matter as the book has done so well. We're so proud of you, aren't we?' She looked towards Bethan's father.

'Yes, of course we are.' Her father picked up one of the copies that Bethan had brought to give to Jack's nieces. 'I can't believe our little girl could be in the bestseller list.'

'I'm very proud too.' Tom put his arm around Bethan's shoulder and kissed her cheek. 'It's a wonderful story.'

'It's Evelyn and Jack's story,' Bethan said, sitting down on the edge of the bed. She put on a pair of 1950s Valentino stilettoes. 'It wouldn't exist without them.'

Tom checked his phone.

'Talking of Evelyn, there's a message to say the car has arrived.'

'It would be awful to be late,' said Bethan's mother.

'I'm all ready.' Bethan stood up and picked up the turquoise shawl. 'How do I look?'

'You look beautiful.' Tom kissed her cheek.

'Don't forget this.' Tilly handed Bethan a long black box tied with a white ribbon.

'Thank you, it would be a shame if I left that behind.' Bethan gave Tilly a hug.

'We'll see you at the church,' said her mother.

'I'm so honoured that she asked me to do this.' Bethan wrapped the shawl around her shoulders. 'I hope I won't mess it up, I'm nervous.'

'You'll be wonderful.' Tom nodded reassuringly as she gave him a last glance before walking out of the room.

Outside, the air was warm. Bethan lifted her face to the sun and took a deep breath before walking towards the vintage Cadillac. The chauffeur was dressed in white; he was standing beside the car making adjustments to the satin ribbon that adorned the bonnet. As Bethan approached, the chauffeur held open the passenger door.

Bethan could see Evelyn sitting inside the car, waving at her in a way that reminded Bethan of the Queen.

Her hair looked perfectly styled with a tiny pearl encrusted band across the top. She was wearing a pale silk jacket and holding a bouquet of deep pink peonies. Bethan slid onto the cream leather seat and was immediately enveloped in the smell of Chanel No. 5.

'Come on,' said Evelyn. 'I don't want to keep him waiting.'

Bethan put the gift-wrapped box down beside her and took Evelyn's hand in hers. Evelyn's nails were iridescent pink and the diamond on her finger sparkled.

'Thank you for asking me to give you away.'

'It was Jack's idea. After all, this day wouldn't be happening without you.' Evelyn squeezed Bethan's hand.

'Have you told Jack where you're spending your honeymoon yet?'

Evelyn shook her head.

'No, but I told him to pack lightly!'

'Jack will be amazed when he realises he's only going a few yards along the shore.'

'I can't wait to see his face,' Evelyn laughed.

The chauffeur turned from the driver's seat.

'All ready to go, Your Ladyship?'

'Just call me Evelyn,' Evelyn said. 'And after we've been to the church you can call me Mrs Valentine.'

'Do we still have time for the detour?' Bethan asked.

The chauffeur started the engine and turned back with a smile.

'Oh yes, it's all part of the day's itinerary. We've got plenty of time to go to the lake before the ceremony, it's not far.'

The car set off smoothly down a wide tree-lined road.

'Jack doesn't suspect a thing,' Evelyn said. 'It was lucky that he had the private view of his exhibition in New York to keep him busy. It meant we could be away when the workmen were assembling it all.'

'And he didn't venture down the track after you came back?'

'I kept him very busy with preparations for today, and Mary persuaded him that he should stay with them last night to give the bride a bit of time on her own. That meant I could make sure all the finishing touches were right.'

'What does it look like?' Bethan asked.

'It looks fabulous.' Evelyn's grin made her look years younger. 'Just the way it did in 1944.'

The car turned from the road and started to bump its way down a rutted track that Bethan remembered from her previous trips to the beautiful lakeside house.

Just as they approached the house the car slowed.

'It's down here.' Evelyn tapped on the glass of the car window, indicating another smaller track. As soon as the car turned, Bethan could see the roof. The gable pointed up against the bright blue sky, the intricately carved weatherboards and the stained-glass window glinting in the morning sunlight.

'Oh my goodness,' she breathed. 'I can't believe it's really here.'

The car came to a halt and the chauffeur walked around to help Evelyn out while Bethan slid out of her side. The two women stood together staring at the pretty little timber building standing on the lakeshore, as though it had always been meant to be there.

'It looks exactly the same,' Bethan said.

'It is exactly the same,' Evelyn replied. 'They've reassembled every piece of it perfectly – except it's now much stronger, no longer about to collapse in the way it would have if it had stayed in Wales.'

'It's such a wonderful idea, Evelyn, such a wonderful present for Jack.'

'It's a present for us both. And the school didn't need it. It was a liability – all those naughty paintings were only ever going to cause trouble!'

'So, they've survived the trip?'

'Come and see for yourself.' Evelyn took Bethan's arm and led her slowly towards the little arched door. She pushed it open and Bethan followed her inside.

Everything was just the same. The bed, the crate beside it, the fireplace and the candles in the jars and the wind-up gramophone on the floor. Even the pile of records with Perry Como on the top. And there were the paintings, as fresh and vibrant as though they had just been painted, Evelyn looking beautiful in every one of them.

'It's perfect,' Bethan whispered as she gazed around.

'Yes.' Evelyn squeezed her arm. 'It is. Our little summer house beside Jack's lake. It's the most perfect thing in the world.'

'It's nearly time,' the chauffeur called from outside.

Bethan smiled at Evelyn's radiant face.

'It's all because of you that this has happened,' Evelyn said. 'It's all because of you that I'm finally going to be Jack's wartime bride.'

The two women turned towards the doorway.

'Oh, I almost forgot! Wait here.' Bethan ran out to the car and returned with the long box. 'This is for you.' She handed it to Evelyn. 'And Jack.'

Evelyn carefully undid the ribbon and opened the box. She drew out a peacock's feather and smiled.

'A lovely reminder of Perry and Penelope.' She walked to the bed and placed it on the blanket. She turned to Bethan.

'After all those years I feel like I am home at last. Jack's house, the lake, and now this special place.'

'We'd better get going, Lady Evelyn,' the chauffeur said from the doorway. 'I pride myself on getting my brides to the church on time.'

'Oh, I'm afraid it would take a bloody miracle to get me there on time for this one.' Evelyn smiled at him as she walked out into the sunlight. 'I'm at least seventy years too late already.' She glanced back towards the summer house. 'But miracles can happen, I really do believe that now.'

Author's Note

The idea for *The Peacock House* came to me when my children and I were living in Dairy Cottage, in the grounds of the National Trust-owned Newton House, near Llandeilo in South West Wales. I discovered that, during the Second World War, Newton House had been used as an army hospital and that, for a short time, American troops had been stationed nearby. A local man, Meurig Jenkins, told me he remembered the excitement in Llandeilo when the GIs arrived. They would come into town to play pool and drink in the pubs, handing out sweets to the children and looking like film stars. He then described how they had vanished overnight and everything had seemed so boring afterwards.

My friend, the artist Sarah Rhys's family had lived in Newton House for many generations. She told me about a room that had been painted with a frieze of female figures during World War Two. Over time the room had fallen into disrepair and the paintings had faded away. She had an exhibition in the space in 2012, and she projected images of the original figures onto the dilapidated walls. I was fascinated by the idea of the paintings re-emerging and also of the American GIs transforming the small Welsh town. I found myself wondering about the hearts they might have broken and the lives they might have changed.

At that time my eldest son, Harry, started boarding school at St David's College in North Wales. Like Tilly he is dyslexic, and their specialist teaching helped transform his life and give him much-needed confidence and self-esteem. (It's very like the school that

Vaughan Court becomes in the novel.) I wish that kind of help was more easily available to all children who need it.

When I picked Harry up at the end of term I sometimes stayed at Bodysgallen Hall, a hotel near to the school. I fell in love with the seventeenth-century pink limestone manor house, with its views out to sea and mountains in the distance. Vaughan Court is loosely based on Bodysgallen, but if you are ever lucky enough to stay there don't expect to find it exactly the same. I also fell in love with the spectacular scenery of Snowdonia and I wanted to use it as a backdrop for a story that was bubbling into my imagination about an old lady in a big house and a secret wartime romance.

In October 2018 I spent a week at Ty Newydd Writing Centre on the North Wales coast. That is where Aberseren began to form in my mind; a fictional seaside village where the magnificent mountains sweep down to meet the Irish Sea. It was during my week at Ty Newydd that I wrote the first few chapters of *The Peacock House*, though I didn't write any more until the spring of 2020.

Like all the other characters in the book, Evelyn is fictional, but she is in part inspired by my mother's great friend, the late Diane Tomlinson. Diane was a renowned art expert and plant photographer in Dublin. As a child I was terrified of her, though as an adult I came to love and admire her hugely. She came from an aristocratic Anglo-Irish family and, like Evelyn, she had been a nurse in the Second World War. Also like Evelyn, she was never one to suffer fools and could be very formidable at times. But underneath her feisty exterior she was one of the kindest and most generous people I have ever known, who encouraged and helped me in many ways over the years. She lived well into her nineties with endless energy and good health until just before her death in 2015. Unlike Evelyn I never heard her swear, she left that to my mother, Biddy, who though she is in her late eighties and looks like the Queen, swears like a trooper!

My knowledge of peacocks comes from our time in Dairy Cottage where we lived with a resident peacock called Perry. Though he technically belonged to the National Trust Estate next door, he often came into our kitchen, getting his great swishy tail stuck in the legs of the chairs as he tried to turn around. He became as much a part of our household as our dog and cats, and I missed him after we moved. It was with great sadness that I heard that he had died of old age in 2019.

Acknowledgements

I would like to thank my wonderful agent Lisa Moylett for believing in me and giving me the faith to keep writing at a difficult time in my life. I am so grateful for her encouragement and support and for everything she's done to further my career as an author. Thank you also to Zoe Apostolides for all her help, ideas and brainstorming Zoom meetings.

Sherise Hobbs has been a truly wonderful editor at Headline. Her enthusiasm for my work has been inspiring, and her editorial advice has really helped to make *The Peacock House* a novel I'm extremely proud of.

Katie Brown has also been fantastic to work with; I very much enjoyed developing her ideas and suggestions.

I'd also like to thank my three amazing children, Harry, Daisy and Tomos. They were so supportive and encouraging while I wrote *The Peacock House*, even though I was often distracted by thoughts of World War Two and 'in a minute' usually meant 'in an hour – or two'. Harry and Tomos were very helpful answering questions about things I'm too old to know about, and Daisy helped me to develop the plot lines and listened patiently to all my different versions of the ending while we were walking the dogs.

My parents, Hugh and Biddy, were, as ever, a huge support – thank you to my mum for reading the very first, very rough draft, and to my dad for saving all the drafts on his computer, so that my nightmares about losing them on my computer didn't come true (it's happened before!).

As it was 2020 when I wrote *The Peacock House*, I didn't get to see my friends as much as I would have liked, but they still found ways to give me unerring amounts of strength and emotional sustenance in a problematic year, as well as practical help to move on with my life so that I can do what I love doing best – writing stories. Thank you so much – all of you.

I'd also like to say a big thank you to the two writing groups I belong to, WWWWWW (Wild Women Who Write in West Wales) and Writers at Wrights – wonderful and inspirational women who have helped and encouraged me both creatively and personally, and who have provided huge amounts of laughter along the way – plus tea, cake, gin and cheese!

Discover more unforgettable stories by

Kate Glanville . . .

**A warm, inviting story of love and family secrets set
in the beautiful French countryside.**

When tragedy struck twenty-five years ago, Martha Morgan lost
everything. Once a member of one of the UK's most prestigious bands,
she now lives in solitude in the beautiful small village of Dordogne.

In an attempt to piece her life back together Martha decides
to rent her idyllic French farmhouse to holidaymakers for
the summer, hiring the mysterious Ben to work as a caretaker
to help reconstruct the dishevelled B&B.

But when a vicious storm makes its way across the small village, tensions
begin to rise. Martha, Ben and her guests are forced to pull together and
they're about to find out that they have more in common than they
realise – but it might mean jeopardising the old secret of Martha's past.

Available to order

ACCENT

It's hard to run away from your deepest secrets . . .

When Phoebe's lover dies in a car accident, their hushed
affair goes with him to the grave.

Heartbroken, she abandons her life in England and searches
out the old boathouse on the west coast of Ireland left to her
by her grandmother. Soon she is embraced by the villagers
of nearby Carraigmore and slowly begins to heal.

But when Phoebe discovers a collection of old diaries hidden
under the floor of the boathouse, she finds herself immersed
in a story of family scandal and a passionate affair between her
grandmother and a young Irish artist.

With so many unanswered questions, Phoebe turns to the locals who
knew her late grandmother best. But when she is met by silence, she
realises she's not the only one (in her family) with something to hide . . .

Available to order

ACCENT

Is home *really* where the heart is?

Claire appears to have it all – the kind of life you read about in
magazines: a beautiful cottage, three gorgeous children, a handsome
husband in William and her own flourishing vintage textile business.

But when an interiors magazine sends a good-looking photographer
to take pictures of Claire's perfect home, he makes her wonder if the
house means more to William than she does . . .

Available to order

ACCENT

Three women connected by one man.

Daniel is father to Seren, husband to Nesta and lover to Frankie.
When he leaves Nesta and their beautiful home in the middle of a
party celebrating their fortieth wedding anniversary, Seren's world
begins to crumble. Only the continuation of the family ideal can
make things right. But Nesta isn't so sure.

And for Frankie, Daniel offers hope of a safe and secure future. But all
three women are carrying secrets that they've kept hidden, even from
those closest to them. Secrets that might threaten a life . . .

Available to order

ACCENT